JOAN FALLON

TOO CLOSE TO THE SUN

SCOTT PUBLISHING
(ESPAÑA)

The Scottish novelist Joan Fallon, currently lives and works in the south of Spain. She writes contemporary, historical and crime fiction and almost all her books have a strong female protagonist. She is the author of:

FICTION:
Spanish Lavender
The House on the Beach
Loving Harry
Santiago Tales
The Only Blue Door
Palette of Secrets
The Thread That Binds Us
Love Is All

The al-Andalus series:
The Shining City (Book 1)
The Eye of the Falcon (Book 2)
The Ring of Flames (Book 3)

The City of Dreams series:
The Apothecary (Book 1)
The Pirate (Book 2)
The Prisoner (Book 3)

The Jacaranda Dunne Mysteries:
Sophie is Still Missing
Dark Heart
Strawberry Moon

NON-FICTION:
Daughters of Spain
(Available in paperback, audiobooks and as ebooks)

TOO CLOSE TO THE SUN

A Jacaranda Dunne Mystery

Joan Fallon

Too Close to the Sun

ISBN 978-84-09-60822-5
First published in 2024
Scott Publishing
España

ACKNOWLEDGMENTS

My sincere thanks to my editor Sara Starbuck for helping me to create an exciting crime series, to Angela Hagenow for proof reading the manuscript and to Alex Allden for the stunning cover. Their advice and support have, as always, been invaluable.

Too Close to the Sun

He instructed the boy as well, saying 'Let me warn you, Icarus, to take the middle way in case the moisture weighs down your wings if you fly too low, or if you go too high, the sun scorches them. Travel between the extremes.'

(Daedalus and Icarus, an ancient Greek myth recorded by the Roman poet Ovid in his Metamorphoses.)

Too Close to the Sun

TOO CLOSE TO THE SUN.
A Jacaranda Dunne Mystery Book Four

PROLOGUE

Rachel stretched her long legs and dug her toes into the warm sand; she had not felt so relaxed for a long time. The beach was almost deserted this morning; most people were still recovering from the annual Feria which had opened the night before with a spectacular display of fireworks. She had watched it from the window of her rented apartment for a while but then had poured herself a glass of whisky and gone to bed; she was getting too old to stay up until all hours of the night. She sighed contentedly. All she could hear was the gentle murmur of the sea as the waves lapped against the harbour wall. She liked this narrow strip of beach; it was close to the apartment and easy to walk to. Unlike the wider, more expansive beaches further along the coastline, it was not a favourite with the tourists nor the foreign tour companies. The warmth from the sun was seeping into her body and making her sleepy; this was just what she needed after the wet and windy summer they had been having in England. The plan was to relax and soak up the sun for a couple of weeks then go back to face the problems she had been trying to ignore. She could feel her back starting to burn now, so she sat up and reached for her bag; there was some suncream in there somewhere. She began to rummage through her collection of 'beach essentials' as she liked to call them: an old paperback she had started to read on the flight over, goggles in case she decided to have a swim, a tube of aftersun cream, her reading glasses, a bottle of water. Where on earth was the suncream? Had she left it in the apartment?

The loud drone of a para-motor made her glance up at the sky. Dreadful, noisy machines, she hated them. And now there were two of the blasted things. Why were they allowed to fly so close to the beach, disturbing everyone's peace and tranquility? She squinted into the sun as she watched the ungainly machines fly past; they seemed far too insubstantial to carry the weight of a man, just a propeller and a small engine attached to their backs. Yet there they were, flying across the waves one behind the other. They were so low that she could see the faces of the pilots; both seemed to be men although it was not easy to be sure with the helmets covering most of their heads. One appeared to be very young but she was sure that the other was much older, despite the fashionable Air Jordan's that he was wearing. She recognised them straight away; her grandson had asked his father for them for his birthday but her son refused to spend over a hundred pounds on something he said would be ruined in a week. She smiled to herself, everyone wanted to look younger these days. The man with the expensive trainers was shouting something to the other one, who shook his head and gestured as if to say that he couldn't hear him. It was no wonder with that awful noise.

As if in answer to her prayers, the noise level had dropped; it was no longer deafening her. In fact one of the para-motors had gone completely silent. What had happened? She looked up and shaded her eyes in order to see it clearly. The younger pilot was looking frightened. Something was definitely wrong; he was no longer moving forward in a purposeful manner, but floating unsteadily beneath the multi-coloured canopy. It looked as though the propeller of his para-motor was slowing down and might stop altogether. Had the engine stalled? She leapt to her feet, her suncream forgotten. What could she do? The young pilot was struggling to control his craft; he tugged on the lines attached to the parachute as though that would help but even she could see that it was making no difference. The para-motor was already beginning to descend. He was going to land right on top of her. She ran further up the beach, desperate to keep out of his way but unable to take her eyes off him. Now she could see the terror on his face as he tugged frantically at the guide lines but his efforts were useless. For a moment the sun was in her eyes and she blinked just as a sudden gust of wind buffeted him and for a moment he was airborne again. She breathed a sigh of relief but it was short lived and once again the para-motor began to lose height. The pilot of the leading vehicle appeared not to have noticed the drama taking place behind him and continued on his journey, gaining height and flying over the harbour then turning eastward along the coast, seemingly unaware that his companion was in trouble. She gasped as she watched the young man's descent; the motor was completely silent now and the propeller barely moved. The man was still struggling with the parachute, desperately trying to catch some wind in the sail. If only there was something she could do to help him. She found herself whispering a Hail Mary, but by now he was completely out of control and was heading straight for her, so close that she could feel his panic. She shrieked and ran towards the road, torn between the fascination of watching his descent and the fear that he would crash on top of her. People at the far end of the beach were on their feet now, but like her there was nothing they could do but stand and watch. Everyone mesmerised by the imminent catastrophe, frozen in time. Suddenly a strong gust of wind pulled the para-motor up into the air and away from the beach; it carried man and machine across the harbour wall and out of sight. There was no sound of the motor starting up again but no sound of a crash either; did this mean he was all right?

People were running along the promenade towards the harbour. She dashed back to where, only minutes before, she had been lazing in the sunshine, grabbed her bag and followed them. She prayed he was all right. He looked too young to die. She knew she had to do something, but what? Her brain was numb; she was unable to think clearly. Should she phone for the police, or the coast guard? The truth was she had no idea how to do either and she didn't speak any Spanish anyway. She was completely helpless.

By the time she arrived at the harbour wall, panting for breath, there was already a small group of people gathered to watch the unfolding drama. 'Where is he?' she gasped, stopping to ease the hammering of her heart. 'What happened to him?'

'I think he's in the sea,' said an English voice. 'He just vanished. Looks like SEMAR are here already.' He pointed to a motorboat with GUARDIA CIVIL on its side. 'It's the marine wing of the police. They'll have some divers on board. I expect they'll soon get him out.' He sounded confident and knowledgable, and although Rachel did not share his confidence, his words made her relax and she watched as a police launch exited the harbour and headed in the direction where she had last seen the para-motorist. Would they be in time? Would they find him? The safety of this unknown man pressed on her conscience as though in some way it was her fault that he had got into difficulty. Just by watching it somehow she had become part of the tragedy.

'Well I'm going back to my lunch,' the Englishman said. 'Me and my wife were in that restaurant when I spotted that he was in trouble.' He pointed to a small fish restaurant in a nearby street.

'Did you see what happened to the other one?' she asked.

'Other one? Oh, the other para-motorist. No, I thought he'd probably landed on the beach and would come back to see what had happened.'

'I don't think he realised what was going on; anyway I can't see him now. I think he just kept going.'

The man slowly shook his head; he looked bewildered. 'That's odd. You'd think he'd have eventually noticed that he was alone and turned around and come back to see what had happened to his friend.'

'Maybe it's not easy to manoeuvre those things. Anyway, they might not even be friends, or even know each other,' Rachel said, but she too thought it was strange. She remained there staring at the sea. The sun was directly overhead; she could feel its rays beating on the back of her neck. She wanted to go back to the beach and lie down under her umbrella, but she couldn't drag herself away from the harbour. The need to know what had happened to him was too compelling. She fingered the silver cross her mother had given her and automatically began to recite the prayer for those in danger, 'May the Father, Son and Holy Spirit hold you safe and hold you strong...' She had not prayed in a long time, since she was a teenager in fact, yet here she was in a foreign country, praying for a man she did not even know.

CHAPTER 1

JD's phone rang and rang. She tried to ignore it but it was impossible. She reached up and pressed the decline button. Almost immediately it started to ring again.

'Are you going to answer that?' a sleepy and rather disgruntled voice asked.

'It's barely six o'clock,' she muttered, pulling the pillow over her ears. 'It's only my mother.'

'Rosa? Well you should speak to her. Maybe she's had an accident. It must be important for her to ring so early.'

'Not really. She probably couldn't sleep.' Nevertheless he was right; maybe her mother did need her urgently. She picked up the mobile phone and pressed accept. 'Mama. Do you know what time it is?'

'Of course I do. I'm not gaga you know.'

'So what do you want?'

'I need to speak to you, Jacaranda. It's urgent.'

'Can't it wait until later? I'm still in bed.'

'No. It's time you were up, anyway. This is important.'

'Well can't you give me a clue to what it's about?' JD asked, swinging her legs out of the bed and searching for her slippers.

'It's a murder case. That's all I'm going to say until I see you. Come straight over. Paola will make you some breakfast when you get here.'

'I take it you don't mind if I have a shower first?' she asked, but her sarcasm was lost on her mother as she had already hung up.

'Well?' asked Federico, attempting to pull her back into bed.

'She says it's about a murder. I'm to go over there right away. Do you have any idea what it's about? Have there been any reports of suspicious deaths lately?'

'No, not that I recall.' He pulled himself into a sitting position. 'Well if you're determined to get up at this ungodly hour, then I will join you in the shower. Do you want me to give you a lift to your mother's?'

'Thanks, but it's better if I take my bike. I'll go straight from there to the agency.' It was at times like this when she wished she still had her Mini.

It took her about twenty minutes to reach her mother's new apartment. Once the entrance door to the block was opened, she wheeled her bicycle into the communal hallway and propped it against the wall. Rosa now lived in a sixth floor penthouse with one of the most spectacular views of the bay of Málaga that she had ever seen. JD did not like to think what her mother had paid for it, a small fortune by normal standards, she was sure; the whole building reeked of opulence and money.

'*Buenos días,* Señora Dunne,' said the doorman. 'Here, let me take care of that.' He wheeled her bicycle into a small lobby. 'You're very early, today. Everything okay?'

She smiled. 'Everything is fine, thank you. Got a lot on this morning.' Since her mother had moved into the centre of Málaga, JD had taken to popping in to see her on the way home from work at least once a week.

This morning Rosa was already waiting for her and opened the door immediately. 'At last, Jacaranda. What took you so long?'

JD didn't bother to reply. It was too early in the day to get into an argument with her mother, besides which her head was thumping, a consequence of too much wine and too little sleep the night before. She was definitely going to have to cut back on her drinking. 'Can you control your dogs, please, Mama,' she said as Rosa's two schnauzers jumped up to greet her.

'They are pleased to see you, *Cariño.*'

'Well can they demonstrate it a little more quietly, please,' she grumbled, but nevertheless bent down to stroke them. The dogs appeared to sense that their mistress's daughter was not in the best of moods and slunk off to the kitchen in search of something to eat.

'*Buenos días, Señora,*' said Paola. 'Would you like some breakfast? A cup of coffee and some toast?'

'Just a little yogurt would be fine; I'm not really hungry. Maybe some orange juice and a couple of paracetamol. I've got a thumping headache.' She smiled at the maid. Paola had worked for JD's mother for years and was now like part of the family. 'So, Mama, who's been murdered?' JD asked, sitting down at the table opposite Rosa.

'The son of a good friend of mine.'

JD stared at her. 'Are you being serious?'

'Of course I am. It's hardly a joking matter, now is it.'

'No, of course not. So, what's the name of this friend of yours? And what do you think happened to his son?'

Her mother gave her a contemptuous look and replied, 'I don't think. I *know* he's been murdered.'

'So who are we talking about?' she asked, as patiently as the throbbing inside her head would allow her.

'Gabriel Francisco Mendoza de Goya. He's the Duque de Roble, an old friend of mine from my younger days. I was very close to his sister, Irina. Before I married your father I went to many parties at their house in Madrid.' Her mother's eyes had that far-away look in them which meant she was about to recount some long and boring story about her scandalous youth.

'Okay, Mama. What about the son? You say he's been murdered.'

'Yes. He was also called Gabriel Francisco, but everyone called him Kiko. He was the duke's oldest child and his heir.'

'And why do you think this Kiko has been murdered? Do you have any evidence?'

'No, of course not. If I had evidence I would have gone straight to the Guardia Civil, but I am convinced that something is not quite right about his death. So I want you to help me get the evidence.'

'Okay, well if you are serious about this you need to come into the agency and we can interview you properly with the rest of the team present.'

'You don't understand. This is urgent. The duke is seriously ill. He's in hospital at the moment and the doctors are only giving him a few weeks to live. Before he dies he wants to know what happened to his son.'

'I'm sorry to hear that, but an investigation takes time.' She was going to add *and money* but thought better of it. 'So if he dies who will inherit the duke's title now that his eldest son is dead?'

'His daughter; she's next in line.'

'And is that a problem for him?'

For a moment Rosa looked bewildered. 'Honestly, Jacaranda, I don't know. According to the dukes's secretary, the police have said his son's death was an accident, but the duke doesn't believe it. He just wants to know what happened to him. It's too much of a coincidence that he should have a fatal accident just when his father has been given only a few weeks to live.'

'Is he rich?' JD asked.

'Who? El Duque de Roble? Very. His son was due to not only inherit the title but also a fortune in land, property and investments. He and his sister would have become very wealthy.'

'Now that all goes to the duke's daughter?'

'The main part, I suppose. There will be something for his wife I expect, but you'd have to speak to his solicitor for the details.'

JD drank the rest of her orange juice and walked across to the window. 'I think I like this apartment better than the one you had in Torremolinos,' she said, as she watched people walking along the promenade and heading for the lighthouse. There was a pair of binoculars hanging by the curtains. She picked them up and focused on the lighthouse. 'These are good. Pretty powerful. Do you use them much?'

'Of course. That's why they're there. I like to watch the birds, and the people,' she added with a smile. 'That's where Kiko died.' Rosa pointed to the harbour. 'He was on one of those noisy glider things and fell into the sea and drowned. If I had been at home I would have seen what happened.'

'I doubt if you could have done anything about it from up here.' JD replaced the binoculars and picked up her helmet. 'I have to go now, but come along to the agency at eleven and you can tell us everything you know about Kiko's death. I can't promise anything, but we will look into it. Maybe someone else was bird watching that morning; they might have seen something. Paola for instance.'

'I think she would have said something to me, but we can ask her.' Rosa walked into the hall and called, 'Paola. Can you come her for a minute.'

'*Si, Señora.* What would you like? More coffee?'

'No. My daughter would just like a word with you.'

'Were you working here last Saturday morning, Paola?'

'Paola works here every morning,' her mother interrupted.

JD looked at Paola.

'Yes, *Señora.*'

'Did you see the man who died in the harbour? He was flying a para-motor.'

'I heard about someone dying but I didn't see anything. I was probably in the kitchen. I usually do some baking on a Saturday.' Was JD imagining it or was Paola deliberately avoiding looking at her.

'Okay, thank you. Well, let's leave it like that for now, Mama. You come down to the agency later and give us all the details.'

'Thank you, *Cariño.* I knew you wouldn't let me down. You will get paid, of course. The duke is a generous man; he wouldn't expect you to investigate for nothing.'

Well that was a relief. She'd had the feeling that her mother was expecting the investigation to be free. 'See you later, then.'

'*Buenos días,* Boss. My, you look rough, this morning,' said Nacho, who was already working on his laptop.

'Thank you. That makes me feel much better. Where's Linda?'

'She'll be here in a minute; she had to drop Jane and the baby at the post natal clinic,' he said, without looking up.

Of course. She still hadn't got used to the fact that Linda now had her duties as a grandmother to fulfil as well as wife, mother and most important of all, as her assistant. While work was slack she had allowed Linda to reduce her hours, but if there was anything in what Rosa was saying about the man being murdered, then she would have to rethink that decision. 'Send her a text. I want you all here in the agency for eleven. We have someone coming in to talk about a new case.'

'Really.' She had Nacho's attention now. He stared at her through his new rimless spectacles. 'Not more lost dogs, I hope.'

'No, much more interesting than that. In the meantime I want you to find out all you can about the current Duque de Roble and his family. I'll explain later.'

Despite the urgency with which she had called JD that morning, The Most Excellent Lady, Rosa María de la Luz, Marquesa de Calderón del Bosque did not arrive at the agency until eleven-thirty.

'You're late,' said JD, ushering her into their meeting room.

'*Buenos días*, everyone. Linda, how's the new baby? A boy, isn't it?' asked Rosa, beaming at everyone and ignoring her daughter's comment. 'I've brought you a little present for him.' She handed Linda a small package wrapped in paper printed with pink elephants. 'Sorry about the colour but I couldn't resist the little elephants. They are so cute.'

JD stared at her mother. This was so unlike Rosa; she usually preferred dogs to babies. This case was obviously very important to her.

'Thank you Rosa; how kind of you. The baby is fine, putting on weight and sleeping through the night, thank goodness.'

'What have they decided to call him?'

'Ramon, after his grandfather.'

'I think it's time we got down to work,' interrupted JD, tired of watching her mother pretending to be interested in Linda's grandson. Besides which she was eager to get started; things had been very quiet lately and it would be good to get her teeth into an interesting case. This one seemed to have distinct possibilities, not the least of which was that the duke could afford to pay her bill. They could do with an influx of cash; a nice fat fee from the duke would not go amiss.

'Of course. I was just being polite. After all it's not every day Linda becomes a grandmother,' said Rosa.

'No it isn't, *gracias a Dios*,' said Linda. 'Although I have to admit, I am enjoying it. He's a delight.'

'Okay, Mama. I haven't told Linda and Nacho anything yet, so can you start from the beginning, please. Nacho, will you write some notes on the evidence board.'

'Right you are, Boss.'

'Shall we start with the name of the deceased?'

'Gabriel Francisco Mendoza de Goya Pérez, the eldest son of the Duque de Roble.'

'Quite a mouthful,' said Linda, scribbling the name in her notebook.

Nacho glanced at JD and raised his eyebrows, then wrote the name on the board.

Rosa repeated what she had already told JD earlier then added, 'His father is convinced that it's too much of a coincidence that his son should die in an accident just five days after he'd received the news that he only had a few weeks to live.'

'So the Duque de Roble is terminally ill?' asked Linda.

'Yes. They moved him into a hospice in Seville, yesterday.'

'But he's still conscious?' asked JD. 'We could talk to him?'

'I don't know. Only his wife is allowed to see him; you will have to speak to her. She's his third wife, by the way. The mother of Kiko and Isabella died in childbirth when they were still quite young.'

'Kiko?' asked Nacho, looking puzzled..

'The dead man. Gabriel Francisco, Kiko to his friends,' JD explained.

'Anyway, the baby survived and seemed healthy enough but then he too died a couple of days later,' continued Rosa. 'Gabriel was heartbroken at the time; he had lost his wife and his new son. Anyway it looked as though he wasn't interested in getting married again and he remained a widower for many years. His remaining two children were brought up by their nanny. Then, when Kiko and Isabella had both finished their education, the duke decided to marry again, this time to a much younger woman.' She gave a snort of derision. 'That didn't last long. They were divorced in no time at all. After that we all thought Gabriel was resigned to living alone and then he met Leticia, his present wife. She is the same age as his daughter, Isabella, and very beautiful. They had a son just before the duke first became ill. That must be...' Rosa hesitated, thinking back over the years. 'He has to be four-years-old by now.'

'So he too could inherit the estate?'

'I suppose so. But the daughter Isabella is the heir now. If anything happened to her, then I suppose it would be little Antonio's turn. As I said before, I think you need to speak to Don Emilio, Gabriel's solicitor. He has all the details of the inheritance, and he can tell you more about the family.'

JD glanced across at Linda. 'You had better do that,' she told her. Before she had joined JD's agency Linda had worked as a secretary for a criminal lawyer in Málaga, and had become very familiar with legal procedures. She would know better than JD which questions to ask. 'Anything else you can tell us about the dead man?' she asked her mother.

Rosa shook her head. 'Not that I can think of.'

'If you are so sure he was murdered, who do you think would want to kill him?' asked Linda. 'You must have some suspicions.'

'No, I don't. I haven't had a lot to do with the family since I got back to Spain. Rebecca had died by then, and Irina had changed. I suppose I was different too; I hadn't lived in Spain for over twenty years.'

'So what was your connection to the duke's family?' asked Nacho.

'It goes back a long way; I was at school with the duke's first wife, Rebecca, and his sister Irina. Anyway as I was saying, I didn't see anything of them for many years—what you have to understand is that we didn't have WhatsApp and Facebook in those days and no mobile phones. Making a phone call was an expensive and complicated process—especially once I was living in Scotland—so we barely kept in touch. We exchanged the odd letter now and then at Christmas. Even when I eventually returned to Spain, it wasn't easy to slot back into my old life. At the time Jacaranda's father had just died and I had a young daughter to bring up. My life was no longer the same.'

'You seem to have managed it well enough now,' JD said.

Her mother laughed. 'Inheriting your grandfather's title helped open a few doors.'

'So you have no idea about Kiko's friends?' Linda persisted.

'None at all.'

'Or whether he had any enemies?'

'I would doubt he had any enemies; he was a sweet boy, shy even.'

'Mama, you've just told us that he was murdered. You have no idea why, and now you say he had no enemies. If what you allege is true, someone wanted him out of the way.' She struggled to control her temper. Why did she allow her mother to irritate her so much?

'Of course. That's what I want you to find out: who did it and why. You're a private investigator, aren't you?'

JD took a deep breath. 'All right, Mama, do you have contact details for any of these people?'

'Yes, some of them. They're all on my phone.' She pushed her mobile phone over to her daughter.

'Check them out, please, Nacho,' JD said, handing him her mother's phone. 'We will have a look at the case, Mama, but like I said, I can't promise you anything. The first thing we need to do is find out if there is any evidence of foul play. If there is, then we can go ahead.'

'That's all I want you to do, *Cariño*. Get me proof that he was murdered and then we can worry about who did it.'

'I need to ask you one thing first, Mama, does the duke know that you are talking to me about his dead son?'

'Not exactly. Now why would I bother him when he is so ill?' She looked across at Linda, as if to say, what a stupid question. 'But before he went into the hospice he rang me and asked me to visit him.'

'And did you go?'

'Of course. He was worried. The doctor had warned him that he did not have long to live and he was concerned about his heirs.'

'But he had that covered by his solicitor, didn't he? A man like that would have had his will in place years ago.'

'Yes, of course. I don't mean that he wanted to change his heirs; it wouldn't be an easy task even if he wanted to. No. Something was worrying him, but he was rather vague about what it was.'

'What did he say? Can you remember his exact words, Mama?'

'He said that things within the family were not quite what they seemed and he was unsure what to do about it.'

'Is that all?'

'Yes.'

'So he asked you to visit him and that's all he had to say to you?'

'I said so, didn't I.'

'So why you? Why not someone else? You haven't had much to do with the family in recent years.'

Her mother gave an elegant shrug of her silk clad shoulders. 'I don't know, *Cariño*. Maybe it's because I am an old friend, but at the same time I am not involved in the same clique as many of his other friends. Remember that for many years I was living abroad. Maybe he thought that made me more impartial and I wouldn't go gossiping about what he told me.'

'Did he say that he was worried that something would happen to his son?'

'Not directly, but I have the feeling that was what he meant.'

'So why didn't you tell someone at the time? His wife for example?'

'If he had wanted her to know, he would have told her. But anyway, I didn't really believe him. I thought it was the medication making him paranoid. Now I regret it bitterly. If I had, maybe Kiko would not be dead now.' She wiped an imaginary tear away from her eye.

'Don't go there, Mama. We don't even know if Kiko's death was deliberate yet. We can't jump to conclusions just because a sick old man was worried about his son's safety. Para-motoring is a dangerous sport and accidents happen.'

'It's also not a popular method for murdering someone,' added Nacho.

Rosa stared at him.

'If he and his family don't know that you've asked us to investigate, how do you think we can go prying into their lives without their permission?'

'Isn't that what you do? Pry into people's private lives?'

JD was about to tell her mother what to do with her murder case, but before she could release the expletives gathering on her tongue, Linda turned to Rosa and said, 'In a way we do, Rosa, but usually with the backing of the police or at least at the request of the family. I think the duke's family might be upset if we went barging in saying that we think a member of their family was murdered and we had no real proof.'

'Well, talk to that captain of yours, Jacaranda and get him to give you the authority. I'm telling you that young man was murdered and I'm not going to rest until you have found his killer.'

'We will do our very best, Rosa. You just leave it to us,' said Linda.

'And you'll keep me informed?'

'Of course. Now I think we need to get started.' Linda looked across at her boss, her eyes pleading for support.

'Yes, indeed. Linda is right. We will get an investigation started and keep you up to date on our progress, Mama.' JD ushered her mother out of the meeting room and opened the door

'Just a minute, Rosa,' called Nacho. 'Your phone.'

'Thank you Ignacio. Ring me this evening, *Cariño*,' her mother said once she was in the street, but JD had already gone back into the office and closed the door.

Now that Rosa had left, she turned to her team. 'Well, what do you think?'

'I don't see how we can investigate it if the police have said it was an accident and the family agrees with them. It's not as though Rosa is a relative of the dead man; she's just an old friend of his father. It sounds as though she barely knew the son,' said Nacho.

'It sounds like an unfortunate accident to me,' said Linda. 'And how are we going to examine the body? He's sure to have been buried by now, or worse still, cremated. There will be no evidence.'

'We need to speak to the family. We are just assuming that they all think it was an accident,' said JD. 'Maybe some of them have their own doubts.'

'According to Rosa, the duke has serious doubts.'

'Yes, but even she admits she didn't take him seriously.'

'But that was before the son died. His death throws a different perspective on events,' said Linda. 'It's quite a coincidence that the heir to a fortune should die while his father is on his deathbed. We need to talk to the duke.'

'Well we can't get to talk to him because he's in a hospice,' said Nacho.

'Well then we need to talk to someone close to the immediate family. What have you found out about the duke, Nacho? Does he have any brothers or sisters?'

'Yes, three brothers and two sisters, but he and a sister are the only ones still alive. He was the eldest brother and that's why he inherited the title; male-preference primogeniture was the law at the time so although both sisters were older than him, the title went to the oldest son, which was Gabriel. Of course nowadays, it's changed. The eldest child inherits regardless of sex.'

'Yes, I know all about that; my mother is always reminding me that the change in the law is why she inherited the title from my grandfather,' interrupted JD.

'Are you going to speak to the captain?' Linda asked.

'Not yet. Let's see what we can come up with ourselves first. Remember, as far as the whole world is concerned it was a straightforward accident.'

'Apart from your mother.'

'Okay, apart from her, and when Rosa gets an idea into her head it is impossible to shift it, but that doesn't mean it's true.'

'So, are you telling her we're not taking it on?' asked Nacho. He looked poised to wipe the board clean.

'No, not unless we find concrete proof that this was just a horrible accident. Have you any idea what my life would be like if I dismissed the idea out of hand?'

'We can imagine. Okay, so what do you want us to do?'

'Get on to the morgue, Nacho, and see if they still have Kiko's body or if the family have claimed it yet. Pretend you're a relative. Tell them that the duke is in Seville and has sent you instead. You'll come up with something, I'm sure.'

'What about me?' asked Linda.

'Nacho has already started looking into the background of the Duque de Roble and his family but I want you to concentrate on the children: Kiko, Isabella and this little Antonio. Get me everything you can. These kind of people like publicity; there's bound to be plenty in the news about them in the celebrity columns.'

'And you?'

'I'm going to talk to Tim; there's got to be something in the paper about Kiko's death.'

'Well, I haven't seen anything,' said Linda. 'You'd think the death of an aristocrat's son would hit the news.'

'Nor me,' added Nacho. 'There's nothing on social media either.'

'So it's not newsworthy. There's nothing strange about that. We'll make a decision tomorrow morning on whether we take the case or not. Okay?'

'Yes, just as you say, Boss. But I think you should speak to the captain, anyway. The police may already be looking into the case and keeping it quiet because the duke or someone in his family have asked them to.'

'Okay Nacho, I'll think about it. Linda?'

'I don't think we'll find anything, but we might as well give it a try; it's not as though we're weighed down with interesting cases. But I agree with Nacho; I can't see the harm in asking Federico what he can tell you about the man's death.'

'We've solved more complicated murders than this,' said Nacho.

'Always the optimist, Nacho. It's not going to be easy if we don't have a body, you know.' They were both looking at her; she knew what they were waiting for. 'Oh, very well. You two get on with what I've asked you to do and I'll speak to the captain. See you both later, then.'

Linda was right; since solving their last investigation into what had appeared to be a suicide pact and turned out to be a double murder, things had been very quiet in the agency. It would be exciting to have another meaty case to investigate, although her head kept telling her that this could just be her mother's over-active imagination. She would speak to Federico, but first she would like a chat with Tim; he had an uncanny knack of sniffing out a good news story.

CHAPTER 2

She found Tim Pierce sitting in a bar opposite the offices of the Voz de Málaga; he was with some colleagues whom she recognised from the newspaper where he worked. JD undid her helmet and shook her long blonde hair loose as she wandered over to him. 'Hi Tim, can I have a quick word with you?'

'JD, what a pleasant surprise. Pull up a chair. These guys are just leaving.' He nodded at his companions.

'Yes, it's time we were going, anyway,' said a tall, lanky youth. 'Nice to see you, JD. Anything exciting happening?'

'I wish. When something does happen, you'll be the first to know, Paco.' She smiled at him.

'I hope you didn't mean that,' whispered Tim as his colleagues left. 'I thought I was your go-to guy.'

'You are. That's why I'm here.' She waved a hand at the waiter and ordered an iced tea. 'So it's work as usual for you? Not going to the Feria?'

'Actually I'm off home in a minute. Some friends have invited us to spend the afternoon at their *casita* in the Feria ground.'

'That sounds nice, if you like that sort of thing. How is the wife? Still floating on a cloud of married bliss?'

'Barbara is fine. You're just jealous because nobody has asked you to marry them.' He dropped his voice and added, 'If you'd played your cards right, you could be Mrs Pierce by now.'

JD choked back the caustic comment she was about to make and said, 'Well, it may take me a bit of time to get used to the idea that you're a married man now Tim, but in the meantime you are still my number one source of good info.' She smiled sweetly at him.

'So, how can I help you?'

'What do you have on the accidental death of the Duque de Roble's son?'

Instantly Tim sat up, all ideas of flirting with her gone from his mind. 'So you don't think it was an accident?'

'I didn't say that. In fact I said the opposite. If you were listening closely, I said accidental death. My mother knows the family and she said, if I saw you to ask you what happened to him. That's all.' She knew he didn't believe her. He was too shrewd for that. Although Tim irritated her enormously at times, he had a great nose for a scoop and this would seem like one to him. If there was anything in it, he would soon find out.

'Well, sorry but I didn't write the piece. In fact it was really only an obituary, a few paragraphs for our sister paper, the Voz de Seville. The family's from Seville, as you probably know. I don't think there was even anything about it in our edition; too many other things happening that weekend. Sorry, so you see there's not much else I can tell you.'

'Well, do you know how he died? My mother heard that he had drowned but no other details.'

Tim's face lit up; he loved a good story. 'Oh, it was much more dramatic than that. He was paramotoring along the coast last Saturday when his engine failed and he fell into the sea. Must have got tangled up in the parachute and by the time anyone could get to him he had drowned. Tragic. I did hear that it was the first time he'd gone up on his own.'

'Isn't that newsworthy? So why didn't you make more of it in yesterday's newspaper? That's not like you.'

'As I said, the man was from Seville.'

'So? He died in Málaga; I'd have thought that was enough for your readers to be interested. Anyway, I thought paramotoring was supposed to be very safe?'

'Well it is usually, but accidents happen. It could have been due to his inexperience. Or maybe he panicked.'

'Why are you so sure he was inexperienced?'

'It's only a guess. Experienced para-motorists wouldn't fly anywhere near the port. It's forbidden, for a start.'

'So you really don't know anything about it then?'

'I know he was a bit stupid to be flying over the harbour; he should have kept to the land. It's always more dangerous over water, even I know that.'

'Have you ever been paramotoring?' she asked.

'Me, no. I went up in an air balloon once, but that was enough for me. The thought of throwing myself off the top of a cliff with only a parachute to keep me from crashing to my death is not my idea of fun.'

'But with paramotoring you have an engine. You don't have to rely on the wind alone.'

'Still too dangerous for me. If you want to know more about it, you should go and talk to Bob Free. He's an Australian guy who has opened a paragliding and paramotoring school in el Torcal. I can give you his number.' Tim pulled out his mobile and forwarded Bob Free's details to her phone. 'We did a piece on him and his school back in the Spring.'

'Thanks. I might get in touch with him. Not sure if it's really my thing, though.' She finished the last of her iced tea. 'So nothing else you can tell me about the duke's son?'

'Ah, well. That wasn't what you asked. You asked about the accident. I can tell you a lot about the son. You know that his father has been very ill for a while, and that the son was due to inherit the estate, well my boss had me pull together some facts about him so we could be straight out with a double page article the moment his father died and he inherited the title. He had quite a reputation, you know, the son, not the father.'

'I didn't, actually. So what had he been up to?'

'What hadn't he. Women, drugs, gambling, he was into it all.'

'I'd heard he was a quiet, shy young man.'

Tim let out a loud laugh. 'You have to be joking. He was anything but that.'

'So, did you find anything particularly interesting?'

'What if I did? Why are you so interested in him if you believe he died in an accident? Is there something you're not telling me, JD?' Tim's internal antennae for a good mystery were already twitching.

'No, I promise you, it's nothing more than idle curiosity.' It wouldn't do to let Tim know her mother's suspicions, not at this early stage. She would tell him later if she needed his help with anything else. 'I ought to go. It's been nice to chat. I'm sure I can put my mother's mind at ease now. Thanks a lot.'

Tim stared at her suspiciously. 'I can understand that your mother would be upset by the death of her friend's son but why would she be so worried?'

Damn it. He didn't miss a thing. 'She's not worried; she's just been pestering me to find out more information. For instance, I'm sure she didn't know that he was a beginner at paramotoring —although I doubt she even knows what that is.'

Tim gave her the look which said he knew there was more going on than she was telling him. 'Okay, have it your way. You should come round one day, JD and meet Barbara. You'd like her. I'm sure you two would get along famously.'

'Good idea. One more thing, whose idea was it not to print it in the Málaga edition?'

He blushed and said, 'Nobody's. We just didn't have any room. As I said, we sent it to the Seville office.'

She could tell from his expression that this was a lie. Someone didn't want to draw attention to the circumstances of the young man's death. But who? 'You give me a ring sometime, Tim.' She wasn't going to ask him any more about the dead man right now. She knew he had some information he was keeping to himself and could contact him later if she needed to. 'Enjoy the Feria.'

She cycled slowly back to the agency. It was very hot and she longed to take off her helmet, but she didn't want to risk another accident. It was barely two months since she had been knocked off her bicycle and broken her arm and her collar bone. Both were now healed but Federico and her mother had joined forces in trying to persuade her not to cycle in the city any more. She had listened to them and even agreed with their point of view, but eventually told them that it was the best means of transport for her and for the environment, so no-one was going to stop her just because she'd had a silly accident.

The annual fair had opened the previous Friday, the night before the man had died. She was not a great fan of the Fería of Málaga even though it was good for the economy; thousands of people descended on the city for the week to party and have a good time. They had been holding a *feria* in August for almost two hundred years; it was supposed to commemorate the re-conquest of the city from the Moors in 1487, but she doubted if even a fraction of the people attending it gave that historical detail a passing thought. These fairs were held all over Spain and, as in most European countries, they were originally a way of showing and selling livestock. Nowadays it was a week of music and song: flamenco dancing, singing, dressing up in traditional costumes and drinking the customary glasses of *fino* —she particularly liked that cold dry sherry. As she weaved her way through the dancers in the narrow streets, dodging the tables and chairs that had spilled out from the crammed restaurants, narrowly missing a guitarist who was too engrossed in his playing to see her, she was grateful that at least nowadays the horses and carriages were restricted to the purpose-built fairground on the periphery of the city and the streets smelled more of jasmine than manure.

Normally she would tell Linda and Nacho not to bother coming into work during Feria week. All the businesses and most of the shops in the city centre were closed and shuttered; only the restaurants and hotels were open and they were full to overflowing. It was as if the whole city was on holiday for the week. It wasn't until she was almost back at the agency that she began to wonder why neither Nacho nor Linda had complained when she had asked them to work today, particularly Nacho. Surely his band had things planned for Feria week, a few concerts, parties to perform at, friends to catch up with. Had she been so engrossed with the possibility of a new case to think of asking them what their plans were? Well, she would ask them now.

Both her assistants were at their desks when she arrived. 'So why don't you two have any plans for Feria this year?' she asked, as she wheeled her bicycle into the office and leant it against her desk.

'I'm too old for that,' snapped Linda. 'And anyway I'm too busy. Phil's got two appointments this week in oncology. He wants me to go with him.'

'Actually we do have a gig tonight, but don't worry I'll be all right for tomorrow,' Nacho said, looking up from his computer. 'You know I don't drink much.' He gave her that look which said it was her turn to say something.

'Okay, I get the message. Why don't you both have the rest of the day off and we'll look at this case fresh tomorrow?'

'You are so generous, Boss. You do realise hardly anyone else is working this week?'

JD laughed. 'Well we could be the exception. You've never liked being one of the herd anyway, Nacho. Tell me, have either of you ever been paragliding or anything similar?' she asked, changing the subject.

'We need a bigger office,' Linda muttered, getting up and removing a pile of magazines and newspapers from her boss's desk.

'Take them into the meeting room. You can spread them out in there,' said JD. 'Well?'

'No, never,' said Linda. 'And I don't have any desire to do so. Why? This isn't going to be my next assignment is it, JD? I think that could be a step too far for me.'

'That depends. What about you, Nacho?' She grinned at her assistant.

'You know me, Boss, the most adventurous thing I do is tuning my guitar. What's this all about?'

'I spoke to Tim. He didn't have a lot to tell me but he did say that Kiko was paramotoring at the time he died, that the engine broke down and he fell into the sea and drowned. He didn't know much about it but he said that Kiko was a novice at that particular sport and shouldn't have been anywhere near the water. He may have panicked and got caught up in the parachute.'

'*Dios mio*, that's dreadful,' said Linda. 'Don't they have instructors to advise them. Well even if I had fancied trying it out I certainly wouldn't go up in a para-motor after hearing that.'

'I'm sending you the contact that Tim gave me.' JD pulled out her phone and forwarded the details about the paramotoring club to their phones. 'He doesn't know if this man knew Kiko or not, but he does run some sort of club, so it's a possibility. It's worth having a word with him. Have either of you found out anything about our dead man yet?'

'Yes, I have an address for him. He owned an apartment not far from here, in La Malagueta, somewhere near the bullring.'

'So he didn't live in Seville?'

'Yes and no. That's his father's house and he often stayed there, but the only place registered in his name is an apartment in Málaga.'

'What about the body? Has it been released to his family yet?'

'It's still in the morgue. Because of his father being so ill, they don't want to collect it until they have arranged the funeral.'

'That's strange; normally they can't wait to get their dead into the ground. What about you, Linda?'

'Tim was right, there are a lot of photos of him with beautiful women on his arm. I don't think Rosa knew him at all, he seems to have been anything but shy. There's one where the paparazzi caught him staggering out of a nightclub one morning, looking much the worse for wear. Not a lot of facts though, just photo opportunities, and they are all at least two years old.' She pointed to the pile of magazines and added, 'I've still got a lot to go through yet. I thought I might take them home with me this afternoon.'

'That's a good idea, and if you find anything that's worth following up, pass it on to Nacho and he can check it out on the internet.'

'Okay. So what do you want me to do with this contact you sent me? And before you ask, I am not signing up for a course.'

'No, no, nothing like that. I want you to drive up there in the morning and chat to him. First of all, find out if he knew Kiko. It's possible that he didn't; there are a lot of these clubs around. Then ask him some general questions about the club and the sport. Do these machines often break down? Are there many fatalities, for example? Why would a novice be flying on his own over water? Find out anything you can which would explain why Kiko crashed and drowned.'

'So you are not discounting the fact that it could have been an accident?' asked Nacho.

'Not at all. At the moment we don't know enough about what we're looking at to make a sensible decision, but if the police aren't investigating it, then it's up to us. How easy would it be for someone to sabotage his equipment and cause his death? That's what we need to find out. Once we know for certain that it was deliberate then we can look for a motive.'

'We need to see the evidence. Do you know what's happened to the broken para-motor?' asked Linda.

'No, but I'm going to make some enquiries.'

'Estrella?'

'Yes, why not. She doesn't finish for another four weeks; I'm sure she'd like to help us.'

'Unless she's at the Feria, like the rest of the city.'

'Shouldn't you speak to Federico first?' asked Nacho.

'Yes, I will. I wish you would both stop nagging me.' Nacho and Linda stopped what they were doing and looked at her expectantly. 'Okay. I'll ring him right now. Satisfied?' They both grinned at her.

After a couple of rings, a familiar voice answered her call, 'Jacaranda, how can I help you? Does this have anything to do with your mother waking us up at an unearthly hour this morning?'

'Good morning, Federico. How are you?' she said, as though it was the first time they had spoken that day. She could see Nacho and Linda watching her closely and hoped they hadn't heard what he had just said. 'Are you free for a chat?'

'Where? I don't fancy meeting in the centre; it will be packed with people. We'd never hear ourselves speak. Why don't you come to the police station?'

She hesitated then said, 'Yes, you're right. That's a much better idea. See you in half an hour?'

'Well?' asked Nacho and Linda simultaneously.

'I'm going to the police station. It makes more sense because I can get Estrella to take me to the morgue as well while I'm there. In the meantime you two can get on with whatever it is you have planned and I'll see you both tomorrow.'

'At your command, Boss,' said Nacho, with a big grin.

Captain Federico Rodriquez Lopez was sifting his way through a pile of papers when JD was shown into his office by his sergeant. He looked up and said, 'Thank you, Luis. Can you bring us a couple of coffees.'

The sergeant looked at JD. 'The usual?' he asked.

'No, I think I'll give it a miss, thanks Luis.' She smiled at him. 'A glass of water would be great.'

The captain motioned for her to sit down. 'Okay, Jacaranda, what's this all about?'

'Well, you guessed right; it is about my mother. Or rather her suspicions.' The captain leaned back in his chair and folded his arms as he waited for her to continue. 'Did you know that the son of the Duque de Roble drowned in the harbour a couple of days ago?'

'Yes, I did hear something about it. Why?'

'My mother went to school with his aunt and his mother.'

'His mother is dead, isn't she? I didn't know he had an aunt.'

'Yes, she died when they were children, but the aunt is very much alive. My mother has lost touch with her but she is still friends with his father.'

'So? Where is this leading, Jacaranda?'

'My mother doesn't believe that Gabriel Francisco Mendoza de Goya Pérez died in an accident; she is convinced that he was murdered.' There now she had said it.

'Rosa sees a crime around every corner. Why on earth would she think that? It looks very much like an unfortunate accident to me.'

'Because the duke's secretary rang her and said the duke found it suspicious that not long after he was told that he was terminally ill, his son and heir drowned.'

'Coincidences happen.'

'You're being very cagey, Federico. I know you. You are not telling me everything you know.'

The captain lifted his hands in protest. 'You're wrong. I don't know anything about it, except that a young man and the remains of his para-motor were fished out of the harbour, last Saturday.'

'So where is the para-motor now?'

The captain shrugged his shoulders. 'I expect it's with the rest of his belongings, waiting for the family to collect them.'

'Have forensics examined it?'

'Now, why would they do that? We have photographed the para-motor and sent the photos to the family in case they want to make an insurance claim, but now it's up to them. Look if you have any evidence that this was more than an accident then let me have it and we will look into it further.'

She could hear the irritation creeping into his voice. 'Well if you had told the forensic team to examine the para-motor then you might have your evidence.'

'Don't get on your high-horse with me, Jacaranda. I am not going to spend the department's resources on a wild goose chase just because your mother knows the Duque de Roble.'

The door to his office opened and a young man in uniform came in. 'Sorry, *Capitán*. I didn't realise you had someone with you.' He turned towards her. 'Oh JD. It's you. How are you?'

'Ricardo? What a surprise. So you are back in Málaga, now.'

'Well, the exchange was for six-months but I decided to come back a couple of weeks early because Estrella was going on leave.'

'Well, it's great to see you. Where's Estrella then, back in the UK?'

'Cycling around Italy, I think,' said Federico. 'Then she's back here to tie up a few loose ends before returning to work at the Met.'

'And her Spanish boyfriend?'

Federico grinned. 'I think that's one of the loose ends she has to sort out. I've told her that there could be a job for her here if she's interested, but she was very non-committal about it.'

'Really? You mean your charm didn't work on her.'

The captain did not answer her but turned to Ricardo instead. 'Well *Cabo*, what is it you want?'

'The funeral parlour just rang. Apparently the Duque de Roble's secretary has been on the telephone to say that they want to hold the funeral for the duke's son next week, so can we keep his body in the morgue until then.'

'Did you point out that we are a police station, not an extension of their funeral parlour?'

'I did say it was rather irregular, but it seems that the duke's condition is deteriorating and his wife wants to wait to see how he is before arranging anything; she thought it would be more respectful to leave his son's body where it is until the funeral.'

'That is their problem, but I suppose, as it's the duke's son, we have to accommodate them. But make sure that the undertaker realises that this is a one-off occasion; I don't want them off-loading all their dead bodies on us whenever they are full.'

'As you will have the body for another week, perhaps we could get the pathologist to look at it,' said JD. 'And maybe look at the remains of the para-motor? Just in case.'

Ricardo looked at the captain.

'Jacaranda's mother thinks the duke's son was murdered,' he told his *cabo*.

'So does the duke. His secretary rang her about it,' she interrupted.

'Do we have any evidence?' asked Ricardo.

'Apart from the word of a sick man, heavily sedated with pain killers and an old woman who has read too many detective stories. No, we don't.'

JD bit her lip. It was a good job that the lance corporal was there or she would have told the captain what she thought of his dismissive attitude. 'You don't know that because you haven't looked at any of his belongings. The evidence could be sitting there, waiting for someone to discover it.'

'What sort of evidence are you talking about?' asked Ricardo.

'The remains of his para-motor. But I'm not going to find anyone to examine it this week. Everyone is on holiday,' said the captain.

'I can have a look at it for you. I'm no expert but I could tell you if anything is missing or looks odd. I go paragliding and paramotoring whenever I get the opportunity, which unfortunately is not that often. The instructors insist on making sure that everyone can do the safety checks on their own equipment. They can be very rigorous,' said Ricardo.

'That would be wonderful,' said JD, beaming at the lance corporal. 'Then if everything looks correct, we will know that it was an accident.'

'Don't you have anything else to do, *Cabo*?'

'Not right now, *Capitán*. I would be happy to help.'

The captain scowled at JD and said, 'All right, but don't spend too much time on it.'

JD beamed at Federico and hurriedly followed Ricardo out before the captain could change his mind.

She let the lance corporal lead the way to the evidence room. 'So what did you think of London?' she asked. 'Did you enjoy working at the Met?'

'Yes, I did. I struggled a bit with my English, but the people there were very helpful. Especially your friend, Bill. He's a really nice guy.'

'No thoughts about staying in the UK, then?'

He shook his head. 'Even if I had wanted to, I don't think it would have been possible. No, I'm pleased to be back in Spain. To be honest I missed the sunshine.'

'Well, we're pleased to have you back.'

He took the key out of his pocket and unlocked the door to the evidence room, then checked the reference number for the dead man's possessions. 'This is it, then.' He pulled out a large tray containing the remains of the para-motor. 'It certainly looks a mess.'

'But that could have happened when they were salvaging it,' JD commented.

'Yes, we need to see if there is any damage that looks suspicious.' He carried the box over to a table and carefully laid out the remains.

JD was not sure what to look for, but Ricardo seemed to know what he was doing. 'There is not really much that can go wrong with the equipment,' he explained as he stretched the guide lines out on the table and examined them. 'Less than one in fifteen-hundred flights end in death and then it's usually due to pilot error, and mostly from inexperience.'

'That seems to be a lot to me.' She watched him for a few more minutes and then asked, 'So, can you see anything suspicious?'

'Not really, but I'm beginning to wonder if they managed to find all his equipment.'

'Why? What's missing?'

'Well there's no safety vest here and there are no flotation pads attached to the motor.'

'Is that odd?'

'Yes, if he was intending to fly over water, it is.'

'Maybe that wasn't the original plan.'

'You need to find out how experienced he was at paramotoring, how many times he had actually flown one of these things. Apart from the fact that he didn't have all the right equipment I can't see anything wrong. However you would need forensics to take a look at it to be sure.'

'The captain won't agree to that unless I have something else to tell him.'

'If his attention was to fly over the harbour then it is very strange that he didn't have a safety vest. And he doesn't seem to have a hook knife either, although that could have been dropped and is now lying at the bottom of the harbour.'

'A hook knife?'

'He probably drowned when he fell into the water and got tangled up in the guide lines. He wouldn't have been able to escape.' Ricardo must have seen her puzzled expression because he added, 'The lines are strong, nylon ropes which attach the parachute to the motor. When he fell in the water the parachute would have collapsed and the lines would have got tangled; he needed to be able to cut through them to get himself free. The hook knife is standard issue; he should have had one.'

'Are there any more of his belongings? Maybe the knife is with them?'

Ricardo went back to investigate and returned with two more trays of Kiko's personal belongings. 'I still don't see any sign of a hook knife, nor a safety vest. I can understand the knife being missing, but not the vest.'

'It sounds as though there could have been a number of reasons he drowned?' she said.

'Yes, but the more I think about it, the evidence, what little there is of it, is all pointing to inexperience and pilot error.'

'So definitely an accident then?'

He nodded. 'What I don't understand is why he was breaking so many rules? Inexperience is one thing but this was recklessness. It is forbidden to fly below 500 metres over cities for a start, and novices are discouraged from flying over water as it's much more dangerous, for the reasons I've just pointed out. That motor is heavy; it must weigh forty-five kilos.' He lifted up the motor and grimaced. 'Imagine falling into the water with that strapped to your back.' He picked a strand of seaweed off the propeller. 'You'd sink like a stone. Even an experienced para-motorist would struggle to get out of that situation.'

'Maybe the wind blew him away from the land. Maybe he didn't intend to fly over the water.'

'Maybe. In which case it supports what I said, he was inexperienced and it was an accident.'

'Okay, thanks Ricardo. That's been really helpful.'

'That's all right, JD. Glad to be of help. Mind you, it wouldn't hurt if you were to talk to a professional about it, hypothetically like. Just to see if he could come up with anything else.'

'Yes, I might do that. I do have someone I could ask.' Maybe she should have a chat with Bob Free, herself. At least now, after listening to Ricardo, she had an idea of the dos and don'ts of paramotoring.

'Well, I'd better get back before the *capitán* accuses me of wasting time.'

'What will you tell him?' she asked. 'Do you think it's worth investigating?'

Ricardo shook his head. 'Sorry JD, but it looks like pilot error to me. He should never have been flying so low and definitely not over water. If the *capitán* asks, that is what I will have to tell him.' He looked embarrassed.

'That's okay. You are probably right. I know my mother's imagination can get the better of her sometimes.' JD felt disappointed; she had been looking forward to having an interesting case to investigate. 'Would you mind telling the captain that I'll speak to him later.'

'Will do, JD.'

As she cycled back to the agency she kept thinking about what Ricardo had told her. Unless Kiko had been drunk, why would he have gone against all the safety advice? It didn't make sense.

They needed to find out if anyone had witnessed the accident and had seen anything strange.

She was just turning off the Alameda Principal and about to take one of the few roads open to traffic during Feria Week, when a man stepped out in front of her. She skidded to a halt. 'Jacobo, what the hell are you playing at? I could have hit you,' she yelled at her old friend.

'No, you're too good a cyclist for that,' he said, giving her a big grin.

'Have you been drinking already?' she asked.

'Just one glass. It is Feria, after all. Come and join me. I'm on my way back to the studio.'

JD dismounted from her bicycle and walked beside him. She could feel the sweat trickling down her forehead and removed her helmet. 'That's better,' she said, shaking her head. 'So you haven't taken the week off?'

'Can't afford to. We have a documentary that's due to be broadcast on the 3rd September and it's nowhere near ready yet.'

'What's it about?'

'Hypnotism.' He looked at her, trying to gauge her reaction. 'Surprised?'

'Not really,' she lied. Jacobo's documentaries were usually about local politics, social issues or well-known celebrities. Why the change?

'No questions?' he asked, looking slightly disappointed at her lack of interest.

She shook her head.

'Not even one?'

'Maybe another time. We might have a new case to investigate. The accidental (or otherwise) drowning of the Duque de Roble's son.'

'Yes, I heard about that. My colleague has been preparing a documentary about the family ever since the duke became ill. I don't think he's got long to go, now.' He stopped and looked at her. 'So you think it's a suspicious death?'

'Personally I'm not sure, but my mother is convinced of it.'

'I see. Well if there is anything you want to know about his family, I'm sure Enzio will be glad to help.'

'Enzio? Do I know him?'

'Yes of course. He's the one with the beard.'

She laughed. 'You've all got beards in that studio, including you. Idiot.' She gave his greying beard a gentle tug. 'But thanks, I'll bear that in mind if we decide to go ahead with an investigation. Now I'd better get back. I told Nacho I would only be half an hour.'

'And?'

'That was at least an hour ago.'

'Take him some breakfast on your way. Then he'll forgive you anything.' He kissed her on both cheeks and added, 'Put your helmet back on and be careful on that bike. You never know who might step out in front of you.'

She grimaced but did as he said. 'I don't suppose you know if there is any CCTV coverage in the port?' she asked.

'It depends what you mean exactly? The Port of Málaga installed a completely IP-based system some years ago. It monitors all the incomings and outgoings of the port, with video surveillance and audio PA and intercoms. It's supposed to provide the port with site-wide security plus support for its logistics operation. It was state of the art when it was installed.'

'And it covers the whole port?'

'Well, it covers all of the working area of the port. If you are talking about the part open to the public, then probably not.

There could be the odd CCTV installation, but I can't say off hand.'

'Okay. Thanks.'

'Why the interest?'

'We need to find someone who actually witnessed the accident.'

'Well, I expect the woman who phoned the coast guards saw what happened.'

She stared at him. 'Of course. SEMAR will have the number and a recording of the call. Thanks.'

'You will have to hurry; I believe she was a tourist. She might have gone home by now.'

'That's all I need, the only witness we know about and she could be on a flight to the UK.' She climbed onto her cycle and said, '*Adios*, Jacobo. I'll let you know if we decide to take up the investigation.'

'Yes, do that.' He waved to her and then weaved his way through a group of middle-aged women dressed as flamenco dancers until he was out of sight.

It took her another fifteen minutes to wend her way through the crowds until at last she turned into the narrow passageway behind the Bishop's Palace, where their office was located.

'Sorry I'm late,' she said. 'It's bedlam out there. And so damned hot.'

'So how did you get on?' asked Linda.

'Not as well as I had hoped?'

'Did you speak to the captain?' asked Nacho, as he removed the paper top from his coffee cup.

'I did, although it didn't do much good. He won't call in forensics unless we can convince him that the death was not accidental. I knew it was a waste of time speaking to him.'

'What about Estrella? Did you see her?'

'No, she's on vacation, but I did see Ricardo.' JD proceeded to tell them how she and Ricardo had examined the dead man's belongings, including the engine of the para-motor.

'Well that's something. Did you find anything suspicious?'

'Not according to Ricardo. In fact, much as I hate to admit it, I'm starting to believe that it was an accident after all.'

'But Rosa said...' began Nacho.

'Listen you two. My mother is not always right.'

'So I don't need to read any more of these boring magazines?' asked Linda, closing the one she had been reading and adding it to the pile.

'I didn't say that. It's just that I don't want you both to get your hopes up.'

Linda grinned at Nacho. 'Well now that's clear.' They both began to laugh.

'I bumped into Jacobo on the way here. Literally. The idiot stepped out in front of me.'

'And?'

'He said we should contact SEMAR and get the details of the person who phoned for help.'

'I did that while I was waiting for you to arrive,' said Nacho. 'It was a foreigner, a man having lunch. He rang them but there was also an English woman who witnessed what happened; she was sunbathing on that little stretch of beach near the port.'

'The Playa de la Malagueta?'

'Yes, but at the end close to the harbour. She saw him blown across the harbour wall and when the coastguard arrived she told them what she had witnessed.'

'Did SEMAR give you any details of who she is and where we can contact her?'

'Yes, eventually.' He gave her his customary grin. 'I'll send the details to your mobile.'

'Send them to Linda as well. Look we'll give it a day, and if we haven't found anything to substantiate my mother's claim by tomorrow evening, then we abandon it.'

'Sounds a good idea. There's only one problem,' said Nacho.

'And that is?'

'Most of Málaga is on holiday this week. It's going to be hard to locate anyone and even if we do, will we get any answers?'

'You've done all right so far, Nacho. I'm sure your charm will work wonders as always. Well I'm off to see my mother and talk to her maid.'

'Your mother has a maid?' Linda's eyes widened in surprise.

'Well, she's her housekeeper and cook, but my mother likes to refer to her as her maid. Paola. She's been with her as long as I can remember, and is like part of the family now. I'm sure you've met her, Linda. That time when Rosa invited us all round for pre-Christmas drinks.'

'The Argentinian woman? Yes, I know whom you mean.'

'Not much gets past Paola. I'm sure she would have seen something if she was home at the time of the accident.'

'What makes you think that?' asked Linda, looking perplexed.

'Because she spends most of her time either cleaning windows or looking out of them.' The others just stared at her.

'And my mother's new flat looks right over the port. There is a slight chance the maid saw something. And if she didn't then the neighbours might have done.'

'It's worth a try, and it'll show Rosa that we are taking her seriously,' said Nacho, closing his laptop and slipping it into his rucksack. 'You did say we could have the afternoon off?'

'Of course. Linda, will you have the car tomorrow?'

'I can do. Why?'

'I think I ought to go with you to talk to Bob Free. I'd like to know if he knew the duke's son, or trained him even.'

'El Torcal, isn't it?'

'Yes, I'm sure Nacho will find the address for us. I'd like to go first thing.'

Linda sighed. 'Okay, JD. I'll pick you up at eight-thirty. Is that early enough for you?'

'You're a star, Linda. Okay guys, see you tomorrow.'

CHAPTER 3

There was nowhere to park outside JD's apartment, so Linda double-parked beside a black BMW and sent her boss a message to say that she had arrived. It was exactly eight-thirty but she hadn't really expected JD to be ready on time, so settled down to read a message from her youngest daughter. Laura was spending the summer in Manchester with her grandparents and according to her frequent texts was enjoying herself, despite the constant rain. There was no mention of her missing them or wanting to come home before school restarted, so all Linda could assume was that her daughter was having a great time and had probably met a boy she liked; Laura had been falling in and out of love since she was twelve. She didn't want to ask her outright because it would lead to an argument and that was the last thing she wanted with her headstrong fifteen-year-old, especially when she was so far away. She would ask Jane; if Laura had her eye on someone then she would want to tell her sister all about it. Before Jane had had the baby, the two of them had been very close, but now that Jane was a married woman and a working mother, their lives were quite different. Maybe Linda should ring her husband and see how he was coping with his grandson. She dialled his number and was pleased that he picked up so quickly.

'What is it, Linda? Ramon has just got off to sleep. I'll murder you if he wakes up,' he whispered.

'Hi Phil, I just wanted to check that you were managing all right?'

'At the moment. Don't worry about me. His other granny is coming over to collect him at lunchtime; I should be able to hang on until then.'

'I'm really sorry about this, but I couldn't say no to JD. This could turn out to be a murder enquiry. I'll be home as soon as I can.' She glanced up; someone was getting into the black BMW. She stared at the tall, bearded man who waved at her cheerily before indicating that he was going to pull out. Federico. 'Sorry, Phil. I've got to go.' She returned Federico's wave then put the car into gear and moved it back so that he could drive off.

Were he and JD living together now? Of course her boss would never admit it, so there was no point asking her. Still it would be nice if they decided to get married. She knew that Federico had asked JD and she had turned him down; he had muttered something about it once at a drunken party then laughed and said she should take no notice of his ramblings. She had never asked JD if it was true; she knew better than to do that.

'At last. I thought you'd slept in. I was just about to phone you,' she said as JD clambered into the car.

'Have you been waiting long?' JD asked.

'No, just a few minutes.' She decided not to mention that she had seen the captain leaving. 'I've put the address in the GPS; it's about three quarters of an hour from here.'

In fact it turned out to be a much slower drive up the windy road to the mountain range of El Torcal. 'Are you sure this is the right way?' JD asked.

'It's what Google maps are telling me.'

'But there's nothing here but bare rock. There's no sign of much going on up here at all, just the occasional goat.'

'Patience. We are apparently only ten minutes away from our destination. Enjoy the view.' It was spectacular scenery. Even though Linda had been there before, she was still impressed by the naturally formed towers and columns of ancient karstic limestone, which millions of years ago had lain beneath the sea. Today they looked as though some prehistoric giant had created them for his own pleasure using an ancient version of Lego. JD was right, there was little sign of life on the bare mountainside. A bird of prey flew over, too high for her to identify clearly, and hovered for a moment scouring the landscape for food.

'I can't see how anyone can run a para-motor school up here. It must be so cold and windy in the winter and baking in the summer,' JD said. As though to emphasise the truth of her statement a strong gust of wind buffeted the car sideways. 'Careful,' she warned Linda.

'Don't panic. Once we get round the next bend we will be sheltered from the wind, and besides which we are almost there.'

'You said that before,' JD muttered.

'You can drive if you want.'

'No, take no notice of me. I didn't get much sleep last night.'

Linda was tempted to ask her the reason for that but decided it was not a good idea. 'There. I told you we were almost there.' To reinforce that, the automated voice on her mobile began to chant 'Destination. Destination.' She quickly turned it off and drove into an open parking area.

'Are you sure this is the right place?' JD asked.

'Pretty sure. This is the visitors centre; it said that his shop was somewhere near here.' She started walking towards a low concrete building. 'We can always ask in there.'

A group of hikers wearing shorts and hiking boots were just setting off up a track between the rocks, flat plates of limestone piled one on top of the other, like man-made steps. The fluorescent rucksacks of the hikers added a ribbon of colour to the uniform grey of the landscape, while peering down at them in curiosity was an Iberian ibex, its long curved horns silhouetted against a cloudless blue sky. It was going to be another hot day.

Bob Free was a tall, pleasant Australian who greeted them with a broad smile and a strong handshake. 'So what can I do for you ladies? Have you come for the paragliding class?' He was looking at their clothes in puzzlement.

Linda stifled a laugh; surely he didn't think they wanted to go paragliding dressed in flimsy dresses and sandals? 'No, we just wanted to talk to you.'

'We believe you knew Gabriel Mendoza?' asked JD, getting straight to the point.

'Kiko? Yes I did. We weren't mates or anything like that, but he came up here a few times. What about him?'

'I expect you heard that he died recently?'

'No, I hadn't. I'm sorry to hear that. What happened to him?'

'That's what we are trying to find out.'

The smile faded from his face. 'So why are you asking me? I hardly knew the bloke. I sold him some equipment once, but that was all.'

JD began to explain about Kiko's death and how the police were inclined to dismiss it as accidental. 'We are trying to find out how such an accident could happen; his family are devastated and want some answers. We are presuming that the young man didn't just decide to buy a para-motor and set off on his own.'

'No, of course not. It isn't classified as a dangerous sport, but like anything else with an element of danger you have to know what you're doing. If someone comes here to buy a para-motor I make sure that they already have some experience, and if not then offer them free lessons before they buy it. Paramotoring is not for everyone. It's exhilarating of course, but basically you are flying maybe 3,000 metres above the ground, with a heavy engine on your back and only a parachute to keep you afloat. You need to be able to keep your nerve and use the natural elements to help you.'

'The wind, you mean?'

'Yes, and the thermals. It helps if you have learnt to paraglide first, but it is not essential; although personally I usually recommend it. If they enjoy paragliding then taking a para-motor up is a lot easier.'

'You will have to explain,' said JD, looking puzzled.

'Well paragliding depends totally on the natural elements and the pilot's experience and skill. With a para-motor, unlike paragliding, the engine provides a constant forward motion which stops the wings folding in on themselves.'

'So it should be safer?'

'In theory, but in both cases, there are lots of things that can go wrong, something as simple as a sudden gust of wind for instance.'

'But what specifically can go wrong with the para-motor?'

'Well the engine can stall if there are rising thermals, or if there's any sudden upward flow of air, or even by flying too slowly. The weather conditions are important too; the para-motorist should avoid gusty conditions, cloudy weather and definitely rain. Also we recommend that they go out either in the evening or early morning; midday is not a good time because there's always a risk of hot thermals then.'

'Goodness. Sounds a dangerous hobby to me. What else can go wrong?'

'Well, it's like most things in life; you have to use your common sense. Don't fly too low, or near trees and bushes. If you're flying with someone else be sure to know where they are at all times so you don't become tangled up in their lines. And don't fly over water unless you have no other choice.' He handed JD a leaflet. 'This is a list of the dos and don't that I give to beginners.'

'To be clear, he bought a new para-motor from you?'

'Yes, and it was under guarantee. Plus he wanted various other bits of kit. He wanted it all perfect. He agreed with me that it was foolish to take chances with faulty or sub-standard equipment.'

JD looked at the leaflet. 'So any of these things could have caused Kiko's death? He was flying low over the harbour for some reason,' she told him. 'And at midday.'

'If he had been more experienced he would never have done that, especially somewhere as crowded as the port of Málaga. Everyone knows they aren't allowed to fly below five hundred metres when they are above a town or city. Maybe he had a blackout. Then he would have definitely lost control of the para-motor and lost altitude. '

'There has been no mention of that. All we have heard is that he got tangled up in his harness and that was why he drowned.'

'Did he attempt to cut himself free?'

'We don't know. The harness was intact and there was no sign of any knife, but then he may have dropped it.'

'No hook knife? Well I know he had one, because it was in the kit with all the other essentials. That's odd. He should have checked that he had it with him. It's normally attached to the belt so that it doesn't get lost, although some guys like to carry it in the pocket of their safety vest.' He paused and added, 'That's something else that can cause accidents, not checking your gear every time you go up. Sometimes a loose screw is enough to bring you down with a crash.'

'One more question, do you run your courses from here?' Linda asked.

'Not all of them. There are a number of sites we use. Why are you asking?'

'We still don't understand why Kiko was flying so low at the time, and why he was flying over water. I thought maybe you had another training area that took them over the sea. On the beach for example. I have seen para-motors taking off from the beach in the winter.'

Bob Free shook his head. 'You can take off from ground level - the engine will lift you into the air eventually - but there are not many suitable sites for that around here, especially at this time of year. The beaches are too busy in summer. You need to be able to have a runway in order to take off, a bit like a plane.'

'So you are telling us that Kiko would have known about all these rules?' JD asked, waving the leaflet in front of him. 'What to do and not to do?'

'Yes, I expect so. As I said at the beginning I didn't know him very well and I didn't give him any training. My mate, Juan Felipe Moreno did that.'

'I heard it suggested that it was the first time he had gone up in a para-motor and that was why he made so many mistakes, which led to the accident. Is that right?'

'Not at all. I don't know where you got that from. He'd been up many times. Although I didn't train him myself, I know that he was having lessons with Juan and you can't learn how to fly a para-motor without actually doing it. They must have flown together many times. No, it definitely was not his first and only time.'

'So the man who trained him, Juan, is he here today?'

'No, he doesn't work for me. To be honest with you, I don't think he should be teaching people at all; he's an unemployed fireman who considers himself an expert in paramotoring.'

'But you don't agree?'

'No, I don't. He has the wrong temperament; the man is a risk taker. He got sacked from the fire-service because he became obsessed with jumping off high buildings in his spare time.'

'So why did you let him teach Kiko?'

Bob stared at her. 'He was a grown man. What was I supposed to do? He and Juan became friends and so he asked him to teach him to para-motor. Nothing to do with me.' He looked decidedly irritated at her comment and added, 'It was Juan who brought him here to buy his gear.'

'Of course. I understand. I'm sorry; I put that badly. Do you have Juan Felipe's number by any chance?'

'I do, in fact. He buys stuff from me from time to time.' He held out his hand for JD's mobile and typed in the number.

'Thanks. You have been most helpful, Bob.'

'That's okay. Glad to help.' He shook her hand again and beamed at them. 'So you Sheilas are sure you don't want to learn to para-motor?'

'Not today, but thanks anyway,' said Linda with a laugh. She had enough in her life to worry about, without fretting about the dos and don'ts of paramotoring.

As they drove back along the mountain road towards Antequera, JD said, 'Well that was very interesting, but I'm not sure if we learnt anything that suggested a suspicious death. If anything it is beginning to look more and more like an accident.'

'I agree. Especially as it sounds as though he wasn't taught properly in the first place. Maybe we should speak to this Juan

Felipe? If he was as big a risk-taker as it sounds then he may have egged Kiko on to do something he shouldn't have attempted.'

'Yes, that's possible. Can you do that tomorrow?'

Linda groaned. Tomorrow she had promised to accompany Phil for his check-up. 'Why don't you ask Nacho to have a chat with him? I bet he'd get a lot more out of him than I would.'

For a moment JD was silent. 'Yes, I think that's a good idea, Linda. They can chat about living dangerously.'

Linda laughed. The most dangerous thing Nacho ever did was hack into government computers.

'Perhaps you could go and see the tourist who witnessed Kiko fall in the harbour, instead,' JD added.

'It will have to be in the afternoon.' She hated refusing JD but she had to put Phil first. He had been very depressed lately, probably due to the chemotherapy treatment, and she wanted to be there for him. He had always been the strong, positive one in the family—their daughter Laura was much the same—but lately she had noticed how much he turned to her for support. She was not going to let him down when he needed her.

'That's okay. Find out if she told SEMAR when she was leaving Málaga. We don't want to find it's too late and she has already left.'

'Okay, Boss. So what are you going to do?'

'I'm going to visit Paola. I'm sure she would have seen something.'

'Oh well, good luck with that.'

'Señora Dunne, come in. I will tell your mother that you are here,' said Paola, opening the door as soon as she rang the bell.

'*Buenos días*, Paola. No need. It's you I would like to speak to.' Paola, an Argentinian immigrant who had arrived in Spain while still a child, stopped and stared at her. For a moment JD saw a flash of fear in her eyes. 'It's okay, Paola, I just want to ask you a few questions about the young man who drowned the other day.'

'Oh, yes, the son of the duke. Poor man. Such a terrible accident. Shall I make some coffee first?' she asked, relief relaxing her face into its usual sunny smile.

'No, don't bother. A glass of water would be fine. It's so hot today.' What was the maid frightened about? Surely not deportation. Rosa would have made sure that all Paola's papers were in order before employing her. Her mother was meticulous about that sort of thing, about most things in fact. JD sat down on an elegant sofa positioned next to one of the large French windows that opened onto a wide terrace filled with pots of red geraniums—her mother's favourite flowers. From this position it was possible to see the holiday makers stretched out below them on the beach and the usual hustle and bustle of activity in the port. She took the binoculars from their hook and adjusted them to suit her eyes. She could make out the faces of the people on the beach quite clearly. She lowered them and viewed the panorama below her; if anyone in the neighbouring flats had been looking out at the port when the accident happened, they would have seen everything from this height. Today the port was crowded with the numerous passengers who had just disembarked from a cruise liner that had recently docked in Málaga; the travellers were heading towards the city centre. Is that what had happened when Kiko died? Had he brought his para-motor down so that he could take a closer look at a cruise liner, then realised he was too low and lost control? It was a possibility, but seemed unlikely. Surely even an inexperienced flyer would know that it could be dangerous; a sudden gust of wind could have blown him against the turrets of the liner. It would be interesting to hear what Nacho finds out from the guy who trained him. There had to be some reason other than inexperience for him to have been flying so low, but what was it and was it intentional on his part?

'*Señora*?'

JD turned round. The maid was standing behind her holding a tray with a carafe of iced water and two glasses. 'Would you like us to sit here, by the window?'

'Yes, thank you.'

'How can I help you, *Señora*?' Paola asked as she poured some water into the glasses.

JD did not reply straight away and for a moment she stared out at the view in silence. Was this all just a waste of time? Her mother could get so obsessed with an idea that she lost all objectivity; JD had to be sure she didn't do the same thing. 'I just wondered if you had been here when the poor man drowned and if you saw anything,' she asked, picking up her glass.

Paola shook her head. 'No, *Señora*. I told you, I saw nothing at all. I was probably in the kitchen at the time.'

'And you didn't hear any of the neighbours commenting on what had happened?'

'No.'

JD waited for her to say more, but Paola avoided looking at her, instead she fiddled with one of the lacy serviettes that she had put on the coffee table. Was she hiding something or was she just nervous at being questioned by her employer's daughter? This was not like Paola; she was usually so chatty. 'That's surprising. I would have thought the gossips would have leapt at the news and it would be buzzing around the building by now. Are you certain nobody saw anything?'

'If they had, I'm sure I would have heard about it,' the maid said at last, a little curtly. She took a sip of water and pursed her lips, something JD had seen her do before when she was annoyed.

'So it's not worth me knocking on their doors to ask them?'

'Maybe, *Señora*. But I think it would be a waste of your time.' Now the maid had begun to look anxious, even fearful, again.

'Is there something you're not telling me, Paola?' JD asked as gently as she could.

'No, *Señora*.' She stood up. 'If that's all, then I ought to get on. Your mother is having guests for dinner tonight and I have a lot to prepare.'

'Okay. Can you tell my mother I am here; I'd like to have a word with her.'

'Yes, *Señora*.'

JD poured herself some more water and leaned back on the moquette cushions. There was definitely something odd about Paola's behaviour today; she could sense that she was not happy being questioned by JD. Surely if she had seen something she would tell her. After all what was there to be frightened about? Not for one minute did she imagine that Paola was involved in Kiko's death. So why was she behaving so strangely?

'Ah, there you are, Jacaranda. Do you have any news?' Rosa glided into the room wearing a long pink housecoat and sat down beside her daughter. 'No coffee today? Didn't Paola offer you any?'

'I didn't really fancy any.'

'How long have you been here?'

'Not long, Mama. I just wanted to have a quiet word with Paola first.'

'Well did she have anything to add to what she told you before?'

JD shook her head. 'No, she says she didn't see anything at all.'

'Well then.' She looked at her daughter. 'What is it?'

'She doesn't want me to bother your neighbours. She reckons that no-one would have seen anything but I find that hard to believe. I know you were out when the accident happened but if you had been here do you think you would have seen something?'

'Yes, I'm positive. The thing about these windows is that your eyes are drawn to them all the time; I walk into the room and instantly I am looking at the sky, or the sea. If a para-motor, or whatever it's called, flew past I would stop and watch it. Maybe Paola didn't see it, but I am certain that someone in this building would have.'

'That's exactly what I thought.'

'Do you want me to make some enquiries?'

'No. I'll ask Linda to come here; she can be very good at getting people to open up.'

'I have a better idea. I'll invite them all round for a drink and bring up the subject then. Someone will have something to say, if only to complain about the noise they make.' She smiled happily at her daughter. 'I have been meaning to do that ever since I moved in. You know the sort of thing. New neighbour wanting to say hello. It will be perfect. I'll invite them this Saturday, just the ones who overlook the port, of course.'

JD stifled a smile. Despite being a wealthy woman now, her mother had held onto her old parsimonious ways. 'That sounds as though it might work.' She stood up. 'And talking about work, it's time I did some.'

'You're not staying for lunch?'

'No, I need to get back to the agency.'

'You'll keep me posted?'

'Of course, but don't get your hopes up. It's looking more and more like a dreadful accident.'

'What does Federico have to say?'

'Just that. There is nothing so far to suggest otherwise.'

'You two seem to be getting on much better lately,' Rosa said, giving her a wide conspiratorial smile.

'I really must be off now, Mama.' She leant forward and gave her mother the customary kiss on both cheeks and almost ran for the door. She did not want to start a discussion about her love life with her mother; she knew exactly where it would lead.

CHAPTER 4

JD had come to terms with the fact that making any rapid progress with the enquiry during Feria week was nigh on impossible—the city had virtually ground to a halt—so she had told Nacho and Linda that they only needed to work in the mornings. She wheeled her bike through the deserted alleyways, still littered with the debris from the night before: empty wine bottles, food cartons, streamers and beer cans mostly. Someone had left a multicoloured shawl draped over one of the statues, and nearby an elderly man lay stretched out on a stone bench, his dog curled up beside him; he was fanning himself with a broken fan and smiled at JD as she walked past. As she turned into the narrow street where she had the agency, she saw the local road cleaner coming towards her.

'*Buenos días*, JD,' he said. 'You're up early. Or is it that you've not been to bed yet?'

'Yes, well some of us have to carry on working, don't we Pedro.'

'True. Have a good day.' He pushed his trolley to one side so she could pass, then carried on sweeping.

The blinds were up at the agency, a sign that Nacho had already arrived. When Antonio's bar had closed earlier that year one of the big chains had bought it and the new owners had tried to turn it into an English pub, but had failed dismally; the Union Jack on the wall looked out of place, as did the various photos of famous places in London and an old poster of the

Beetles. The cosy, grimy comfort of a typical English pub, with horse brasses on the walls and a long bar with old fashioned beer pumps on the counter had been attempted but not succeeded. Even the coffee was not as good as it had been before; as far as she was concerned it just wasn't the old familiar place any more. They had frequented Antonio's bar daily since the time that she had opened the detective agency. It was part of their life and they all thought of Antonio as a friend and even at times, when things were not going well, as a confidante. Now he was retired and had moved to Pontevedra to be nearer to his wife's family, and they were left with a pseudo-English public house which just happened to sell coffee. They would have to find somewhere else.

She pushed open the door and wheeled her bicycle into the office. '*Buenos días*, Nacho.'

'Buenos días Boss. No Linda?'

'Linda has to take Phil to the hospital this morning, but Jane is coming over to stay with him when they get home, so she'll go and talk to Rachel, the tourist who saw the accident, at midday. Have you found out anything?

'I spoke to SEMAR, the *Servicio Marítimo de la Guardia Civil*, and they said that she is supposed to be leaving tomorrow evening; her flight is booked for 20.30. So it's just as well that Linda gets to speak to her today.'

'She says she will come in this afternoon and let us know how she got on.' Phil's illness was making JD realise just how much she relied on Linda. 'I see you got some coffee.' She parked her bike in its usual place and helped herself to one of the styrofoam mugs on his desk. 'Mmn. So where did you buy it this morning?' Nacho had been conducting his own personal survey of the local coffee shops ever since Antonio's had closed down.

He gave her a wide grin. 'You won't believe this but just next door. Well, down the alley and round the corner, to be precise. I think our problem is solved; we have a new coffee house at last.'

She smiled at him. 'Good, so now you can start to concentrate on our next problem. Was Kiko murdered or not? Until we establish whether or not a crime has been committed we can't go much further forward.' She replaced the styrofoam mug of coffee on his desk and said, 'Actually I don't think I fancy it today. I'm sure you could manage a second one.'

'No problem, Boss.'

'What time are you seeing Juan Felipe?'

Nacho glanced at his watch. 'In an hour. He lives in Málaga, near the Malagueta, so it won't take me long to get there.'

'That's good. Now let's go over what the officer from SEMAR told you, in detail.'

'Okay, although really he didn't have much to tell me. The coast guards were quick to reach the scene but there was no sign of the man or his para-motor. The police divers were brought in to recover his body and the damaged para-motor, but the police could find nothing unusual about the death and that's why they declared it an accident. The body was taken to the morgue and the damaged para-motor went to the police station,' he read from his notes. 'You know the rest.'

'Nothing else?'

'No. To be honest JD, I don't think they were looking for anything else. They were more concerned about saving a life, then when they realised he was already dead, it was all about recovering his remains.'

'Apparently SEMAR were there very quickly. Do we know why? They're based in Benalmadena aren't they?'

'The port authorities had already contacted them because they had spotted the para-motors heading for the harbour; they thought they might be terrorists. As they knew a team from SEMAR were already close by, investigating some incident with the local fishermen in El Palo they told them to investigate.'

'*Dios mio*, so they could have been shot down. Hang on, para-motors? Plural? Did he say that?'

'Yes. Why?'

'Well we have always assumed that Kiko was alone, but you are saying that the officers from SEMAR referred to para-motors, plural. How many did he see? And were they together? Get on to them right away and let's get this clarified. Also get more details about the incident with the fishermen; I want to know if it was just a coincidence that SEMAR were in the area at the time he drowned.'

While Nacho rang SEMAR again, JD started writing a list of possible suspects on the white board. First she listed the family members who would benefit from his death: Kiko's sister, Doña Isabella and her husband, Jorge. Their children would now be eligible to inherit, but not until their mother was dead and anyway they were far too young to really be considered as suspects, as was four-year-old Antonio. Then there was Kiko's stepmother, Leticia, Kiko's aunt Irina, her husband Armando and their son Pablo; Kiko's cousin was eighteen, old enough to qualify for the suspect list.

'Yes, JD, it's confirmed,' Nacho informed her. 'There were two para-motorists that morning and according to the chap I spoke to, they were flying one behind the other. He said that, in his opinion, they were flying too close together and it looked as though the one at the back was trying to pass the other one for some reason. So he wasn't that surprised when they got the call to say that one of them had gone into the harbour.'

'Well that changes everything. Why hasn't this person come forward to say that he was there?'

'He might have had nothing to do with him. In fact, I think his presence suggests an accident was the more likely cause of death. From what the officer said Kiko sounds as though he was not able to control his para-motor properly, and the witness had told him that he was flying erratically.'

'But it could have just been the wind. What about the fishing incident?'

'It was nothing really, just someone who had reported a couple of fishing boats being too close to the beach; they had drifted inside the buoys and an irate swimmer had telephoned SEMAR to complain.' Nacho looked at his watch. 'I'd better go. I'll see you later.'

'Okay. Try to find out exactly how much flying experience Kiko had with para-motors. I can't believe he was the novice that Tim suggested. And send me what you have found out about the duke before you leave and I'll go through it.'

'Sending it to you now.'

JD went back to the evidence board and scrawled *Mystery man*, then crossed out *man* and wrote *person*. So who was this person and were they connected to Kiko's death? Or was it, as Nacho was suggesting, nothing more than an unfortunate accident? She sat back and studied the board then stood up and crossed out inexperienced and wrote erratic. Their conversation with Bob Free had convinced her that Tim was wrong when he had suggested that Kiko had not flown a para-motor before. Let's see what Nacho could find to back that up.

She opened the file that her assistant had sent her and then remembered that Jacobo had told her that they were preparing a documentary about the duke. What was the guy's name? Enzio. She took out her mobile and rang Jacobo's number.

'JD, nice to hear from you, as always. Is this a work call or a fun call, because you do realise it's Feria week don't you?'

'I do, but I need some information and I know you will have it, because you have already told me that Enzio is preparing a documentary about the duke's life.'

'Okay, so what do you want?'

'I want to have a chat with Enzio. Can you arrange that for me?'

'I can, but it will cost you lunch.'

'I'll put it down on my expenses.' They both laughed at this, as they knew JD did not have an expense account and Jacobo always ended up paying for lunch.

'I'll ring you when I've spoken to him. When did you have in mind?'

'As soon as possible. The man is dying; I would like to let him know that we are taking his fears seriously before it's too late.'

'I'll see what I can do. Got to go now.' She could hear a woman laughing in the background and for a moment felt a twinge of jealousy. How ridiculous; her affair with Jacobo had been years ago, and after a few euphoric months she had soon come to the conclusion that he was better as a friend than a lover. They had remained close friends ever since.

'Thanks, speak tomorrow,' she replied, but by now the phone had gone dead. She turned back to the file that Nacho had sent her. He hadn't come up with a lot of information but some of it was very interesting, and what with Enzio's contribution she should have a clear picture of *el Duque* before finally meeting him. And the only way that could happen was if her mother arranged it. She groaned. What was she doing? She was planning to interview a dying man about his son's death when she still wasn't sure whether it had been an accident or not. She had to prioritise. Was it murder or was it an accident? That single fact had to be established before she could go chasing around the country interviewing suspects. She turned back to the evidence board; all the suspects had something to gain from Kiko's death, but that didn't mean they had caused it.

She opened her mobile and dialled Federico's number.

'Jacaranda? Everything all right?'

'Yes, all fine. I need to speak to you and I thought we could have lunch at the same time. We could go somewhere quiet, away from the centre?'

'Is this about the dead man?'

She sighed. He knew her so well. 'Actually it is. I just need to ask your opinion.'

'Ask my opinion? Well, that's a first. Do I need to buy you lunch for you to be able to do that?'

'No, but I am rather hungry; I didn't have time for breakfast this morning.'

'And whose fault is that?'

She could imagine him sitting there in his office, with a big smile on his face and felt a surge of love for him. 'Yours, of course,' she said with a laugh. 'So what about it? Lunch at two o'clock? Nacho and Linda are only working in the mornings this week, so the office will be closed.'

'You've given them the afternoon off? Now I know that something is bothering you. I'll meet you at one-thirty at the end of the port; there's a nice little restaurant there called La Lonja.'

'Yes, I know it. See you later then.' It had been a regular haunt for her and Jacobo when she had first opened the agency. That all seemed a long time ago now; it was just after her husband had been killed and she was a mess. Jacobo had been a great help to her in those early days, then they had drifted apart and she had met Federico and fallen in love. Federico. She had to make a decision soon or she would lose him; she was certain of that. For years she had told herself she could never have a permanent relationship again until she had found out who was behind her husband's death. Well, now she knew and it was thanks to Federico. He had said nothing about his role in solving the crime, but Estrella had let it slip one day when they were celebrating having solved their latest case. JD had been astounded but never said anything to him. So what was she waiting for? Maybe she would tell him that she knew, today, over lunch. Or was she still going to hang on to the only excuse she had for refusing to marry him?

At one-thirty she closed and locked the agency then headed off towards the port. The centre of Málaga was already filling up with hundreds of people enjoying the Feria, tables were set ready for lunch, enormous blinds shaded the crowded streets from the hot, midday sun and the music and dancing had already started. She wended her way through the back streets and alleyways until she reached the park and began to cycle happily along its cool, shady paths, past rows of botanical plants, trees and bushes imported from all over the world, eucalyptus from Australia, Yucca trees from Central America, palm trees from Mexico, China and India. It was a beautiful day and despite the dilemma about the case, she was feeling positive. Today was the day when she would get her personal life back on track. Steed had disappeared off the radar but that didn't mean she had to spend the rest of her life worrying about him. If Federico still wanted to marry her then she would accept him; she might even propose herself. A buzz in her back pocket told her she had a message, so she pulled up under the shade of an English oak tree and pulled out her mobile phone. Was lunch cancelled? She felt a tinge of disappointment. No, the message was from Nacho. All it said was, 'You'll want to hear this, JD.' She considered ignoring it, but then remembered that Nacho wouldn't be sending her a message this afternoon unless he thought it was important. 'Nacho? What's up? Is Juan Felipe a suspect now?'

'It's nothing to do with the case. Something much more interesting, JD. You remember I was routinely checking to see what they were going to do with Antonio's bar? Out of curiosity, nothing more.'

'Yes. I do. So?' Why would Nacho think that was of any interest to her? He was the coffee freak in the team.

'The new owners have closed down the English style pub they had set up and the estate agents have sent me a notification to tell me that the site is available on a three-monthly basis as a pop-up coffee shop until they can find a new buyer. They wanted to see if I was interested. So I thought I would check out the owner of the pop-up shop, just out of interest you know. At first it was not listed but, you know me, I have ways of finding out what I want. Well, you are not going to believe this.'

'I'm not if you don't tell me. Hurry up, Nacho. I'm stopped under an oak tree and the squirrels are bombarding me with acorns.'

'Too soon for acorns.'

'Nacho.'

'It's an Englishman called Thomas Steed. Now, do you think that is a coincidence?' he asked. 'Doesn't sound like it to me.'

Despite temperatures of nearly forty degrees JD felt herself go cold. She couldn't speak. Her mind was spinning. How could this be happening? Was this a vendetta on his part? How come nobody knew what he was doing? And where the hell was he? Was he in Málaga right now, invisible amongst the thousands of tourists here for Feria week? She automatically looked around her, half expecting to see him leering at her from amongst the trees. No, this could not be happening.

'JD? Are you all right? JD?'

She forced herself back into the present and replied, as calmly as she could, 'Yes, I'm fine. Well, that is a surprise. Thanks, Nacho. Don't speak about this to anyone, please.' She hung up, and climbed on to her bicycle and pedalled slowly towards the port. Just when she thought it was all over, here he was again, haunting her. What on earth was she going to do about it? If anything.

Federico was already at the restaurant when she arrived. 'What is it? What's happened?' he asked, taking the bicycle from her and propping it against the wall. 'You look as though you've seen a ghost.'

'I have in a way, I suppose. Pour me a glass of wine, please. Then I'll tell you.'

Federico poured her a large glass of Rioja and sat back and waited for her to speak. 'Is it to do with the dead man?' he asked, eventually.

'If only. No, it's to do with someone who is very much alive, unfortunately.'

'Not Steed again.'

She nodded. 'Yes, He's opened a pop-up coffee shop in Málaga. Actually it's registered under the name of someone else, but Nacho—you know how he can't resist delving into the roots of everything—found that the actual owner of the pop-up shop is a Thomas Steed. I just can't believe it. Why would he open a pop-up shop in Antonio's old bar unless he was watching us?'

'Antonio's bar? Your old haunt? That can't be a coincidence. He has to either be here in Málaga or someone here is working for him. I think it is probably the latter; he wouldn't risk coming so close and besides I already have a friend in Interpol keeping a lookout for him.'

'Yes, but if he was in France then it's no problem for him to come to Málaga without anyone knowing, thanks to the Schengen Agreement.'

'True. Leave this with me, *Cariño*, I'll look into it. Relax. It's nothing to worry about; he is trying to spook you, that's all. I'll have a word with Jean-Paul and let him know what we've found out. I can't believe that Steed would risk coming to Málaga himself,' he repeated.

'I hope you're right. The thought of him being so close, in the city where I live and work, makes me feel quite sick.' All her old fears and inhibitions had returned; there was no way she could talk to Federico about marriage now. At least not until she had a clearer picture of where Thomas Steed actually was and what he wanted from her.

'Now, what else did you want to talk to me about?'

'Let's order first and then I want to talk about the duke's dead son.'

Federico sighed. 'Very well. But you have to tell me everything that you have learned so far. No secrets.'

JD's hunger had disappeared, so she ordered a tuna salad, while Federico enquired about the fish of the day. Once the waiter had left and Federico had refilled her glass, she said, 'The truth is, we still can't establish if a crime has been committed or if he was just a very foolish young man. It could be either. We are trying to find more witnesses.'

'So you're no further forward?'

'Yes, we are, but we still have no clear proof that he was murdered.' She proceeded to tell him about their talk with Bob Free and how the dead man seemed to have ignored all the normal safety precautions. 'Beside which, the duke's son does not appear to have been someone who was into extreme sports. My mother described him as shy and retiring.'

'But how old was he when she met him? Boys change. Especially when they grow into young men. Do we really have a clear picture of this young man? Have you looked into his finances, for example? Is there someone who might have had a motive to kill him?'

'No, that's just it. We know there are plenty of family members who would gain from his death, particularly his sister, but we can't go much further until we have established that his death was suspicious. For that we need a post mortem examination of the body and a full forensic analysis of his clothing and the para-motor. We know that certain safety procedures were not taken and safety equipment was missing or lost. What we don't know is why.'

'So, you want me to agree to a full investigation although it might turn out to be a waste of money?'

'Yes. He is the duke's son and heir, after all. It's impossible for us to move forward without your help, Federico.'

'Well, I never expected to hear you admit that, Jacaranda. Can I have that last statement in writing, please?'

'No, you can't.' She grinned at him. 'Also we have discovered something interesting; Kiko was not alone. There was another para-motor in the air at the same time. Now why didn't that person come forward when they saw that he was missing? Why didn't he or she stop and try to find out what had happened to him?'

'Is that so? Well that does makes a difference. I think I could now make a good case for investigating the death of the duke's son. You can liaise with Ricardo on this; I'll brief him tomorrow as soon as he gets in.'

'Damn Feria. I suppose he's gone off duty, now.'

Federico nodded. 'As you say, it is Feria Week. The only people working overtime are the uniformed staff. But it won't hurt to wait a few more hours.'

'As long as the duke doesn't die before we have had time to speak to him.'

'You are welcome to try and see him, but I bet his wife won't let you near his bedside.'

'My mother has ways of getting what she wants.'

'Don't I know it. And it appears that particular trait runs in the family.' He smiled at her and squeezed her hand. 'You concentrate on the death of the duke's son and leave me to worry about Steed. Okay?'

'Okay.' So now they could get started in earnest. She crossed her fingers that her hunch—because it was no more than that—would turn out to be correct.

CHAPTER 5

Phil's appointment was at eight-thirty. His session usually lasted about two hours by the time they had checked in, seen the nurse and he was hooked up to the infusion. He didn't really need to be accompanied but he liked to have someone with him; sometimes it was Jane but mostly it was Linda. And on one occasion, Jane's mother-in-law had taken him because there was no-one else available; he had explained to Linda that having someone else there meant that he didn't feel quite so vulnerable. Not that he talked much; usually, like today he would sit there with the drip in his arm and do the daily crossword while she read a book. Only today she couldn't concentrate. The words on the page kept blurring as her mind returned again and again to Kiko's death. She didn't believe for one moment that it was an accident; he was young but he was no fool. So far she had found no references to Kiko in the more recent magazines. There was nothing more about his love life, nor his hobbies; there were no photographs of him attending the bullfights, or at the races, no sign of him attending society weddings, or sailing a luxurious yacht. It was as if he'd already died and there was nothing for them to write about. Kiko seemed to have been deleted from all the usual paparazzi lists. Maybe he had become a recluse, but Rosa had not said anything about that. There had to be something about him somewhere, something more recent than when he was in his twenties. She put the magazines to one side and decided to search the usual social media platforms. She pulled out her phone and logged into her favourite search engine then typed in Kiko's full name: Gabriel Francisco Mendoza de Goya but all that came up were articles about his father. She added his mother's name to the end of it, Pérez, but still nothing. How strange. She then logged into Facebook and tried to locate him on that but without success. There was no trace of him on Instagram, nor TikTok, nor Twitter, not with his full name nor as Kiko Pérez or any other combinations of his name. She glanced across at her husband; he had closed his eyes and was quietly snoring. The crossword lay across his knees and his pen had fallen on the floor. Carefully she removed them both and put them on the side table. It pained her to see him like this; the chemotherapy was essential according to his oncologist, but they all knew that it would take its toll on his body before it did any good. Careful not to wake him, she dialled Nacho's number.

'Hi Nacho. Just a quick question. Have you found any trace of our dead man on social media? I've been searching for him and I can't find anything. When you get a minute can you have a look?'

'Yes, no problem. The boss has sent me to see Juan Felipe, but I've got a few minutes before I meet him; I'll have a look now. Is there anything in particular you have in mind?'

'Nothing special. I just find it strange that a man of his age doesn't appear on social media.'

'Yes, you're right. You'd expect to find him somewhere. I'll get back to you. How is Phil?'

'He's dropped off. But he doesn't seem too bad today. I'll let him know you were asking after him. Look I'd better go, the nurse is giving me a dirty look.'

'Okay, *hasta pronto*.

By mid- morning she and Phil were back at home, so she messaged Jane to let her know. 'Would you like a cup of tea?' she asked her husband, as she switched on the kettle.

'No, nothing for me, thanks. I think I will just lie down for a while. You go off to work. I'll be fine until Jane arrives.'

'All right. If you are sure.' She glanced at her phone. 'Jane's on her way. She won't be long. I'll tell her not to wake you if you're asleep.'

He nodded his head. Already he had his eyes closed and was stretched out on the sofa. She wanted to weep; it was so sad to see the change in him. The strong, active man he had been before the cancer struck was no more. Now, the man lying exhausted on the sofa was a shadow of the man she married, his body wasted by the disease that was consuming him, his once thick hair now thinning rapidly. She forced herself to be more positive; after all lots of men had prostate cancer and survived. It was just the awful chemotherapy that was draining him of his strength. She bent down and kissed him on the forehead. 'I won't be long, Darling. I promise. You have a rest. Jane will make you some lunch if you feel like eating.'

Phil grunted and turned on his side. She knew it was likely that he would still be there when she returned and Jane would tell her that he hadn't eaten anything. Jane was a good girl; she had her hands full with the new baby but she always found time to be with her father. Without her help Linda would have no option but to resign from her job and she didn't want to do that; financially things were hard enough, what with Phil on sick leave and her already working part-time.

She glanced back at her husband and closed the door quietly behind her. Rachel had agreed to meet her by the beach near the apartment where she was staying; she thought it might be useful if Linda saw exactly where she had been sitting when the para-motors went over. That alone had intrigued Linda; it sounded as though there was more than one para-motor, but if so, why had no-one mentioned it before.

Rachel Rogers was a woman in her early sixties, her greying hair lightened with blonde streaks and pulled back into a short pony tail. Her week in Málaga had given her a deep even tan and when she removed her sunglasses she looked at Linda with penetrating, blue eyes. 'I was wondering if anyone was going to ask me about the poor man,' she said, getting up from where she had been sitting on a low wall by the beach. 'I don't speak any Spanish, you see and the police preferred to talk to a man who had been watching from over there. He was the one who called the coast guards.' She pointed to a small restaurant on the other side of the road.

'Well, thank you for taking the time to speak to me,' said Linda. 'I realise this is your last day and I imagine you won't want to spend it talking about a stranger's death.'

'Actually I don't mind at all. I feel very sorry for the man and his family. I have a son about the same age and if he had an accident I know I would want to know every detail of what happened.' She stared at Linda's blue and white spotted, cotton dress, clearly not police uniform. 'Did you say you were from the police?'

'Not exactly, I work for a private detective agency. The family of the dead boy want to know more about what happened to him.'

'Didn't the police explain?'

'Yes, but I think they want more details than the police are prepared to give them. They heard that there had been another witness to his death and wondered if you could tell them anything more about what happened.' It wasn't exactly a lie,

Linda told herself. She knew the duke certainly wanted more information even if no-one in the family was aware that JD had already started investigating his son's death.

'Well, I don't think I can add much to what the other witness said.'

'So what did you see, exactly?' asked Linda. 'Can you talk me through it?'

'Well, I was lying down there, sunbathing,' She pointed to the beach in front of them. 'When two para-motors went past, very low. They were making a dreadful noise. I could hardly hear myself think.'

'So there were two of them? Were they together, do you think?'

'Oh, I think so. The older man was trying to tell the young one something but he couldn't hear him. He waved his arms about a bit then he carried on flying in that direction, out to sea.'

'Was he angry with him, do you think?'

'No, I don't think so. He didn't look angry. Maybe frustrated.' She frowned, as though trying to recall the man's expression in detail.

'Can you describe him? The other para-motorist?'

'Not really. The sun was half-blinding me. If I saw him again I might recognise him, but I can't be sure. I did notice one thing though, he was wearing expensive trainers. Air Jordan's, in a bright lime green. The sort of things a teenager would wear if they could afford them. I just found it a bit strange.'

'And the younger one didn't follow him?'

'No, he was really struggling by now. He couldn't have followed him, even if he wanted to. There seemed to be a problem with his engine and the propeller was moving more slowly; you know, you could see the individual blades instead of a blur of movement. By then he was very low, almost touching the water and I could see how scared he was; he was so close to the beach that I was frightened he would crash into me. He kept tugging at the ropes but it didn't make a lot of difference, and then suddenly there was a strong gust of wind which lifted the parachute into the air and took him and the motor with it. Then he disappeared over the harbour wall and I lost sight of him. I ran round to see if he was all right, but it took me a few minutes to get there and when I arrived there was no sign of him. He must have gone straight into the sea.'

'And what about the man who was with him?'

'He had gone. I could still see him in the distance, quite high up and heading east, away from the port and the city.'

'Did you tell the police about the other para-motorist?'

'No, as I said the man from the restaurant did the talking, but he must have seen him too,' she replied then added, 'He was English but spoke passable Spanish.'

'Then what?'

'Nothing. The coast guards, or whatever they were, arrived and pulled the para-motorist's body out of the water. There were quite a few people gathered round by then, so I went back to the beach; there was nothing more I could do. To be honest, I just wanted to get away. It really upset me; I kept seeing that look of terror on the boy's face. So in the end I decided to go back to the apartment.'

'So you can't tell me anything else about the other para-motorist?'

'Not really. The sun was so strong that most of the time I was blinded.'

Linda put her notebook back in her pocket. 'Thank you so much for talking to me, Rachel. I do appreciate it, and I'm sure the family will, as well.'

The woman shrugged. 'I keep asking myself if I could have done anything more, but I don't even swim.'

'Even if you could swim, I don't think it would have been a good idea to jump in after him. The maritime police would have been pulling you out of the harbour as well. You did what you could. Now, enjoy the rest of your stay, short though it is,' said Linda. 'And thanks, again.'

She walked back towards her car, leaving Rachel staring at the sea. Poor woman, certainly not what she was expecting from her beach holiday. So had it been worth driving over here to talk to her? Yes, it had, but now instead of answers, there was another question. Who was the second para-motorist and why did he keep going when he must have been aware that Kiko was in trouble? And where was he now? Why hadn't he come forward; he must have realised that Kiko had disappeared.

She pulled out her phone and rang her daughter. 'Hi, it's me. Everything all right?'

'Yes, fine, Mum. Stop fussing. Dad is asleep, and so is Ramon, and I'm preparing a bit of lunch for when they both wake up. How did your interview go?'

'Okay. Look, do I have time to pop into the agency? I just need to pick up a few things.'

'Of course. I'm planning on staying here at least until the baby wakes up and I can give him his feed.'

'And Dad?'

'Yes, I won't go without waking him. Do what you have to do, Mum. See you later.'

Linda felt so proud of Jane; she had made some tough decisions this year and got her life back on track. Okay it wasn't what she would have chosen for her daughter; becoming a mother at seventeen was hard, but Jane was coping much better than she could ever have imagined. She thought of little Ramon and felt so happy that Jane and her husband had made the choices they had, otherwise that little chap would not be here to give them all such pleasure.

It was quicker to leave the car in the carpark and walk to the agency. She would pick up the rest of the magazines and spend the afternoon at home looking for information on the reclusive Gabriel Francisco Mendoza Pérez; there had to be something more recent about him somewhere. These magazines survived on gossip about film stars, royalty and especially the aristocracy. He had to be in one of them.

Linda chose the back streets in order to avoid the crowds of revellers that were gradually filling the centre of the city. As she walked, she rang Nacho to see if he had found out why there was nothing about Kiko on social media, but his mobile went to voice mail; that was not like him. She expected to have received a message from him at least, so she concluded that he must still be interviewing Juan Felipe. She would ring him later, when she got home.

Phil was watching the television in the sitting room when Linda returned. She dumped the magazines on the coffee table and sat down beside him. 'Everything okay?'

'Yes, I think so. I've been asleep most of the time. Jane woke me up to have something to eat, but I couldn't face any food.'

'How was the baby?'

'Fine. What's all that about?' he asked, pointing at the pile of magazines.

'I'm trying to find out if our dead man had a social life or not. So far there's not much in the magazines and absolutely nothing on social media, which I think is very strange.'

'How old is this guy?'

'Thirty-six. Not exactly young, but I would have expected him to be on Instagram or somewhere.'

'What does Nacho say? He's usually good at that sort of thing.'

'I can't get hold of him.'

'Speak to Jane, she might have an idea.' He picked up one of the magazines and began to flick through it. 'I'll give you a hand, otherwise it will take you hours to go through all these.'

'Thanks. Want a cup of tea?'

'Yes, okay.'

While she waited for the kettle to boil she dialled Jane's number. 'Hi, Sweetheart. Thanks for looking after Dad.'

'That's okay, Mum. No need to phone.'

'Well actually, I need to pick your brains. It's about social media.'

'Really. What about it?'

'The case we're working on…'

'The man who drowned in the harbour?'

'Yes. Don't you think it's strange that I cannot find a single trace of him on social media? I do. I think it's very odd.'

'Maybe you're not putting his name in correctly.'

'I've tried all combinations of his name and nothing comes up.'

'Sometimes people don't put in their real names; they prefer to use a nickname.'

'Well that's impossible then; I can't guess a nickname for a man I don't know.'

'Some people go to a lot of trouble to keep their accounts secure but it doesn't mean they are hiding anything; they just don't want to be bombarded by a load of junk messages. Maybe the dead man valued his privacy. he was the son of a duke after all.'

'So what can I do?'

'You know, it is possible that he didn't like social media and doesn't have any accounts. Haven't you asked Nacho to help?'

'Your dad suggested that but I can't get hold of him. He's talking to a man about paramotoring.'

'Wow. That's exciting. I wouldn't have thought that was his thing.'

'It isn't. Look, I'd better get on with some work. Thanks anyway. If you get any bright ideas give me a call.'

'Linda, I may have found something. Come and look at this,' Phil called from the living room.

She stirred a spoonful of sugar into his mug, the one with *BEST DAD IN THE WORLD* painted on it—a present from Jane one Christmas—and took it through to him. 'What is it?'

'Look, an interview your man gave to a magazine called Top Table. It might prove useful.'

'Top Table? That's interesting. They interview all the establishment elite; politicians, aristocrats, important business men. Thanks, my love. I'll read it now.' The article was entitled 'My Biggest Worry: How to spend my inheritance,' and next to it was the grinning face of Gabriel Francisco Mendoza Pérez. As soon as she began to read it, she realised it was a provocation on his part. Kiko was staking his claim and declaring that no-one was going to deprive him of his inheritance. No-one. It was a message to someone, a warning maybe, but to whom?

'So? Is it useful?' Phil asked. As he sipped his tea, his eyes never left her face.

'I think it is. You can never be sure how accurate it is; the press love to embellish things. However it could be a link to his murder. After all he's boasting about what he will do when he inherits his father's title.'

'How old is it? The article.'

She flipped back to the front cover. 'Last year. December.'

'So, does this mean that JD has decided it wasn't an accident after all?'

'If she hasn't already, she soon will when she reads this article. Thanks, Phil. This is just what we needed.'

He looked at her expectantly. 'Well, does it prove anything about his death?'

'No, not exactly but it does show that the inheritance was important to him, and possibly to someone else. Maybe someone who was trying to disinherit him.'

'His father?'

She frowned. 'No, I don't think so. If it was his father he wouldn't have been so concerned about us discovering the reason behind his death. No someone else close to him.'

'Maybe he had a secret and someone had discovered it.'

'Or maybe it was the other way around. Perhaps Kiko had discovered somebody else's secret.' She handed him a few more magazines. 'Here, you seem to be good at this. See what else you can find out about him.'

'I hope I'm getting paid for this,' he said, with a big grin.

'I'd speak to JD,' she said, 'but you know what she's like.' Whether Phil found anything else or not, the task was taking his mind off his treatment and that could only be good. 'Talking of whom, I ought to ring her and see what's happening.'

'You are supposed to be having the afternoon off.'

'I know.' She looked at her husband; the look he gave her was the same as the one their old dog used to give her whenever she left for work. 'You're right. It can wait until tomorrow. It's not as though anything much will happen between now and then. But in the meantime I think I'll take a closer look at what he said in this interview. Maybe it will give me a clue as to who the duke's son really was.'

'I knew you would find it impossible to leave it until tomorrow,' said Phil, but he smiled as he said it.

'I won't be long, then I'll make us some lunch, all right?'

'That's fine by me. I'm not really hungry anyway.'

Linda spread the magazine out on the kitchen table and began to go through it methodically, marking the significant passages with a yellow marker pen as she read. The article was one of a series that questioned the Great and the Good on what they had planned for the coming year and what impact they hoped it would have on their lives. One interview with a top fashion model, which Linda had read in the November issue, had talked about the model's aspirations to move to the United States and maybe try her luck in the movie business. The series of interviews resembled an early New Year's resolutions list. Kiko, on the other hand, had decided to tell the readers that his biggest worry was how to spend his inheritance, when he received it. As she reread the article, she realised this was a direct challenge to someone. A "catch me if you can" type of challenge. But to whom was it directed? Someone in his family? All of his family? Or was it nothing to do with family, was it a personal challenge to someone who had tried to humiliate him? They knew so little about the deceased, and now of course, they had to rely on what others could tell them. They had to piece his story together for themselves from whatever they could find but at least, here in this interview, they had his words and thoughts, and what sounded like his aspirations too.

From Kiko's statements, it seemed as though someone had threatened him that he would never live long enough to inherit his father's estate, and not only that but he did not deserve to inherit it, anyway. Kiko did not contest the statements directly but his reply could only be construed as an attack on the aristocracy, referring to outdated traditions which only served to bolster a dying privileged class. It was strong stuff for the son of a duke to declare publicly. Maybe too strong for some readers. Maybe his lack of humility and what sounded as dismissive arrogance on his part had triggered an attack on his life. If that was the case, then his murderer had taken his time to fulfil his promise. Eight months to be exact.

CHAPTER 6

Nacho pulled out his mobile phone and checked the address again. It was obviously the right place but how did you get in? There was no intercom outside. There was nothing for it; he would have to telephone him.

'Yes?' a gruff voice answered.

'Señor Moreno?'

'Yes.'

'It's Ignacio from the detective agency. I'm downstairs.'

'And?'

'You agreed to talk to me about Gabriel Francisco Mendoza Pérez.'

'Oh, yes, the dead guy. Well come on up. I'm on the sixth floor. Sorry you will have to use the stairs. You'll see a door on your right; the stairs are opposite.'

The door to the building clicked open and Nacho went in. Sure enough the lift had an out-of-action sign on the door so he headed up the stairs to the sixth floor. Considering its location, in one of the best parts of Málaga, the building looked rather dilapidated and in need of a good clean, however when he reached apartment 6B and waited outside, trying to get his breath back, he soon realised that Juan Felipe lived in style.

'Sorry about the lift. The landlord has promised to get it mended, but he's taking his time,' said Juan Felipe, holding the door wide open. He was a well built man in his early forties, not tall but stocky, his dark hair had signs of premature balding and, as though to compensate for that, his face was obscured with a thick, black beard. 'Do come in.'

Although Juan Felipe was very much as Nacho had expected and he could easily imagine him in his fireman's uniform, and even jumping off tall buildings, the apartment was definitely a surprise. It was very spacious, with high ceilings and big windows, through which was a view of the city's iconic 19th century bullring. Although the building itself probably dated back to the 19th century, the interior of the apartment was very modern, painted in simple tones of white and grey and decorated with what seemed to Nacho to be very expensive works of modern art. 'You've got a nice place here,' he said. 'I like your paintings.'

'Yes, it's all right for the time being. I'm looking for something a bit bigger, with a good view of the sea,' Juan Felipe replied, stroking his beard. 'But they are all so expensive these days.'

Nacho didn't bother to answer but he did wonder how Juan Felipe could afford to live in such a luxurious apartment. The marble floor was covered with expensive Persian rugs, his sound system was top-of-the-range and the furnishings were definitely not from Ikea. 'Is that a Barefoot Sound Masterstack?' he asked, sounding rather like an excited child in a toyshop.

'Yes, so you know your sound systems, I see.'

'I'm a musician, well part-time.'

'A hobby?'

'A bit more than that; I play guitar in a flamenco band.'

'Please sit down.' Juan Felipe indicated an elegant sofa which faced the window. 'Can I get you something to drink?'

'A glass of water would be good. Thanks.' While Juan Felipe disappeared to the kitchen to get the water, Nacho sat down and looked at the view, puzzling how he was going to interview this man; already he felt he was on the back foot. How could an out-of-work fireman afford to own such expensive equipment and live in a place like this? Did he inherit from his parents? He just didn't seem to fit the part.

'Nice and cold,' the ex-fireman said, handing Nacho a glass of water. 'So, remind me. Why are you here today?'

'I expect you heard about the death of the Duque de Roble's son; he drowned in the port?'

'Yes, I think I heard something about it. Tragic accident.' He stared at Nacho. 'So, what has this to do with me?'

'I believe he was a friend of yours.'

'Now, why would you say that?'

'Maybe you don't know the details of his death; he was paramotoring and fell into the harbour and drowned. I believe you taught him how to para-motor?'

'Me? I don't know any of the aristocracy, never mind the son of a duke.'

'But you do like to para-motor?'

'Yes, but so do hundreds of other people. It's very popular nowadays. It's not a crime, is it?'

Nacho decided to take a different tack. 'Do you know Bob Free?'

'Yes. I've known Bob a long time; I buy a lot of stuff from him. There aren't many places where you can buy decent gear and I'm not keen on buying it on-line. I like to see what I'm paying for.'

'Bob told me that you and the dead man were friends and that you trained him to para-motor.'

'Oh, in that case you must be talking about Kiko. He's not aristocracy, is he?' He looked surprised. 'Well I wouldn't say we were friends exactly, but I met him one day in a bar and we started talking. He said he really fancied paramotoring, so I offered to take him up to Bob's shop. He was desperate to get started but Bob said he was too busy so I offered to show him the ropes. We met a few times and I gave him some basic instructions and that was it.'

'How many lessons did you give him?'

'Oh, I don't remember. I was just doing the guy a favour. He appeared to think he could read the leaflets and watch a video on YouTube and that was all he needed to do. No wonder he fell in the drink.'

'Where were you last weekend?' Nacho asked.

'Me, I wasn't in Málaga. I hate Feria week. I just had to get away from the crowds; the city was packed with tourists.'

'So where did you go?'

'I went to a conference in Seville. An LGBT conference. Why? Surely you don't think I had anything to do with his death?'

'I just need to check everyone who was in contact with the deceased,' Nacho explained. He felt uncomfortable about questioning him as though he was a suspect, so decided to change tack. 'Look, I'm a complete dunce about paramotoring. I've no idea what's involved. Can you run me through what you told him?'

'Better than that, I'll take you out for a trial; I've got an extra motor in the garage. That way you can see for yourself.'

'Well, I'm not sure about that,' Nacho replied. He looked at his watch. 'I need to be back by eight. We have a gig tonight.' He wasn't certain that going paramotoring with this guy was a good idea, but it was one way to understand what had happened to Kiko and to see exactly what sort of training he had been given.

'We'll easily be back by then. Anyway I have a beach party to go to tonight, so I don't want to be late. Unless you decide to do something stupid that is, like crash into a tree.' He laughed. 'No, don't worry, you'll be as safe as houses with me.'

'Okay. I'm just going to message my boss to let her know where I'm going.' He had growing doubts about this venture. Nacho was not a great one for physical activity; riding his moped was about as much as he had time for. Besides which he didn't really have a good head for heights; so why on earth was he agreeing to this.

Juan Felipe grinned. 'Likes to keep a close watch on her employees does she? Doesn't she know it's Feria week?' He looked at Nacho's standard attire of jeans and tee-shirt and added, 'No need to worry about clothes; what you're wearing will be fine. I've got a spare safety vest in the jeep.' He went into another room and came back wearing a red teeshirt in place of the neatly ironed shirt he had on previously. 'You look worried. If you want we can go up together on the same machine? That might be easier for your first time.'

Nacho looked up from typing his message to JD and said, 'No, it's better if I fly on my own and get to experience what is actually involved.'

Juan Felipe shrugged his shoulders. 'As you wish. You know it would be better to go earlier in the day before it gets too hot. Would you like to leave it until tomorrow?'

'No, now is fine.' If he delayed, he was not sure he would be able to keep his nerve and go through with it. Nacho followed him out of the apartment and down the stairs. 'Do you usually go paramotoring at the weekends?' he asked. 'When you're not at conferences, that is.'

'Me? Sometimes, it depends on what's going on. Why do you ask?'

'No reason, just there always seems to be a lot of activity at the weekends.'

'Is that when Kiko had his crash?'

Nacho nodded. All he could concentrate on now was getting this ordeal over.

They drove east along the motorway then turned inland towards Velez Málaga. 'Where are we going?' asked Nacho. His stomach was already churning with anxiety.

'Up into the mountains; there are a couple of paramotoring schools up there near Periana. But don't worry we aren't going to a school; I can teach you all you need to know.'

Juan Felipe had loaded up his jeep with his own equipment and a set for Nacho to borrow. He seemed to be fairly confident that Nacho would be capable of flying after a few rudimentary instructions; he prayed he was right.

The road began to narrow as the jeep wound its way up the side of the mountain. 'It's beautiful up here,' said Nacho.

'You've never been in the Sierra de Alhama before?' asked Juan Felipe. 'There are a couple of places here where it's great for flying and perfectly safe for landing, if anything goes wrong. We will launch off from about eight hundred metres. That should be adequate.' He sounded very enthusiastic but all Nacho could think about was how to stop the butterflies racing around in his stomach. 'You okay? You've gone very quiet.'

'I'm fine,' he lied. 'Just enjoying the ride.'

'It's always a bit scary the first time, but I can guarantee that once you have experienced it you will be hooked.'

Nacho did not reply. They were turning off the mountain road now and crossing a stretch of reasonably flat terrain. The jeep suddenly pulled to a halt and Juan Felipe said, 'Well this is it. Out you get and I'll show you where you are going?' Nacho clambered out of the jeep and followed him towards the cliff edge. His knees were shaking and he started to feel sick. 'Are you sure you are all right?' Juan asked.

'Yes, just a bit nervous.'

'That's normal,' his companion said, dismissively. 'Come and look at this. Isn't that wonderful?'

Nacho edged his way closer to Juan Felipe. The view was indeed very impressive.

'This is the launch area. You will be flying out there and then I want you to land down there.' He pointed to a flat stretch of land which seemed to be an incredibly long way below them. 'I will come down with the car and pick you up. Are you happy with that?'

'Yes, I understand. I hope you're going to show me how to work this contraption,' he said as he helped Juan Felipe lift the equipment from the boot of the jeep.

'I think you might as well use my para-motor.'

'So you are not going with me?' Nacho was feeling really nervous now.

'No. I thought you wanted to experience it as Kiko had, solo. Like I said, I'll drive down and pick you up.' He walked to the edge of the cliff and pointed to where he would be waiting. 'But you don't land there, you want to aim for that wide, flat space and land there.' He walked away from the edge and said, 'Come on, let's get you dressed for the party and then I'll go through what you have to do. For this first flight all you want to achieve is to launch yourself into the air, fly around for a couple of minutes and then bring it down to land where I've told you. And don't rush the landing; you don't want to break an ankle because you've landed awkwardly. Remember to bend your knees.'

'Got it,' Nacho said, putting on his safety vest and then struggling into the harness. He watched as Juan Felipe walked over to the jeep and pulled out the parachutes and laid them flat on the ground then beckoned Nacho towards the edge of the cliff again. Already he felt constricted with the gear he was wearing, but stood still to allow Juan Felipe to strap the motor to his back.

He handed him a helmet and said, 'Put this on. Now let me show you how to control the lines.'

Nacho was so nervous he feared he wouldn't remember what the man was telling him. So he repeated the instructions word for word. 'That's it. You've got it. It's quite simple isn't it.'

Nacho would have liked to believe that, but he was not at all confident. He looked around him. The air was still, without the slightest breath of wind. That was good, wasn't it.

'Are you all right?'

He nodded.

'Okay, let's just go through the final safety checks once again; I don't want you getting separated from the para-motor.' He went over everything a second time, tightening and checking all the fastenings. 'That all looks fine, so now we're ready to go. Come and stand over here, away from the edge.' Nacho did as he was told; he was now about ten metres away from the launch point. 'Once the motor starts I want you to run towards the edge and don't stop. Just keep running. I'll start the motor for you, okay. Remember, don't stop. Keep running.' Suddenly Nacho heard the roar of the engine and felt his whole body begin to vibrate. 'Off you go.' Juan Felipe shouted as he gave him a gentle push forward. 'I will come down with the car and pick you up.'

Nacho was no longer listening; he was running and before he knew it he was in the air, the parachute wings had opened behind him and he was soaring away from the launch area. The ground spread out far below him, green swathes of grass and bushes, grey outcrops of rock. The sun glinted on a narrow stream that tumbled down the hillside. He was flying high. It was exhilarating. He looked around him as he soared over the adjacent hills, the excitement growing inside him. It was a long way down to the landing area, but he was no longer afraid. He felt no panic, just an overwhelming sense of calm; there was nothing between him and the fields below. He was free. He was a bird, just him and the sky. It was indescribable; he was flying and the ground was fast disappearing beneath him. He spotted the jeep on the hillside, throwing up tiny clouds of dust as it made its way down to the landing area and he dipped towards it. For a moment he was so amazed at what was happening he almost forgot the instructions that Juan Felipe had given him, but his instinct kicked in and he pulled on the hand toggles, working the controls as he had been taught. It was not very difficult, but he was well aware that, at that height, a simple error could have tragic consequences. He flew upwards again and then swooped back towards the landing area. Suddenly it was as if something had been taken away from him and he felt his stomach dropping towards the ground. He felt panic grip at his heart but then reminded himself that it was just a little turbulence; Juan had warned him about it. He pulled on the toggles and once again was soaring up and over the hills. The jeep had reached the landing area now and Juan was waving for him to come down. What had he told him to do? Not to rush the landing. Bend his knees. So Nacho slowed down his descent until all of a sudden his feet were on the ground and he was running again. It was over. He had landed.

'Well done, mate. That was excellent for a first flight. You're a natural, young man. We'll have to get you into the club.'

Nacho was not listening. His feet were on the ground but his head was still in the clouds. It was much more than he had ever expected, more exhilarating than he could ever have imagined. He was hooked.

When Nacho collected his moped from outside Juan Felipe's apartment and set off for home, his mind was still racing. He was elated. What an experience it had been. He wanted to turn circles in the road, stick out his legs and drive in the central lane, like he used to do when he was a teenager. He wanted to shout and sing. He wanted to whoop out loud. He was buzzing. Paramotoring had captivated him; it had got under his skin from the moment he realised that he was airborne. Flying high. He was never going to forget that experience, first the anticipation, the fear, the roar of the motor and the canopy billowing out behind him and then, miraculously, all of a sudden he was airborne. Nacho was not a timid man, but he was cautious and although he had played most sports at school, it was usually because he had no choice. Music was his thing. He did not need extreme sports to get an adrenalin rush; he could get that from his live concerts. But now he knew there was another way to get high. He was mesmerised. Flying like a bird was something he had never contemplated before but now he could think of nothing else.

Juan Felipe had been caught up in his enthusiasm. When they had finished he immediately suggested that Nacho try paragliding as well, as it was cheaper and less cumbersome. Nacho had been on the verge of agreeing and making a date to meet Juan Felipe again when he remembered why he was there in the first place; this was work and that meant he had to keep his distance, at least until they were sure that Juan Felipe was not a suspect. He tried not to let his enthusiasm for the sport and his liking for the man cloud his judgement, but after an afternoon with Juan Felipe he just couldn't believe that Kiko's crash had been caused by lack of training. There had to be another reason. He would stop and have a coffee and collect his thoughts.

Now that the overall feeling of euphoria had died down, Nacho decided to return to the agency and follow up on a couple of things that were bothering him. He still hadn't given Linda an answer for why the deceased man had so little exposure on social media. For someone in his social position and of his age, it was, to say the least, a little unusual. There had to be something somewhere, some evidence of a presence on one of the social platforms; he just had to find it.

Two hours later, he decided that he had exhausted all the sites that he could find; he hadn't discovered the reason why Kiko was not currently active on social media, but at least he had found evidence of a previous presence. Until this year, there was evidence that the duke's son had been quite an active participant on Twitter, Instagram and Snapchat but then he or someone else had deleted all his social media accounts. Nacho couldn't retrieve anything from Twitter or Snapchat but he did manage to recover some of the original posts on Instagram; these were mostly of young women, and surprise, surprise photos of Kiko paragliding. So the duke's son was not a complete novice; he certainly knew how to paraglide although there were no shots of him with a para-motor. Nacho typed a quick message to Linda and forwarded the photos.

CHAPTER 7

As Rachel lined up to pass through passport control, she silently cursed the extra—and in her opinion unnecessary— number of delays they had to endure since the UK had decided to leave the European Union. She looked at her watch; the boarding gate would be closing soon. Well there was nothing she could do about it, except relax and go with the flow. She reminded herself that if she let herself get wound up over a slight delay then she would undo all the benefits of this relaxing week in the sun. All of a sudden she saw something which literally took her breath away. She had a feeling that she had neglected to tell that private detective everything—it had been niggling away in the back of her mind all the way to the airport— but the shock of the poor young man dying so tragically had numbed her brain. She could be mistaken, but the longer she stood there, staring at the policeman deep in conversation with the woman checking passports, the surer she became that the dead para-motorist had been wearing a body-cam. She remember seeing the tiny green light. It was attached to the frame of his glasses. In the chaos of the moment it hadn't registered with her that it was a camera and it was filming, but now as she stared at the green light on the policeman's body-cam, she realised what she had seen. A body-cam. Why on earth would the para-motorist be wearing a body-cam?

She closed her eyes and willed herself to revisit the scene at the beach, when the para-motor had spun out of control and it and its pilot were heading straight towards her. Her attention had been on the young man's face, contorted with terror. She had barely noticed what he had been wearing, but just as a gust of wind had lifted the para-motor and its pilot into the air, something green had glinted in the sunshine. She concentrated on that single moment in time. Yes, it was then that she found herself looking into his terrified face; his glasses fell off and she could see the panic in his eyes. Now, she was sure. But what had happened to the glasses and the tiny camera?

'*Señora*, is everything all right?' The policeman asked, walking over to her. 'You look upset.'

'No, sorry. Everything is fine. I was just wondering how much longer we will have to wait.'

'I think the queue is moving now. Here, give me your passport and boarding card.' He held out his hand for her documents and then led her to the front of the queue where he handed it to the policewoman behind the desk.

She could not understand what he told her, but suddenly she found herself heading for the boarding gate and half running, half walking down the ramp towards the aeroplane. She appeared to be the last one to board; all eyes turned to look her as she hurried to take her seat. There was no time to contact the detective now; she would do it once she was back in Surrey.

The flight was smooth and after all the excitement and a large glass of white wine, Rachel slept most of the journey, despite having two boisterous five-year olds sitting behind her. Her friend, Moira was waiting at arrivals for her.

'You look wonderful, Rachel. You've had a great time by the look of it.'

'Well, it was different, I'll give you that.'

'In what way,' Moira asked, taking one of her bags and leading the way to the carpark.

'I'll tell you when we get home. I'm still puzzling over something and what to do about it.'

'That sounds intriguing.'

'So how has your week been?' Rachel asked, not keen to continue the conversation about her holiday. While the two friends chatted, Rachel's thoughts kept going back to the body-cam. Maybe she was giving it too much importance. He had probably only worn it to get some aerial shots of the coastline; it wasn't as though it would shine any light on his accident. She and the other witness had seen what had happened very clearly, so what further information could it provide.

'You're not listening to me, Rachel. Why don't you tell me what is bothering you. Two heads are often better than one,' said Moira.

'Sorry, you're right. Okay. It's not a very pleasant story, I warn you.' While Moira drove her home, Rachel recounted what had happened to the para-motorist and how she had neglected to mention that she had seen him wearing a body-cam.

'Oh, don't worry about that. I'm sure the police will have found it by now. There's not much you can do about it anyway.'

'So, you don't think it's important?'

'No. After all, you said you saw what happened and so did another witness. The body-cam is unlikely to give any more information than that, even if it's still working.'

'That's true. Anyway, I can't remember the detective's name. I think it was Lynn, or something like that. And she didn't give me her phone number so I can't get in touch with her anyway.'

'Well there you are. Stop worrying about it. They have your number, don't they? Someone will get in touch with you if they need any more information.'

They pulled into Rachel's drive and parked behind her own, rather dilapidated Citroen. 'Do you want to come in?' she asked.

'I won't thanks. I'd sooner get straight home, but I'll see you tomorrow.'

'Okay. Thanks for picking me up.' She was glad she had spoken to Moira. Now it didn't seem such a big deal; she no longer felt she had let the young man down. If the police got in touch with her again, she'd tell them all about the camera then.

CHAPTER 8

The next morning they were all in the office before JD arrived. Even Ricardo was there, sitting on her desk, drinking coffee.

'Ricardo. This is a surprise.'

'*Buenos días* JD. The *capitán* thinks you should visit the forensic department; they have some news for you and he's asked me to go with you.'

'Do you know what it is?'

Ricardo shook his head. 'But he thinks you will be interested to hear it.'

'So he didn't even say if it was good or bad?'

'No. What's good news? That it was an accident or that he was murdered?'

'Either way it wasn't good news for Kiko, was it,' said Nacho.

JD parked her bike in its usual spot and said, 'I hope you've got your car; I'm exhausted.'

Ricardo looked at Nacho who raised his eyebrows and explained, 'She's been to her Aikido group.'

'Oh, okay. So that's why the *capitán* told me to take the car.'

'No coffee, Nacho?' JD asked, grabbing a folder from her desk and sitting down in the meeting room. Did everyone know her business? It certainly sounded like it. She decided to ignore their remarks and said, 'I want us to run through what we know before I go to talk to the forensics team. You can listen in Ricardo; maybe you can help.'

'And what we don't know,' added Nacho.

JD gave him one of her *'don't push me too hard'* looks. 'Coffee?'

'Sorry JD, I drank yours,' said Ricardo. 'I'll get you one at the station.'

'No thank you; the coffee there is undrinkable. I'll pick something up on the way. Right. Let's start with you Nacho. How did you get on with our friend Juan Felipe?'

'What can I say? He explained everything very clearly and was very insistent about safety procedures. I couldn't fault him and remember I'm not at all familiar with mechanical things, so if I could understand what to do then I'm sure Kiko could.'

'So, we can rule out lack of preparation?'

'Yes.' He crossed it off the list on the board. 'That leaves carelessness, freak accident, malfunction etc. I don't know how we can measure the first two, but if the machine malfunctioned then the forensics team should be able to spot that.'

'So what opinion did you have of this Juan Felipe? Is he someone who could have sabotaged Kiko's para-motor?'

'I can't see that he would have had any motive to do that; but he would have had the opportunity. He just doesn't seem to be that sort of bloke.'

'You liked him?' She could see Nacho blushing.

'To be honest, I did. He is obsessed with paramotoring and now, after going up with him, I can understand why.' He looked at them and beamed. 'It was the most wonderful thing I have ever done. It was amazing.'

'Really?' asked Linda. She looked astounded. 'I thought you would hate it. I fully expected you to come in this morning and make some excuse for why you hadn't gone, say you weren't able to go up because of the wind, or it was too hot, or you didn't have the right clothes. Not that it was bloody amazing.'

'Linda. How could you even think that? All right, I admit I was scared rigid when I knew what we were going to do, but I truly enjoyed the afternoon and I thought Juan Felipe was an excellent teacher.'

'Does that mean you will be going again?' asked JD.

'Not until we've solved the case. I'm not that reckless, you know.'

'Well we know that Kiko was no novice to this sport, thanks to the photo you found on Instagram, Nacho. So I think we can eliminate inexperience. Okay, Linda, anything to report?'

'Well, I spoke to Rachel and she took me through everything she saw, including the second man on a para-motor—but you know about him, anyway.'

'Do you think she could identify him?'

'It's possible; she said he was older than Kiko and appeared to be irritated about something. Also he was wearing a pair of those expensive trainers, Air Jordans. She noticed them because they were lime green and stood out. At first he seemed to be headed west then changed his mind and turned around and flew back along the coast.'

'Eastwards?'

'Yes.'

'Do you think it could have been Juan Felipe?'

'I don't know; it's possible. Do we have a photo of him?' They both looked at Nacho.

'There's one on my phone. Here, have a look.'

'Send it to Rachel and ask her if this could be the man she saw?' said JD.

'I can't believe Juan Felipe would fly on if his companion was in danger,' said Nacho. 'He doesn't seem the type.'

'Also she seemed to think there was something wrong with Kiko's motor. The blades were turning very slowly and he probably would have crashed on the beach but a strong gust of wind took him up and over the harbour wall. Much the same as the SEMAR guys said,' Linda continued. 'Thanks Nacho. I'll forward it to her now.'

'So in a way, it was an accident. If the wind hadn't blown him into the harbour, then he wouldn't have drowned. Thanks, Linda, anything else?' asked JD.

'Yes, Phil was helping me go through the magazines and he found this article about Kiko. It's from last year. It's quite short but it's worth reading.' She handed the magazine to JD. 'What do you think that's all about?'

JD took the magazine and began to read. After a few minutes she handed it to Nacho and said, 'What's your opinion? It sounds to me as though he knew someone else was after the inheritance and he was staking his claim, loud and clear.'

'Yes, the title is very arrogant,' said Linda. She opened her notebook and added, 'I marked a few passages. It doesn't read like a general diatribe against the aristocracy, more like a direct challenge to someone in particular. But who?'

'Well the journalist will have written that title, but he would have had a reason to do so. We ought to speak to him.' She turned back to the evidence board and added, 'I think we need to look more closely at the duke's family and see who is actually going to inherit when he dies. Nacho, I know you have already started looking into the family, but now I want you to do it more thoroughly. Are there any other potential heirs out there, lurking in the shadows and waiting for his death before they appear?'

'So you are sure it's a murder now, Boss?'

'It's certainly starting to look that way.'

'But…' Nacho began to say.

'What? You look unhappy about something, Nacho.'

'I agree with you that we need to look at the family more closely, but don't you think we should let them know that we are investigating Kiko's death? It's only right. What would the *capitán* say if he found out?'

'You can leave the captain to me. However I think you have a good point. They may not like us poking about in their lives. They might go straight to the *comandante*.'

'They are the aristocracy. They will go directly to the top, the General of the Division.'

'I agree. *Dios* knows what secrets we might discover once we start asking questions. We need permission from the duke, or at least we need him to officially invite us to look into his son's death. We can't just go crashing in there because Rosa says so. Leave it with me. I'll go and see the duke and Rosa can arrange it. In the meantime, we carry on investigating, but discreetly.'

'Do you want me to speak to this journalist, Adolfo Ruiz?' asked Linda, retrieving the article from the desk. 'Maybe he has some opinions about our victim that he couldn't put into the article.'

'Yes, good idea. Add him to our list, Nacho.' She smiled broadly. This was looking more promising. If they could find a clear motive then it would be easier to identify the perpetrator. 'Once I've spoken to the duke then I'll report back to the captain. Happy Nacho?'

'Just don't want us treading on anyone's toes, that's all, Boss.'

'What do you think, Ricardo?'

The lance corporal looked slightly embarrassed. 'It's always a good idea to keep on the right side of the law, JD.'

'*Dios mio*, you sound just like the captain. Come on, *Cabo* let's go and have a look at this motor. And maybe you could stop at the chemist on your way.'

'Of course, JD. No problem.'

The pathologist greeted JD in the usual Spanish manner, with a kiss on each cheek and a big hug. He was a new member of the team, having been transferred there from Córdoba, but he and JD had met before.

'*Buenos días*, Leonardo. You drew the short straw then? No time off for Feria?'

'No, but I don't mind. I'm not a great one for Feria. So, JD, I suppose you want to know how this young man died. Well, it was clearly death by drowning. A tragic death actually; he struggled desperately to free himself, but you can see from the bruises and rope cuts he wasn't able to, so he drowned.' He pulled back the white sheet. 'Do you want to see him? He's not in a bad condition; he wasn't in the water long enough.'

'Long enough to drown.' She looked at the slightly bloated face of the young man.

'True.'

'Who identified him?'

'His sister. His father was too ill to do it, and his step-mother couldn't face it. I felt sorry for her, the sister. She appeared to be holding it together until she saw the body and then she broke down. Not that he looks too bad; there are some bruises on his face and arm, as though he had a fall, but they are definitely ante-mortem, possibly a few hours before he drowned. The rest of his injuries were caused as he struggled to get free from the harness.'

'What happened? Can you talk me through it?'

'Of course. Well, it appears that his engine failed for some reason. It might just have been caused by wear and tear or lack of maintenance; the motor was old and not in good condition. Now the idea behind para-motors is that the motor provides a constant forward speed which keeps the wings inflated and prevents them from folding in on themselves. If the motor stops it can be bad news, as we have seen here. He would have immediately begun to lose height, the wings would have surged forward and he would have found it hard to control. However, that doesn't necessarily mean a crash; he should have been able to eventually take control of the wings by using the lines and steering himself out of trouble. In this particular case, a number of things made it impossible. First of all he was flying at midday and was far too low; both of which are not recommended because of the risk of rising air currents. And then he was very unlucky; we know from what the witnesses said that he was swept over the harbour wall and fell into the sea. By then he was probably completely out of control. Once in the water the weight of the para-motor would have pulled him under and he would have become tangled up in the wings and the lines. He would have found it very hard to get free of the harness and swim to the surface. We can tell from the state of his hands that he must have been desperately pulling at the lines to get them loose. He was caught like a fish in a net. The more he struggled, the worse it became.'

'That's awful.' JD shuddered at the image the pathologist had conjured up.

'Yes, not a nice death. When we examined the debris after the crash, we saw that one of his lines would not have worked properly because the nylon riser attaching it to the para-motor was damaged. At first I thought the damage had occurred when it hit the harbour wall, but closer examination showed that it may have been sawn through, not completely but enough to weaken it; if he had been flying higher, or in rougher conditions it would very likely have snapped in two. That and the fact that he was flying so close to the water without any safety gear, makes me wonder if it was foul play. But the forensics team will tell you more about that.'

'What about the toxicology report?'

'Well, it was what I would have expected for a young man with expensive tastes and too much money. He was obviously a cocaine user at some time.' He indicated the man's nose. 'There's some old tissue damage here, but nothing excessive. Probably not an addict, but definitely a recreational user. He smoked and he drank, but not to excess. As I said, there was no sign of addiction, no needle marks or tell-tale bruising and I couldn't find traces of any drugs in his system. As far as my report is concerned he was clean.'

'But that doesn't mean that there weren't any?'

'What are you saying?'

'Well I'm trying to explain his erratic behaviour. Some drugs leave no trace in the body.'

'True, but it's unlikely. I suppose he could have taken something like GHB, but I doubt it.'

'So, apart from the damage to the riser, there is nothing that could explain his accident?'

'Not that I could find. I do think it strange however that he should have been flying so low over the harbour. He would have known that went against all common sense.'

'Okay.' She was disappointed; she had expected him to find something that they could work with.

'There was mention of another para-motorist who was with him, what news of him?' Leonardo asked.

'Nothing so far. We have yet to identify him.'

'Well good luck with that. If he didn't care enough to come back and check on his friend then he's not going to turn himself into the police, is he. My conclusion is that it was sheer bad luck on the part of our dead man, and maybe a bit of carelessness too. You know the sort of thing, not looking after his equipment, lack of preparation. But María will show you what she has discovered.'

'Thanks, Leonardo. That's been very helpful, although I'm not sure I agree with you about it being an accident. Why would he be using an old motor, when I know that he only bought a brand new one just a few months ago? And the information about the risers is interesting as well.'

'You're welcome, JD. Glad I could help. I don't suppose you're free for a drink one evening? I haven't got to know many people in Málaga, yet. It would be nice to catch up on old times.'

She looked at him in surprise. 'Yes, why not. Here's my number. Give me a ring when you're free, although I must admit, I'm rather busy right now with this case, and it looks as though it's going to get busier.'

'*Buenos días*, JD. Come to look at that heap of metal, have you?' asked María, one of the forensic team. 'We have some good news for you. Come with me.'

'So Ricardo said. Keep it simple though.'

'It's simple all right. We couldn't find any deliberate damage to the motor, just the usual wear and tear. It wasn't a new motor though; it had been used quite a lot. Probably bought it second-hand. Looks to me as though it had been reconditioned.'

'Are you sure about that, María?'

María's only answer was a raised eyebrow. 'I'll send you the full report. You are going to have to find another reason for the accident; it's not the motor.'

'Maybe not mechanical failure, but I'd like to know where that motor came from. Does it have a serial number or any other kind of identification?'

'Of course. It will be in the report.'

'What about his other equipment? Any evidence of foul play there?'

'Well if there was any evidence, fingerprints, DNA, it was all destroyed in the water. And what wasn't removed by the water was destroyed by the ham-fisted life-guards.'

'What about the risers? Anyone been tampering with them?'

'It's difficult to say. One of them does have what could be a cut across it. It wasn't enough to cause the crash, but it would have weakened the riser and it wouldn't have responded so well in a crisis. For an experienced flyer, it probably would not have made a lot of difference, but for someone new to the sport or in a state of panic, it could well have contributed to the crash.'

'Was it a deliberate cut? Or accidental?'

'Oh deliberate, for sure. You can see the saw marks. Look.' She directed her to the microscope.

'Yes, I can see the damage. Not enough to saw right through it, but as you say, to weaken it. What about his other stuff?'

'What other stuff? His clothes, you mean? Well there wasn't much there. His wallet was in the back pocket of his trousers with his identity card, a couple of credit cards, his mobile phone and two hundred euros. There was a bit of jewellery: a gold necklace and a very expensive Cartier watch. To be honest, he looked dressed for a walk along the promenade.'

'Nothing else? No safety vest? No hook knife?'

'No, I told you. That's all. He had the harness but no helmet. I don't think he intended to go up in a para-motor that morning at all. Everything is pointing against it. Oh, and this of course. Easy to overlook.' She handed her an evidence bag.

'What is it?'

'An elastic band, of course. It was on his wrist.'

JD looked puzzled. 'I don't understand the significance.'

'People sometimes wear them to help themselves break a habit. It's aversion therapy.' She picked one up from her desk and slipped it on her wrist. 'If I was trying to give up smoking, for example, every time I went to smoke a cigarette, I'd snap the band to remind me not to.' She snapped the band on her wrist.

'Does it work?'

'They say it does. And it looks like our deceased thought so too.'

'So he was trying to give up something. What do you think it was?'

'Could be anything.'

'Cocaine, maybe? Leonardo said that he had been a user but there was no sign of current use.'

'In that case, yes it probably was cocaine.'

'Okay. Thanks, María.'

'You're welcome. Give me a ring if you need anything else, or send Ricardo round to see me.' She winked at the lance corporal and JD was amused to see him blush.

As she and Ricardo walked back to the car, she asked, 'So what do you think? Was it an accident?'

'That is still a possibility, but I admit it is looking more and more unlikely. What on earth was that about the motor? Did he really buy a new one only a few months ago?'

'That's what Bob Free told us, and I expect he has the paperwork to prove it. Anyway, Kiko does not seem the kind of man to buy a reconditioned motor, especially one in such a poor state. I think we have a few more questions for Señor Free.'

'Do you want me to help? I could go and see this Bob Free for you.'

'That would be good. And while you are at it, can you check with Juan Felipe? He should know what sort of motor Kiko owned. Nacho will give you their contact numbers.'

'Back to the agency, JD?'

'No, I'll see if the captain is still working. Maybe I can persuade him to buy me lunch.'

CHAPTER 9

The restaurant was packed, but Federico had rung the owner beforehand and somehow he had a table for them, as usual. JD had once asked Federico how he always managed to get a table at one of the most popular restaurants in Málaga, and he had replied that the owner liked having a captain of the Guardia Civil as a regular client. She hoped that was true and he wasn't putting any undue pressure on Mario.

'So how did you get on with the new pathologist?' Federico asked, once they were sitting at their usual table.

'Leonardo? He was very thorough, as you might expect.'

'And?'

'Well, I don't have a copy of the report yet; it will probably go to you first. Although he wouldn't commit to it being a homicide, he does agree that the death looks suspicious. Certainly enough to warrant further investigation.'

'Okay. Tell me why he thinks it could be suspicious.'

JD proceeded to explain to him about the motor and how the forensic scientist who examined it commented on the unlikelihood that anyone would go paramotoring with so little preparation.

'So that is all you have? Doesn't seem a lot to go on.'

'I know, but it is very strange about the reconditioned motor. Ricardo is going to get the serial number of the one Kiko bought and he will try to trace the number on this old machine. There has to be a reason why Kiko went out with an old machine, when he had recently bought a brand new one.'

'Maybe this was all a spontaneous thing. He decided to go up for a spin and didn't want to go back to get his own para-motor. That would explain his lack of appropriate clothing and safety gear. Somebody probably lent him the machine. Or someone stole his new motor and all he could get hold of was this old one.'

'If it was lent to him, then why haven't they come to collect it? Why haven't they tried to contact him? And if it was stolen then why didn't he report it?'

'Maybe they have tried to get in touch. You've got his mobile, haven't you?'

'Yes, but it is too damaged to recover any calls.'

'Send me his number and I'll get someone to look at his call log for the past few days.'

'A month would be better.'

'Okay, a month. And I'll check to see if it was reported stolen. Machines like that cost a lot of money; he would have needed to have a police report in order to claim the insurance. Satisfied?'

She nodded and tried not to look too pleased with herself.

'Now how about we order some food?'

While they waited for their usual seafood platter to arrive, JD asked, 'Not drinking anything today?'

'Just water, I'm going back to work. I've got some things I need to tie up this afternoon.'

'Nothing to do with Thomas Steed, I suppose?' she asked.

'Why do you ask that?'

She stretched across the table and took his hand. 'I know what you and Estrella did for me. She let it slip the night we were celebrating the end of our last case; she thought I already knew about it. I can't believe you did all that for me, Federico. I am so grateful, but I don't understand why didn't you tell me? Why keep it a secret?'

'I didn't want to disappoint you if we couldn't find out the truth.'

'But later, when you had the truth, why didn't you tell me then? Why make it look like the Met had solved it?'

'Well they had, really. I used their resources and even had Estrella working for me; I couldn't have got to the bottom of it without their help. Bill was only too happy when I suggested we try to bring this nightmare to an end for you. He was very supportive throughout—he thinks a lot of you, you know.'

'He was always a good boss. But, I think for some reason he felt guilty about what happened to Andrew.'

'Guilty? That's an odd thing to say. He wasn't even there, was he? I thought he was away on a training course at the time of the murder.'

'He was, but it was such a shock for us all, and for it to happen right outside the station made it worse. Don't we all feel a little guilty to still be alive when someone close to us dies?'

'I don't. I feel grateful.' He leaned across and poured some wine into an empty glass. 'Maybe I will manage one glass.'

'Do you think he will come to Málaga?' she asked.

'Who? Steed? You're not still worrying about him, are you?'

'Well, I don't like to think that he is so close. I would be much happier if he was behind bars.'

'I doubt if he is in Málaga or even been here. This will just be a move on his part to rattle you, just like when he put the spyware on your laptop, but don't worry I am looking into it. I rang Jean-Paul and he confirmed that Steed's details are on the Interpol network; he says they've been there since he escaped arrest. He reckons Steed is somewhere in Europe and it's only a matter of time before they find him. Someone will give us some information about him soon, you'll see.'

'And in the meantime, I am looking over my shoulder all the time, wondering if he is there.'

'Honestly Jacaranda, I doubt that he will try anything. My guess is that he wants to frighten you, to interfere with your life. Don't give in to it, Jacaranda. You're tougher than that. Relax. Let's enjoy these delicious scallops.' He smiled at the waiter who placed a large plate of scallops and prawns on the table between them.

'Can I have some chips with the fish, please Mario. I'm starving.'

'Of course, *Señora*.'

Federico's phone buzzed. 'It's Ricardo, I'd better get this,' he explained. 'Yes, *Cabo*? I understand. Yes. Tell them it will be released when we are satisfied and not before. I don't care what his sister says.'

'Kiko's body?'

'Yes, the sister is making a fuss because we haven't released his body yet.'

'I thought they asked us to keep it until the duke died?'

'That was his wife. His sister wants to get on with it.'

'Is there any reason to keep it longer? Hasn't the pathologist finished with it?'

'Ricardo said Leonardo was being awkward and had told the sister that forensics is the voice of the victim and he needs to be sure he has listened to all it has to say. Pompous prat.'

'I don't think it has much more to tell him,' said JD, with a big smile. 'But I'm glad he isn't releasing it until we have a clearer picture of why Kiko behaved in the way he did. Something still doesn't add up. If they had found alcohol or drugs in his system that would have explained what can only be described as erratic behaviour. But they didn't.'

'I'll send you a copy of the report as soon as I get it.'

'No need. Leonardo says he'll give me a copy.'

'I see, personal service; I don't remember you getting that from the old pathologist.'

JD felt she was blushing. 'Well I know him from the old days, when I was at Uni. He was in Edinburgh studying medicine and I was doing criminology. We went around with the same crowd for a while but I didn't have a lot to do with them. My closest friend was in love with one of his mates but when that ended we stopped seeing them.'

'So, not an old boyfriend then?'

She laughed. 'No. You're not jealous are you, Federico?'

'What would be the point?'

She stared at him but decided not to answer.

'That's your mobile, isn't it?' he said.

'It's my mother. I'd better take it.' She pressed speaker and put the phone on the table between them.

Her mother spoke immediately, 'Jacaranda. Be at my house at 6pm. All the neighbours are coming round for a drink, so you will be able to chat to them. Bring Federico.'

'That's not a good idea, Mama. If they think the police are there, people will be more reluctant to talk. I'll bring Linda, if she is free.'

'All right, just as you wish. Give him my regards, anyway.' Then she rang off.

'So that's organised then. Sorry about that, *Cariño*, but if somebody recognised you then nobody would tell us anything.'

'No need to apologise. I understand. I can't say I'm disappointed; it doesn't sound like my idea of an enjoyable evening anyway. Do you want me to pick you up later?'

'I'll let you know. If Linda can make it, she will probably drive me home.'

'Well good luck. Hope you find someone who had a good view of what actually happened that day.'

'Thanks. You know I'm not keen on that kind of party, but it was a good idea of my mothers and it would look odd if I wasn't there.'

'Talking of family-get-togethers, my brother wants us to join them for a barbecue.' He waited for her response.

JD knew that his family had taken a while to get used to the idea that he was going out with her; they had all been very fond of his ex-wife, his brother in particular. 'That sounds nice. Which day?'

'Sunday at 2pm. You don't need to go if you don't want to; I can always make up some excuse for you.'

'No, I'd like to go. It's not often you get the time to see your brother, after all.'

'Okay, I'll tell them.'

JD and Linda had planned a strategy, of sorts; JD would chat casually about the weather and the crowds at Feria while Linda would pursue the topic of Kiko's crash and what had been seen, if anything. Linda was good at getting people to talk to her, whereas they tended to do the opposite when JD questioned them.

'Linda, this is a nice surprise. And how is that beautiful grandson of yours?'

'*Buenas tardes*, Rosa. He's fine, thank you. I must say you have a lovely apartment. The view is amazing.'

'Thank you, my dear. I have to admit that I am very pleased with it; these places don't come on the market very often. Now let me get you a drink and then I will introduce you to some of my neighbours.'

Within minutes Linda was standing, a glass in her hand, chatting to an immaculately dressed woman and her sister. 'Do all the apartments have the same amazing view?' she asked, sipping her sparkling white wine.

'Yes, more or less,' said the younger of the two women.

'But they are not all the same; Rosa's apartment is one of the biggest.'

'Yes, ours has just two bedrooms, which is a nuisance if anyone comes to stay.'

'Not that it often happens,' muttered the older one. Her name was Encarni and her iron grey hair, was pulled back from her face giving her a permanent look of severity.

Linda moved a little closer to the window. 'Amazing,' she murmured. 'Is that where the man drowned a few days ago?'

'You heard about that, did you?'

'It must have been a dreadful thing to witness.'

'No, we didn't actually see it, but the whole place was talking about it when we got back from the Corte Inglés. Dreadful accident.'

'Did anyone actually see what happened?' Linda asked. She glanced around the room, hoping to locate JD. At last she spotted her, talking to a bespectacled man in a linen jacket; he looked English.

'Oh, Margo saw it all. You couldn't get her to shut up about it. She had her binoculars out, you know.'

'She says she uses them to watch the shipping; her husband —he's dead now—had a luxury yacht. Margo would never go out on it; she said it made her seasick, but she liked to watch him sail it. She would sit at the window for hours waiting for him to return and as soon as he came into the harbour she would go down and meet him.'

'Quite romantic,' said Linda.

'Not really,' said the older woman. 'She was convinced that he had another woman on board and wanted to catch him out.'

'And did she?'

The woman shook her head. 'She was always too slow. Anyway the rumour was that the husband always stopped at the marina in Benalmadena before returning home. Nobody actually saw another woman, but Margo was convinced there was one.'

'So, is Margo here?'

'No, she's not well. Influenza, I think.'

This was not going well. There seemed to be plenty of gossip being exchanged but not a lot about the duke's son. Linda moved along to join a couple further along. The man was studying the lighthouse through a pair of binoculars. '*Buenos tardes*, I'm Linda,' she said in her perfect Spanish. 'Can you see much through those?'

'Indeed. They are very good. Would you like to try them? I am Borg, and this is my wife Karina. We live on the third floor.'

Linda placed her glass on an immaculately polished table and accepted the binoculars. 'So you are from Sweden?' she asked as she scoured the sea with them.

'Denmark.'

'These are very good. I can see every detail on that boat. They must be very expensive. What do you use them for?'

'Yes I think they are good, too. They are not mine. I wish they were. I do a lot of bird watching from my own apartment, but my binoculars are not as good as these.' He sounded irritated with her, or maybe with the fact that he had inferior binoculars.

'Isn't that a bit boring? Seagulls and more seagulls.'

'Gulls. And they are not all the same. There are plenty of different birds to see, I can assure you.'

'Oh, so I expect you witnessed the accident a few days ago?' Linda said, handing the binoculars back to Borg. 'I bet that was exciting.'

'Exciting? No it was dreadful watching that poor man fighting for his life.'

'So you saw it then?'

'Yes. Well, Borg did,' replied his wife. 'My husband spends a lot of time looking at sea birds.' She did not look particularly pleased about his pastime.

'I heard about it on the news, but they said very little and gave almost no details at all of how it happened.'

'Well, I can describe it to you, but it's not pleasant.' Unfortunately he had little more to add to what Linda had already gleaned from Rachel, with the exception that he had seen over the harbour wall and had a good look at the second para-motorist.

'Interesting, said Linda, finishing her glass of wine. 'So you would recognise him again if you saw him?'

'I think so. Why?'

'Just interested.

'Can I get you another drink?' asked Borg.

'No thank you, I'm the driver and I'm sure there will be plenty of police on the lookout for drunk drivers tonight.'

'So you don't live in the apartment block? I thought I hadn't seen you before.'

'No, I'm a friend of Rosa's daughter.' She pointed at JD who was now chatting to a young Spanish couple. 'In fact I think I had better see if she is ready to leave. Nice meeting you both.'

'And you.'

His wife said nothing.

As Linda squeezed her way through to JD, Rosa caught her arm and whispered, 'Did you find out anything?'

'Not really. You?'

'Yes, I did. You are not going to believe this, but Leticia is pregnant.'

'The duke's wife? So, what's so important about that?'

'The duke had prostate cancer two years ago and is unable to father any more children. She must have been hiding it from him.'

'So how did you find out?'

'One of the midwives from the hospital saw her having a scan a few weeks ago. She told her sister, who works here as a cleaner for one of my neighbours.'

'And I suppose she told her employer and that's how you know. We should tell JD. I'll go and look for her.'

JD gave Linda a huge smile when she saw her pushing her way through the throng of people around the dining table. 'Just the person I wanted to see,' she said, putting a savoury pastry into her mouth. 'I must admit, my mother knows how to throw a party; no wonder this place is so crowded. Here, try one of these; they are delicious.'

Linda picked up an *empanada* and bit into it. 'You're right. It's like a mini meat pie only tastier.'

'These are better still; they're filled with scallops.' She helped herself to another and then filled up her empty glass.

'Good job I'm driving you home,' said Linda.

'Any luck?'

'A little, but your mother has some interesting news for us. The duke's wife is pregnant and it's not his.'

'What?' The *empanada* on its way into JD's mouth stopped in mid-air. 'How does she know it isn't the duke's baby?'

'Because he had prostate cancer two years ago.'

'He could have frozen some of his sperm. Sick people often do that.'

'Well we need to find out if he did. Have you asked your mother to arrange for you to see the duke?'

'Yes, we're going tomorrow morning, early, before his wife gets there. She usually arrives at eleven when he's been washed and had his meds.'

'Okay. Will your mother pick you up?'

'Yes, you don't need to worry, Linda. Can you ring the solicitor and find out when you can make an appointment to speak to him.'

'I need something to back me up. I can't just swan in there and start asking him about the duke's will without some sort of permission.'

'Don't worry I'll get that for you. I hope. That's if the duke is able to speak to us.'

'He will be,' said Rosa, joining them and selecting a date filled with marzipan from the table. 'I'll pick you up from home, Jacaranda. Six o'clock all right?' She held out her glass to the waiter and waited while he filled it up with champagne.

'I'll be there.'

'Are you leaving already?'

'I think so. Linda has to get home to Phil and I have some things to go over before tomorrow.' She kissed her mother on the cheek and added, 'It was a lovely party, Mama. Paola excelled herself with the food.'

'It was Alejandro's restaurant, actually.'

'Whatever. It was all delicious. See you in the morning. Come on Linda, time we were on our way.'

'Just a moment, Linda. I have something for your husband.' Rosa turned and went into the kitchen. 'Here, I thought he'd like a few pastries. Something to tempt his appetite.' She handed Linda two small cardboard boxes. 'Sweet and savoury, some of each.'

'Oh thank you, Rosa. He'll enjoy that. How kind of you.'

'Not at all.'

'Well I'd better hurry, as the boss is waiting. *Adios*, Rosa. Thanks for inviting me,' Linda said, hurrying out after JD.

As Linda drove through the centre towards JD's apartment, her boss checked her phone for any messages.

'Ricardo says that Kiko's para-motor was definitely new; the registration is February this year and he says that Juan Felipe confirms it. He even sent Ricardo a photograph of it, with Kiko standing beside it. Apparently it's not even the same colour; the new one was red. Anyway, now Ricardo has logged it as stolen and will tell us more tomorrow. I suggested he join us at the agency at about midday; it's time we had another review of where we are. I might even have persuaded the duke to officially ask us to investigate by then. What about you, Linda? Did you learn anything new this evening?'

'I have found a man who says he had a clear look at the other para-motorist. He reckons he could identify him.'

'Did you get his name and address?'

'In a way. He's called Borg and she's Karina and they live on the third floor. I'm sure Rosa will tell you which apartment it is.'

'So not a bad evening's work,' said JD.

CHAPTER 10

At six o'clock the next morning JD was standing in the street outside her apartment block when her mother's Audi screeched to a stop in front of her. 'I'm glad you are here; I wasn't looking forward to searching for a parking space at this time of the morning, or driving around the block until you woke up. Jump in.'

'Okay, Mama. What's the hurry?'

'I'm worried that they won't let us in to see him.'

'So why does getting there a few minutes earlier make any difference? Anyway I don't understand why we are going so early. You said his wife doesn't visit him until eleven.' Although she had slept for at least eight hours last night, JD still felt exhausted.

'Because it's a long drive and we have to arrive while Teresa is still on duty; she does the night shift and goes home at nine each morning.'

'Do I know Teresa?'

'No. I don't think so; she is Adolfo's sister.'

JD groaned. This could go on forever. She had no idea who these people were, but she knew her mother had a wide and varied network of contacts, either people she knew personally or people one of her friends knew. It was best not to ask too many questions. The main thing was that her mother could open many doors. 'I hope the duke is able to talk to us and is not too heavily medicated.'

'Teresa will see to that. Don't worry.'

'Where are we going, exactly?' JD asked, when her mother signalled right and headed towards the dual carriageway.

'A small town just outside Seville. I thought you knew. They wouldn't send him to Málaga now, would they, not when his family are all living in Seville. It's a nice place, the hospice. Very exclusive and expensive, as you might expect.'

'So, at least two hours drive then?'

'Maybe a bit less; but we don't need to go through the city.'

'So I can have a sleep? Or do you want me to navigate?'

'Absolutely not. You go to sleep. It looks as though you need it.' Rosa turned on the radio, fiddling with the channels until she found some music she liked.

It was nice to be getting out of Málaga for a few hours, away from the noise and the crowds. JD closed her eyes and tried to think about the case, but her thoughts kept drifting back to her new condition and how it was going to affect her life. She had already started to think something was wrong with her, the nausea in the mornings, wanting to stay in bed longer than usual but it wasn't until she did the pregnancy test that it became real. Pregnant at her age; she had been so sure it was never going to happen to her that now she didn't know how she felt about it. It wasn't that she didn't want to be a mother, it was more that she had just never considered it a possibility. She had her work, her friends and her lover. Federico. Her life was complete just as it was. Did she want it to change? She was feeling very confused. Was that the reason this case seemed to be harder than usual? They said that pregnant women became more emotional, but she had always dismissed that as an old wives' tale. Perhaps it was true. She just never expected it to apply to her; she was not normally an emotional person, she told herself. She was logical and practical; those were her strong points. So what would her advice be to someone else in her position? '*Take your time. Don't rush into anything. Weigh up the pros and cons.*' Sensible advice but it all seemed so clinical when inside her heart was racing like mad, whether with excitement or fear, she couldn't be sure. Then there was the big question. Should she tell Federico? He deserved to know, no matter what her final decision was. But if she told him he would be so delighted at the prospect of being a father that he would have her marching down the aisle before she could say anything to stop him. Was that what she wanted? At the moment she did not know what she wanted, but she would have to decide soon. She groaned.

'What's that, Jacaranda? Are you okay? You're looking a bit peaky, you know. Perhaps you shouldn't drink so much during the week,' said Rosa, looking across at her daughter.

'Keep your eyes on the road, Mama. I'm fine. I was just thinking about the case.'

'So what is your opinion?'

'It's too soon to say, but I am now pretty confident that Kiko's death was not an accident. All we have to do is prove it.'

It wasn't long before they were pulling up outside a large stone building surrounded by immaculate lawns and well established Cypress trees. It looked as though it used to be the stately home of a local landowner; there were a lot of big estates in this part of Andalusia, olive plantations, sunflowers and wine. This one had obviously once been part of an olive plantation. 'Very impressive,' said JD as the wrought iron gates slowly opened onto a long driveway flanked by ancient olive trees, bent and twisted with their years, that led up towards the house.

'When I was a girl, this was a consular building. I remember we came to a garden party here once, but that was a long time ago. And before that it belonged to the Arcos family; you know them, big producers of olive oil.' JD grunted a reply; her mother didn't really want an answer, she was just reminiscing again. 'It's been a hospice for about fifteen years I should think,' Rosa continued.

JD was surprised to realise that she was actually feeling nervous about this meeting; somehow it didn't seem right to be bothering a man who was lying on his death bed.

'I can see what you're thinking, Jacaranda. Just remember it was the duke who contacted me. He wants to be able to die in peace and he can't do that if he doesn't know how and why his son died.'

'I realise that. Well we can tell him how Kiko died, but we can't tell him why, not yet.'

'But you will. I have every faith in you, *hija mia*.' She pressed a bell on the wall and then stepped back to wait. They stood side by side in front of a huge double door made of Spanish oak, with a large brass knocker in the shape of a wolf's head.

'Maybe we should knock,' suggested JD, eager to touch the wolf's head.

'They would never hear us. Anyway there's someone coming now.' As she spoke the door swung open and a man in a white coat beckoned them inside.

'*Bienvenida* Most Illustrious Señora Calderón del Bosque. I will take you to the duke's room. Would you like me to send someone to see to your car?'

'Thank you, Enrique. We will not be staying long; the car is fine in the drive where I left it.'

As they followed the man up the wide oak staircase, JD felt she was entering a different world. Here money was no object. You may be about to die, but you would die surrounded by luxury. She wondered what the duke was like; her mother had often spoken of him but JD had always kept well away from that part of her mother's life.

'The duke is very weak,' said Enrique. 'Please try not to tire him.'

'We will not disturb him for long, I promise,' Rosa replied. 'We have only come because he asked us to.'

'Yes, I know. He is very anxious to talk to you.' They stopped outside a white painted door. Everything upstairs was white, the ceiling, the walls, the window frames, even the floor was made of white marble. Enrique tapped gently on the door then opened it for them. 'Teresa is in there with him. Please go in, *Mi Señora.*'

JD found it strange that he never addressed her, nor even looked at her. She was not just in her mother's aristocratic shadow, she was invisible. Perhaps he thought she was Rosa's maidservant.

'Thank you Enrique,' Rosa said and glided into the room as though she was going to a grand reception; she blended into her surroundings perfectly whereas JD felt completely out of place.

The duke's room was spacious and airy; her first impression was of floating in a white cloud as the colour scheme continued towards the tall French windows framed by long flowing muslin curtains. Outside the well tended green lawns and brightly coloured plants stood out in stark contrast to the unbroken sea of white that surrounded her.

A white-coated nurse who had been sitting by the duke's bedside stood up and bobbed in greeting to Rosa. 'I am so pleased you could come, *Mi Señora*. He asks for you every day. It is making him very anxious.'

'How is he, Teresa?'

'Not good. The doctor thinks it won't be long now.'

'But I can talk to him?'

'Yes. I'll wake him up.' But there was no need, the old man was already aware that he had visitors and was trying to pull himself upright to see them. '*Momento, Mi Señor*. Let me help you.' Teresa deftly manoeuvred the duke into a sitting position and placed some pillows behind him.

'Rosa. I am so happy to see you,' he said, his breath coming in sharp bursts, making his words barely audible. He turned towards JD and extended his hand. 'Your daughter? She doesn't look like you.' He tried to smile, but his lips could no longer move as he would have liked.

JD took the old man's hand in hers; it was dry, like a dead leaf and she could feel his gentle pulse throbbing under her fingers. '*Buenos días, Mi Señor*.'

He beckoned for her to bend closer and whispered, 'Do you know why my son died?'

'Not yet, *Mi Señor*. We need your permission to investigate before we can get any further with our enquiries. I have brought a document for you to sign which says that you would like us to find out all that we can about the unexpected death of your son, Gabriel Francisco Mendoza de Goya Pérez.'

'My poor Kiko,' he sighed. 'My poor, poor boy.'

'You understand, don't you Gabriel? The police are not looking into his death; they say it was an accident. If you want my daughter to investigate it for you, you need to give her official permission.'

'Yes, Rosa, I understand.' He stretched out his hand and took the pen from JD. 'Teresa, help me please.' The nurse placed his tray in position and helped him lean forward so that he could sign his signature. Once completed, he fell back on the pillows and closed his eyes.

'Is he okay? asked JD. 'Will I be able to ask him a few questions?' The duke looked at least ten years older than his seventy-eight years.

'Yes, just give him a minute.'

JD moved her chair closer to the sick man, while Teresa removed the tray and plumped up his pillows. His uneven breathing gradually slowed down and returned to normal.

'Are you feeling better, Gabriel?' asked Rosa. 'We need to ask you a couple of questions if you don't mind.' The duke opened his eyes and nodded. 'Was Kiko going to inherit your title when you died?'

'Yes, of course.'

'So who will inherit it now that he is dead?'

He looked at her, seemingly unsure of what to answer. 'I don't remember. Isabella, I suppose. Not right that. Should be a male heir. Lovely girl, my Isabella, but not strong enough, not like a man. Has to be a man. No more male heirs, now. End of the line.' He shut his eyes and lay back on the pillows.

'Do you remember what you put in your will? If anything should happen to Kiko, who would become the next duke?'

'My solicitor will tell you. All changed these days. Can't keep up with the changes.' He looked at JD and whispered, 'I have told Don Emilio you will get in touch with him.'

'What about your other son?' asked JD, thinking about his comment about having no more male heirs.

He looked at her blankly. 'Other son? What other son?'

'Antonio. Leticia's boy,' said Rosa.

'He's just a child. He doesn't count. Gabriel was the one.' A tear trickled down his wrinkled cheek.

'Can you think of anyone who might have wanted to harm Gabriel?' she asked. 'Did he have any enemies? Did he owe anyone money? Can you think of any reason why someone would want him dead?'

He looked at her through rheumy eyes and shook his head. 'He was a lovely boy.'

'But someone didn't think so.'

'So you agree with me; someone killed him. I knew it. I told Rosa; he was a sensible boy. He would never have flown over the harbour like that. Never. Was he on his own?'

'We are not sure but we think someone might have been with him. Would you have any idea who that could have been? Did he have any close friends?'

'There was a girlfriend, but I haven't heard anything about her in a while. Lavinia, or something like that.' He turned to Rosa. 'You knew her father. Count something or other. Very keen on the horses. I'm sure you knew him. He was a rich man but lost everything at the races. All he had left was his title.'

'I know who you mean, but I don't remember his name. Auguste, maybe.'

'This Lavinia does she live in Málaga?' asked JD.

'I'm sorry; I don't remember. Leticia will know. She was a good friend of hers for a while until they fell out. Not sure what happened there. Some silly women's squabble.' He spoke in gasps, a subdued staccato broken by the wheezing from his chest. 'Leticia, where is she? Isn't she coming today?' He looked around him, anxiously.

'Yes, she is coming. It's still early, *Mi Señor*. You know how Leticia likes to take her time in the mornings. She will be here in a little while,' said Teresa.

'Do you think your wife knew any of Kiko's friends?' JD asked.

'My wife? Leticia you mean? She might well have. She is nearer to his age than mine, you know. Yes, she will have known some of them. You must ask her. She is coming, isn't she?' he asked again, turning back to Teresa. 'My wife isn't here yet. But she is coming, isn't she?'

'Of course she is, *Mi Señor*. Don't worry. She will soon be here.'

'Good, because I think she can help us find who killed my boy.'

'How is your sister, Irina,' Rosa asked. 'I haven't seen her in a long, long time.'

'As grumpy as ever. She didn't like it when I married Leticia. Said I was still married to that other one. Did I think I could just go around how and when I liked getting rid of my wives, sending them all over the world? Stupid woman, she made it sound as though I was in the habit of getting divorced. If my beautiful Rebecca was still alive, she would be sitting here by my side right now. There was never any other woman for me.'

'Has Irina been to see you?'

'No, and I don't want her or her sneaky son anywhere near me.'

'Pablo? I thought you liked Pablo?'

'I did, when he was eight years old. But he grew into an objectionable boy, always hanging around my Isabella, and he and Kiko never got on.' His breathing was very fast now, and he was struggling to get his words out.

'Now don't get yourself into a state, *Mi Señor*. I think it's about time for your medicine,' said Teresa. She looked at Rosa. 'If there's anything else you want to ask him, you should do it now, but don't mention his sister again. He's very upset that she hasn't been to see him.'

'No, I don't think we want to ask anything else.' Rosa looked at JD, who shook her head.

'The morphine makes him very sleepy and confused. I like to give it to him now, just before I go home and then he is usually awake by the time his wife arrives.'

'I understand. We're on our way. Thank you for arranging this, Teresa. I hope it makes him feel better to know that someone is looking into Kiko's death.'

'It seems he was very fond of his son,' JD said. The old man was lying back on the pillows with his eyes shut and his face screwed tight with pain. She watched as the nurse adjusted the drip in his arm.

'Sometimes the pain hits him so hard he can't bear it,' the nurse said. 'It's sad to see. He used to be such an active man.'

'You've known him a long time?' asked JD.

'Quite a few years now. I helped nurse his first wife when she was ill. That was a very sad time. The duke took it hard losing his wife and the new baby.' She looked at her watch. 'I'm sorry, but you will have to leave now; my relief will be arriving soon.' She looked down at the duke; his face had relaxed now and he was sleeping peacefully. 'He won't last much longer, you know. It's really sad. He is a nice man. Always very kind to me and my brother. I was very upset when I heard about Kiko; I had known him all his life. He could be a bit wild, but there wasn't a bad bone in his body. I really don't know who could have done this to him.'

'Well I hope we will soon find out. Thank you again for your help.'

'Yes, thank you Teresa. If you think of anything that might be of use to our investigation, please phone me,' said JD handing her a business card.

As soon as they were outside, and out of earshot, Rosa asked, 'Well. Did you learn anything useful?'

'I think I did. I certainly have a few more questions that need answering, particularly regarding his current wife and what her relationship with Kiko was really like.'

'And the sister, don't forget Irina and her son.'

'Is it all right if you drop me off at the office? I can message the team to tell them what time we will arrive and then we can go over the case together. That way, Linda will be free to spend the rest of the day with Phil.' Having seen the duke lying in that bed, struggling to tell them what little he could, not knowing if he would last another day, reminded her just how quickly someone you loved could be taken from you. She hoped Phil was going to recover from his cancer but whether he did or not, time was precious for him and his family, and Linda needed to spend as much time as possible with him.

'Sounds like a plan, but you know how it doesn't always work out the way we want,' said Rosa, almost as if she had been reading JD's thoughts. 'Anyway, if you're going to discuss the duke, I think I should join you.'

JD stared at her mother. It made sense. Once they started going over the duke's background they would certainly raise as many new questions as they had answers to the original ones. 'Of course, Mama. That's a good idea.' She beamed at her.

They arrived in Málaga at half-past-eleven and everyone was already at the agency. Nacho had not only arranged coffee for them, but pastries as well.

'You are a star, young man,' said JD. 'I am starving. Breakfast seems a long time ago.' She picked up a Danish pastry and took a bite.

'So what have you found out?' asked Nacho, handing a coffee to JD's mother. 'Nice to see you, Rosa.'

'My mother is going to sit in while we go over the duke's background, in case there is anything that is relevant to this case.'

'Or incorrect,' Rosa interrupted.

'Exactly.' JD began to relate their conversation at the hospice while Nacho scribbled on the evidence board. It was not looking quite so bare now.

'So do we have some new suspects?' Linda asked.

'Possibly, there are certainly some people worth looking at more closely; the second wife, Ana María for example. Do we know if she stands to inherit anything? Why were they divorced? Who was to blame? Him or her? And how come they got a divorce when the duke is supposed to be a staunch Catholic? That should keep you going for a bit, Linda.' She grinned.

'Can you tell us anything about her, Rosa? Did you know her?' asked Nacho.

'Not really. I wasn't living in Spain when she was on the scene, but I did meet her once when I was over for a friend's wedding. She was young and very pretty, coquettish, if you know what I mean, and seemed to be giving the duke a lot of attention. That was when I learned that he had been on his own since Rebecca's death, so maybe after meeting her he felt it was time to start afresh. The next thing I heard was that they were getting married. It was very sudden and the immediate family were not happy about it, apparently.' She paused, a frown creasing her perfectly made-up forehead.

'What is it, Mama?'

'Well now I remember; one of my friends wrote to me to say how shocked everyone was because the couple didn't get married in Seville, not even in Spain. They flew to Argentina for the wedding. That's virtually unheard of; it should have been a big society wedding, so why wasn't it here in Spain?'

'Well the marriage doesn't seem to have lasted very long, anyway,' said Linda.

'Two years and three months, according to the papers. Then he managed to get the marriage annulled,' Nacho chipped in.

'Not divorced then?' asked Linda.

'Gabriel was a very devout Catholic. He would have been against divorce,' added Rosa.

'But you have to have a valid reason to have an annulment. Do we know what it was?' asked JD.

Rosa shook her head. 'No, but I admit I wasn't surprised when I heard they were no longer married; she wasn't his type. Seemed too flighty to me. However I don't know any of the details. You could try to speak to the Bishop of Seville; the reason for the annulment should be recorded somewhere.'

'I think I might find it a bit difficult to get an audience with the Bishop,' said JD, grinning at her mother. 'The duke's sister would know, wouldn't she?' You said you were going to contact her, Mama. Ask her what she thought of Ana María.'

'She didn't have any children with the duke so what's the point?' asked Nacho. 'She didn't have anything to gain by Kiko's death.'

'I'm not so sure. If she can prove that they were still legally married then she would be his spouse and would get her inheritance. That would make Leticia's marriage null and void.'

'*Dios mio*, what a mess. What about his first wife? I assume there's nothing suspicious there?'

'No, I think that was a genuine tragedy. Rebecca had a history of difficult pregnancies; she had a terrible time with both Isabel and Kiko, and she had had a couple of miscarriages as well.'

'Poor woman. They had Kiko and Isabella, so why didn't they stop there?'

'I think he probably wanted another son.'

'Well, he's got one now, whether he acknowledges him or not.'

'What do you mean, Boss?' asked Nacho.

Rosa explained how the duke appeared to have forgotten that little Antonio was also his son. 'I expect it was the morphine, confusing him.'

'I wonder. He didn't seem confused about the rest of what he told us.'

Nacho picked up the marker and drew a question mark on the evidence board next to Antonio's name.

'Anything to add about the duke's background, Nacho? Anything that might suggest a motive for killing his son?'

'Well, you can trace the duke's family, Mendoza de Goya, back a hundred years and there has been a Duque de Roble for even longer; the line is steeped in tradition, so in a way he's a bit of a dinosaur if the truth be told.'

'Any relation to the painter?'

'Goya? No, not that I could see. The painter's father was an artisan, although I think the grandparents on his mother's side were petty nobility from somewhere in the north of Spain. Anyway, the duke's family, like the majority of aristocratic families at the time were strong supporters of the Nationalists during the civil war, and of Franco in particular. They are all still very right wing—the duke voted for Vox during the last elections and was interviewed only recently, giving the party his support—except for Kiko that is. Although the duke's son did not seem very interested in politics he has been recorded as saying on a number of occasions that, in his opinion, it was time to do away with outdated institutions such as the monarchy and the aristocracy. Now whether he really believed that or said it to annoy his father, I can't be sure. I couldn't find any evidence to say that Kiko belonged to any left-wing organisations. He wasn't affiliated to the Communist party or even P.S.O.E.'

'So you're saying he was apolitical. I don't see that as a reason to murder him.'

'Maybe not, but remember he was the heir apparent. Would the family, or any of their aristocratic friends be happy for the next Duque de Roble to be a Communist?'

'So, why didn't the duke disinherit him?' asked Linda.

'That is not possible in Spain. The law regarding inheritance is very strict.'

'So we have a rich, aristocratic family with its feet firmly stuck in the past and an heir apparent who looks likely to turn everything upside down.'

'And a sick man who didn't approve of the modern aristocracy's behaviour, with their photos spread all over social media, living the good life and spending money like water. That wasn't the legacy he wanted for his family. Maybe he thought Kiko's behaviour would bring the family name into disrepute?'

'And that from a man with three wives,' said Nacho, with a laugh.

'You are not suggesting that the duke was behind his son's death, JD?'

'No, Linda, but I think the aristocracy would close ranks even if one of them was a serial killer. And anyway, if the duke was behind his son's death then why did he contact Rosa to ask us to investigate it? No, he's definitely not a suspect. But what if it is about the inheritance? What if someone else in the family felt that they were much better equipped than Kiko to inherit the duke's title? We have to keep digging into their backgrounds. All of them.'

'Actually, Jacaranda, the duke didn't ask me to speak to you. He didn't know my daughter was a detective then. I just put it like that so that you would agree to look into it.'

JD could not believe what she was hearing. 'So the duke didn't ask for me to investigate?'

Her mother shook her head. 'But he did want to know what had happened to his son. You saw him; he is desperate to find out how the boy died.'

'But is he going to pay us?'

'Jacaranda, why do you always bring it back to money. This is more important than money. I expect someone in the family will pay you for your time. Anyway you have the contract signed, so that's okay.'

JD could not find the words to answer her mother. She turned to Nacho and said, 'If there's no more to report, we'll call it a day.'

'Okay, Boss. It looks like we've moved from no motive for Kiko's death to 'Take your pick.'

'But so far they are all pointing to Kiko's inheritance,' added Linda.

JD looked at her watch; it was only one-thirty. She dialled Jacobo's number and waited impatiently for him to answer. 'Jacobo? It's JD.'

'*Hola, Cariño*. Are you ringing to invite me to lunch?'

'Not exactly. Is Enzio still there?'

'I believe so. Why?'

'I wondered if I could pop round and have a word with him. I won't keep him long; it's just that we have found out a lot more about the family and I'd like to double check a couple of things with him.'

'Hang on and I'll see what he says. You realise that we're only working half a day during August?'

'Yes, you told me.' She could hear voices in the background but couldn't make out what was being said. After a few minutes, a voice she didn't recognise answered.

'Señora Dunne? How can I help you?'

'Enzio? *Buenas tardes.* I wondered if we could have a chat about the Duque de Roble and his family? Jacobo told me that you were working on a documentary about them.'

'That's right. To be honest, there's been a bit of a rush on to get it finished. We knew he was ill but we were not expecting him to deteriorate quite so quickly. He's only seventy-five after all; his father lived well into his eighties.'

'Would it be possible to meet up today?'

'Today? You are in a hurry.' There was a pause and then he continued, 'Okay, can you meet me in Álvaro's bar in half an hour? Then I can have my lunch while we chat; I'd like to get back to work by three o'clock.'

'That's great. I'll go straight there.'

Álvaro's bar was not far from the agency but despite the fact that the celebrations had been going on for almost a week now, there was no let up in the amount of revellers thronging the city eager to enjoy themselves; the music and dancing were already in full flow as she walked through the narrow back streets where tired looking waiters were busy setting up tables for lunch. The heat at midday was intense and alleviated only slightly by the brightly coloured canopies strung between the buildings to serve as sunshades. She stopped for a moment, her way blocked by a handsome, older couple in full flamenco dress, dancing a *Sevillana;* they were surrounded by friends clapping and clicking castanets in time to the music. She wondered if Federico had ever learned to dance the *Sevillana;* originally from Seville this dance was now popular all over

Spain, even with the younger generation. He would make a handsome figure in the narrow trousers and short jacket; for a moment the unlikely image of the captain in high-heeled boots made her smile. A brief pause in the music allowed her to squeeze past the dancers and continue towards the bar. The smell of someone barbecuing meat reminded her of how hungry she was; she had eaten a big breakfast this morning before she left home, but still felt ready for more.

The bar was crowded and all the tables were taken. She waited, scanning the occupants and wondering which of the young men sitting there was Enzio, when a tall, thin man in his twenties stood up and beckoned her towards him. 'Enzio?' she asked.

'Yes, you must be JD,' he said and smiled at her. 'No bicycle? I was told to look out for a lovely blonde with a bicycle.'

'Well, you should know better than to believe what Jacobo tells you. Looks as though you were lucky to get a table.'

'I'm a regular. The owner looks after his regulars, even during Feria Week.'

'Sensible man.'

'So what is it you want to know about the duke? Anything in particular?'

'I suppose I just want some background on the family. We spoke to the duke yesterday.'

'Did you, indeed. I thought he was too ill to see anyone except immediate family?'

JD hesitated. Should she share what she had found out with this man? He was a reporter, of sorts. Was it wise? 'My mother is an old family friend, she took me with her to see him.'

'Ah, yes. Jacobo said something about you being related to the aristocracy. Well that's one way to open doors.' He sounded slightly peeved; from what she now knew about the duke's family, she imagined that it couldn't have been easy for him to research into their background. 'How was he? Please don't tell me he won't last the week.'

'He is very ill, but he was quite coherent most of the time. Who knows how long he will last. He is very upset about his son's death and is desperate to know why he died, so I think that's why he is still clinging to life.'

'And you're the one with the job of finding out for him? Does that mean you think his son's death was suspicious?' There was a gleam in his eye.

Again JD hesitated. Her police training reminded her that revealing how much you knew to someone not directly involved in the investigation, could hamper it and even make it hard to get a conviction. She had to go carefully. 'We don't know. I am just doing this as a favour to my mother; she wants her friend's mind to be at rest before he dies. And he will die, that much we do know; the doctors all agree that there is nothing more they can do for him. I am just trying to make things easier for him and the relatives, but as you have probably already found out, they do not want to talk to outsiders about family matters.'

'Yes, you're right. And that's exactly what we are, JD, outsiders. How am I supposed to make an interesting documentary about the man, if no-one will tell me anything.' He waved across to the waiter. 'The usual, please Álvaro.'

JD ordered a salad and some *boquerones*. She had lost her appetite since talking to Enzio, who was making her realise just how hard this investigation was going to be, and although she liked a challenge she did not like to accept defeat.

'I'll go through what I've found out so far; it's mostly about the duke's career, although that was not very distinguished.'

'Yes, I know about his politics and how it was his father who made the family rich. Look, I understand that you don't have a lot of time, so maybe we could start with what you have found out about his son? If anything. What I need to know is his relationship with the rest of his family. I get the impression that he was the black sheep of the family?'

'The *oveja negra*? Yes, I think he was. From what I have found out he was always a bit of a rebel. He didn't conform in the way the heir to a dukedom was expected to; for example he had no interest in politics at all.'

'So he wasn't right-wing, like his father?'

'No, but then he didn't appear to support any particular party. At a guess, if he had to vote for anyone it would be the Green Party. *Los Verdes*. He was someone who loved the countryside and the outdoor life. That's what eventually led to his death.'

'What do you mean by that?'

'Well he joined the paragliding club. Didn't you know?'

'No. You're sure you don't mean paramotoring?'

'No. I think that was a quite recent venture; he has been paragliding since he was a teenager. Not on a regular basis, but occasional weekends when he wanted to get away from everything. When you think about it, paragliding makes more sense because of his love of the countryside; there's no noise pollution and no contamination to the environment. It's an environmentally friendly sport which is why I found it very strange to hear that he had died in a paramotoring accident.'

'So do I, now. Do you have the details of the paragliding club?'

'Not on me, but I'll send them to you when I get back to the office.' He checked his watch. 'Yes, what was I saying? Ah yes, about his lack of interest in politics.'

'I expect that didn't go down very well with the duke?'

'No, of course not. He wanted his son to be preparing himself as his successor and part of that meant being active in politics, both local and national.'

'You said, part of it, what else was expected of Kiko?'

'Well, he was due to inherit a very lucrative business, but he had no interest in it. The duke had accountants and estate managers to do the majority of the work but he still kept very close control over what was happening, which was why the business continued to grow and prosper. We are talking about a lot of money here and that doesn't include the various properties the family owned.'

'I know about that. So you are saying that Kiko was not interested in managing the family business?'

'No, and never had been. It was Doña Isabella and her husband who did all the work, especially since the duke became ill.'

'So does that mean Kiko would have been happy to leave it to them to continue managing the business? He really didn't want it?'

'Who knows. He was an enigma. You do realise that he was rated as one of Spain's most eligible bachelors? Mind you, that was before the scandal.'

'What scandal?'

'Oh, you haven't heard about it? It was all over the news at the time. A year ago, he was due to marry an Italian heiress, a young woman he had met when he was holidaying in Rome. The family were all delighted. Bianca was a beautiful girl, well educated and from a very well-connected family. It was in all the gossip columns; it seemed that the *oveja negra* was going to settle down at last. The duke settled a large amount of money on the couple and gave them one of the larger of his properties as a wedding present. Then two days before the wedding, Kiko announced that he was not ready to get married and broke it off. The shock waves could be felt across the country. At least he didn't leave her standing at the altar, but it was nearly as bad; both families had spent a fortune on the wedding arrangements and the duke was left with the task of explaining to the Bishop that they did not require the use of the cathedral after all. Can you imagine it.' He grinned. 'You see Kiko was not a practising Catholic; I heard that he didn't even want to get married in a church, never mind the cathedral. Of course both families insisted and the duke supported them. It was to be a Catholic wedding or nothing. And it turned out to be nothing.'

'What about Bianca? It must have been a dreadful shock for her and her family.'

'She went back to Verona, heartbroken, it is said. Personally I think she probably had a lucky escape if truth be told. Men like him don't really ever settle into a conventional life style.'

'Are you sure about that? Maybe he just didn't love her, and had succumbed to pressure from the family?'

'Maybe.'

'Was he gay, do you think? His father would definitely not have approved if he was.'

'Well if he was homosexual, he hid it very well. The coverage I have found on him always seemed to include a beautiful young woman hanging on his arm, and it was hardly ever the same one twice running. I think he was just scared of getting married and settling down.' He paused while the waiter served their lunch and then continued, 'That's about all I have on the son.'

'What about his girlfriend, Lavinia?'

'His step-mother's friend? Well ex-friend. Oh, she didn't last long. Not a lot to tell about her; she was very much like all the girls who hung out with him.'

'In what way?'

'Only with him for the publicity. You know, to get her name in the gossip columns, have her picture in glossy magazines, that sort of thing.'

'Did you say that she was an ex-girlfriend of Leticia? What happened there?'

'Sorry, I wish I knew. Maybe Mama warned her off her step-son. Maybe Leticia was scared that it was getting serious and she didn't want her old schoolfriend as part of the family.'

JD pushed her half-eaten salad to one side. She picked up one of the *boquerones* and ate it. 'You can finish these if you want; they're delicious but I've had enough.'

'Are you off then?'

'Yes, I need to get back to the office. Thank you so much for finding the time to talk to me.'

'I hope it's been useful.'

'It has. I look forward to seeing the documentary when it's finished.'

'Well, it will probably be redacted in places, but I can't do much about that; the powers that be are in charge. I am just a humble reporter. If you want to come and see it before the censor gets to it, just let Jacobo know and we will fit you in for a private viewing.'

'I would like that. Thanks. Good luck with your deadline.'

'Thanks. Have a good weekend.'

She smiled. On Sunday they were going to the barbecue with Federico's family and she was feeling a bit apprehensive. They didn't often socialise with them; Federico and his brother seemed to rub each other up the wrong way and his mother definitely did not think JD was right for her son. She half hoped that something would come up that prevented her from going but she didn't really want to leave Federico to face them on his own. She knew the first topic of conversation from his mother would be about marriage—Federico's.

CHAPTER 11

When JD returned from her early morning run along the promenade, Federico was still stretched out in her bed, one arm hanging over the side and fast asleep. She slipped into the bed beside him and whispered in his ear, 'It's almost two o'clock. We'll be late for the barbecue.'

'What the hell? Why didn't you wake me up earlier?' He leapt out of bed and grabbed his watch from the bedside table. 'Not funny, Jacaranda; it's not even ten yet. You nearly gave me a heart attack saying that.' He sat down on the edge of the bed and added, 'Well I suppose I might as well get up now, as I've been so rudely awakened.'

'You looked so peaceful lying there,' she said, laughing at him. 'Quite out of character.'

'I suppose we have to go to this thing, do we?' he asked. 'Don't you have something urgent to look into regarding the case. It is a murder, after all. Higher priority than a family barbecue.'

'Not according to your mother.' She stretched out her legs. 'But there's no rush, we can have a leisurely breakfast and relax.'

'I like the sound of that,' he said, lying back on the bed and stroking her hair. 'Perhaps later.'

'Your mother wouldn't approve,' she murmured as his hands started to move slowly down her body.

'My mother doesn't approve of anything I do,' he said. 'It's her automatic reaction to everything I say or do.'

She knew it was pointless being on time; punctuality was not a custom many Spaniards adopted and certainly not Eloy. Federico's eldest brother lived in a modern house in Alhaurin de la Torre; it was separated from its neighbours by a high hedge of scarlet *bougainvillia* and had a view of the distant hills. Surrounded by other similar styled houses, there was only a glimpse of the blue Mediterranean on the horizon. Nevertheless, she liked their garden; it was neither ostentatious nor neglected. It lay somewhere in between; there was a rectangular pool that was obviously well used by Federico's nephews and the lawn which stretched around the house like a weathered green scarf, was anything but immaculate; there were bicycles propped up against the garden wall and signs of a recent game of football. A large barbecue sat in one corner, shaded by two parasols, and a long table and numerous chairs had been set out ready for lunch on the patio at the back of the house. It was, in short, a garden thoughtfully designed to be enjoyed and used by everyone and that included the two long-haired German Shepherd dogs who were currently lying at the feet of an old lady, resting in the shade of a medlar tree. The woman appeared to be sleeping while the dogs kept a watchful eye on everything that was going on.

'Federico. How are you, *hermano*?' An older version of the captain came across and grabbed his brother in an affectionate hug. 'It's ages since we've seen you. The boys are always asking about you; you promised to take them to a basketball match. Remember?'

'I know, I'm sorry, Eloy; I have just been so busy lately. As soon as the season starts again I'll get tickets for all of us. It's good to see you too, *hermano*.'

'Hi Jacaranda, you're looking lovely as always. So you are still managing to put up with my brother are you? I would have thought you were fed up of him by now.'

'Not yet.' JD smiled and kissed Eloy on the cheeks. 'Your garden looks lovely, Eloy.'

'Thank you; as you can see we don't do much with it. It could be better cared for, and the gardener does try but with two teenage boys and two dogs, it's hardly worth the effort.'

'Who is that sitting with your dogs?'

'That's our great aunt, Anita. She's ninety today.'

'So this is a birthday party. Why didn't you say and we could have brought her a gift.'

'No, it's not really a party; she wouldn't appreciate it. She's not really with it these days.'

'I'll go over later and say hello,' said Federico.

'She probably won't recognise you. Depends on the sort of day she is having.'

'So she's living here as well?' asked JD.

'For now. I think she may have to go into a residential home if she gets any worse, but for now, Mama and Julia look after her between them.'

'I can't notice any smell of cooking,' said Federico, eyeing the empty barbecue.

'I'm going to start now. Just waiting for Mama to come outside; she and Julia are preparing some things in the kitchen.'

'Would you like me to help?' JD asked.

'No, they have it all covered. Let me pour you a drink.'

'Uncle Fede,' a boy's voice called and two teenagers ran across and threw themselves at Federico. 'Come and play football with us. You can be in goal.'

'I'm always in goal,' she heard Federico grumble, as he allowed himself to be dragged away by his nephews.

'He needs to take more exercise,' said his brother, handing her a glass of cava. 'He's definitely getting a middle-aged spread; he'll soon be worse than me.' He patted his plump stomach lovingly. 'By the way, you're not vegan or anything, are you?'

'No. I eat almost anything.' Was that strictly true she asked herself. It had been her standard reply for years, but lately she had noticed that in actual fact there were quite a few things that she no longer liked: peppers were one and bacon was another, even the smell of it made her feel sick. Was this because of the pregnancy?

'Phew, that's good. I never thought to ask Federico. So, you and he have been going out for a while now?'

'Yes, I suppose we have. Not sure how long, exactly. We aren't counting.'

'And what is it you do?'

'For a living?' He nodded at her, and began to smear oil over the hotplate of the barbecue. 'I am a private detective. I have an agency in Málaga.'

'Really. That's interesting,' Eloy said, but from his tone of voice she knew he was thinking the opposite. 'Do you get much work?'

'A steady amount.' She sipped some of the cava. It looked as though this was going to turn into a Spanish inquisition and she was the heretic. Good job it was an electric barbecue so they couldn't burn her at the stake. She giggled.

'Sorry?' Eloy asked, looking up at her.

'Nothing, I just choked on the bubbles.'

'I can get you something else if you prefer?'

'No, I'm fine. Oh, I think they're bringing the meat out now.' Federico's mother, whom she had met on only a couple of occasions but would never forget a single moment of either of them, carried a wide tray covered with a selection of chicken legs, kebabs, sausages and beef burgers.

'Let me take that, Mama.' Eloy grabbed the tray from his mother and placed it near the barbecue. 'Did Antonio say what time they were coming?' he asked, beginning to lather the meat with his home-made barbecue sauce.

'Your brothers are a law unto themselves. I see Federico at least made it this time.' She turned to JD as though she had only just noticed her. '*Buenas tardes*, my dear. I'm glad you were able to come. Have you been enjoying the *feria*?'

'No, I haven't had time to go this year; we have been quite busy at the agency.'

'Busy? More lost dogs?' The sarcasm was obvious in her tone.

'Amongst other things.' There was absolutely no point in correcting her; she had made up her mind about the value of JD's work and nothing was going to change that preconception.

'*Buenas tardes* Jacaranda.' A woman about her own age came rushing towards her and gave her an enormous hug. 'I'm so glad you could make it; we'd never get to see Federico if it wasn't for you.' She stepped back and looked at her. 'You look lovely, my dear. Absolutely glowing. Have you done something to your hair?'

JD was tempted to say that she had combed it, but instead she smiled pleasantly and replied, 'Thank you. No, it hasn't changed; it's probably because I haven't tied it back this afternoon.'

'Well, it looks very nice.' She turned to her husband. 'Cook a few without that ghastly sauce, *Cariño*,' she said. 'You know your mother can't eat anything spicy.'

'I will.' He leant across and kissed her. 'Can you give Antonio a ring and see where he has got to.'

'No need. I think I can hear a car now. That's probably him. I wonder who he's bringing with him this time.'

'No idea. It was Mama who invited him.'

Julia leant towards JD and whispered, 'Antonio has left his wife, you know. He came out a few months ago; I expect Fede told you.'

JD frowned. 'Came out? As in he's gay?'

'Yes, surely Fede said something about it?'

'No, I don't think he mentioned it. He doesn't talk very much about his family.'

'Oh.' Julia looked disappointed. 'I think I'll get myself a drink. Can I top yours up?'

'Yes, please.' She knew she shouldn't be drinking, not just because she was pregnant, but because she had to behave herself in front of Federico's family, for his sake. She would make this her last, she told herself as she followed Julia to the makeshift bar. 'Have you been married a long time?' she asked her. She was beginning to realise how little she knew about Federico's family and that she knew nothing at all about his ex-wife. Perhaps she would learn something this afternoon.

'Fifteen years. It seems like a lifetime. It was never the plan to have a family straight away, but Pepe came along a year after the wedding, followed almost immediately by Rafa. It was hard work when they were babies, but later it was lovely to have the two of them so close together in age. And look at them now. They are inseparable; it's wonderful. It's almost as if they were twins.'

JD looked across at where Federico was playing with the boys; the football had been abandoned and now they were taking it in turns to shoot a basket ball into a rather ragged net that was hanging on the back wall of the house. Julia was right, the boys were very similar in looks; they could easily be twins. JD felt a pang of regret as she watched the three of them joking and laughing; this was a different Federico to the one she was used to seeing. So this is what he meant when he said he wanted to get married and have a family, but was this what she wanted? She still didn't know.

'Here he is now, just in time,' said Julia, looking towards the front gate.

JD remembered meeting Antonio and his wife a few years before but he hadn't made much impression on her; she recalled that he was a quiet young man who seemed in awe of his elder brothers, but not much else. '*Buenas tardes* Antonio,' she said and greeted him in the customary way. 'Is this your daughter? She's grown.'

'Jackie, isn't it?' he asked, returning her embrace.

'Jacaranda.'

'Sorry. Nice to see you, Jacaranda. Yes, this is Ellie. She's five now, Say hello, Ellie.' The little girl smiled shyly at JD, while her father greeted his sister-in-law. 'Hi there, Julia. Looking lovely as always.' Lastly he turned to Eloy. 'Do you have anything other than meat, *hermano*? My partner is vegetarian.'

Eloy looked at his wife. 'Yes, I can find something for him, Antonio.'

'Is that Patrice, now?' Julia asked.

'Yes.' Antonio waved across at a tall, thin man with long grey hair who was coming towards them. 'He's from Germany.'

'Living in Málaga?'

'Yes, for now. We might decide to go and live in Berlin, if I can find work there.'

'For goodness sake don't talk about that in front of Mama; she'll go on about it all afternoon,' said Eloy. 'She moans enough about Federico going out with an English woman and constantly worries he'll leave Spain and go to the UK to live.'

'I'm half Scottish and half Spanish,' JD reminded them. 'And I don't see what business it is of your mother's, whom her sons go out with or where they decide to live; they are all over the age of consent as far as I can see.'

Eloy looked embarrassed but didn't apologise and merely said, 'You don't have to live with Mama. You don't know what she can be like. She's worse than a bloody sheep dog the way she has to monitor everyone's movements all the time.'

JD wanted to say more, but Federico and his nephews were heading towards them. 'Is that meat cooked yet? We're starving, aren't we lads?' he shouted.

'It is. Help yourself to a beer, Fede. No, not you two, orange juice for you,' Eloy told his sons as they ran towards the cooler box. 'You look absolutely whacked, Fede. The boys been getting the better of you?'

'You could say that. Don't they every slow down?' He took a sausage from the barbecue and began to eat it. 'These are good.'

'Well, you can take them across to the table; we're going to eat now.'

It was almost midnight when they left the barbecue. Federico had insisted on driving, so now JD felt full, contented and sleepy as she curled up in the passenger seat. It had been a lovely afternoon, and as far as she could remember she had not upset any of his family, well not intentionally.

'I suppose you're going to go to sleep now?' Federico said.

'Probably. Are you staying at my place?'

'No. It's work tomorrow and my uniform is at my apartment.'

'You could get up early and go home in the morning.'

'No, I prefer to sleep in my own bed tonight.' He sounded a little disgruntled. She knew what it was; he had suggested on more than one occasion that he move in with her but she had told him it was too soon. She hadn't even allowed him to leave anything more than a few toiletries and a toothbrush in her apartment. No wonder he was grumpy.

CHAPTER 12

On Monday morning Linda headed straight for the offices of "Vega, Vega y Garcia (*Abogados*)" and asked for Don Emilio Vega, the senior partner. When she had telephoned them the previous afternoon and said that the duke had told her to get in touch with his solicitor, there had been no problem getting an appointment at such short notice. What it was to have wealth and power, she thought as she climbed the steps of a nineteenth century building in the old part of Málaga.

The receptionist gave her a cursory look up and down, then looked surprised when she gave her name and said she had an appointment with Don Emilio. Her demeanour changed instantly. 'You're here on behalf of the duke, I understand,' she said. 'How is he? I was so sorry to hear that he was ill. He has been a client of Don Emilio's for many years, you know.'

Linda made no comment but followed her into an enormous office with a high ceiling and sash windows overlooking the cathedral. Don Emilio was exactly as she had imagined, a man in his fifties, balding and wearing rimless spectacles; he was dressed immaculately in a pale grey suit and white shirt, his only concession to the scorching hot day being the absence of a tie but she was sure he had one in his desk drawer for more important clients. She obviously did not fall into that category.

'*Buenos días*, Señora Prewitt. Please take a seat.' Linda seated herself in a blue leather armchair opposite his desk while he opened his computer and scrolled through his files. 'So you are investigating the recent death of the duke's son. Well, I don't know if I can be of very much help; I didn't really know the young man. Although I'm the family's solicitor, I never had anything to do with him personally. If he required the services of a solicitor then he went elsewhere.'

'I understand,' said Linda. 'Actually I am more interested in the duke's "Declaration of Heirs." We would like to know who stands to inherit the title and the duke's considerable fortune when he dies.'

'I'm not sure I can do that, *Señora*. Not without the duke's permission.'

Linda placed an envelope on the desk in front of him. 'He has given his express permission for you to give me any information which could help us to find out why his son died; I am sure that document is included in his instructions. The duke is a very sick man and he would like to know what happened to his son before he himself dies. I don't think you would want to prevent that, Don Emilio.'

The solicitor picked up the letter and read it carefully. 'In that case, I would be happy to help, although I don't have anything unusual to tell you. It was all very straightforward as far as I can remember.' He studied his computer screen for a few minutes then said, 'Yes, here it is. His son, Gabriel Francisco (Kiko as he was known) was to inherit the title; he was to be the next Duque de Roble. Regarding his last will and testament, well that follows the usual laws of inheritance. The duke's wife would inherit half of any money and assets, and the two children, Isabella and Kiko would get the other fifty percent between them.'

'Two children? I thought there were three? Isn't there a boy called Antonio?'

'Yes, of course. How stupid of me. So the three children would get a sixth of the current duke's estate each. It may not sound a lot, but the duke has accumulated a considerable fortune over the years, or rather I should say his father did, and the present duke has managed it very well ever since.'

'What do you mean by a fortune?' Linda asked.

Don Emilio looked rather uncomfortable at that question, but eventually said, 'Suffice to say it runs into a few billion euros. I take it you do not need the specific sum involved?'

'No, that's sufficient. So now that the duke's heir is deceased, who will succeed to the title?'

'That's not very complicated. Isabella will inherit the title; she will be known as Señora María Isabella Mendoza de Goya Pérez, Duquesa de Roble.'

'So it won't go to Antonio, his second son?'

The solicitor shook head firmly, 'No, definitely not. The new law on that is quite clear; the first born child inherits the title. As he is now dead, then the next in line is Doña Isabella.'

Linda already knew all this, but she listened intently and then asked, 'And if Doña Isabella dies? Would the title go to Antonio?'

'That depends. If the duke was still alive then, yes it would possibly go to Antonio, but if the title had already passed to Doña Isabella then it would continue down through her family. It would go to her eldest child. Araceli is the oldest I believe.' Don Emilio was looking even more agitated than ever. This conversation was obviously not going the way he wished. He was torn between fulfilling his client's wishes and not wanting to reveal too many details to a virtual stranger.

'Sorry, I don't understand. What aren't you telling me, Don Emilio? Is it something that could hinder our investigation? Is a question mark over Antonio's parentage?'

'No, no, no. Of course not. The duke's sister had his DNA checked as soon as he was born. He is the duke's son all right.'

'What? Are you telling me that the duke's sister checked the child's DNA? What did the baby's parents have to say about that?'

'Well, as you can imagine, the duke was furious with his sister and so was his new wife. She really had no right to do that.'

'So, if he is the duke's flesh and blood, then what is the problem?'

'You probably know that the duke was married three times.'

'Yes, his first wife died.'

'Tragic. She was the most delightful woman, elegant, witty and beautiful. He adored her and so did most of their friends. We were all distraught when she died.'

'So?' She was getting the feeling that Don Emilio had been a little in love with the delightful Rebecca.

'Yes, well when the duke married again, the family were all very surprised. His new wife was nothing like the *duquesa*. She was brash, loud and glitzy. And much younger than him. Personally I could not see what the duke saw in her. I rather think he was lonely and wanted some female company again; I can't imagine any other reason. The children were away at school at the time, and his sister had moved to Madrid, so in a way, I could understand it.'

Linda was beginning to realise that Don Emilio enjoyed talking about his illustrious clients but he probably didn't realise quite how much he was revealing about them. 'How would that affect the inheritance?' she asked.

'As it stands, it probably wouldn't, but his second wife wants to have the annulment squashed—you may already know that the duke had their marriage annulled because he doesn't believe in divorce—she says her conscience is bothering her and that the marriage was not only consummated but that they had a child together.'

'The duke has another child?' This was a surprise.

'So she says. A girl. So far, Ana María has not provided me with any proof of her claim, which is why I was reluctant to discuss it with you. Apparently, she is having a problem getting hold of the girl's birth certificate. The baby was born in Argentina, you see.'

'So there could be another child to share the inheritance, and if anything happened to Doña Isabella before the duke died, she would be next in line to inherit the title.'

'Exactly Señora Prewitt. So you can see it is rather complicated at the moment.'

'And what about his current wife? If the annulment was squashed, how would that affect her?'

He leant back in his chair and lifted his hands up in a gesture of despair. 'She would no longer be his legal wife and the duke would be considered a bigamist. Antonio of course would be illegitimate. A complete disgrace for the family.'

'I thought that illegitimacy didn't matter anymore?'

'Legally it doesn't; the law has recently changed to allow illegitimate children to claim their inheritances. But the stigma would still be there. Years ago almost every aristocratic family had a few illegitimate children hidden away; it was nothing exceptional, but nowadays it is frowned upon.'

'Can she do that? Ask for an annulment to be cancelled?'

'Oh yes. She has appealed directly to the Bishop to review her case.' He reached across and switched off his computer. 'Well, that's about all I can tell you.'

'My goodness, what a mess for the family,' Linda said as she handed one of her business cards to him and added, 'Thank you for your time, Don Emilio and please let me know if there any developments regarding the annulment.'

He stood up and held out his hand. 'I will indeed, Señora Prewitt. It has been a pleasure to meet you. Please give my regards to the duke when you next see him. *Adios.*'

As she walked back to her car, Linda went over what she had learned from the solicitor. It was quite a web of intrigue. Don Emilio had not mentioned Leticia's pregnancy, so did that mean he had not heard about it or didn't want to pass on any gossip. No, he seemed to enjoy a bit of gossip; she would guess that he didn't know about it. So who knew about it, other than Rosa and her neighbour? Half the neighbourhood, she guessed; that sort of juicy titbit would do the rounds very quickly. The duke? She doubted it because the woman was playing the devoted wife at the moment, spending every minute she could at his bedside. She was also controlling who was able to visit him. Surely he wouldn't want her near him if he thought she had been unfaithful to him.

She climbed into her car and pulled out her phone but her call went straight to the answerphone. 'Hi Phil, it's me. I hope everything is okay. I just wanted to let you know that I'm going into the office now but I will be back home in time to make the lunch, so you just relax. No need to prepare anything. Love you.'

JD and Nacho were eager to know how she had got on with Don Emilio, so they all, Ricardo and Rosa included, squashed into the meeting room.

'Boss, you're going to have to find somewhere else to store your bike. There just isn't room for it in here,' said Nacho, rubbing his shin which had just banged against one of the pedals.

'I agree,' said Linda, moving JD's helmet and looking around for a big enough space to store it. Eventually she put it on the floor under the table.

'I'll never find it under there,' JD moaned. 'Anyway, if you are all comfortable now, can we get on with the investigation. Nacho, you can do the board.'

He pulled a face at her, but took up the marker pen, nevertheless. 'Right, you are.'

'Linda, do you want to start?'

'All right. There wasn't a lot that we didn't already know; it was more a case of confirming what we'd worked out. However there were a couple of surprises.' She proceeded to tell them about Anna Maria's intention to squash the annulment of her marriage to the duke.

'On what grounds?'

'According to Don Emilio, she has become very religious and said it had been wrong to have forced the duke to annul their marriage; it goes against her conscience as a good Catholic. She also claims there was nothing wrong with their marriage; it had been consummated and there's a child to prove it. A girl. I reckon she'll be about ten-years-old now.'

'So where has she been hiding her all this time?' asked Nacho.

'I'm not sure, but I can look into that. I do know she was born in Argentina.'

'That sounds about right; I had a feeling from something the duke said, that she was not living in Spain,' said JD. 'Well done, Linda; we've got a few things to go on now. What did the duke's sister have to say when you went to see her, Mama?'

'Well, she wasn't very welcoming but she could hardly shut the door in my face. It seems that Irina and the duke haven't spoken since Antonio was born.'

'The DNA test,' interrupted Linda.

'Exactly. She tested the baby's DNA without speaking to her brother or his wife and they were furious. He has not spoken to her since.'

'But why did she do that?' asked Nacho.

'She was doing it for the family, she said. She didn't trust Leticia and she had heard from one of her maids that her sister-in-law had been seen in a night club in Córdoba with a well-known bullfighter. She didn't say anything to her brother, because it could have just been malicious gossip, but when Leticia announced that she was having a baby, she wanted to make sure that the duke was the father.'

'And was he?'

'Apparently so. He only found out about what his sister had done when his doctor asked him why he had had a DNA test done. Irina said she couldn't understand why he was so angry with her.'

'So the fact that there is a rift between them has nothing to do with her son?'

'No. But that's a bit strange too, because Kiko and Pablo were as close as thieves according to Irina, but one day, when they were in their early twenties, there was a tremendous fight between the two of them and the gardener had to be called in to separate them. As far as she knows, there was no contact between them after that. She questioned Pablo at the time, but all he would say was that it was nothing, a scrap over a girl they both knew.'

'In their twenties? So it's unlikely to have anything to do with Kiko's murder. How old was Kiko when he died? Thirty-six? And this Pablo is?'

Rosa hesitated a minute then said, 'Thirty-three, I think.'

'So I don't think a ten-year-old fight is going to be behind his death, do you?'

'By the way, Nacho, have you discovered why Kiko deleted his social media accounts? I still find that very odd. Was he frightened of something, do you think?'

'Or someone?' asked Linda.

'I'm not sure of the reason, but everything was deleted about eight months ago,' Nacho replied.

'So what happened eight months ago?' asked JD. 'Linda, what was the date of that magazine article? The one with the interview, "My Biggest Worry: How to spend my inheritance."'

'January. It was to do with New Year's resolutions. He wasn't the only one in the article; there were a number of celebrities. Why do you want it? Do you think he deleted all his social media accounts because of this article?'

'It's a possibility. It's certainly an eye-catching headline; maybe he didn't want so much public attention. Go and talk to that journalist and get his opinion of Kiko. I still don't have a clear picture of our dead man but it does look as though everything is pointing towards the inheritance.'

'I'll see what I can do, but it might have to wait until tomorrow.' Linda picked up the magazine in question and put it in her bag.

'That's okay. What are you up to, Nacho?'

'Why?'

'This mystery man is bothering me. Who is he and why did he continue flying away from Kiko? He must have known he was in trouble, so why didn't he stop and help him? Even if it was a coincidence that he was there, you would think he would go to his aid.'

'Maybe he didn't know Kiko was in trouble. Remember he was ahead of him. Why would he turn around and look for him? It's possible that he just wanted to get away from that area as quickly as possible before the Port Security caught him,' said Linda. 'Then by the time he turned around he would have seen that the coast guards were there and just kept going.'

'No, I don't buy it. Nacho, see if you can get photos of all the possible males who knew Kiko and we'll see if Rachel can identify one of them as our mystery para-motorist.'

'She'll be on the plane back home, by now,' Nacho protested. 'It's a waste of time.' JD said nothing. 'Oh, all right. I'll do it now, but then I'm off home; we have a rehearsal tonight.'

'Thanks. Message me if you find anything useful.'

'Right, well I'm off home too, Boss. I'll see you tomorrow,' said Linda.

'Have a good evening, both of you,' JD said. She knew she was being unreasonable wanting them to work in the evening, especially during August while the weather was exceptionally hot and humid, but now that she was sure that Kiko had been murdered she wanted to get on with finding his killer.

Instead of cycling straight home as she had originally planned, JD sat down in their meeting room and studied the evidence board. She couldn't wait until tomorrow when the rest of the team would be in; she had to clarify her thoughts now. She was convinced that the evidence was pointing to a deliberate intent to murder the duke's son. But the reason for his murder was still eluding her. Was it to do with the inheritance or did he have enemies they didn't yet know about? She was also finding it hard to get a clear impression of the dead man; her mother described him as shy and quiet, yet Tim had said he had a reputation for enjoying the high-life, gambling and taking drugs. Somehow neither description fitted. They could find almost nothing about him in the papers nor on social media. Maybe he had been hiding from someone, or maybe, as her mother maintained, he was simply a retiring young man. She decided to go through the list of suspects and see who really had something to gain from Kiko's death. First was the duke. No, now that she had met him she did not think he would have had his son killed, although he might well have written a codicil into the will that meant Isabella should continue to manage the estate. He certainly didn't want to leave her the title unless he had to; he had expressed his opinion about primogeniture quite vehemently. She put a red line through his name. Next was the new heir apparent, Isabella and her husband Jorge, who were currently carrying the burden of managing the extensive estate. But did Kiko's sister want to inherit a title so desperately that she would have her own brother murdered? It seemed a bit extreme, but then they were looking at an enormous amount of money, and with the title and the wealth together came a great deal of power. It was a possibility but, in her opinion, a slight one. She left Isabella's name intact and moved down to the next one in line, the duke's sister Irina. Now she would only inherit if both of Isabella's children were dead. JD couldn't see her organising the death of all her brother's immediate family in order to claim the title of Duchess; for a start it was too risky, never mind callous. No, she could go. The next one on the list was a much more likely suspect, Leticia. But if she wanted her son Antonio to become Duque de Roble, she needed to get rid of Doña Isabella *before* her husband died. Afterwards would be too late. In fact Isabella stood in the way of not only Antonio, but this unknown daughter of Ana María. Despite the heat JD felt a shiver run down her back; Isabella could be in real danger.

She picked up her mobile and rang Federico. 'Are you still at the police station?' she asked as soon as he answered.

'Jacaranda? What's wrong? Yes, I am, why?'

'I think Doña Isabella, the duke's daughter, might be in danger.' She hurriedly explained her hypothesis to the captain. 'Can you contact the Guardia Civil in Seville and get someone to keep an eye on her?'

'This sounds a bit extreme, Jacaranda. I hope you have more evidence than just one of your hunches. I can't go to another division and expect them to send out a protection team without a bit more to go on.'

'Please, Federico. It's important. If she is not behind her brother's murder, then that could mean that she is the next victim.' She heard him heave a deep sigh. 'Please Federico, I don't mind looking stupid if I'm wrong; I'd sooner that than have her death on my conscience. Anyway, it wouldn't look good for you or your department if something happened to her and it came out that you already had a reason to suspect she might be attacked. We're talking about someone's life here, remember. And not just anyone, but the duke's sister, a member of the privileged class, could be in danger.'

'Straight to the point, Jacaranda, as always. You are the one with the suspicions, remember, not me. Well okay. I will speak to someone, just leave it with me.'

She knew he wasn't happy with her. If this was all a wild goose chase, he would get it in the neck from the *comandante*, but he also knew that most of the time her hunches were correct. She turned her attention back to the evidence board. There were still a couple of suspects left. Leticia's ex-lover Salvador Blanco could possibly have been responsible, but that still meant he would have to get rid of Doña Isabella. Then there was Juan Felipe; he might have had the opportunity but what motive did he have? No she did not think he was a strong candidate. A red line for him as well. That left her with just three groups of suspects: Leticia and/or her ex-boyfriend, Doña Isabella and/or her husband and Ana María. JD stared at the board for a while then stood up and wrote anther name on the board. There was someone else to consider, the heiress Bianca; it was a long-shot as it was over a year since the woman had been jilted. If someone wanted revenge why wait until now? On Monday JD would ask Nacho to find out where Bianca was currently living and if she had since married.

There was still a lot to uncover but now they had two possible motives, either the duke's inheritance or revenge. Neither of them were what she would classify as a strong motive, especially as they still had not identified the true cause of Kiko's death. They were going to have to focus their attention on that for a while longer.

CHAPTER 13

There was something worrying the captain, and he couldn't quite put his finger on it; this niggling little suspicion had started when he was having lunch with Jacaranda. Why had she said that Bill felt guilty about Andrew's death? Upset maybe, shocked, angry, many things but guilty? Did Bill know more about Andrew's murder than he was letting on? He pulled out his phone and looked for Estrella's number. Was it worth speaking to her; she wouldn't have even known Bill at the time. How long had she been working for the Met, eighteen months? Despite his misgivings, he dialled her number.

'*Capitán*? What a surprise?'

'*Buenas tardes*, Estrella. Are you enjoying your holiday?'

'I am. We're having a wonderful time; I will be sorry when it's over. But I am sure my holiday is not the reason that you've rung me.'

'This may sound a bit odd—and by the way, it's just between you and me—but I wanted to ask you about Bill.'

'Okay. What about the Super?'

'I know you weren't at the station when JD's husband was shot, but did you ever hear any rumours about why they closed the case so quickly? I know they labelled it a random killing, but as you and I both proved recently, there was nothing random about it. It's bothering me that if we could find the evidence to prove it was a murder five years after the event, then why couldn't they find it at the time?'

'Luck? I'm not sure what you are suggesting, Captain. Do you think someone in the Met wanted to deliberately hinder the investigation?'

'No, I think it was more than that. I think that maybe—and at this juncture it is only a maybe—someone dismissed it as a random mugging in order to close the investigation down as quickly as possible.' He knew his words sounded outrageous, but he had witnessed it happen in the Guardia Civil when someone with money and power had put pressure on a corrupt officer, so why not in the Met. 'After all it was a serving officer who was killed and that would normally mean that the case would get more attention, not less.'

'But not in that particular instance, is what you're saying?'

'Yes.'

'What do you want me to do? Make some enquiries when I get back to London?'

'Yes, but only if you think you can do it without alerting anyone.'

'What about Bill? Are you suggesting he might have been involved in shutting the case down?'

'I don't know. I admit I find it hard to believe because he and Andrew were friends as well as colleagues, but he had to know more than he has told us.'

'He wasn't there when the officer was shot. You know that.'

'Look, I don't think for a moment that he pulled the trigger, nor gave anyone information about Andrew's movements that day, but being away on a course is an excellent alibi.' There was silence at the other end of the line. 'Estrella, I can tell you're not happy with this train of thought. Just forget I phoned you. I'm probably reading too much into it. I just needed to speak to someone who was familiar with the case, and there is no way that I can discuss it with Jacaranda; she would be straight on the first flight to London. I'm sorry. I shouldn't have involved you.'

'It's not a problem, Captain. I start back at work on 1st September, so I will let you know if I hear anything then, but at the moment I am finding it hard to believe that the Super would have been involved in anything criminal, especially as he was so encouraging to you when you wanted to re-open the investigation. If he was involved he could have found a number of excuses to stop you.'

'I agree.'

'So JD doesn't know about your suspicions?'

'No, and please don't say anything to her. If I am totally wrong about this, and Bill was not involved in a cover-up, then it is better that she never knows.'

'I won't mention it to anyone.'

'Good. Enjoy the rest of your holiday, Estrella. Where have you got to now?'

'Thanks. We've had a few days in Florence and tomorrow we are cycling down to Pisa.'

'Sounds good. See you when you get back to Málaga.' He rang off and sat for a moment wondering if he had been wise to discuss it with her; he was putting her in an awkward position. However, the more he thought about it, the more questions he had. Why had Steed been given early release when he was in a high security prison? Were English prisons so lax that convicted criminals could have early release? He struggled to remember hearing of any such cases before? It was certainly not something that happened very often. Also, why had there been no trace of Thomas Steed, other than possible sightings which were never confirmed? He picked up his phone again and sent a message to Jean-Paul to ask him if he had any news of Steed's current whereabouts. Maybe it would be a good idea to contact Europol as well; after all if Steed had managed to get to France then he was more likely to stay in Europe where Schengen meant he would be able to move across borders more freely. Jean-Paul would know the best person to speak to at Europol; the captain knew that Interpol were regularly in touch with them. Of course he could go through the normal channels; the Guardia Civil and the Policía Nacional had their own people who were in regular contact with Europol but this was a personal enquiry and he did not want to involve too many people, especially if he was mistaken about Bill. Once Federico had an idea in his head, he couldn't ignore it; it was like an itch that you know you should leave alone but you can't stop scratching it.

No sooner had he put his phone away, when Ricardo put his head round the door. 'Excuse me, *Capitán*, Señora Dunne rang while you were on the telephone. She wants you to ring her back.'

'Thank you, *Cabo*. Did she say what she wanted?'

'No, but it's to do with the murder investigation.'

The captain sighed. 'Of course.' He still was not convinced that Jacaranda was right about it being a murder; there seemed to be so many loose ends, not least of which was the reason for the man's death. If they had found traces of drugs or even alcohol in his blood it would have provided some sort of explanation for his behaviour, but toxicology had found nothing. They had even tested his hair for traces of GHB but he was clean. He pulled up the report on his computer; what it did include was that the man's body showed signs of previous drug use, possibly cocaine and maybe heroin. The pathologist would not commit himself to any particular time line, but his comments stated that, in his opinion, the deceased hadn't taken any drugs within the last few months. So what was he? A druggie who was trying to get clean? Or just a party-goer who overindulged from time to time? He dialled the internal number for the pathologist. '*Buenas tardes* Leonardo, it's Capitán Rodriguez. I have the report on Don Gabriel Francisco Mendoza de Goya Pérez in front of me; it is all very clear but I do have one question for you. In your experience, does the deceased look like a drug addict in remission or just your average young man who takes recreational drugs?'

'I think to get an accurate answer to that you need to widen your investigation,' the pathologist replied.

'How do you mean?'

'You need to look not just at his corpse but at his history. Is he in remission because he had a drug addiction, or does his body look as though it's in remission because he has changed his life style?'

'In other words, you can't tell.'

'Exactly. But, off the record, I don't think he was an addict. There are hardly any needle tracks and what there are, are old, but there is some damage to the nasal tissue. However that doesn't necessarily mean that he was an addict and there is definitely no evidence of current use.'

'So we are leaning towards a fun-loving partygoer?'

'Probably, when he was younger.'

Federico could see the pathologist was not going to commit himself to anything other than what he had written in his report. 'Okay I'll take that as an "inconclusive." Do you have any hypothesis as to why someone who is not under the influence of drugs or alcohol would behave so erratically?'

'I deal with evidence, *Capitán*, not supposition. Now, if you'll excuse me I have a customer waiting.'

A customer? Federico knew he meant a cadaver. Every pathologist he had ever met had that sick sense of humour; it must go with the job. He hung up and then immediately called Ricardo. 'Do you have a minute?'

'*Si, Capitán*?'

'Have the forensic team been to the dead man's apartment yet?'

'No, *Capitán*. They only visited the crime scene. You should have their report on your computer.'

'But not his apartment?'

'No, *Señor*.'

'Arrange for them to do it as soon as possible and go with them yourself. And get them to go over the para-motor again and all the equipment that we were able to recover. I want a thorough examination of it all. We need to have clear evidence for why that para-motor failed.'

'And if it was just pilot error?'

'If that's what it was, then I want indisputable proof of it.'

Ricardo started to leave then hesitated in the doorway. 'What is it now, man?'

'Señora Dunne. Have you telephoned her?'

'No. I'll do it now.' *Dios mio*, even his own officers were frightened of Jacaranda. He waited until his *cabo* had left the office and closed the door behind him then rang her number. 'You wanted something, *Cariño*?'

'Federico. At last. Did you speak to the Guardia Civil in Seville about Isabella?'

'I did and they have sent a man round to check on her. I think it is a waste of the tax-payers' money, but as you so bluntly pointed out, we have to be seen to be doing our duty.'

'Don't be grumpy. You'll thank me if you manage to prevent anything from happening to her.'

'Is that all you wanted?'

'No, there's one more thing. Do you have any contacts in the department of immigration?'

'Yes, one or two; you remember I used to work there when I first joined the force. Why? You don't think Kiko was mixed up with illegal immigrants, do you? Possibly flying them into Spain on para-motors?' He grinned to himself.

'Don't be stupid. This is serious. Well actually, I hope it's not serious.'

'Okay, Jacaranda, I have a busy morning. I've no time for riddles. Just explain to me why you want me to contact Immigration?'

'It's about Paola, my mother's maid.'

'I know who she is. What about her? She's here quite legally, I believe.'

'Yes, that's what I think as well. But she was acting very strangely when I was asked if anyone had witnessed Kiko's death. It is probably nothing, but I want to explore every avenue.'

'Very well, I'll see what I can find out. Things should be a bit easier now that Feria is over. I'll ring someone now.'

'Thank you, *Cariño*. See you at home, later.'

Home. She said that as though it was their home, not hers; so why did she insist on keeping him at arm's length. The captain walked out to the coffee vending machine in the hall and poured himself an expresso; he would have preferred to go across to the bar opposite and and buy one, but he didn't have time. If he was going to speak to anyone in the Immigration department he needed to ring them before 5pm. He remembered how good they were at time-keeping when he worked there, and how there would almost be a stampede when it was time to clock off.

He drank the strong black liquid down in two mouthfuls and then returned to his desk. He hoped that Ruben was on duty; he had known him when he was in the National Police, investigating human trafficking, but he hadn't been in touch very much since he had transferred to the Guardia Civil. However he did know that things had changed since Spain had become a member of the EU and that now there were various departments dedicated to different immigration issues. He had no idea where to start. His call was answered swiftly and he asked to be put through to Ruben Garcia—he did not know his current rank— so was surprised when the voice asked, 'Who shall I say wants to speak to Comandante Garcia?'

'Capitán Federico Rodriguez of the Guardia Civil.'

'One moment, please.'

This was ridiculous, he was ringing an old colleague and he had no idea what to say to him. Damn Jacaranda and her hunches. Paola was probably just nervous of the police asking her questions; many immigrants were, even when they had nothing to hide. They automatically mistrusted anyone in authority, and who could blame them.

'Federico, is that you? Well, it's been a long time. How are you, my friend?'

'Ruben. I see you've been promoted. I thought they had put me through to the wrong person, for a moment.'

'No that's me, all right. I was made *comandante* a few years ago when they reorganised the department. Well, I don't expect that this is a social call, so what can I do for you?'

'To be honest, Ruben, I have no idea if you can help me or not. There is an Argentinian immigrant who works for my friend's mother; she's called Paola Caceres.'

'And you want me to check if she's illegal?'

'No. I am certain that her papers are in order, identity card, passport, the lot. I just want to know if she has sponsored anyone, or if her name comes up in connection with anyone dodgy. Sorry I know that's a bit vague, but we think she might have seen something which could help us with our current case but when we questioned her, she seemed rather too nervous about something. It's likely that whatever is worrying her doesn't have anything to do with our murder case, but I would like to eliminate her from our enquiries.'

'Well, you certainly like to give me a challenge, don't you. I'll see what I can find, but it does seem like a long-shot. What if nothing comes up in a blanket search?'

'That's it then. There's probably nothing in it after all.'

'Is this to do with the duke's son, the one who was fished out of the port?'

'So you've heard about that?' He didn't know why he was surprised. The police services were known for the dissemination of gossip, or as they were usually referred to, leaky sieves.

'Yes, I heard it on the grapevine. No details, mind you. In fact it sounds as though you are struggling with this one. Still got that female private detective doing all the work for you?'

'Sounds as though you know all about it,' Federico said, biting his tongue. 'Look, I have to go. Let me know if you find anything.'

'Will do. And look, we should have lunch one day. My treat.'

'Yes, good idea. *Adios*.' He hung up, cursing JD under his breath for getting him to make that call. He could sense that Ruben was delighted that he was still only a captain while he had been promoted to *comandante*. He hoped his humiliation was worth the while. 'You still here, Ricardo? I thought I told you to go to the deceased's apartment.'

'Yes, *capitán*, but there is a complication.'

'What sort of complication, damn it?'

'Someone is living in his apartment.'

'What, a squatter?'

'No, a friend of his, or so he says. A Juan Felipe Moreno. I think JD's assistant may have spoken to him before, but I can't get hold of Nacho to ask him.'

'So where are the forensic team now?'

'I left them there, but I'm on my way back right now. I just don't know how we can do a proper forensic check when someone has been living there all week.'

'We bloody can't.' Federico threw his empty, paper coffee cup across the room. 'What a mess. We should have sent them in as soon as we knew Kiko was dead.'

'But we thought it was an accident, *Capitán*.'

'Where is Juan Felipe now?'

'He's in the apartment. He said he had some valuable things in there and he didn't want the forensic team to break anything.'

'Get back there, right away and remove him from the apartment. I don't care what he says; it is still a potential crime scene. And make sure he doesn't take anything with him.'

'But *Capitán*, the crime scene was at the port.'

'I don't care,' he bellowed. 'At the moment we don't know what happened to the deceased. Until we have a clear picture of how he died, both places are to be cordoned off and treated as crime scenes. Remove Juan Felipe from the apartment and if he refuses to go, arrest him. Have I made myself clear?'

'Perfectly, *Capitán*.'

'And do it now.' This was getting out of hand. It was his own fault for dismissing Jacaranda's theories so readily, but he was not going to admit that, not even to Ricardo. He got up and walked into the main office. 'Luis, I have to go out and then I'm going home. Ring me if there are any messages.'

'Will do, *Capitán*.'

As he drove back to his apartment he thought back to the barbecue they had gone to at the weekend; all his family were there, even his great aunt, who had recently celebrated her ninetieth birthday. Jacaranda appeared to have enjoyed herself at the time, but hadn't commented on it afterwards, except to say how grey his brother's hair had become. He had felt like telling her that was because he had to listen to their mother nagging at him, every day. Then he remembered just in time that he was trying to convince Jacaranda of the joys of family life and marriage in particular, so merely reminded her that Eloy was the eldest in the family.

He had spent the entire afternoon dodging his mother, who would sidle up to him at every opportunity to ask him when he and Jacaranda were going to set a date for the wedding. He couldn't bring himself to admit to her that if he had his way they would get married tomorrow. He knew she would pity him, and he couldn't bear that. It had been bad enough when Adele had filed for a divorce on the grounds of incompatibility; by that she had meant that he spent too much time at work, but his mother thought it went deeper than that and blamed him for the breakup. Federico hadn't thought such a thing was grounds for divorce, but the judge granted it to her on the tenuous evidence of there being irreconcilable differences which had led to an irretrievable breakdown of their marriage. It was a lot of gobbledygook as far as he was concerned but he had not contested the divorce; another thing that earned him his mother's disapproval. For her, life was not complete unless all her children were happily married and she had a horde of grandchildren. He had disappointed her on that latter point as well, although it had not been his fault; Adele had not wanted a family. That was what she had told him when she had the miscarriage; it had happened when he was in Madrid attending a conference on community policing but later he wondered if in fact she had taken that opportunity to have an abortion. It was ironic however, because now he had heard that she and her new partner recently had twin girls.

One of his mother's recent comments had stuck in his mind. She had reminded him that motherhood was a ticking clock; one day Jacaranda would be too old to have any children. He loved Jacaranda but he was not happy with their casual relationship even though it seemed to suit her perfectly. He would be fifty before long and he wanted to settle down and raise a family. For years he had watched his two brothers playing with their children, his nephews and nieces, laughing and joking with them, shouting at them when they misbehaved, cleaning scabbed knees when they fell over, cheering them on at football matches, and he envied them. But he never said a word of this to Jacaranda. Perhaps now was the time to do so. Now it was time to bring it out into the open and find out what she really wanted from him.

His mobile began to ring. He pressed the Accept Call button on his dashboard.

'*Si, digame.*'

'*Capitán*, it's Luis.'

'Yes, *sargento*?

'The duke's daughter has been taken to hospital. I thought you should know.'

'Doña Isabella? What the hell? What happened to her?' It sounded as though Jacaranda had been right, yet again.

'I don't have many details but it looks as though she was mugged. The woman who found her sent for an ambulance straight away.'

'I thought someone was supposed to be keeping an eye on her?'

'They were, but they thought she was at home; someone was stationed outside her house. In fact she had been to the hospital to see her father and on her way back, stopped in the city. She was just strolling along by the river when a man attacked her. He hit her with an iron bar and snatched her handbag.'

'A bit brutal for a mugging.'

'Oh, it could have been much worse but a woman walking her dog, shouted for help and then set the dog on the man. He ran off with the handbag while she called for the ambulance.'

'Brave woman. Can she give any details about the man, a description for instance?'

'I don't know, but I do know that her dog ripped a piece out of the man's trousers. They may get something from that. I'll keep you informed if I get any more news.'

'Good man. In the meantime send me the name of the hospital where Doña Isabella has been taken. I'll get someone to go over there as soon as I can. Has Ricardo returned yet?'

'No, *Capitán*. I'll tell him to ring you when he gets back.'

Federico pulled into a side street and stopped the car. This could not be a coincidence. The threat to Kiko's sister had been real. Any doubts he had had about Kiko's death being a murder were now wiped away.

CHAPTER 14

JD had already phoned Nacho and told him to meet her at Kiko's apartment, but when she arrived, hot and sweating he was already waiting for her under the shade of an acacia tree.

'Didn't take you long to get here,' she said.

'I know you keep fit, Boss, but even your bicycle cannot beat my moped.' He patted the red moped affectionately.

'Well, do you know what's happening here?'

'No more than you've told me, Boss. I have to admit, I'm struggling to believe that Juan Felipe lied to me. Barefaced lies, all of it. So this is Kiko's apartment, not Juan Felipe's; well that explains the luxurious interior. I did wonder where he found the money to furnish it so lavishly.'

'He lied to all of us. So let's find out what else he has been lying about? Is the forensic team still here?'

'Nobody has come out, so I imagine so. Come on, I'll lead the way.'

JD could see that Nacho was upset by the revelation that someone he had considered to be trustworthy had been squatting in the dead man's home. 'We're going to have to go over all his statements again, carefully. If you like, I can ask Linda to double check them?'

'No, it's my mess. I'll clean it up.'

One of the forensic scientists stopped them at the door of the apartment and handed them footwear protectors and latex gloves. 'Just in case there is any evidence left uncorrupted,' she said.

'Do you think you'll find anything useful, Ana?' JD asked her as she pulled on the gloves.

'You never know. There may be something that will tell us why his behaviour was erratic. Maybe traces of drugs or other substances. Hard to tell when there has been someone living here for over a week.'

'Where is he? Juan Felipe?' asked Nacho.

'He refused to leave, so he's been arrested and taken down to the police station. I believe they're going to question him,' Ana replied.

'Ricardo asked if you could join them later, JD,' said Tito, another member of the forensic team. 'There's no hurry. They plan to put him in a cell and let him stew for a bit.'

'Okay, I'll go down there when we've finished here,' said JD. 'In the meantime let's take a look in the bedrooms. It wouldn't surprise me if he was using Kiko's bedroom.' She opened one of the doors from the hallway. 'This was probably Kiko's; it's got an en-suite bathroom.' She pulled open a drawer in the closet. There were socks and underpants neatly folded, but nothing else.

'We've done the bedrooms,' Ana said. 'In fact we're almost finished, so you can take your time.'

'Okay, thanks.' JD wasn't sure what they were looking for; it was hard to distinguish which of the things belonged to Kiko and which to Juan Felipe, if any. 'There are some very expensive items in this apartment,' she said to Nacho. 'I wonder if he has sold any of them? You know that antique shop near the English Cemetery? *Antiguidades Cristóbal*, I think it's called. They often have items like this in their window.' She held up a bronze statue of a bull. 'Do we know how Juan Felipe earns a living?'

'No. Sorry, I never asked. It looked as though he had plenty of money, though.'

'Yes, but now we know that none of the stuff in this apartment is his.' Nacho looked so crestfallen that she added, 'Don't worry. You were not to know he was living in someone else's home. Let's assume, for now, that he doesn't have a job. How did he live? He didn't have to pay any rent, because the flat belonged to Kiko, but he still had to eat.' She picked up another small statue, this time of a horse rearing on its back legs. 'Feel the weight of that,' she added, handing it to Nacho.

'Heavy.'

'Yes, that would cost at least ten thousand euros, in Madrid or London. Go over to the antiques shop now, while we're in the area, and ask them if anyone has been in during the last week trying to sell items of value.'

'Okay, Boss. It's certainly worth enquiring.' He shook his head, sadly. 'Just to think that twenty-four hours ago I would have said it was impossible to believe that Juan Felipe was a thief.'

'That's life. He was a conman, and a convincing one. Who knows, he may have done something similar before; we ought to check that out with Federico.'

While Nacho went to question the jeweller, JD continued wandering around the apartment, keeping out of the way of the forensic team but trying to get a general feel for the place and for its previous owner. There were a number of photos, framed and hanging in the hall. She studied them one by one. What did they tell her about Kiko? She couldn't be sure. There were a number of sporting photos, groups of young men playing beach volleyball, attending a Formula One motor race, Kiko on horseback with a young woman, posing with friends with a drink in his hand. There were two taken in the countryside; she looked at them closely. The figures in the photos were small and hard to identify, but they were definitely para-gliders. She removed all the photos and put them into evidence bags. 'Ana, I'm going to take these with me, is that okay?'

'Yes, I've logged all those.'

Her mobile phone began to ring. 'Federico?'

'Are you still in Kiko's apartment?'

'Yes. I was just going to ring you. Can you do a check on Juan Felipe; it's possible that he has a record. I have a feeling that he has done this before. He has all the signs of a conman to me. I'm getting Nacho to check if he's been trying to sell any of Kiko's possessions. There's a bronze statute here, and I'm sure I've seen it before in an arts magazine, but it was part of a pair then.'

'Okay, let me know how you get on. But that's not why I'm ringing you. You were right about Doña Isabella being in danger; she was mugged this afternoon as she was walking by the Guadalquivir River, in the middle of Seville.'

'Is she okay?'

'She has a chipped bone in her shoulder and a lot of bruising but she'll live.'

'*Dios mio.* In broad daylight. Who do you think attacked her?'

'An idiot, if you ask me. Not your regular mugger, for sure. He took a car-jack with him, to scare her.'

'Maybe he intended to kill her. Any witnesses?'

'Yes, one. A woman who saved her life, and her dog. Or maybe it was the dog who saved her life. We're hoping to get the man's DNA.' He went on to explain what Luis had told him.

'So it was a vicious attack. Did he steal anything?'

'Her handbag.'

'I suppose we can eliminate her and her husband from our enquiries, now,' she said, thinking of the list of suspects on the wall in the evidence room.

'I imagine so. I'll make sure there's a constant police presence outside her home from now on and ask them to explain to her the dangers of wandering about on her own at the moment.'

'When are you going to interview Juan Felipe?'

'This evening probably. Why?'

'Ricardo suggested I sit in?'

'Did he indeed. You can observe from outside, by all means, but no, you can't take part in the interview. The *comandante* made enough fuss last time when he saw you observing the last interview. What do you think would happen if he saw you actually taking part this time? And before you start arguing with me, the answer is still no.'

'All right. Keep your shirt on.'

'Did you find anything else in the apartment?'

'Possibly. For a start, I'm sure Juan didn't want Nacho snooping about the apartment, which is why he diverted his attention by insisting on taking him out to para-motor.'

'What do you think he was worried that Nacho would find?'

'I'm not sure. The fact that he'd been stealing? Or maybe there's something he doesn't want us to see in the photos that were hanging in the hall. I'll keep on looking; there's something he is not telling us, I'm sure of that.'

'See you tonight?'

'Maybe. Let's see how the interview goes first. It's been a long day and I still have to check in with Linda.'

'Fine.'

'Federico?' He had rung off. Great, she'd offended him now. She was about to call him back, when Nacho came through the front door, a big smile all over his face.

'You were right, JD. He had been trying to sell one of those bronzes.'

'Did he say it was Juan Felipe?'

'He didn't know his name, but he identified his photo.'

'And did the dealer buy the bronze?'

'No, he said he rarely buys from people he doesn't know. He likes to be one hundred per cent sure the items are not stolen. Apparently he got caught out like that once before, and he had a dreadful job convincing the police that he wasn't a fence.'

'So I wonder what happened to the other horse.'

'You think there were two?'

'Positive. This sculptor is known for making his sculptures in pairs. It's his signature, if you like. So, somewhere there is another horse and another bull. He has probably already sold them.'

'But if they are known for being in pairs why would anyone want to pay all that money for one?'

'God knows, Nacho. Why do people pay that sort of money for a piece of brass, anyway?' She looked at her watch and said, 'Come on, let's get back to the office. We have a lot of loose ends to sort out.'

'Before you go, JD, you may want to see these. They were stuffed behind a cushion.' Ana held out an evidence bag with half a dozen poker chips in it.

'Gambling? The thing is, whose are they, Juan Felipe's or Kiko's? '

'You will have to wait until we've examined them. They were pushed down between the sofa seat and the cushion, pretty well concealed.'

'So hidden in a hurry, do you think?'

'I would imagine so, otherwise why not put them in the safe?'

'Safe? What safe?'

There's a wall safe in the kitchen. Really neat, it's hidden behind one of the cupboards. Come on. I'll show you.'

JD and Nacho followed Ana into the kitchen and watched as she opened a small wall cupboard which contained detergents and cleaning products. She pressed against a wooden strip at the back and the cupboard swung forward to reveal a small strongbox. 'We don't know what it contains yet. Someone is coming up now to open it.' She swung the cupboard back into position. 'It will all be in our report. I'm sure the *capitán* will fill you in.'

'Nacho, are you any good at safe cracking?' JD asked her assistant.

He shook his head and laughed. 'Sorry. I prefer hacking to cracking.'

'I wonder if Juan Felipe knew about the safe?' she asked.

'Well, I've dusted for prints so we will soon find out,' Ana replied. 'We've nearly finished now. Just got to wait for them to open the safe and then we will be done.'

'Okay. Well we're off now anyway.'

'I'll see you at the agency, JD. Do you want me to ring Linda?' Nacho asked.

'Yes please. I want to have a quick word with Tim; there's something that's been bugging me.'

She stopped in the park and sat in the shade while she rang Tim. 'Hi, it's JD.'

'I know it's you. What do you want?'

'How do you know I want anything? Maybe I was just going to ask about your weekend.'

'Don't mess me around, JD, I've got a meeting with the editor in two minutes. What do you want?'

'I want you to explain to me why a very newsworthy story about the death, accidental or otherwise, of the Duque de Roble's son didn't warrant even a mention in the Voz de Málaga.'

'I told you. It was in the Seville edition.'

'The truth now, Tim. This is looking like a murder case.'

'Murder? Is that true, JD or as you just saying that so I will tell you what you want know?'

'Yes.' She waited, knowing Tim would not be able to resist.

'Okay, but you have to promise me that you'll tell me what's going on.'

'So?'

'I had direct orders from my editor not to publish anything about the death of the duke's son.'

'Did he say why?'

'He just gave me the same spiel that I passed on to you.'

'Nothing more?'

'No, honestly. Well, he might have mentioned that someone from the duke's family had asked him to keep it quiet because it would upset the duke. As the man was so ill, he agreed. I expect he thought he could make something of it later, after the duke had died.'

'Thank you. And I don't suppose you know who made this request?'

'No. All I will say is that the duquesa was hanging around the office one morning. Maybe she asked him.'

'Maybe she did. Well thanks, Tim. I owe you.'

'Hang on. Don't you have anything for me?'

'Okay. Why don't you ask your sister paper in Seville about the attack on the duke's daughter.'

'What? Doña Isabella was attacked? When? Why?'

'Got to go. Bye Tim.'

So Leticia had prevented the news about Kiko getting out. Now why was that? She wheeled her bicycle out onto the road and began to cycle towards the agency.

Nacho and Linda were already at their desks by the time she arrived. She pushed her bicycle into the office, deliberately ignoring the look of exasperation on Linda's face and asked, 'Is Ricardo joining us?'

'Yes, he'll be along in a minute,' said Nacho. 'He's got the call log for Kiko's mobile.'

'Good, anything else?'

'He didn't say.'

'How are things at home, Linda?'

'Much the same. Some good days and some not so good. Phil seems to be going through a good patch at the moment.'

'I'm pleased to hear it; I hope it lasts. Okay, I think it's time that we collated our results.' She moved into the meeting room and sat down. 'At last we are getting a much clearer picture of the family and what makes them tick, but we still have nothing that points to a strong enough motive to murder a family member. Nacho, can you do the honours again, please.' Her assistant picked up the marker pen and moved over to the evidence board. 'I'll start by bringing Linda up to date on the fact that Doña Isabella was mugged today.'

'Is she okay?'

'She'll live but it was a vicious attack. It could have been a coincidence, but as you know, I don't believe in them.

Nevertheless I think we can remove her from the list of suspects, Nacho.'

The door to the agency opened. 'Sorry I'm late, JD.' The *capitán* needed some information from me,' said Ricardo.

'Sit down, if you can find a space. We've only just started and I expect you've already heard about Doña Isabella?'

'Yes.'

'I know you are aware of what has been happening this morning, but I'm going to go through it for Linda's benefit.' JD began to explain that Juan Felipe was now in custody and how he had been squatting in Kiko's apartment. 'What you might not know, Ricardo, is that we found a safe in his kitchen. Forensics were waiting for someone to open it when we left; so we should get some information about its contents later today.'

'So does that mean that Juan Felipe is a murder suspect now?' asked Linda. 'It's a big jump from being a thief and a squatter.'

'I know, but we can't rule him out; one thing we are sure about is that he is a very proficient liar. We found some poker chips in the apartment, so it looks as though either Kiko or Juan were gamblers. We need to find out which one.'

'I'll look into that, JD. I know the usual haunts on the Costa,' said Ricardo. He handed a sheet of paper to JD. 'This is the list of calls we got from Kiko's phone records. I haven't been through them; I thought Nacho might want to do that.'

'Thanks. We'll go through them later. Anything new on the para-motor?'

'Yes, but I'm not sure if it's much use. We traced it back to a wholesaler in Antequera but he says he doesn't remember exactly who bought it, but according to his records it was sold in the year 2001.'

'So it's ancient,' said Nacho. 'I didn't think they even used para-motors back then.'

'The sport has been going since the eighties. Maybe it just wasn't as popular as it is now,' said Ricardo. 'Anyway he also said that most of his sales are to retail stores, so I think that's probably a dead-end.'

'And we won't find any fingerprints on it because of it being immersed in the harbour,' said Nacho.

'Well at least we know Kiko was not using his own, brand new para-motor the day he died. So where is it now?' asked JD.

'We are checking all the shops that sell second-hand para-motors to see if either of the serial numbers turn up.'

'Can you also check the local insurance companies to see if Kiko's machine was insured, either by him or its new owner, Ricardo. I can't believe an expensive item like that would be dumped; it will have been sold to someone.'

'Will do, JD.'

'What about Bob Free? Do you think he might have it?' asked Linda.

'It's possible,' said Ricardo. 'I'll get a warrant and send some men up there to have a look.'

'Will the captain agree to that?' asked JD. She knew they didn't have any evidence against Bob, so this was just a speculative search.

'Probably not. But there's a way round it without a warrant. I'll tell him that we're looking for some faulty machines that need to be withdrawn, and the inspection is just a precaution.'

'So you will lie to him?' If the captain found out he would think JD had put Ricardo up to it.

'No, I just won't tell him the whole truth. Don't worry, JD, the *capitán* will never know.'

'Unless you find it, of course. Then what?'

'We'll worry about that if it happens.' He checked his watch. 'Anything else, JD?'

'Ricardo, I think we are having a bad influence on you, but I won't tell the captain if you don't. No, there's nothing else for now.'

Once Ricardo had left, she turned to Nacho and Linda and said, 'Someone who has been on our list since the beginning and about whom we still know very little, is the duke's wife, Leticia. I spoke to Tim this morning and he said she was hanging about the offices of the Voz de Málaga on the morning when they heard of Kiko's death. And soon after she left, his editor told him to leave the story, that the Seville edition would cover it. So I think it's time we all looked a bit more closely at the grieving step-mother. Linda and Nacho, find out all you can about her. Where does her son go to school? Who are her friends? What's the name of the ex-boyfriend and is he still on the scene? Anything at all, however insignificant.'

'Okay, Boss.'

'Now, another matter. I didn't want to bring this up in front of Ricardo, but can anyone think of a way to discover if the duke had his sperm frozen?' She saw them staring at her. 'Well? We know that Leticia is pregnant, but we are just assuming that she was having an affair. We need to confirm it.'

'And if she was then it's probable that the baby is not the duke's,' said Nacho.

'I don't buy it. The family are bound to want a DNA test done and then they will know for certain.'

'That won't help us. We can't afford to wait for months before we catch this murderer. The plan is to put the duke's mind at rest before he dies.'

'Let's ask Rosa to help. She will probably know who his doctor is; she may even have spoken to him already,' said Linda with a grin.

'Much as it grieves me to ask my mother for help, I think you are right in this case, Linda. I'll ring her tonight. Maybe you and she can go over to see Leticia tomorrow morning?'

Linda hesitated for a moment, 'Yes, that's fine. Tomorrow is Wednesday; Phil's next appointment is on Thursday. In the meantime, Nacho can you send me all you can find on Leticia, please.'

'No problem, Linda.' He turned to JD. 'Do you want me to hack into the Duque de Roble's medical records?'

'I'm tempted to say yes, but it's too risky for you. Let's see what we can find out by conventional means first. But you could find out who his doctor is and which health company he uses; that would be useful.'

'Okay, I can do that.'

'We also need to identify the second para-motorist. I was sure that someone would know who he was and tell us, but so far nobody has come forward. Nacho, can you get together photographs of all our suspects and make three sets of them, one for each of us. We need to ask everyone who has anything to do with this case if they can identify him. Linda, you can start with Borg and Paula. The neighbour, Borg said he saw him clearly, and wasn't there another neighbour who alleged she had seen him, but she couldn't make it that night?'

'Yes, Margo. She had the flu,' said Linda.

'Do you just want photos of the men?'

'No Nacho, copies of all the people in the photos. I'm sure there are female para-motorists as well as men.'

'So that's the plan for today, Boss. You want me to make copies of the photos of our suspects, go through Kiko's phone records and prepare some stuff on Leticia, is that it?'

'Yes, that reminds me, the photographs I took from Kiko's apartment, where are they?'

'In your saddle bag?' He pointed to her bicycle and the bulging saddle bag.

'We need these images blown up. At the moment it's difficult to make out all the faces. They must have meant something to Kiko if he put them on his wall.'

'I'll see to them now and send them over to Ricardo.'

'Thanks. In the meantime, I'll speak to my mother and then go over to the station and see how the captain is getting on with Juan Felipe.' She looked across at Linda.

'I'm off to speak to Adolfo Ruiz,' Linda told her. JD looked puzzled. 'The journalist who interviewed Kiko for the magazine.'

'Of course. I'd forgotten about him. Well good luck and don't let him worm any information out of you about the case.'

'As if.'

Once Linda had grabbed her things and left, JD rang her mother. 'Mama, we need your help again,' she said.

'Of course, *Cariño*, what can I do?'

'We need to talk to Leticia. I know it's not a good time for her, but if we are to get a result before her husband dies, then we can't wait much longer. You do understand, don't you. She could be a suspect. It's imperative that we interview her.'

'Do you really think she would murder her step-son? I find that hard to accept.'

'So who did then? The only people to gain from his death are family members.' She decided not to complicate things by bringing up Bianca's name. 'Anyway, I think it would be easier for her if you were present at the interview.'

'Yes, I understand. Of course I'll come along. What time do you want me to pick you up?'

'I'm not going. Linda will interview her. You said that Leticia usually visits her husband around eleven o'clock. How about if you get there about ten-thirty? I'll ask Linda to pick you up at eight. Is that okay?'

'That sounds all right with me. Have you found out any more about the baby yet?'

'Not yet Mama. Have you?'

'Nothing at all.'

'Okay. Well thanks for doing this. I'll let Linda know. *Adios.*' As soon as she finished the call she texted Linda to tell her the plan.

'Are you off, now?' asked Nacho. 'When will you be back?'

'In an hour, maybe a little more. Why?' He lifted up his empty coffee cup and smiled at her. 'Yes, of course I'll bring you a coffee.'

Luis was at his desk when JD walked into the station. '*Buenas tardes*, Señora Dunne. Are you looking for the *capitán*?'

'*Buenas tardes,* Luis. Yes, is he around?'

'He is just about to interview the guy they brought in this morning. Shall I tell him you're here?'

'Please. He said I could observe the interview.'

'Wait here and I'll go and check.'

She perched on the side of Luis's desk and looked around her; there were two officers working at the far end of the room, but the rest of the desks were empty. Where was everybody? She walked over to the vending machine and poured herself an iced tea; she knew it wouldn't be very good, Federico had complained about the vending machine on numerous occasions.

'Ah, there you are,' said Luis coming back into the room. 'The capitán said you can watch but that's all. I'm to take you to the observation room, and…' he hesitated.

'What?'

'He said you were not to bang on the window if you disagreed with something.'

'I don't know how you can work with him,' she said with a laugh. 'He stifles all creativity.'

'Follow me and I'll show you where it is.' The stiffness of his back as he walked away told her that he was not amused at her comment, so she refrained from telling him that she already knew the way and followed meekly behind him. But before they arrived, Ricardo intercepted them. 'It's okay Luis, I'll take JD along to the interview room. It's 3B isn't it?'

'Yes, *Cabo*.'

'I thought I'd bring you up to date on what we've found before you watch the interview,' he explained.

'Thanks, Ricardo. That's very thoughtful. So what have you found?'

'Well, it seems that our friend Juan Felipe has run this scam before. Two years ago he was accused of stealing from a friend's apartment. Apparently he met this guy at a paragliding club in Granada and struck up a friendship with him, and then offered to house sit for him while he was in China for a month on business. The guy was completely taken in by Juan Felipe and was delighted to leave his home in safe hands, or so he thought. However, when he returned to Granada, Juan Felipe was gone and so were most of the man's possessions, including some expensive works of art.'

'So Juan Felipe was arrested?'

'No. There was no way the man could prove that Juan had stolen them, or even provide the police with his name as he'd used a false identity at the time. They had plenty of his prints and an identikit of him, but they didn't match anything on file. It is only now when we ran Juan Felipe's prints through the system that this has come up.'

'So he could be facing charges from the police in Granada?'

'Yes, and of course that victim is still alive, so he'll be able to identify him in a line-up.'

'Thanks for telling me. Are you taking part in the interview?'

'Yes.' He opened the door to the observation room. 'I'll leave you here, then. The *capitán* says he'll have a word with you when he's finished. And you are to stay here.' He smiled at her. 'I'll come and get you, JD.'

'Okay, Ricardo. I don't know what everyone is so worried about. I'm not going to barge in on the interview. I promise.' The smile Ricardo gave her suggested that he was not wholly convinced of that.

She sat herself down in front of the viewing window and studied the man sitting across from her. It was an eery sensation to be staring at someone and knowing that they could not see you. He didn't look like a criminal—Juan Felipe just seemed to be an ordinary man, a likeable one at that—but she had been in this game long enough to realise that appearance was not everything. The most innocent looking people could be revealed as serial killers, bank robbers or even child molesters. The eyes were not the gateway to the soul, despite what the poets claimed. In order to convict someone, you needed rigorous and systematic investigation to uncover the necessary evidence. She just hoped they were going to get that evidence now.

Federico and his *cabo* entered the interview room and sat down. Juan Felipe was not alone; she assumed that the balding man sitting next to him was his lawyer. Federico started straight away to question him about how he had met Kiko, and why he had denied knowing him.

'I didn't,' Juan Felipe replied. 'I didn't realise they were talking about Kiko. That guy from the detective agency kept rambling on about a duke's son. I don't know any dukes or their sons.'

'Well, it seems that you do. You have been living in his house for the past week. So what was your plan, to continue living there for nothing and hope that nobody noticed, or to sell off everything of value and then disappear?' He paused and then added, 'Like you did in Granada.' She saw Juan stiffen and she half expected him to say 'No comment' but instead he remained tight lipped.

'There's no point sitting there in silence, the Guardia Civil in Granada have your fingerprints all over the house you stayed in. You will be going to prison anyway, so you might as well do yourself a favour and help us with our murder enquiries. You don't look to me like someone who would commit murder just so that you could take over their home. So why not explain to me what was going on. Was this supposed to be another robbery? Or is there something deeper behind it, something darker that led you to murder Don Gabriel Francisco Mendoza de Goya Pérez? Or as you affectionately knew him, Kiko?'

The man sitting next to Juan Felipe leaned across and whispered in his ear.

'Well?' asked the captain. 'I'm waiting for a reply.'

'I didn't have anything to do with his death, I promise you. Kiko invited me to stay in his apartment.'

'But why would he do that? He hardly knew you.'

Juan Felipe was looking embarrassed now; he looked at his lawyer, who nodded encouragingly at him. 'All right, I wasn't telling the truth when I said I didn't know Kiko. We had been friends for some time.'

'So this is you, in this photograph?' Ricardo placed one of the photographs that JD had taken from the apartment in front of him.

'Yes,' he mumbled. 'I didn't know he was an aristocrat at first. He was just like one of us. Mad about paragliding. And women,' he added with a smile.

'Tell me more about that. Did he have a girlfriend?'

'He had quite a few. Sometimes more than one at a time. And even one who was married; mind you he never spoke about her much.'

'Did you ever see him with these women?'

'Sometimes.'

'What about the married one?'

'No, he kept very quiet about her. Didn't bring her up to the club, or anything like that.' Juan Felipe seemed more relaxed now. Perhaps he felt that the danger had passed and he would be sent home. If so, he was soon disappointed. JD could see what the captain was doing; he would get as much information from him as he could and then slam back into the charges of squatting and theft.

'So, do you know what happened to his para-motor? Or why he was not using it on the day he drowned?' asked the captain.

'It was stolen. He was very upset about it; it had cost a lot of money and he had barely used it.'

'I can believe it was stolen, and most likely by you. You were happy to help yourself to the rest of his belongings, so why not a brand new para-motor?'

'You're wrong there. I didn't steal it. He told me it had been stolen and he was going to speak to the insurance company about it.'

'And did he?'

'I don't know. I don't know what he did; I went to Seville for the weekend.'

'So where did he get the old one from? Did Bob Free give it to him?'

'I told you, I don't know. I didn't even know he was going paramotoring that day. Do I have to keep repeating myself?' He looked at his solicitor, hoping he would intervene. 'As I just said, I was in Seville that weekend. I had to get away from the Feria crowds.'

'Can you prove that?'

'Well, I don't have my train ticket but I did keep the programme from the conference. It should be in the apartment.'

'What was it called, this conference?'

'Come Out and Shout Out. It was a LGBT conference. I go every year.'

'This one?' The captain placed a brightly coloured brochure on the table in front of him.

'Yes, that's it. You can check. I was there from Friday morning until Sunday evening.'

'We will, don't worry.'

'Can I go, now?'

'One more thing, we found some poker chips in the apartment. Are they yours or were they Kiko's?'

She saw Juan hesitate, as though he wanted to claim them, then he said, 'They were Kiko's. I don't gamble; it's too risky.'

'So Kiko had a gambling problem?'

'I wouldn't have said it was a problem; he was very successful at it from what I could see.'

'Is that why he had a safe behind the kitchen cupboards? To keep his winnings safe from people like you?'

'What safe? I don't know anything about a safe.' He looked genuinely surprised and annoyed.

'Did you ever go with him?'

'No. I just told you; I don't like gambling.'

'So you never saw him open the safe?'

'I told you, I know nothing about a safe. Now, can I go?'

'Yes. *Capo*, take Señor Moreno back to his cell.' The solicitor stood up, about to protest but the captain added, 'We will check out his alibi and then decide on the charges.'

'What charges?' asked Juan Felipe. 'I haven't done anything.'

'Let me just give you a flavour of what we are preparing for you while we check out your alibi—and this is before we hand you over to the Guardia Civil in Granada—theft, identity fraud, illegal entry into a building and interfering with a murder enquiry.'

'What the hell?'

The solicitor put his hand on his client's arm. 'Best to just go along with them for now; I'll sort this out later.'

The captain waited until the solicitor had left and Ricardo had escorted the prisoner from the interview room, then he opened the door into the observation room. 'Well? What did you think? Is he our murderer?' he asked JD.

'Somehow I don't think so. He's just a conman who got involved with the wrong person. Did you believe him when he said he wasn't a gambler?'

'Hard to say, but we can check that out. He will be registered somewhere, if he is. Somehow I think those chips belonged to the deceased. It will be interesting to see what is in the safe, if anything. Did you notice his face when I mentioned it?'

'Yes, he looked really annoyed, as if he had missed a good opportunity there. I'm sure he didn't know about it.'

'I think you're right; if he had known about it he would have tried to get into it some way or other.'

'So what are you going to do with him?' she asked Federico.

'Hang on to him for now. We need to check out a few things before we can eliminate him as a suspect. Check out his alibi for one. Do you think Nacho has ever been to that Come Out and Stay Out conference?'

'I don't know. Maybe. He tries to keep his personal life private, you know.'

'That can't be easy when he works for you,' he said with a laugh.

'Ricardo said that when he was in Granada, Juan Felipe used a false identity. How sure are we that he really is whom he says he is now?'

'Because he was born in Málaga, and all his paperwork checks out. But, it's a good point. I'll get one of my men to double check his passport and identity papers again, just in case.' JD got up to leave when he added, 'We've heard back from Seville, by the way. The police have found the man who attacked Doña Isabella; he has a record as long as your arm, but all petty stuff, mostly minor burglaries and shop lifting. One conviction for selling drugs a few years back, but apart from that nothing that suggests he is a potential murderer.'

'Did they find the weapon he used to attack her?' asked JD.

'Yes. An old car-jack. I thought it was a bit extreme to use in a mugging; he could have killed her if he had hit her on the head. As it was, the dog leaping up at him, knocked him off balance and the blow struck her shoulders.'

'Has he been questioned?'

'Yes. He admits he attacked her, but he says he didn't intend to hurt her, just frighten her and take her handbag. He says a man gave him €500 and told him to steal her bag; he told him that he could keep anything that was in the handbag, but he wanted the bag back. In fact when the thief opened the handbag there was only some loose change and a couple of credit cards in it.'

'Didn't the man you caught think that was a bit odd? Someone paying him to steal an empty handbag?'

'Yes, he did. He said he thought that the man wanted to frighten his wife—he was sure he was the husband—you know, give her a scare. He thought she had probably been playing around.'

'So where did the car-jack come from?' JD asked.

'Our mugger thought he would use that to scare her.'

'Well, it did that all right. Does he know who the man was that paid him?'

Federico shook his head. 'No, but they are doing a photofit image and will send it over as soon as it is done. Maybe we will recognise him. Maybe it's Jorge.'

'Do you really think it was Isabella's husband? But why would he do that?'

'Maybe he is fed up with her. Maybe she has been cheating on him. We shouldn't get too fixated on the inheritance; there could be other motives, you know.'

'No, I can't see that. So who would hire someone to attack her? Leticia, perhaps. Her son is next in line, after Doña Isabella.'

'That's what you suggested before, but somehow I can't see it being her. Her son is too young.'

'Maybe. Thanks for letting me observe,' she added. 'Will you send me the transcript later?'

'Of course. See you tomorrow.'

CHAPTER 15

Linda had tried ringing Rachel but there was no reply; she wanted to send her the photos and ask her if she could identify the mystery para-motorist. She stopped outside the 'Top Table' offices and rang her number one more time but all she heard was 'This number is out of service or unavailable.' She groaned. Did that mean that Rachel had changed her number? Oh well, she would have to do without Rachel's help and hope that one of the others could identify the second para-motorist. She switched off her phone and walked through the swing doors and asked the receptionist for Adolfo Ruiz. Despite the glossy, glitzy image of this popular magazine, its premises were grey and uninspiring, as was the rather scruffy reporter who came out to meet her.

'You must be Linda. *Buenas tardes.*' He held out his hand for her to shake. 'I believe you are some sort of detective. So how can I help you?'

She handed him her card and said, '*Buenas tardes*, Adolfo. I work for Jacaranda Dunne; I'm her legal assistant.' She was nothing of the kind, but she didn't like the way the journalist seemed to be patronising her. 'I just wanted a few words with you about an article you published last December referring to our client's son.'

He looked at her attentively now. 'Who is your client? I publish a lot of articles.'

'The Duque de Roble,' she replied. 'You interviewed his son, now deceased, Don Gabriel Francisco Mendoza de Goya Pérez.'

'You mean Kiko, I suppose. Well you'd better come into my office. We can't talk here.' He looked across at the receptionist who was obviously listening to every word they said.

Linda followed him into the small cubicle which was his office, and sat down on a chair opposite him. 'I apologise for the cramped space,' he said. 'The editor's plan is to make us all so damned uncomfortable in the office that we are forced to go out and find more stories. And it works. If nothing else it saves on the air conditioning bills.' He smiled at her and asked, 'So what would you like to know about our dead friend? I suppose that's why you are here in this dilapidated building asking questions, instead of lying on the beach on this beautiful summer's afternoon. You are hoping to find out who killed him, no doubt.'

'Exactly. However I am curious to hear you say he was killed; his death was reported as an accident.'

'It wasn't reported for a start. Not a line in all the Málaga papers and barely a mention in Seville. Don't you think that's odd? The heir to a dukedom is killed in unusual—I won't say suspicious because that would be presupposing something illegal—circumstances and nothing is reported.'

'Apparently the family wanted to keep it quiet in case the duke got upset.'

'If that's the story then you'd better stick to it. So, *Señora*, where do you want to start?'

'Whose idea was it to do the interview? I was under the impression that Kiko was a shy and retiring man.'

'Well, I don't know who told you that. He may have been once upon a time, but he was anything but that when I interviewed him. It wasn't a big deal, you know. The objective of this magazine is to make money. It's as simple as that. We have no aim to win literary prizes. The owners decided on that objective from the very beginning. Its focus would be on the rich and famous because the rest of the world, those of us who toil for our daily bread, just love to read about them. Well, to be honest there are only so many themes you can explore without repeating yourself too often: weekends in Monaco, Doña X having an affair with Don Y, a film star dining at the opera, bull fights, motor racing, Doña X having her first baby. You get my drift?'

'Yes. But why Kiko?'

'Well we, that is me and my colleague, decided that this time we would get a number of celebrities to talk about their New Year's resolutions and then a year later we would interview them again to see if they had kept any of them.'

'So that was what was behind the interview in December?'

'Yes. We went through the list of "interesting celebrities" that we pull out from time to time and selected six of them; three men and three women. Kiko just happened to be one of them.'

'So what was his New Year's resolution? I don't think it came over very clearly in the interview.'

'How diplomatic of you, Linda. The interview was a complete shambles. I didn't want to publish it, but my editor insisted. He said, it might not be what I had hoped for but it was, in fact, much better. It was an attack on the people at the top table, as he put it.' He paused and then added in a low voice, 'You see my editor is a communist at heart. He cannot abide the sort of people we write about every month.'

'So why doesn't he work for another magazine?'

Adolfo shrugged his shoulders. 'Who knows. Anyway, I'm assuming you have read the article, so you can see that Kiko was talking about someone in particular, although he would mention no names. I tried to find out, but he was very cagey.'

'Do you think he believed that someone was trying to stop him becoming the next Duque de Roble?'

'It sounded like it. To be honest I couldn't quite make out if he was just taking the opportunity to throw a few stones at his family, or at the aristocracy in general. He was certainly pissed off with someone.'

'Tell me about the day you interviewed him. How was his behaviour? Had he been drinking, or did you think he might have taken something. Cocaine perhaps?'

'He was angry about something, that was clear, but no, there was no smell of alcohol on his breath. We did the interview at nine-thirty in the morning.'

'Here?' she asked.

'Yes, but not in my office. We have set of rooms for that; sometimes we video the interviews as well, as a kind of insurance.'

'So you could see no reason for him to suddenly start attacking his family? And how did he think that his replies related to new year resolutions?'

'Let's be clear about this. He never mentioned his family specifically, but as they are all members of the aristocracy I can only assume they were included in his rant. I challenged him about what he was saying, but his reply was, and I quote, "You'll be bloody lucky if I'm around next December to tell you whether I've kept the stupid resolutions or not.'

'That wasn't in your article.'

'No, well it didn't seem appropriate. I wanted to pursue it further, and maybe even talk to the Guardia Civil, but the editor said not to make a fuss. He thought, like you, that Kiko was under the influence of drugs.'

'But you don't?'

'No. I'm sure he wasn't taking anything. I've seen enough of these people under the influence of cocaine and other so-called recreational drugs to know the symptoms when I see them. He was angry about something, and possibly scared.'

'With hindsight it looks as though he was right to be,' said Linda.

'So, you do think he was murdered?' asked Adolfo.

'This is an ongoing police investigation, so I really can't tell you anything, but thank you for talking to me. It has been useful.'

'I believe your boss is a member of the aristocracy,' he suddenly said. 'Do you think she would agree to be interviewed?'

Linda burst out laughing. 'Sorry. How rude of me. No, I'm pretty sure she wouldn't agree to be interviewed. Anyway it's her mother who is the *marquesa*.'

'Oh, that's a pity. Here take another of my cards, just in case she wants to chat sometime.'

'Thank you, but don't hold your breath.'

Linda was still chuckling by the time she reached her car. She checked her mobile; there was an attachment from Nacho. Good she would look through Leticia's background this evening, so that she could prep Rosa on the way to the hospice. She was not looking forward to it; she was tired of hospitals and everything to do with them.

Nacho had sent Linda all he could find on Leticia, and there had been quite a lot; he hoped it was sufficient to help them interview her the next day. His next task was to go through Kiko's call log; it was a tedious job but could produce some revealing results if he was lucky, so he took a swig of cold coffee and set to work.

It wasn't long before a pattern began to emerge. Kiko had made quite a few phone calls in the week leading up to his death, the majority of which were to an unknown number. He had also made a couple of calls to Juan Felipe, including one on the Friday evening before he died, which had not been answered. And there were a number of phone calls to Bob Free's shop; the first of these was five minutes long and then Kiko had rung the number six times in succession and received no reply. It looked as though Bob was ignoring him. So what had that first call been about?

He carried on through the list, checking and double checking; there were a couple of calls to his insurance company, one to a hospital in Seville and the rest were to the unknown number. Nacho picked up his mobile and rang Ricardo.

'Nacho, everything okay? You got the list I sent you? Anything useful?'

'Hi Ricardo. Do me a favour and see if you can tell me who owns this number; I've tried putting it through my system but it seems to be protected in some way.' He read out the phone number and waited for the lance corporal to respond.

'Yes, I can see why that is; it's the duke's personal number. It's unlisted and there is some kind of security protection on it which means that only someone close to the duke can contact him.'

'The duke? Why would Kiko be ringing the duke so often?'

'Well he's his father and he's ill. He would be wanting to check on him, I expect. Not sure what you're getting at here, Nacho.'

'Something feels wrong. Don't worry, Ricardo; I'll check it out.' He rang off then dialled the number in the call log. There was no way that Kiko was ringing his father at two o'clock in the morning, five nights in a row. Someone else must have had his mobile phone. The number rang and rang but nobody answered it. So where was it? It was unlikely it was by the duke's bedside because someone would have answered it by now. He pulled up his version of Find My Phone on his laptop and typed in the number of the duke's mobile. Within seconds it had been located; it was in Seville at the hospice. So maybe Kiko had been ringing his father during the night. Nevertheless he sent a message to Linda to tell her what he had discovered, just in case it was relevant. As JD always said, we don't dismiss anything until we are sure it is irrelevant to the case.

So far he had only looked at the calls Kiko had made in the week prior to his death, but it could be worth looking further back. It would be a big job, but he decided to go back to December of the previous year, at the date of Kiko's interview in Top Table. There was something about that article which Nacho had found very revealing; this was a man who had nothing to lose. He had been born into a role that did not fit him and he knew there was no way out of it, unless he hit out at the establishment first. But what had happened to push him to the edge? The article itself was a general attack on the privileged classes; no-one was specifically targeted. Maybe his call log would suggest something.

CHAPTER 16

Wednesday morning was cloudy and very humid. Linda had a raging headache, mostly due to lack of sleep but also to the humidity. Phil had had a very restless night and now she was feeling guilty about leaving him. Luckily Jane didn't start work until three o'clock this week, so she had promised to come round and sit with him until her mother got home.

Linda took a couple of paracetamol and washed them down with some cold tea. Rosa had offered to drive today, but she had declined; the marquesa rarely managed to go above fifty kilometres an hour and she didn't want to be away from home any longer than necessary. She looked at her husband; at last he had fallen asleep. She bent down and kissed his forehead gently, careful not to wake him.

When she entered the city, Linda immediately saw Rosa standing by the roundabout, waving at her. She pulled over, indicators flashing and ignoring the irate drivers following her.

'*Buenos días* Rosa. Get in,' she said, looking at the growing queue of cars in her rear-view mirror. Linda moved her papers out of the way so that the older woman could get in the front seat, something she did with some difficulty. 'Are you okay?'

'Fine. Just a bit stiff in the mornings.'

Linda switched off the hazard warning lights and pulled out into the traffic. 'Did JD explain what we have to do?'

'Good morning, Linda,' she said in flawless English, with just a hint of a Scottish accent. Rosa rarely spoke Spanish when she was alone with Linda; she liked to practise her English, she would tell her. 'Not really. I know she wants to eliminate Leticia from her enquiries, but to be honest, I'm surprised that she is even considering her as a suspect. Why would the woman want to murder her stepson? It doesn't make sense. Antonio is far too young to inherit the title anyway, and I can't see his mother being able to manage the estate for him until he comes of age. No, Doña Isabella is a much better choice for that.'

'You heard about what happened to her?'

'Yes. How dreadful. The poor woman must have been terrified. Surely you don't think Leticia had anything to do with that?'

'You know what your daughter is like, Rosa; JD likes to keep an open mind. Everyone is a suspect until she has eliminated them.'

'A waste of time, if you ask me.'

Linda glanced at her companion. She hoped Rosa was not going to let Leticia's position as Duquesa de Roble stand in their way of questioning her. 'We have some specific information we need to get from her. Some of it may seem rather personal and intrusive, which is why JD wanted you to come with me. You know this family and how best to approach them.'

'Well, I don't really know Leticia, but I understand what you mean. We don't want to antagonise her, or make her feel like a suspect, even if she is.'

'Exactly, Rosa. There are a couple of important things that we need to clarify. Who is the baby's father and does the duke know she is pregnant? We also need to find out if the duke had any of his sperm frozen before he started the treatment.'

'Well, I can tell you that.'

'You can?' Linda was so surprised to hear this that she almost missed the slip road to the motorway. 'How do you know?'

'He told me.'

'So? Did he have it frozen or not?'

'Of course not. The duke would never do something like that. He told me she asked him to do it, but he refused. He was convinced that the operation would not make him infertile.'

'But surely the doctors explained that there was strong evidence that it could happen, and very often did.'

'They may well have done, but I don't think the duke wanted to have any more children, anyway. He muttered something about there being enough heirs to ensure that the family title would continue, and that he had done his bit for the Mendoza de Goya inheritance.'

'So that's why there is nothing in his medical records. I thought that maybe the doctor was being discreet about it.'

'Not at all. He explained the risks to the duke in front of his wife. But the duke would have none of it. He can be very stubborn, you know, like all the Mendoza family.'

'So Leticia must know that he is not the father of her baby.'

'Of course she does. What we should be asking is does she know who is the father?'

'You're not suggesting there could be more than one contestant for the title?' Linda laughed.

'I'm not suggesting anything, but it is something we need to find out. Now if you don't mind, I'd like to put the radio on for a bit; it's a long drive.'

While Rosa dozed and listened to the music, a medley of old-fashioned Spanish songs, Linda began to plan how she was going to tackle the duke's wife. It could turn out to be very difficult; Leticia was probably unused to being challenged by someone like Linda, and most certainly not about her personal life.

They arrived at the hospice just before eleven o'clock, thanks to the car's navigation system; she was glad she had set it before she left home because the marquesa had managed to sleep all the way.

'Rosa. Wake up. We're here and I think that is Leticia now; she's just arrived.' Linda hurriedly parked her car alongside a vintage Bentley. An elegantly dressed woman in her late thirties, whom she recognised from the photographs at the agency, had just got out of a chauffeur driven Mercedes and started to walk towards the entrance to the hospice. While Rosa checked her makeup in the passenger mirror and smoothed her hair, Linda sprinted across to the front door. 'Excuse me,' she called. 'Are you the Duquesa de Roble?'

Leticia stopped and turned to look at her. 'I am. Who are you?'

'It's all right, Leticia, she is with me,' called Rosa, now her usual elegant self as she walked calmly towards them and embraced the duke's wife.

'Rosa, isn't it?'

'Yes, I'm an old friend of the family. We met at your son's christening.'

'Oh yes.' She clearly did not remember her. 'Well, what can I do for you? I'm just about to go in to see my husband.'

'I wondered if you could spare a few minutes of your time to talk to us? We won't take long.'

Leticia did not look at all happy at this suggestion, and said, 'Well my husband will be expecting me. I'm always here at eleven. I don't want him to worry.'

'I'm sure he won't mind if you are a little late, especially as it was him who suggested we talk to you.' Linda stared at Rosa in surprise. Was that true? Had she already confirmed their visit with the duke?

'Well, in that case, let's go in together. I'll get them to make us some coffee while we talk,' said Leticia.

'Excellent idea. We've had a long journey and I for one, am parched,' said Rosa, following her up the steps. Leticia stopped and stared back at Linda. 'Oh, how rude of me, please let me introduce my companion, Doña Linda Prewitt,' continued Rosa.

'*Encantada, Duquesa,*' Linda said, resisting the urge to curtsey.

'*Encantada, Señora.* Please call me Leticia.' She led them into a reception area and called for the receptionist to make them coffee. 'We'll take it outside,' she instructed her. 'By the mulberry tree. It is so much cooler out there.' She smiled at Rosa, 'I will be glad when this summer is over; I find the heat overpowering at the moment. Don't you?'

As they sat in the garden, drinking iced coffee and eating almond pastries, Leticia seemed to change; she was no longer playing the role of a duchess, but had relaxed into who she really was, a pretty young woman from a middle-class background. The airs and graces that she assumed as the duchess, fell away as she told them how worried she was about her husband. Linda watched her carefully and couldn't decide if she was an excellent actress or completely innocent of any crime. She took out her mobile and typed a quick message to Nacho, to tell him they were with Leticia. Almost immediately she could hear a phone ringing. Leticia looked a bit perplexed but didn't move.

'Is that your phone, Linda?' Rosa asked.

'No. Maybe it's yours, Leticia?'

'I don't think so.' For a brief moment she looked confused then put her hand in her bag and pulled out a mobile. 'Oh, it's my husband's phone. It's nothing. Nobody I know.'

'Your husband's mobile?'

'Yes, I don't like him to be bothered. You ask people not to call him but they take no notice. I think they don't realise just how ill he really is.'

'Have the doctors said anything lately about his condition?' Rosa asked.

'Just the same prognosis. It could be days or it could be weeks.'

'How dreadful for you,' said Linda. 'I know just what you're going through. My husband is very ill at the moment. Cancer.'

'I'm sorry to hear that. I hope they have caught it in time; cancer is such an unforgiving illness.' She wiped her eyes with a tissue and said, 'Now, what exactly is it you want to ask me?'

'Tell us about your step-son,' said Linda. There was not enough time for small talk; the duchess could get up and go to visit her husband at any moment.

'Kiko? What do you mean? He died in a terrible accident.'

'We have come to believe that it wasn't an accident; we think he was deliberately murdered. What we don't understand is who would want the young man dead. And why?'

'So you think I might know? I'm as baffled as you are.'

'Well it has been suggested that you and he were particularly close. Is that true?'

'We were, but not in the way you are suggesting. I was his mother after all. Okay, not his birth mother, but I looked upon him as my son.'

'Did he feel the same way about you? Or did he have other ideas?'

'No, he didn't.' Her eyes flashed in anger and for a minute Linda thought she would get up and leave. Maybe she had been too direct in her questioning.

'So in what way were you close?'

'Kiko had a gambling addiction. To be honest when I first met him he had a number of addictions; he was a mess. I understood. I knew what that was like; when I first met Gabriel I was a gambler. I would bet on anything. Sometimes I'd win but more often than not I would lose. It was Gabriel who helped me to give it up. I couldn't have done it without his support.'

'So was Kiko still gambling at the time of his death?'

'No, not that I know of anyway.'

'So what changed?'

'Last winter, Kiko was at a really low ebb. He heard a rumour that his father had been speaking to Don Emilio about finding a way to disinherit him unless he stopped gambling. I think my husband thought that leaving him so much money would be a mistake; that he would gamble it all away. Anyway it was enough of a shock to make Kiko decide that he had to stop, and so he asked me to help him; he knew that I had managed it so he thought he would be able to stop too. In a way, I suppose we became each other's sponsors. He'd ring me if the temptation was getting too great and I'd do the same. But I had Antonio, you see, and that gave me the strength to fight my addiction. Kiko had nobody special in his life, not then.'

'What about this girlfriend he had, Lavinia? I believe she was a friend of yours?'

'Yes, but that was a long time ago, before I married Gabriel.'

'Did you fall out?'

'Not really. It was more like we drifted apart. I moved in different circles once I became the Duquesa de Roble. I just didn't have much time to keep up with my old friends; there was Antonio to look after and then, of course Gabriel became ill. No, I'm a different person to the carefree girl who used to be Lavinia's friend.'

'Did you introduce her to Kiko?'

'No, I didn't even know that they were going out together until it was over. It didn't last long, anyway.'

'Did Kiko have money problems? Was he short of money? Was that why he gambled, for the cash?'

'Oh no. It's not just about the money; it's the excitement, the adventure, the buzz you get when you win. It's like any other addiction; you want to stop but you can't give it up. No, Kiko did not gamble just for the money. Not that it wasn't important to him; if his father managed to cut him out of his will it would have affected his lifestyle dramatically.'

'But you've stopped gambling now?' asked Rosa.

'I have, but it's still a struggle sometimes. Gabriel has been very understanding.'

'Your husband knows you are still struggling?'

'Yes, of course. I could hardly hide it from him as it was his money I was using.'

'Did he know about you sponsoring Kiko?'

'No. I wanted Kiko to tell him, but he was too ashamed to talk to him about it, and he wouldn't allow me to tell him either. He was determined to do it himself. He said when he had managed a whole year without placing a single bet, then he'd tell his father how I'd helped him.'

'Forgive me for this question, Leticia, but why didn't you answer your husband's phone just now? Was it because you knew it couldn't be Kiko?' Leticia frowned. 'We found that number in the call log for Kiko's phone. Did he use that phone to call you when he was tempted to place a bet?'

'Yes. My husband hardly ever used his mobile. He was very old fashioned in a lot of ways. So Kiko and I would communicate like that. I knew it wasn't for me when I heard it ring. Dead men don't make phone calls.'

'But why didn't you use your own phone?' asked Linda.

Leticia smiled. The first time he rang me, it was by mistake. He rang his father's number and I answered it. We got chatting and he told me how dreadful he was feeling. It just became a habit after that.'

'Did anyone else in the family know about Kiko's gambling?'

'I don't think so.' She frowned again as if trying to remember something. 'He did say that he may have discovered a way to kick the gambling habit forever, and if it worked he'd take me along as well.'

'Do you remember anything else?'

'No. If I do, then I'll let you know. I've always known it wasn't an accident. Basically Kiko was a careful man; he liked his sports but he wasn't a risk taker, except when he was gambling. But that's the strange thing; he didn't see that as a risk. To him it was a calculated choice. Sometimes it worked and sometimes it didn't.' There were tears in her eyes by now. 'I'm sorry. It makes me so sad to think of him dying needlessly.'

'One more question before we go, and again I must apologise for probing into your personal life, but we need to know in order to ensure that you had no motive to kill your step-son.'

'Who is the baby's father? Is that what you want to know?' Linda nodded. 'Well I will tell you, but you must promise to keep it quiet.'

'I'm sorry, I can't make any promises about that.'

'The truth is that I don't know. I had artificial insemination. My husband refused to freeze his sperm—I told you he was old fashioned—but he knew that I wanted a brother or sister for Antonio, so he paid for me to have IVF.'

'He knows you are pregnant then?' asked Rosa. For once she looked amazed at the news.

'He does and he is happy about it. The child will be brought up as though he is Gabriel's son, with his blessing. The only thing that worries him is that he might not be here for the birth.' She looked at her watch. 'Is there anything else? He will be worried if I'm too late.' She turned to Rosa, 'Did you want to speak to him while you are here?'

'No, but thank you. I think we have kept you away from him for long enough.'

'Thank you for talking to us.' Linda said. 'If you remember anything more about Kiko and his gambling addiction, please get in touch. This is my card.'

'Oh, you work for Rosa's daughter. Gabriel told me about her.' She placed the card in her handbag and walked into the hospice.

'Well, that was interesting,' said Rosa. 'Not what I was expecting at all.'

Linda dropped the *marquesa* off at her apartment then parked the car as near to the agency as possible. She couldn't go home yet; she had to speak to Nacho and JD and tell them to cross Leticia off the list of suspects.

'Linda, I didn't expect to see you today. Weren't you going to interview the wife this morning?' asked JD, looking up from her computer.

'*Buenos días* JD. Yes, I've just dropped your mother off at her apartment.'

'How did it go?' asked Nacho, 'I take it you got all the background bumph I sent you?'

'Yes, thanks Nacho. Well you can cross Leticia off the suspects list, for a start. She was very forthcoming and we learnt a lot. She is not the cheating wife, waiting for her husband to die so she can swan off with her lover. Quite the opposite.' Linda proceeded to recount what Leticia had told them.

'So the duke knew about the baby all the time; well that surprises me. Are you sure about that? Maybe she was just saying that, knowing it would be hard for you to prove otherwise,' said JD.

'Maybe, but Rosa could always ask him outright. No, she was very convincing. I mean, why would she admit to us that she had a gambling problem, for example? And it does explain the phone calls. There was one thing though, which I didn't pick up on at the time. She said that having Antonio to care for, was the reason she had to cure her addiction, but that Kiko had nobody special in his life, not then. Those were her words, *not then*. There had been someone special by the sound of it.'

'You didn't ask her whom she meant?'

'No, the conversation moved on to the monetary gains or otherwise of gambling. I'm sorry.'

'It probably isn't important,' said JD. 'After all we know he jilted his fiancé, perhaps she was referring to Bianca. Which reminds me, we need to look at that episode of his life more closely.' She pointed to the evidence board. 'The only family suspect left up there is the duke's second wife, Ana María. So we need to find out more about her as well.'

'Maybe his murder was nothing to do with the inheritance. Maybe the killer is not a member of his family,' said Nacho.

'You could be right. Stick Bob Free's name up there again. Let's concentrate on finding where Kiko's para-motor is now,' said JD.

'Well, according to Ricardo, the forensics team have re-checked the evidence that they rescued from the port and their verdict has not changed; even if someone had tried to tamper with the old para-motor, they hadn't done enough damage to make it behave as erratically as everyone seems to believe. They say there has to be another reason.'

'Have they checked the post-mortem report again?'

'No sign of drugs, alcohol, nothing to suggest his reactions were impaired. It's a mystery.' His mobile began to ring. 'Sorry, it's Ricardo.' Linda watched Nacho's face as he listened to the *cabo* at the other end of the phone; he looked pleased about something.

'What is it, Nacho? Has he found the para-motor?'

He grinned at them. 'He has indeed.'

'Well, where was it?'

'In an outbuilding at Bob Free's place. They have taken him and the para-motor to the police station for questioning.'

'So he was lying to us. He knew where it was all the time,' said Linda. 'What's the matter, JD? You don't look very happy.'

'I'm not. Ricardo did not have a search warrant; there was not enough evidence to justify one, and the captain didn't know that Ricardo was going to search Bob Free's premises. He's bound to think I put him up to it.'

'And did you?' asked Nacho.

'Well, let's say I didn't stop him.'

'Don't worry, the captain will be so pleased we are making progress with the investigation, that he won't say anything,' said Linda.

'You think? This is the captain we're talking about; he doesn't let anything like that slip by him.'

CHAPTER 17

Federico stared at his *cabo*. He couldn't believe that Ricardo would do this; he was always so strict about rules and regulations. Damn Jacaranda, she must have sweet-talked him into searching Bob Free's shop. 'So where is he, this Bob Free?'

'I left him in interview room B2 with Luis. I thought you'd like to speak to him.'

'Did he ask for a lawyer?'

'I offered him one but he said he hadn't done anything illegal. He was just looking after the para-motor for someone.'

Federico gave a big sigh and stood up. 'Okay, let's get this over with. But don't think this is the end of it, *Cabo*. You and I still have things to discuss.'

'Of course, *Capitán*.'

'Get me a coffee, first. A strong one. And one for our guest.'

'Okay, *Capitán*.' He almost looked contrite as he walked towards the coffee machine.

Bob Free was sitting in the interview room, unperturbed. He glanced up as the two officers came in, but didn't say anything when they sat down in front of him and the captain switched on the recording machine.

'You're an Australian, I believe Mr Free. Would you like me to conduct this interview in English?' The Australian shrugged his shoulders. 'Please give me a spoken answer Mr Free, for the benefit of the recording.' He passed the coffee across to him.

'Thanks. I don't mind, but I suppose English would be best as my Spanish is not that brilliant.'

'Very well, I'll take that as a yes.' Federico went through the usual precautionary statements in English and then said, I believe my lance corporal offered you the services of a lawyer and you refused them. Is that correct?'

'It is. I haven't done anything wrong, mate, so why would I need a lawyer.'

'I believe you knew Gabriel Francisco Mendoza de Goya Pérez?'

The Australian grinned, revealing a gold crown on one of his upper teeth. 'Kiko, you mean. You know I do. You sent that female detective up to see what she could find out about me. I told her, and I'm telling you, that I barely knew the man. And I certainly didn't teach him to para-motor.'

'We know all that, Bob. What I want to know is if you sold him a para-motor?'

'Again, you know I did. Why are you asking me all these damn fool questions when you already know the answers?'

'So can you explain why my lance corporal here,' he looked towards Ricardo, 'found that same para-motor hidden under some old sacking, in a shed behind your shop?'

'I don't know anything about that,' he replied, shifting in his chair.

'Are you uncomfortable, Mr Free? Would you like another chair?'

'No. I'm fine.' He scowled at the captain.

'According to the registration number this is the same para-motor that you sold to Kiko, is that right?' Federico placed a photo on the table in front of him.

'If you say so.'

'Can you explain why it is painted in black, when the one Kiko bought was red, as stated in the receipt that we found in the deceased's apartment?'

'Okay. Yes I sold him the para-motor, but he didn't like the fact that it was red. He wanted a black one but I couldn't get hold of one for weeks. He said he couldn't wait that long. So I offered to have it painted black for him. We had only got the undercoat on it when I heard that he had died. I didn't know what to do, so I put it in the shed while I thought about it. And that's the truth. I thought I'd wait until everything had calmed down and then I'd finish painting it and sell it.'

'Even though it wasn't yours?'

'It wasn't going to be any use to him, now was it?'

'Where did he get the other one? Did you lend it to him?'

'Yes, I was just helping him out. He wanted to go paramotoring that weekend and so I lent him an old one I sometimes used for the classes. It might have looked dilapidated but it worked perfectly well. I've used it myself, many a time.'

'If that is the case, Mr Free, then why did Kiko report his para-motor stolen two days before he died?' The Australian turned pale. 'Nothing to say, Mr Free?'

'Okay. I was lying; he didn't ask me to paint it black. But that doesn't mean I killed him.'

'So how did you get it?'

'It was last Wednesday, this bloke came in and asked if I bought second-hand motors. I told him it depended on the condition. He said it was almost brand new. So I went out to his car and took a look. I knew it was Kiko's the minute I saw it.'

'And you didn't think to report it to the police?'

'What good would that have done? Anyway, what I told you about Kiko hiring an old machine was the truth and I didn't want to get involved with that. It wouldn't be good for my reputation, now would it. I hire out a para-motor to someone and they crash and drown. No, I didn't want to tell the police that it was mine.'

'So you decided to make the man an offer for Kiko's machine?'

'Yes. I offered him €1,000 and he accepted it.'

'That sounds cheap.'

'It was, but he was happy with it.'

'And you didn't think it was strange?'

'Yes, of course I did. It was obviously stolen. Kiko had paid six times that amount. This guy clearly knew nothing about paramotoring. It was an opportunity and I took it. Not a crime is it?'

'Buying stolen property? Yes, I'm afraid that is a crime, Mr Free.'

'But how was I to know it was stolen?'

'I think you have already answered your own question. Now that we have established that Kiko did not want his para-motor painted black, can you tell me why he needed to hire an old machine from you?' asked the captain.

'He said he was meeting someone on the Sunday, a sheila I think. He said he wanted to make an impression.'

'How was he planning on making an impression? Not on that worn out machine, surely?'

'The sheilas are usually impressed by a guy who can para-motor. The condition of the para-motor doesn't really count.'

'Yet it was on the Saturday that he died. Did he mention anything about going up on the Saturday? Or meeting anyone?'

The Australian shook his head, then pushed his long straggly hair out of his eyes. 'Like I said, we weren't friends. He wasn't going to confide in me, now was he. His new para-motor had been stolen and he needed to hire one of mine. It was as straightforward as that.'

'By the way, where were you on the Saturday when he crashed, Mr Free?'

'I was instructing a group of eight para-gliders. They were here from seven in the morning and the last ones left at two o'clock. They can all vouch for me.'

'I thought you didn't take them out at midday, because of the thermals?' interrupted Ricardo.

'Oh, so you can speak, then. Yes, you are quite right about that. We finished the gliding at about eleven, then we had a session on safety and flying techniques, followed by lunch. It was a weekend course. They were here to learn, but also to relax. We only actually flew the para-gliders in the morning. The rest was theory.'

'We will need a list of all the people who were on your course that weekend. Now we have discovered that Kiko was not alone when he was paramotoring on Saturday. Do you have any idea who might have been with him? Or why that person didn't stop to help him?' asked the captain.

'No. But I can say this, it wasn't anybody who had been on one of my courses. I always stress the necessity of looking out for your partner. That's for a number of reasons; you don't want to crash into him and if you get into trouble it's good to know that someone is there for you.'

'Not in this case, sadly. One more thing, Mr Free, why did Kiko telephone you seven times in the week before his death?'

'Why do you think? He wanted to tell me that his new para-motor had been stolen. For some reason he thought I had something to do with it. He got quite aggressive about it, saying that he had paid for it, and he hadn't even had an opportunity to try it out. I told him he should discuss it with his insurance company and if they needed proof of the transaction I could send it to them. He was very upset, but there wasn't any more that I could do. After that I didn't bother to answer his calls.' He leant back in his chair and smiled at them.

'So he thought you were behind the theft of his new machine? Any idea why that might be?'

'None whatsoever.'

'Do you sell many new para-motors?'

'Not really. Maybe two or three a year, if I'm lucky.'

'So it's possible that you told someone about the sale? In conversation, maybe? One of your regular customers?'

'Well, I suppose it is possible, but not intentionally.'

'What about your friend Juan Felipe? Did you mention it to him?' Bob folded his arms and looked down at the table. 'Nothing to say? Well, we already know that your old mate Juan is a thief; he doesn't just steal para-motors. In fact he isn't that fussy; he will steal anything that he knows he can sell. And of course once he heard about the new and very expensive para-motor that Kiko had bought he knew exactly where he could sell it.'

'The bloke told me he was selling it for a friend. I didn't realise it was the one Kiko had bought until I saw the registration number.'

'Do I look like an idiot, Mr Free.' The captain stood up. He was tired of listening to the man's lies. 'Take him down to the custody cells and process him, Lance Corporal. And you can start with a charge of perverting the course of justice and hiding evidence in a murder investigation.'

'Hey, that's not fair. I didn't even know the guy was dead until that sheila came up asking questions. How was I to know the para-motor was evidence?'

'Nevertheless, it was,' said Federico.

'Hey, you can't do that. I've done nothing wrong. I've told you all I know, I swear.'

Federico did not reply; he was working out what to say to Ricardo about the illegal search.

Luis looked up from his desk as the captain walked into the main office. '*Capitán*, I've just heard back from the conference centre. Juan Felipe Moreno was telling the truth for once; his alibi holds up. He was at the conference in Seville from the Friday night until after lunch on the Sunday; he cannot have been our killer.'

'Thank you, *Sargento*.'

'Do you want me to ring Señora Dunne and let her know?'

'No, I'll tell her. I have to speak to her anyway.'

'Oh, and someone from the *Policía Nacional* rang. Would you call them back.'

'Anything else?'

'No, *Capitán*.'

Federico scrolled through his recent calls until he came to Comandante Garcia's number. His old colleague answered as soon as he rang the number. 'That was quick. Does this mean it's bad news?'

'*Buenas tardes*, Federico, no quite the opposite. I'm in a hurry to leave, that's all. My wife has arranged something special for tonight and if I'm late, there will be all hell to pay.'

'So, what did you find out?'

'Your friend's maid is completely legit, just as you said. She has no criminal record, not even a speeding fine. But what she has been doing, is standing as a sponsor for her nephew, one Bautista Diaz Caceres, from Argentina, aged nineteen. His application is currently being processed and there seems to be no reason to reject it. So you can set her mind at ease.'

'So, it looks as though she didn't want to get involved as a witness in case it backfired on her sponsorship.'

'Probably, but it wouldn't have made any difference if she had.'

'Thanks for that, Ruben. I appreciate it.'

'Don't forget that drink.'

'I won't. Have a good evening.'

So they could remove Rosa's maid from the list of suspects/ witnesses; he would let Jacaranda know right away. He needed to speak to her anyway.

'Federico? Any news?' she asked, picking up the phone after the first ring. He knew she had been waiting for him to telephone her and why.

'Yes. But before I tell you what I've found out, I'd like to remind you that Ricardo does not work for you; he is a serving member of the Guardia Civil. I am happy to give you some police help, but you are not, I repeat not, to manipulate him into working outside the law.'

'I knew you'd blame me. I can assure you, Ricardo decided to search the premises on his own. I didn't ask him to do it.'

'You didn't need to, Jacaranda. I know exactly how you work. So, unless you want to ruin the young man's career, don't do it again.'

'Well, you've said what you wanted to say, now tell me what you have found out.'

'I don't think Bob Free is your murderer. He is in cahoots with Juan Felipe, who I am pretty sure stole Kiko's new para-motor and took it up to Bob Free's shop for him to sell. He paid him €1,000 and then I imagine was planning to sell it and split the profit with him. But I can't see how either of them fit the profile for Kiko's killer. They both have alibis. Juan Felipe was definitely in Seville at the time of Kiko's death and Bob Free was running a weekend course en El Torcal, although we still have to confirm that. More importantly, neither of them had anything to gain from Kiko's death.'

'What a pair. Anything else?'

'Yes, you can stop worrying about your mother's maid. It was as we thought; she was just nervous about you mentioning her name to the authorities.' He gave her a quick summary of what Ruben had discovered. 'So you can put her mind at rest and then maybe she will be able to tell you what you want to know.'

'Thank you, Federico. We are starting to make progress.' She gave him a brief review of what else they had discovered. 'However, now that we have eliminated Kiko's sister and his step-mother, our list of suspects is rapidly diminishing.'

'What about wife number two?'

'Yes, Nacho is trying to locate her now. I'll let you know how we get on.'

'Do that, Jacaranda. I'm expecting the *Comandante* to knock on my door any time now. And it won't be to congratulate us on our work.'

CHAPTER 18

JD decided to drop in at her mother's apartment on her way home. She wanted to tell Paola that she had nothing to fear from talking to her, but she still had her doubts that the maid would believe her.

'Señora Dunne.' Paola greeted her more formally than usual. 'Your mother is not at home.'

'That's okay Paola, I just wanted a quick word with you. Nothing to worry about and I promise I won't keep you long.'

'Shall I make you some coffee, *Señora*, or some tea?' She was getting that defensive look again.

'Nothing, thank you. Like I said I won't keep you long.' She followed Paola into the kitchen.

'How can I help you, *Señora*?'

'The last time I was here, I asked you if you had seen the second para-motorist, and you said that you hadn't.'

'That's right.' She avoided looking straight at her and began wiping down one of the work surfaces.

'Well, I don't believe you. And now I want you to tell me the truth. You have nothing to worry about; I have spoken to the immigration people and they told me that you are helping your nephew to get a visa to come to Spain. Telling me the truth won't affect his application. You understand?'

She nodded, but still didn't look at JD.

'Well, did you recognise the man or not?'

She hesitated then said, 'I thought he was one of the immigration officers who had interviewed me.'

'Do you remember his name?'

'Señor Campos.'

'Thank you, Paola. That wasn't so hard was it?'

'Shall I tell your mother than you called?'

'No need; I expect I'll be talking to her later this evening.'

So how was a local immigration officer involved with this case? Well there was only one way to find out.

She waited until she had left the apartment and phoned Federico. 'I know who the mystery para-motorist is,' she said, before he could moan about something else she had done.

'Really? So you have spoken to the maid?'

'Yes, she recognised him because he interviewed her at the immigration office, recently. Can you ask him what his connection was to Kiko, please. His name is Rodrigo Campos.'

'I'll send Ricardo round to see him in the morning.'

'And let me know?'

'Of course. But only if you let me take you out to dinner this evening.'

'Can I think about that?'

'You have ten seconds.'

'Okay, I have to put the investigation first I suppose, so yes. Pick me up at nine o'clock.'

The next morning as JD cycled through the city, her thoughts went back to the evening before; it had been a perfect dinner. Well almost. The food was excellent, the restaurant was right by the beach and as they ate they watched the sun slip below the horizon and the sky turn to orange and scarlet. The sea was a mirror of calmness with hardly a ripple on the surface, and the restaurant was playing some of her favourite music; it couldn't have been better. That was the problem. She had been sure Federico was going to propose to her again, but he didn't. She was not exactly disappointed; she was very happy with the relationship that they had. What was worrying her was, if he had asked her to marry him what would she have said? Maybe she ought to meet him halfway, suggest that he at least leave some clothes at her place from time to time.

'Nacho, we have some updates to put on the evidence board,' she said as soon as she walked into the agency.

'Let me get my helmet off and drink some coffee first. You know I don't function quite so early. And why are you here, already? You know it's only just gone seven?' said Nacho, pulling at his helmet and slipping it under his desk.

'Is it? No wonder I still feel half asleep.'

'So what's new then?' he asked.

'I'll wait until Linda is here, then bring you both up to date. By the way, it looks as though we have identified the mystery man.'

'That's good. So who is he?'

'Someone working in the Immigration Department. Ah, here's Linda now. We'll let her get settled and then we can go through it together.' She sat at her desk and switched on her computer. 'Did you send me the photos I asked for, Nacho?'

'Yes, they should be on your computer and your phone. They are pretty clear, so I hope that someone recognises one of them as the mystery man, or should I call him the immigration man, now.' He laughed.

'According to Paola, he's Sargento Campos.'

'Morning everyone. Am I late, or are you early JD?'

'Hi, Linda. Let's go straight into the meeting room and go over what we've got; there have been a few developments since yesterday lunchtime.' She was buzzing with energy this morning. The investigation was coming together and she was sure it wouldn't be long before they had solved the case. She waited while Nacho took up his usual position by the evidence board and proceeded to update them on the stolen para-motor and both Bob and Juan Felipe's involvement.

'I just can't believe that man. He seems to think he is invincible. First he steals Kiko's para-motor, then he moves into his apartment and starts selling his works of art.' Nacho was still clearly annoyed that he had been taken in by Juan Felipe.

'But did he kill him? I think not. Both Bob's alibi and Juan Felipe's check out. Unless they paid someone to do it for them, I can't see how they are involved. And, besides which I can't see any motive for either of them to kill him.'

'Well, I hope the judge throws the book at him,' said Nacho, reluctantly putting a line through both their names. 'What were you going to tell us about the mystery man?'

'Señor Campos. You can put his name on the board for now, until we find out what his connection to Kiko is all about. Ricardo is going to interview him and let us know what he has to say for himself.'

'And why he didn't stop and help him?' added Linda.

'Exactly.'

'By the way, did the captain have anything to say about the illegal search of Bob Free's premises?' asked Nacho.

'Just a little.' She grinned. 'But we were right, weren't we.'

'So, is that why Paola was frightened to say anything? She didn't want the immigration police to get involved?' asked Linda.

'Yes, but she didn't have any reason to be frightened.' JD explained about Paola's nephew and what she was trying to do for him.

'So, I can cross her off the list as well?'

'Well she was never a suspect but yes, cross her name off.'

'Linda, did you send the photos of the para-gliders to Rachel? Did she recognise any of them?'

'No. I've tried ringing her but I've had no luck so far. I will do it as soon as I can.'

'All right. What about Borg?'

'No. He didn't recognise any of them, either.'

'And that other neighbour. The one who was ill and didn't come to my mother's party?'

'No, she said not.'

'So it looks as though our mystery man is from the immigration police,' said Nacho.

'Well, we will have to see what he has to say for himself, and how he knew the duke's son.' JD looked across at Nacho. 'Have we heard anything back from the forensic team about the safe?'

'Yes. Our friend Juan Felipe wasn't lying when he said he didn't know about the safe. His fingerprints are not on it; and it hadn't been wiped clean. There are lots of prints and they all belong to Kiko.'

'So what was in it?'

'Nothing very exciting, just what you might expect. Cash, about six hundred euros, another thousand euros worth of poker chips, Kiko's passport and a few love letters.'

'Love letters? Who from? Lavinia? Leticia?' asked Linda.

'No, from the Italian heiress.'

'Why would he keep love letters from the woman he had jilted?'

'We will find out when we read them. Forensics are running some tests on them and will send them over to us when they have finished. In the meantime, I think you should pay a visit to the paragliding club where Kiko was a member, Nacho. Far from being a novice to this sport, Kiko had been paragliding since he was in his teens.'

'Okay. What do you want me to do when I get there, JD?'

'Take these photos with you and just ask around. Did anyone know him well? Was he popular? Was he good at paragliding? Just see what you can find out about him. And when did he decide to switch to paramotoring? Now that we know he was no novice, it makes it all the harder to understand his behaviour the day he died.

'Anything else?'

'Yes, see if there is a membership list and get a copy if you can.'

'Okay, Boss. I'll go this evening; there will be more people there then.'

'Good, so in the meantime, I'd like you and Linda to find out all you can about Ana Maria; she is one of the few suspects we still have on the board.' She studied the board for a few minutes. They had made a lot of progress, but it was mostly in eliminating suspects not finding the killer.

JD's phone began to ring. It was Federico. '*Si, digame,*' she said.

'Very formal, Jacaranda. Are you with a client?'

'No, sorry *Cariño*. We are just going through our list of suspects.'

'And?'

'It's getting shorter.'

'That's good, isn't it?'

'It should be, but I don't feel that confident. Anyway, what do you want?' She could feel the team's eyes on her.

'Just to tell you that I have been talking to Ruben. He will ask Sargento Campos to come along to the agency and talk to you this afternoon, if that is convenient.'

'That's fine, but why do you want us to interview him? I thought Ricardo was going to do it officially?'

'No. Comandante Garcia was not happy at the idea of us interviewing one of his men. I tried to explain that he wasn't being charged with anything.'

'Yet?' interjected JD.

'That he wasn't being charged but he could be a useful witness for our investigation.'

'Okay. I'll record the interview, so you and Ruben can listen to it afterwards. Any idea what time he is coming here?'

'Four o'clock.'

She looked at her watch. Not long to get everything set up. 'Fine. I'll let you know when it's over.' She hung up.

'Was that about the immigration man?' asked Linda.

'It was, and you'd better get used to calling him Sargento Campos, because he'll be here this afternoon. We have to interview him. I suppose it's an opportunity to double check that we have the right man. I want you to bring Paola, Margo and Borg here to identify him, Linda.'

'What an identity parade? Not sure how you're going to do that in this shoe box.'

'Well I had planned on asking the captain to set one up at the station, but now we are going to have to improvise. Collect our witnesses before Sargento Campos arrives and they can be sitting in the office as though they are new clients when he gets here. All they have to do is identify him as the man they saw flying the second para-motor and then they can go.'

'Have you cleared that with the *capitán*?' asked Nacho.

'I don't have to. If we still think he was involved in Kiko's death after we have interviewed him, then we will go through the proper channels.'

'Get the captain to do it, you mean,' said Linda. 'Okay. Well I'll ring them both and see if they are available. I suppose we only need one of them to confirm that Sargento Campos was with Kiko.'

'Yes, but I would prefer at least two of them, if they are available. Paola might get an attack of nerves again. Especially when she sees his uniform'

By a quarter to four everyone was in place. Linda was sitting at her desk with Paola, Margo and Borg sitting opposite. They had both been happy to go along with JD's plan, even Paola, as soon as she knew the police were not involved.

At four o'clock precisely a stocky man with a bushy, black beard and wearing the uniform of the National Police rang the bell and was escorted into the meeting room. 'Would you like to take a seat. I'll only be a couple of minutes,' JD told him, making sure that he sat facing the outer office. 'Can I get you anything to drink?'

'A glass of water would be good.'

JD walked across to the water dispenser and filled two glasses, all the time watching the faces of the witnesses. Both Borg and Margo shook their heads in a very definite manner and Paula whispered something to Linda. So it looked as though maybe Sargento Campos was not their man after all.

'It's very good of you to come and speak to me, *sargento*,' JD said. 'I expect you were told that we are looking into the suspicious death of the Duque de Roble's son.'

'Yes, the *comandante* said as much, but I don't see what it has to do with me. I never knew the man.'

'So, the thing is, that when the duke's son crashed his para-motor, he was not alone and I have a witness has identified you as that para-motorist.' She watched carefully for his reaction. It was unequivocally a look of amazement. He seemed genuinely astonished by her words.

'I have never been up in a para-motor in my life, and am not likely to. I suffer from vertigo. I can't even go up in one of those glass lifts, and if I go in an aeroplane—and that's only at the insistence of my wife—I am so drugged up that I sleep for the whole journey. So, sorry but I am not your suspect.'

'May I ask you where you were the Saturday before last?'

'You may. I was in Galicia with my family and some friends. My wife will vouch for me, as will my friends. Sorry Señora Dunne, your witness was mistaken.'

'Well, I am very sorry for taking up your time, but being a policeman you will understand that we need to follow up every lead, however unlikely.'

'Of course. I hope you soon find your man.' He chuckled to himself. 'Wait until I tell my wife about this; she'll laugh her socks off at the thought of me paramotoring.' He shook her hand and was gone.

JD walked over to the three witnesses and said, 'Thank you all very much for coming in and doing that. So it looks as though he isn't our man.'

'I am very sorry, *Señora*, I don't know why I thought it was him. Something about him reminded me straight away of Señor Campos,' said Paola. She looked very embarrassed. 'I just panicked when I saw him.'

'That's okay, Paola. You have nothing to worry about.'

Once the witnesses had left, Nacho went across to the evidence board and wiped out Rodrigo Campos and rewrote Mystery Man. 'So what now?' asked Nacho.

'I have no idea. I feel that the identity of this mystery man, as you like to call him, is crucial to the investigation. But how do we find out who he is?'

'Maybe it's not so crucial. Maybe we should focus on the evidence and find our killer that way. I'm already finding out some interesting facts about our Italian heiress,' said Nacho.

'Talking of which, I think it's about time I phoned Enzio to see how his documentary is coming along.' She picked up her mobile and dialled his number.

'JD, nice to hear from you. How's the investigation going?'

'*Buenas tardes*, Enzio. I thought I'd give you a call and see if the documentary was finished.'

'Yes and no. I've finished all that I can do. Now the editor will go through it with his red pencil, so to speak, and cut out all the bits he thinks are controversial. Do you want to come over and have a look at it before I give it to him?'

'I would love to. When?'

'Well, I have to hand it over to the editor next week, so I'll give you a ring when it's ready. Is the morning good for you?'

'Yes, that would be fine.'

'All right, bring some breakfast and we can eat it while you watch it. I would enjoy having some feedback from someone who will be looking at it from a different perspective.'

'Okay. Ring me when it's ready.'

'What's that all about?' asked Nacho, closing his computer and getting ready to leave.

'It's a guy who works with Jacobo. He's just finishing a documentary about the Duque de Roble and his family. I'm going to see the preview, before they cut out all the juicy bits.'

'Sounded a bit cloak and dagger, to me.'

'Apparently there are a few things in it that he is certain his editor will slash because he won't want to offend the duke's family. I'm hoping to see them before they are cut.'

'Well good luck.'

'Where are you off to? It's only half-past-four.'

'I'm going to visit the paragliding club, like you ordered.'

'Oh, I forgot. Enjoy yourself.'

He put on his helmet and grinned at her. 'It's work, Boss.'

CHAPTER 19

Nacho aimed to arrive at the paragliding club in the early evening. There was no point going too early, but neither did he want to arrive there when the members were already airborne. He had learned from their website that they met socially once a month in a wooden club house somewhere in the mountains of Málaga, a spot which provided the right conditions for paragliding. He located their headquarters—luckily it was not as far away as the place that Juan Felipe had taken him to before, but it would still take him forty-five minutes to get there—and set off along a road that appeared to wind forever up the side of the mountains.

The members were already gathering at the clubhouse by the time he arrived, and one or two gave him a passing glance as they busied themselves with sorting out their equipment.

'*Buenas tardes*,' he said to one of the members. 'I'm looking for Marco. Is he here?'

'*El Presidente*? That's him over there.'

'Thanks.'

'I haven't seen you before. Are you a new member?' he asked. He held out his hand. 'I'm Alejandro.'

'Nacho. Well, Ignacio actually. No I'm not a member yet, but I'm thinking of joining.'

'You should. We are a very friendly bunch. Most para-gliders are.'

'Yes, I had heard that. Wasn't the Duque de Roble's son a member here?'

'That's right. Poor sod. I still can't believe he's dead. He had been a member here for a few years, but it wasn't until he died that we found out he was part of the aristocracy. And so was the guy he sometimes came with.'

'Who was that?'

'Not sure of his name. He didn't come up here that often but someone said he was related to Kiko. He was a member of the club, but I don't suppose we'll see him again now that Kiko is dead; he didn't really mix with any of the other members. Anyway if you want to speak to Marco, you'd better hurry. He'll be going up soon.'

'Marco,' he called, running across to him. 'I'm Nacho. I phoned you earlier.'

'Oh yes, you're from the detective agency. I believe you wanted to ask me some questions about Kiko. Dreadful case. He was really well liked here. Kept himself to himself and was passionate about paragliding. He fitted in very well. I was sorry to hear about what happened to him.' He put his pack on the ground and asked, 'So how can I help you?'

'I just wanted to ask if he had any particular friends in the club, anyone he might have confided in. We're finding it difficult to understand how an experienced paraglider could have died like he did.'

'So you think it might have been suicide? Personally I think there are easier ways to commit suicide than that. I have to admit I was staggered when I heard what had happened. I know that paragliding and paramotoring are different, but the rules of flight are very similar.'

'What makes you say it could have been suicide?' asked Nacho.

'I just don't think Kiko would have been that careless. He was always so meticulous in his preparation that I cannot imagine why he did what he did.'

'So you don't believe it was an accident then?'

Marco shook his head. 'Now his brother-in-law, he was different; he was a risk taker. More than once I had to pull him up because he hadn't checked his gear properly before taking off. I told him time and again that this was a paragliding club, not a paragliding school. He should already know all the safety features without me having to remind him.'

'But if Kiko's death wasn't an accident, why do you think it was suicide?'

'What else could it be? You know a few of our members have mental health issues; more often than not they join the club to get away from the pressures of their daily life. Although I must admit we've never had anyone commit suicide before. In fact we have had very few accidents.'

'Tell me about Kiko's brother-in-law. I believe he was a member here as well?'

'Yes, and I can tell you, if he hadn't been married to Doña Isabella I would probably have kicked him out of the club long ago.'

'So you knew that Kiko was the son of the Duque de Roble?'

'Yes, of course, but when he joined the club he asked me to keep it secret. He said he just wanted to be one of the guys. So I kept it to myself.'

'How did Kiko get along with his brother-in-law then?'

'As far as I could tell, all right. I wouldn't say that they were the greatest of friends; Jorge was a bit aloof if you ask me, but maybe that's how the aristocracy are.' He looked across at the launch area and added, 'Look I need to get going now. Is there anything else I can help you with? You are welcome to chat to the other members while you're here, if you wish.'

'Thanks. Just one more thing. I'm thinking of joining a club. I think this one would suit me fine.'

'You would be very welcome, but you need to have a few lessons first then come back and pay your money. It's as simple as that. You've got my number, just ring when you're ready.' He picked up his gear and walked over to the launch area.

'Well, how did you get on?' asked Alejandro. 'Are you joining the club?'

'When I've had a few lessons, definitely. Actually the reason I'm here at the moment is to find out more about Kiko. I work for a detective agency and we're helping Kiko's family understand how and why he died. Did Kiko ever say anything to you about learning to para-motor?'

'No, I thought he was happy with paragliding. People tend to fall into one of the two groups; it's rare that anyone does both.'

'Do you know someone called Juan Felipe Moreno? Did Kiko ever come here with him?' Alejandro shook his head. 'What about Bob Free?'

'He's the one that has a shop in El Torcal, isn't he? I know of him, but as far as I'm aware he never came here with Kiko. Why?'

'Just curious. Did you ever see Kiko get into a fight with anyone?' Nacho asked, thinking of the bruises that the pathologist had found on Kiko's body.

'Yes, but it was a few weeks before he died. He and the guy were arguing about something and Kiko turned and walked away from him. That's when the other guy lost it, and grabbed him from behind and began to beat him up.'

Nacho took the photograph that JD had found in Kiko's apartment from his pocket and showed it to Alejandro. 'Is he in this photo? The man you are talking about?'

Alejandro squinted at the photograph. 'It's not very clear, but that could be him,' he said, pointing to a burly looking man standing on Kiko's left.

'Do you recognise any of the other men in the photo?'

'That's Marco,' he said pointing to the image of the club president, 'That looks like Eduardo, and that's Richard, an Englishman who was here for a while last summer. I've never seen that guy before,' he said, stabbing his finger at Juan Felipe. He took a closer look at the photograph. 'Where was it taken? I don't recognise the location. I'm pretty sure it's not around here.'

'So these two men, are they still members?'

'I think Eduardo has kept his membership but he works in Bilbao these days, so doesn't often come down here, and never in the summer. I don't know about Richard; I doubt it because he has moved back to England. Marco will confirm that.'

'Have you any idea what Kiko and the man were fighting about?' he asked, indicating the burly figure in the photograph. 'Or who he was?'

'I don't know his name, but he is the one who came up with Kiko occasionally and who turned out to be related to him in some way. I heard him threaten to tell Kiko's sister about something if he didn't do what he wanted.'

'He was blackmailing him?'

'I don't know if it was actually blackmail, but it did sound serious.'

I don't suppose you know what it was about?'

Alejandro shook his head. 'No, but I do know that money was involved, because when they had finished scrapping, the guy yelled at Kiko "Don't think this is over, you mean bastard." Everyone heard them.'

'One last question, do you know if Kiko liked to gamble?' Alejandro looked away. He seemed uncomfortable with the question. 'Well?'

'Yes, he used to have quite a problem with gambling, mostly on the horses but also in casinos, and on anything else where he could place a bet. He got into trouble with Marco last year, because he caught him taking bets on who could stay in the air the longest. Marco told him that if he caught him doing it again, he would be chucked out of the club.'

'So what happened?'

'Nothing, he stopped. The funny thing was that he was desperate to give it up, but sometimes the urge was just too strong. I felt sorry for him. My father had a gambling addiction; it affected all our lives when I was a child. So I know what a struggle it can be.'

'Thanks Alejandro. You've been very helpful.'

'No problem. I hope we'll see you again when you're not working?'

'You will indeed.'

As Nacho drove down through the forest that covered the lower slopes of the mountains, he thought about what he had learned that afternoon. Kiko was emerging as a complicated character. Was he the fun-loving, cocaine-snorting young man who was hooked on gambling, who enjoyed going to night clubs and casinos and had a different girl every night of the week? Or was he a quiet man, who shunned publicity, loved the solitude of paragliding, appreciated art and was desperately trying to give up gambling? And how did jilting his Italian girlfriend right before their wedding fit into either of those profiles?

He may have learned a bit more about the duke's dead son, but his visit had created even more questions. Did Juan Felipe know that Kiko belonged to the club? If so, why hadn't he mentioned it? What was he trying to hide? And Bob Free, why didn't he say anything about it? There was also the question of the brother-in-law; although Alejandro hadn't confirmed that it was his brother-in-law, it was certainly implied. He needed to find a photograph of him to be sure.

By the time he got back to Málaga it was too late to go into the agency, so he decided to go home, have a shower and ring Ricardo from there. He wanted to know if Kiko had managed to kick his gambling habit before he died, or not, and the only way to do that was to check with the casinos.

'Nacho, how can I help you?' Ricardo answered almost immediately.

'*Hola* Ricardo. Have you found out anything about Kiko's gambling habits? Is there any sign of recent activity?'

'Only that he placed most of his bets on line and sometimes went to a casino just outside Seville. To be honest, he doesn't seem to have visited his usual haunts for a couple of months, but that doesn't mean he wasn't placing his bets elsewhere. I'm going over to the casino later to see what they can tell me about him. Do you want to come? I can pick you up, if you like. Are you at home?'

'Yes, that would be good. See you later then.'

It didn't take them long to get to the casino, but it was after ten when they arrived and the car park was almost full.

'They won't be happy with a police car parked outside,' said Nacho, as a red Mercedes drove in behind them and then immediately drove out again. 'It won't be good for business.'

'Well the sooner they tell us what we want to know, the sooner we can leave,' said Ricardo, putting on his cap and straightening his uniform.

'So, you reckon that Kiko was a regular here?'

'It looks like it, but as I said, not recently.'

'Well that fits with what I heard at the paragliding club where they seemed to think that he was trying to give up gambling altogether.'

'That's not easy. Once a gambler always a gambler. You can't help thinking that this time luck will be on your side. This time you will make your fortune and then you can stop. And the next time, and the next. We see a lot of men turn to petty crime because it's the only alternative they can see to get out of the mess that they are in; it's like quicksand pulling them in deeper and deeper,' said Ricardo. 'However, as far as I can find out, Kiko didn't owe anything to the bookies at the moment, although he had a big betting tab going. Unlike his brother-in-law, who is deep in debt with just about everyone, including Kiko.'

'Doña Isabella's husband?'

'Yes.'

'Do we have a photo of him?' Ricardo shook his head. 'Do you think this could be him?' Nacho continued, showing the lance corporal the group photo of the para-gliders. 'The one on the right, a rather burly chap.'

'I don't know. We'll see if anyone recognises him.'

The manager was definitely not pleased to see them, and marched across instantly to ask what they wanted.

'Just a few questions about one of your old regulars,' said Ricardo. 'The husband of Doña Isabella. I believe you know him?'

'Not him again? I haven't seen him in a while and I don't expect to. If you find him tell him that he owes me big-time.'

Ricardo handed the photograph to the casino manager. 'Is he in this photograph?'

'Jorge? Yes that's him. You can't miss him, great ugly bastard. What's he been up to now?'

'I didn't say he'd been up to anything. I just wanted you to identify him.'

'Well I have. So you can go now.'

'Just a couple of more questions, then we'll leave you in peace. Did he come here with this man?' He pointed to Kiko.

'I haven't seen him lately, but yes they did sometimes come here together. Jorge would sit for hours playing roulette and the other one mostly played the slot machines. Neither of them were very successful.'

'How did they get on? Were they friends?'

'Well they knew each other, but I can't say if they were friends or not; I don't have time for social chit chat.' He paused, then added, 'I did see that guy give Jorge a huge wad of money once.'

'Do you know what it was for?'

'No, but Jorge always ran up a big gambling tab when he was here. Goodness knows what he did elsewhere. I can tell you, he wouldn't have got away with it if he hadn't been married to Doña Isabella. Maybe it was a loan. One thing I do know is that he didn't want his wife to find out about his gambling.'

'The other guy, did he owe you money too?'

'No. He lost a lot of money but he always had enough to cover his losses.'

'You said that you hadn't seen him recently, what about Jorge? Does he still come on his own?'

'Yes, at least two or three times a week. In fact he will very likely come in tonight.'

'Thank you, Señor Martin,' Ricardo said, reading the name tag in his lapel. 'I would prefer it if you didn't mention to Jorge that you have been talking to us. Agreed?'

The manager nodded. 'Agreed. Now clear off before you scare off any more of my customers.'

As they walked back to the car, Nacho said, 'I thought you would have wanted to stay, in case Jorge did turn up this evening. We could have asked him about the money Kiko gave him.'

'No, I don't think it would be wise to speak to him yet. We need more background on him first, especially as he and his wife have already been crossed off the suspect list.'

'Yes, you're right. Maybe we were too hasty doing that. We may have been wrong about the attack on Doña Isabella; there could have been another motive which has nothing to do with Kiko's death. Perhaps we need to look at their whereabouts on the Saturday when Kiko died.'

'Yes, and I think we need to get some photos of all our male suspects to the Guardia Civil in Seville for them to show to the mugger. Then maybe we can eliminate Doña Isabella's husband from our enquiries.'

'I'll look for some photos of him tomorrow and see if any of our witnesses recognise him,' said Nacho. All they had on him so far was—and this was only hearsay—that he regularly borrowed money from Kiko, who it seemed had decided that enough was enough. But at the moment they had nothing to connect Jorge to the day of Kiko's death.

CHAPTER 20

Linda helped herself to a glass of water from a fountain in the hospital waiting room and wandered back down the corridor towards the oncology department. She was beginning to despair about the lack of progress they were making with the case; they seemed to be going round and round in circles. She knew JD was feeling the same; she was becoming moody and more impatient than usual with those around her. Maybe she was having problems with Federico again. If only her boss could accept that the captain loved her, but she still continued to keep him at arm's length. Linda was very fond of JD and she was worried that her intransigent attitude was going to cost her the man she obviously loved.

The mobile in her pocket began to vibrate. '*Si, digame*,' she said.

'*Buenos días*, Señora Prewitt, this is Don Emilio. I have some news for you. Do you have a few minutes to speak to me?'

'Yes, of course. Just give me a moment while I find somewhere quieter.' She walked back to the hospital entrance and went outside. 'That's better. So what did you want to talk to me about, Don Emilio?'

'I have discovered some information about the duke's second wife which may be of interest to you.'

'Ana María?'

'Yes, it seems that the woman is an outright liar. She does have a daughter, but she is not the duke's child. She is fourteen years old, not ten as her mother claimed, and was born even before Ana María and the duke knew each other.'

'I'm surprised she could get away with that.'

'The child is small for her age and has been living in Argentina with her grandmother. Ana María claimed that the Duque de Roble paid her a lot of money to take the child there but I don't believe the duke knew anything about it. There is nothing to suggest that he was aware that he had another daughter. I have known the duke for many years; he was a very religious man and if he thought he had another child he would have had her christened and welcomed into the family. He would not have sent her to Argentina and denied all knowledge of her, unless he was certain that he was not her father. Anyway, I am going to go to the hospice today and I will try to speak to him, but I am pretty certain that he was ignorant of it all.'

'So how will that affect the annulment?'

'The Church have refused to change it. It will stand.'

'So I imagine that the Duquesa de Roble is happy about that?'

'Of course. It is one less worry for her, poor woman.'

'May I ask you a question about Kiko's aborted wedding?'

'You mean when he cancelled it at the last minute? That was a dreadful day. His father was furious.'

'Really. I thought maybe it was his father who had forbidden it?'

'Well yes, it's true he did not want his son to marry an Italian heiress; he wanted him to marry someone from the Spanish aristocracy but when he realised that Kiko was going ahead anyway, he capitulated and gave them his blessing.'

'So why was he furious?'

'You have to realise the importance of the duke's position in society. He wasn't furious about the wedding, he was furious because of the way Kiko cancelled it at the last minute. His son humiliated him and insulted the Italian family. It was telling the world that the Duque de Roble had no control over his own family, not even his son and heir. At one point I know he was so angry with Kiko that he would have disinherited him if it had been possible.'

'So what happened?'

'Nothing. I think that was when the duke began to realise that his health was failing and he didn't want a rift between him and his children, especially his son.'

'Thank you for telling me all this.'

'You are most welcome, Señora Prewitt. I will let you know if I find out anything to the contrary about Ana María. *Adios*.'

Linda closed her mobile and walked back into the hospital. So now it seemed it was time to look a bit more closely at the Italian heiress. Once she had taken Phil home she would go into the agency and see what Nacho had discovered about the lovely Bianca.

Nacho was working on his computer when she arrived and JD was looking at what seemed to be photocopies of some handwritten letters.

'Hi, what's that you're reading, JD?' she asked, putting her bottle of water on her desk and slumping into her chair. 'It's so hot out there. I hope you haven't got any job for me that means I have to go out again until this evening.'

'I'm reading about the unfortunate girl that Kiko dumped on her wedding day.'

'It wasn't exactly on her wedding day,' said Nacho.

'Okay. Two days before her wedding. I imagine it felt just as bad. These are the letters she wrote to Kiko. They were in his safe.' JD replaced the letters in the folder. 'You can look at these later. First let's go over what we have found out. I know Nacho has quite a lot to add. What about you Linda?'

'Yes, I had a phone call this morning from the duke's solicitor.' She recounted what Don Emilio had told her while Nacho updated the board. 'So, I think it's time we talked to the heiress, don't you?'

'I agree. As I am not paying for either of you to go to Verona, Nacho I want you to arrange a video call with Bianca as soon as possible.'

'I'll do what I can, but it might not be easy.'

'Why do you say that?' asked Linda. 'What have you found out about her?'

'Well, for a start, Bianca was pregnant which was why there was pressure to have a quick wedding. Apparently her parents were not happy about it and were virtually chasing her down the aisle,' JD told her.

'So maybe this was a revenge killing,' suggested Linda.

'Maybe, because that wasn't the end of it. When Kiko dumped her, Bianca's parents made her have an abortion. The poor woman was so traumatised by it all she ended up having a nervous breakdown,' said Nacho.

'So where is Bianca now?'

'She wanted nothing to do with her parents and refused to continue living at home. She moved into a convent in a small town just outside Verona.'

'The poor girl. What a bastard Kiko was, to abandon her like that,' said Linda.

'Well that's just it. When he called off the wedding he didn't know about the baby. Her parents wouldn't let her tell anyone, not even Kiko. They said it was a stain on the family name. Of course she told him about it later in one of her letters.'

'*Dios mio,* in what century are they living?' said Linda.

'You need to read these letters. He was trying to change. He was still in love with her.' JD handed the folder to Linda. 'It's tragic. Romeo and Juliet all over again.'

'What did forensics say about the contents of the safe?'

'Not much more than we already knew: his passport, some money and a few poker chips. There was a recent phone number for Bianca, but it seems as though they never spoke, only sent WhatsApp messages to each other and we have no record of what they said. But the letters give a clear indication of how they both felt.'

'Were Juan Felipe's finger prints on the safe or the poker chips?'

'No, the only clear prints were Kiko's. And on the letters, the prints of an unidentifiable woman, whom I assume was Bianca. I think Juan was telling the truth for once, when he said he didn't know anything about a safe.'

As Linda began to read through the carefully handwritten letters she couldn't help feeling that she was intruding into the lives of these two young people. Some of the letters were written before he jilted her, and were very intimate but there were a couple written after the breakup. It was heartbreaking to read his words.

'My dearest Bianca, I know I have hurt you terribly but I want to try to explain. I love you dearly and I always will. You can be certain of that. My heart is yours now and for always, but the way things are at the moment I am not worthy of you. You deserve a better man. And I intend to be that man. I am going to change, I promise. I have already given up all those stupid drugs and am working on my worst addiction, gambling. But I have a plan and I hope that very soon I will be someone who deserves to have such a beautiful woman as you for my wife. I know I cannot ask you to wait for this transformation to

happen, *Cariño, but I can only pray that you believe me and give me a chance to be worthy of you, my dearest love. Just give me time and we will have the wedding that we both spoke about, without the meddling of our parents.'*

This letter was folded inside another one, written by Bianca.

'*Do not blame yourself, amore mio. We are both under the rule of our fathers. Even in the twenty-first century we cannot disappoint them. You have a responsibility to your role as the heir to a dukedom and I have my duty to uphold the honour of my family. I have read your letter and returned it to you, not because I don't want it, but because I want you to keep it with you always, to remind you of your promise to me. Soon we will be together again and all this heartache will seem like a bad dream. Il mio cuore sarà sempre tuo Bianca.'*

'Does anyone speak Italian?' Linda asked, wiping a tear from her eye. Bianca was obviously a very sentimental young woman.

'I do,' said Nacho. He lent over her shoulder. 'My heart will always be yours,' he translated. 'Very romantic. I don't think she was planning on killing him.'

'But maybe her father was,' said JD. 'Get the zoom call organised as soon as you can, Nacho. I'm going out, so I will leave it to you and Linda to speak to Bianca.'

'Okay Boss. Where are you going?'

'To see a documentary. I probably won't be back until mid afternoon.'

'Is that the one the guy phoned about?'

'Enzio, you mean? Yes. I don't think there will be anything new about the duke's family in it, but you never know. There may be something we have missed.' She turned to Linda. 'Have you been able to get in touch with Rachel yet?'

'No. She still isn't answering her phone. Maybe you could check if her number is still active, Nacho.'

'Okay, I'll have a look, later.'

Linda read through all the love letters looking in vain for some clue as to why Kiko had ended up dead. It was like JD had said, they were like a modern Romeo and Juliet being kept apart by their families, except this was the twenty-first century not sixteenth century Verona. Bianca's family may have been angry that Kiko had made their daughter pregnant then jilted her, but to take revenge in this way was hard to believe. There had to be something they were missing.

'We're in luck. Bianca has agreed to speak to us on Zoom in half an hour,' said Nacho.

'In that case I have time to go out and buy a sandwich. I'm starving. Do you want anything?'

Nacho gave her a big grin. 'Thanks Linda. I'll have the usual. While you're out I'll set up the link and send it to her. Don't be late back.'

Linda had no intention of being out in the heat any longer than necessary. She made straight for their new favourite bar and ordered a glass of orange juice and a ham and cheese roll and sat by the bar to eat it. It was approaching lunchtime and the bar was crowded with tourists. From the badges that most of them were wearing it looked as though they had just come off one of the cruise ships and were about to set off on a walking tour round the city. Well sooner them than me, she thought, calling the waiter across.

'Something else, Linda?' he asked.

'Just the usual for Nacho, please.'

'He is too busy this morning to come himself?' he asked as he started to make the coffee.

'Yes, we have a lot to do this week.'

'The death of the young man in the port?' he asked.

Now how did he know they were investigating Kiko's death? They had all tried to keep the case secret, even Nacho wouldn't have said anything to him. Maybe he didn't know anything. Maybe he was just fishing. 'The accident at the port you mean?'

The waiter grinned at her and nodded. 'How is it going?'

'I think the police have closed the case.'

He looked disappointed at this news and at her obvious reluctance to talk about it, so went into the kitchen and returned with a ham and tomato baguette for Nacho.

'I see your old haunt has been taken over by new owners again,' he said.

'Yes, do you know anything about them?'

'Only that they appear to be very curious about your detective agency.'

'Really? What makes you say that?'

'Well they knew that you were investigating the death of the duke's son, for a start. I've not heard anyone else mention that. Not even Nacho.'

'Who told you?'

'The barman. I've started going there during my break. It's good to get away from here for a bit, and I was curious about what the new people were planning to do with the place. It's in a prime spot, you know. In fact I was quite surprised when he told me that it's one of those pop-up shops now. They will only be there for a few months, unless the owners can't find a buyer, in which case they can continue renting it.'

'Really. How do you think they found out about the investigation?' There was no point denying it now.

'I don't know, but I'll ask around for you. They had a lot of questions about JD, you know.'

'Such as?'

'Does she live in Málaga centre? Does she always cycle to work? Is she married? Is there a boyfriend?'

'What did you tell them?' Linda was beginning to get worried now.

'Nothing. I don't get involved in my customers' affairs. If someone wants to tell me something, I'm happy to listen, but I always assume that it's in confidence. A barman's role can be like that, you know. Sometimes people will tell their barman things that they don't like to discuss with their families, a bit like their barber. Which is why I found this guy's questioning to be out of order.'

'Is he from around here?' Linda asked.

'No, I think he's a foreigner, but I'm not sure where from exactly. Do you want me to find out?'

'Only if you can do it, discreetly.' She put some coins on the bar to pay for the breakfast and added, 'Thanks, see you tomorrow. Looks as though you are going to be busy,' as another group of tourists began to squeeze their way inside. She walked swiftly down the alleyway and back into the office. 'It's like an oven out there,' she told Nacho as she quickly shut the door behind her. 'It has to be forty degrees today.'

'Thirty-nine,' said Nacho, taking the coffee from her and removing the lid. 'That's great. Just what I needed.'

'Have you never wondered if you drink too much coffee?'

'Is there such a thing as too much coffee?' He laughed. 'Anyway, down to business. Everything is set up, we just need to agree on what we want to get from her. I think it would be best if you led the interview and I'll help where necessary.'

'Okay. But I have something to tell you first.' She related what the barman had told her. 'Do you think this is another attack on JD, like the spy-ware one? Is that awful man still pestering her?'

'It sounds like it. There's something I haven't told you, Linda, because JD asked me not to.'

'What?' Linda did not approve of secrets, but made no comment as Nacho told her what he had found out about the current ownership of Antonio's bar. 'So why didn't she want you to tell me?' she asked.

'I think it's partly because she didn't want to think about it happening again and also she said you had too much on your plate already without worrying about her.'

'Well she needs to know this. I'll leave it to you to tell her, Nacho. Now let's get this zoom call under way. I assume that Bianca speaks as well as writes Spanish.'

'I would think so, but if not then I'll take over and translate.'

'Okay. Shall we give her a call then?' said Linda.

CHAPTER 21

She waited until the three of them were visible on the screen and then introduced herself, 'Good morning Bianca, I am Linda from the Jacaranda Dunne Detective Agency, and this is my colleague Ignacio. We are investigating the unexpected death of your late fiancé Gabriel Francisco Mendoza de Goya Pérez. It is very good of you to talk to us. I understand that you must be very upset about his death and although we don't want to intrude, we do need to ask you a few questions about him. Are you happy with that?'

'*Si, Señora.*' The Italian heiress was indeed beautiful; her glossy black hair fell like a curtain across her shoulders and her eyes were the colour of nutmegs and slanted upwards at the corners.

'No need to call me *señora*, Linda is fine. First of all I'd like to ask you when you were last in touch with Kiko?'

Bianca heaved a big sigh and said, 'It was a few days before he died. He had written to me to tell me how much he loved me and that he was going to change. He wanted me to give him another chance. He said he had a plan.'

'Did he explain what sort of plan?'

'It was to stop gambling. He had become addicted to it, and no matter what he tried he always found himself returning to it, at first in small ways but then it would escalate again. But this time he sounded convinced that he would manage to give it up. That's all he told me.'

'Why this change in him? I heard he was a quite different person when he was younger.'

'Yes, so I believe. I think it was an accumulation of things, but mostly when he learned that his father was seriously ill. It seemed to make him grow up. He realised that becoming the Duque de Roble was no longer something that would happen sometime in the future, but that it could happen any day. He was not prepared for that. At first he just wanted to run away from it all. He wanted us to leave Spain. He talked of travelling to Asia, to Australia; he even suggested that we move to California and live there, anywhere in fact as long as it was a long way from Spain. Then something inside him changed. He told me that he had to face up to his responsibilities; his father relied on him and he didn't want to let him down.'

'That's when he decided to give up gambling?'

'I suppose so. To be honest, I had other things on my mind. I had my own battle to fight with my parents, which sadly I lost.'

'Did you blame Kiko for that?'

'Blame Kiko? No, why would I? Kiko knew nothing about what was happening between me and my family.'

'You said that Kiko wanted the two of you to run away. Didn't he want to get married?'

'No. He didn't believe in marriage. He believed in love, in trust and loyalty but he thought that marriage was unnecessary when two people loved each other.'

'Were you upset about that?'

'Not upset. I could understand his opinion but for me, marriage meant showing all that love and loyalty to the world. It wasn't about the fuss and the expense. That was why we decided to have a simple wedding, but even that was hard as both families had so much to say about what we should do.

Kiko's father wanted us to wait, while my father wanted it over as soon as possible.'

'Was that because of the baby?' Linda asked. She had been nervous about mentioning the pregnancy as so far Bianca had said nothing about it.

For a moment the heiress said nothing, then all she replied was, 'So you know about that.'

Linda nodded. 'It must have been very hard for you.'

'It was.' For a few minutes she said nothing then she asked, 'Is there anything else you want to know?'

'Did Kiko have any enemies? Was there anyone who might have wanted him dead?'

'Apart from his family, you mean?'

Linda looked at her in surprise. 'I don't understand. Didn't he get on with his family?'

'Well, let's say they weren't very close but, having said that, I think one of his new resolutions was to mend the bridges between them. I know he was making an effort to be more friendly with one of them. He saw that as part of his responsibilities if his father died.'

'Did he mention anyone in particular?'

'Not really.'

'What about his step-mother? Did he get on with her?'

'Leticia? Oh yes. He was very fond of her. He said she made his father happy and took good care of him. Other than that there's not much else I can tell you.'

Linda could see that by now Bianca was struggling to hold back the tears, so she said, 'That's fine. You have been really helpful, Bianca. I am so sorry to put you through all this again.'

'You will let me know if you find out what happened to Kiko, won't you?'

'Of course. We will contact you right away. Are you coming to Spain for the funeral?'

Bianca shook her head. 'No, I don't think I could bear it. But I will be thinking of him. He will be here in my heart forever.' She touched her breast and smiled sadly. '*Arrivederci.*' Then her image disappeared from the screen.

'Well, how sad,' said Linda.

'Yes, but what have we learned?'

'Not a lot of concrete facts but I think now we can understand a bit more about what made Kiko tick. He was a complicated man who was emerging from being a rich playboy into becoming the responsible heir to a dukedom.'

'Does that bring us any closer to finding his killer? As far as I can see we don't have any suspects left.' He walked over to the evidence board and crossed out Bianca's name.

'Maybe it does, Nacho. Maybe it does. Let's see what JD thinks about the interview. Did you record it?'

'I did, but don't tell anyone except JD.'

Linda's phone began to ring. 'Excuse me, Nacho, I need to get this.' She accepted the call and said, 'Can I help you?'

'Is that Linda?'

'Yes, who is this?'

'It's Borg. We spoke the other day at the party in the Marquesa's apartment.'

'Hello Borg. What can I do for you?'

'I have some information for you. I was watching a news programme this morning and they were talking about the rise in the number of muggings in the big cities. It mentioned how even the duke's daughter, Doña Isabella was mugged just recently, and then there he was on the television screen, the man who was paramotoring with Kiko on the day he died. The one who left him to drown.'

'That's fantastic. Did they say if it was the same man who mugged Doña Isabella?'

'No, that's what is so strange. It was her husband, Don Jorge Domingo Montero. He was the one I saw with the para-motor. I wrote down his name so I wouldn't forget it.'

'Are you sure it was him?'

'One hundred percent.'

'Would you be able to pick him out in a police line-up?'

'Of course.'

'Thank you very much for that information, Borg. I will get back to you as soon as I can.'

'What was that all about?' asked Nacho.

'That was Borg. He's identified our mystery man. It's Jorge, Doña Isabella's husband.'

'Really? I take it he's willing to identify him in an official police line-up?'

'Yes, I'm sure he is. I'll send a message to JD. She'll be delighted to have the news.'

'And no need for you to phone Rachel again.'

'No. But I'll get Margo to come along and identify him as well. We don't want to screw this up.'

CHAPTER 22

Jacobo was talking to Enzio when JD arrived at the studio. '*Buenos días* JD, have you come to see the documentary before all the good bits are cut out?' He kissed her on the cheeks and continued, 'He's done a great job and I doubt it was easy. A bit like talking to a load of clams, trying to get information out of that family, but he did it.' He slapped Enzio on the back. 'Well enjoy yourself. Do you fancy a spot of lunch afterwards?'

'*Buenos días*, Jacobo. Yes that would be nice.' She looked across at Enzio, 'It's a bit late for breakfast but I brought you coffee and some pastries.'

'What a star.' He beamed at her. 'I can't understand how you let her get away, Jacobo.'

She stared at him. Now what had Jacobo been saying about her? He was such a gossip. 'How long is the documentary?' she asked, deliberately ignoring the silly grin on Jacobo's face.

'At the moment about two hours, but if you're only interested in the more recent stuff then probably about an hour.'

'Okay, I'll pick you up at two. Want to join us Enzio?' asked Jacobo.

'Thanks, but no. I have to see the editor before the end of the day, and there's still plenty to tidy up.'

Enzio accompanied JD into the viewing room. 'I'll stay with you, if that's all right. I need to have a look at some parts again, but I won't interrupt you.'

'That's fine.' She waited as he forwarded the documentary to what he referred to as 'the death of the first wife' and pressed play.

The documentary was impressive, alternating scenes shot in black and white with some in colour, and background music that was very evocative. Most of the content was information she already knew about, but then there was a scene where Enzio interviewed Doña Isabella.

'I believe your brother has a bit of a drug problem, Doña Isabella?' Enzio asked her.

The duke's daughter looked surprised at this direct question, but replied as coolly as if he were enquiring about the health of her dogs. *'There are a lot of young people who take recreational drugs and think nothing of it, but sometimes, sadly, they find that they are no longer in control of their habit and the drugs begin to take over their lives. Unfortunately my brother was one of those.'*

'Was? Does he no longer use cocaine?'

'He has conquered his addiction. He no longer takes cocaine or any other illegal substance. Gracias a Dios.' She crossed herself.

'That is indeed good news. Did he go away to a rehabilitation centre to be cured?'

'Not exactly. My husband has a friend who is a well respected psychiatrist and therapist. He works with many famous people who suffer from drug addiction, some who are in a much worse state than Kiko ever was.'

'And that's how he became cured?'

JD could hear the scepticism in the interviewer's voice.

'Yes. Mind you it was not an overnight cure. It took many months and he had to stay in the rehab centre until he could be trusted not to have a relapse. But Jorge kept an eye on him and

*so far he has kept away from any drugs; he doesn't even drink
alcohol these days.'*

'It sounds like a miracle cure.'

'I'm not a gullible woman, Señor Cabello. I know very well
that if he is not supervised he could slip back into his old ways.
Jorge is in constant touch with him, as is Doctor Delgado.'

'Would you mind stopping it for a minute,' JD asked.

'Of course. Why?'

'When did this interview take place?'

'It must have been six months ago.'

'So after he jilted his fiancé?'

'Yes, quite a while. Please feel free to make any notes before
we move on; I can guarantee the editor will chop a lot out of
this interview.'

'Did you interview Kiko?'

'No, I was hoping to, but he was locked away in that rehab
centre for a lot of the time and when he wasn't he refused to be
interviewed. On the advice of his family, I believe. Shall we
move on?'

'Yes, please.'

When she had finished viewing the uncut version of the
documentary and thanked Enzio for his time, she went in search
of Jacobo.

'Finished already?' he asked. 'I'm sorry but I'll be at least
another half hour.'

'Don't worry, Jacobo. I'll take a rain check. I need to get
straight back to the office.'

'Was it useful?'

'Yes, I think it was. I'll let you know.' She kissed him
goodbye, got on her bicycle and headed for the agency. It was
all coming together, now. She could feel her heart begin to race

as she realised that she had identified their killer; it had been staring them in face all along.

She flung open the door of the agency and rushed inside. 'What's up?' asked a surprised Nacho. 'Is everything all right, Boss? You look as though you've won the lottery.'

'We may have done just that. Where's Linda?'

'I'm here, JD. Trying to get this air conditioning unit to work more efficiently; it's like a sauna in here,' she said, coming out of the meeting room. 'So, what's all the excitement about?'

'I think we may have identified our killer. We just have to prove it.' She walked over to the evidence board and wiped it clean.

'Hey, why are you doing that? We still had some useful information up there,' Nacho protested.

'You can put it back later. We are going to take a different approach.' She scrawled Jorge's name in the centre of the board. 'Okay, what do we know about this man?'

'He's our mystery man, for a start,' said Linda. 'Borg saw him on the television and identified him. Ricardo is arranging for an official police line-up.'

'Really. That's excellent news. I'm glad we have identified him at last. What else?' she asked, handing the marker pen to Nacho and sitting down.

'He's Doña Isabella's husband, but we had eliminated them both after the attack on her. Are you suggesting they are in this together?'

'Let's just concentrate on the husband for the moment.'

'Well we know he was a gambler and he was in debt,' said Nacho. 'According to the manager of the casino, Kiko had been lending him money.'

'He has profited by Kiko's death,' added Linda. 'Both financially and socially. Not only will his wife become the new Duquesa de Roble but they will now receive a larger portion of the inheritance.'

JD stared at the evidence board. It was all moving very fast now, and the case against Kiko's brother-in-law was building up block by block, but they still did not have any hard evidence to link him to Kiko's murder. 'Did the Italian heiress have anything new to tell us about Kiko or his relationship with his brother-in-law?'

'She said that he was trying to improve his relationship with his family, to build bridges between them.'

'Anyone in particular?'

'Yes, she thought so, but didn't know who exactly. It could have been Jorge, but I can't say for sure.'

'We shouldn't jump to conclusions but he was seeing a lot of his brother-in-law,' said Nacho. 'They were both members of the paragliding club, and then there was the gambling. But I had the feeling from what the casino manager said, that Kiko was beginning to feel used.'

'Why do you say that?'

'Well they were often at the casino together, but the manager didn't think they were close friends. Maybe Kiko was getting tired of Jorge constantly asking for money to pay his debts.'

'Nacho, see if you can trace any payments to Jorge's bank account from Kiko.'

'Okay, JD, but I think they would have been cash payments, harder to trace. By the way, what was the documentary like? Anything useful?'

'Which documentary?' asked Linda.

'One that is being prepared for release when the duke dies. I went along to see the uncut version.'

'And?'

'It was useful. Very useful. I didn't watch all two hours of it, but there was an interview with Kiko's sister which was very revealing. She talked about Kiko's drug addiction and how he had managed to recover with the help of a rehabilitation centre and a certain Dr Delgado. Nacho, I want you to find out all you can about this doctor and arrange for me to visit him, as soon as possible. No need to tell him we are private investigators. Tell him I have an addiction and need some help.'

'So why is that important? Do you think this doctor had anything to do with Kiko's death?'

'Indirectly he might have. Doña Isabella said that he was a friend of her husband's. You know the one thing that has been puzzling us all along is why Kiko put himself in such a dangerous situation. The damage to the para-motor was minimal, certainly not enough to cause a fatal crash. It was his behaviour that we needed to look at more closely, and now it transpires that he was seeing a psychiatrist a few months prior to his death. Maybe that is where our answer lies. Anything else?'

'Yes, when I was at the paragliding club I talked to one of the guys, Alejandro. He confirmed that Kiko had a gambling problem but was trying to give it up, and he said that a week before he died Kiko had a fight with someone he hadn't seen before. I showed him the group photo and he thought it might be Jorge, but he wouldn't say for sure. He didn't know what the fight was about but this guy got really angry and called Kiko a mean bastard. He also threatened him.'

'So that's where the ante-mortem bruises on his body came from. It looks as though you were right, Nacho, Kiko had decided to stop bank-rolling Jorge's gambling debts,' said Linda.

'Yes, but we still don't have any concrete proof. It is all still circumstantial.' JD knew exactly what Federico's reaction would be. So far nothing they had would stand up in court.

'Nevertheless I think it's time you spoke to the captain. We have a good enough case to bring in the police,' said Linda. 'We just need our witnesses to officially identify Jorge as the man who arranged to have his wife mugged and who was with Kiko just moments before he died. Those two events alone should be enough to open an official investigation.'

'All right. I'll speak to the captain right away; it's time I gave him an update on where we have got to, anyway. And then I'm going to have a chat with Doña Isabella.' She looked at her watch. 'Time for lunch, anyway. You get off home, Linda.' She looked at Nacho.

'Okay, Boss. I know, arrange the appointment with the psychiatrist for you. I'll do that now.'

JD was already sitting at a table in Mario's when Federico arrived. She stood up and kissed him. 'Thanks for coming.'

'Well, it sounded urgent. What's happened?' He waved across at the waiter. 'Have you ordered?'

'Not yet. Just order something simple for me. I need to get back to work.' She saw the captain raise his eyebrows. 'No, really. I think we may have found our murderer, and I might need your help.'

'Really? I'm intrigued. Tell me what you have found so far, and I'll see what I can do.' He turned to Mario who had placed a plate of olives and a bottle of Rioja on the table, and said, 'No wine today, Mario, just a large bottle of water, and the house salad.'

'Nothing else Capitán?'

'Not today, thank you, Mario. Too much work to do; I need to keep a clear head.'

JD began to update the captain on the investigation, while he made an occasional note on his pad.

'So you want to put the duchess's husband in a police line-up? You don't want much, Jacaranda, do you?'

'Two line-ups actually. The other one is in Seville. The man who mugged Doña Isabella said he had the feeling that the man who paid him to mug his wife was her husband.'

'But why did he think that?'

'Just by the way he spoke about her. And that he was paying for someone to mug her.' She grinned. 'He says a true mugger would do the job himself, not pay someone else to do it for him.'

'But he's in custody, isn't he?'

'Yes, on remand at the moment. He's been charged but not tried yet.'

'Well I'll speak to the Guardia Civil in Seville and get them to ask Jorge Domingo to go into the police station there. They are not going to like it.'

'Would they prefer that we let a murderer go free?'

'To be honest, as your suspect is the duke's son-in-law, I expect they would. I hope to God you are right, Jacaranda. Accusing a senior member of the aristocracy of murder can bring consequences you may not want. Can't we just use the mugger's description of the man who paid him and compare it to the photo of Jorge?'

'No, he needs to be identified in person. Don't worry, I am pretty confident that he's the one.'

'I would be happier to hear you say that you were one hundred percent certain.' He sat back and looked at her. 'So what is your next move?'

JD decided not to tell him she was visiting a psychiatrist; she knew what his comments would be. 'I'm going to see Doña Isabella.' She then told him about the interview she had watched. 'I doubt if they will show that in the final version, but I want to speak to her about Kiko's mental state just before he died. We still don't know why he was behaving so erratically.'

'*Dios mio*, don't tell me that after all this work, you might declare the death a suicide. If I remember correctly it was you who was so certain it was murder.'

'No, I only said it was not an accident, that it was a suspicious death and needed investigating. But now we know that Kiko was being treated by a psychiatrist, we have to take suicide into account.'

'Well, you had better hurry up, because I have heard that the duke is barely hanging in there. His death is imminent.'

'I rang my mother while I was waiting for you. We are going to see Doña Isabella this afternoon. With your help, Federico, we can have this investigation closed in a couple of days. We are so close,' she said.

The captain pulled out his phone and dialled his *cabo's* number. 'Ricardo, I have a sensitive job for you. We need to ask the husband of Doña Isabella to take part in a line-up. Well, two actually. Phone Nacho and he will give you the details.'

'I have them already, *Capitán*. Nacho phoned me earlier. I was just waiting for you to authorise it.'

'Well, it's authorised.' He scowled at JD, who shrugged her shoulders. Why was he always so sensitive.

'Just a minute Capitán. Is JD with you?' asked Ricardo.

'Yes, why?'

'Can you tell her we found out who bought the bronzes that were stolen from Kiko's apartment. It was a collector in Madrid and he thought he was buying directly from the owner.'

'I don't suppose he was very happy when he heard that the owner was already dead. Yes, I'll tell her.' Federico snapped his phone shut and put it back in his pocket. 'It seems that Nacho had already organised the line-up with Ricardo.'

'Don't put on that face. Nothing would have happened without your say-so.'

'I'm not so sure. What about the unauthorised search of Bob Free's premises?'

'That was different. We had to make the search before he disposed of the para-motor.' Before the captain could reply, Mario returned with the salad and placed it on the table between them. 'Thank you, Mario. That looks delicious,' JD continued with a beaming smile at the waiter. She began to serve the salad to both of them. 'What was it that Ricardo wanted to tell me?'

'Ricardo put photos of the stolen bronzes in the police bulletin and a collector got in touch to say he had bought them. Thought he was buying directly from the duke's son, although he admitted he was a bit suspicious of the sale because the bronzes weren't in pairs. So he said he checked the bulletin to see if they came up.'

'And they did. I wonder if he is telling the whole truth there.'

'What does it matter? It's unlikely that Kiko was murdered for two bronze figures. He's probably a collector who couldn't resist a bargain, even though he suspected they were stolen. But he's never going to admit that.' He began to pick at his salad. 'So, you had better tell me now, is there anything else you want us to do for you?'

'I would like to know if Kiko had been paying money into Jorge Domingo Montero's bank account. We believe he had been giving him money in cash to pay off his gambling debts, but I am hoping that he also transferred some into his account.'

'We can take a look, but I doubt it. If he is the killer, he would not want to leave a trail of bank receipts. I'll get them to check Kiko's bank account as well. Now, if there is no more urgent business, can we relax and enjoy our lunch.'

'I thought you were in a hurry to get back to work?'

'I was, but that was before I heard your news.'

JD did not have much appetite; she was so sure that they had found the killer that she couldn't think about anything other than the case.

CHAPTER 23

Rosa had arranged to collect JD by the bullring, a two minute walk from her apartment.

'*Buenos tardes*, Federico, how nice to see you. Are you coming with us?' Rosa asked, stretching up on her toes so that the captain could give her a kiss.

'No, I'm afraid not, Rosa. Your daughter is keeping me very busy with this case.' He smiled at her. 'Well, I must be off. Have a successful afternoon.'

'Everything all right between you two?' she whispered as he walked away towards his parked car.

'Yes, why do you ask?' JD asked, increasingly irritated by her mother's constant curiosity about her love life. 'What time did you say we would be there? And where exactly are we meeting her?'

'I said we would be at her home before six o'clock. She has arranged to meet Leticia at the hospice at seven. The doctors don't think he will last the night.'

'Well, I hope he hangs on just a day or two more; I'm sure we know who killed his son.'

'Do you? Really? That would be wonderful if we could tell him. Give him the peace of mind that he craves.' She climbed into the car and asked, 'Is that why we are going to see Isabella?'

'In a way. I need to ask her some questions and I thought it would be easier if you were with me.' She didn't know whether to tell her mother about her suspicions in case she was wrong, so she said instead, 'I heard an interview she gave recently where she spoke about Kiko going into rehab; I want to ask her for more details.'

'I take it you want me to drive?' asked Rosa, pulling out into the traffic.

'Well, you're in the driving seat, so it would be easier if you did.'

'Very funny.'

When they arrived at Doña Isabella's home, a luxurious apartment in a large Gothic building in the centre of Seville, Rosa turned to her daughter and said, 'If there's something you are not telling me, you had better let me know, now. I don't want to lose all credibility with this family; they have been my friends for many years and I'd like it to stay that way.'

'All right, Mama. We think, in fact we're almost certain, that Jorge is behind Kiko's death. Why and how are still to be decided, but he is our main suspect.'

'That's ridiculous. Why would he want to hurt his brother-in-law?'

'A witness from your apartment block has identified him as the second para-motorist, and I intend to send his photograph to the other witnesses to see if they recognise him.'

'Even if he is, that doesn't mean he intended to hurt Kiko.'

'Maybe not, but he did intend to hurt Doña Isabella.' JD explained how the man who had mugged Kiko's sister, had been paid to do so by her husband.

'I don't understand. Why would he do that? His own wife?'

'I expect it was so that we would no longer think of them as suspects and more as victims. Anyway, it was a positive identification. Federico is going to put him in a police line-up so that there can be no doubt.'

'Does she know? Isabella, does she know?' Rosa was looking very distressed now.

'I don't know. I would expect so. They were taking him down to the police station today.'

'Do you think we should cancel our visit? I mean she will be very upset.'

'I expect she is, and, like you, I don't think she is involved in any of it, but we do need her help. I am convinced that Jorge has something to do with Kiko's death and I need to find out what it is.'

'I think you had better do all the talking, Jacaranda. I don't think I can face it.'

'That's okay, Mama. You just charm your way inside and then leave it to me.'

Doña Isabella's teenage daughter opened the door and smiled at Rosa. 'Mama isn't feeling well; she says she can't see anyone this afternoon.'

'I'm sorry to hear that, Araceli. Please tell her it's Rosa and I have to speak to her urgently. I wouldn't disturb her if it wasn't really important.' The girl hesitated, looking at JD suspiciously. 'This is my daughter,' Rosa explained. 'We're helping your grandfather find out what happened to uncle Kiko.'

'Wait a minute then. I'll speak to her.' She ushered them into a wide hallway and disappeared, only to return a few minutes later. 'It's okay. You can come in; she's in the lounge.' They followed her along the hallway and through some ornate double doors. 'Mama, it's Rosa and her daughter. They just want to help.'

Doña Isabella was lying on the sofa, looking very unlike her usual immaculate self; her hair was uncombed and her make-up was streaked with tear stains. A half-empty glass of sherry was on the rosewood table next to her. Rosa was instantly by her side, and took her hand in hers. 'My dear Isabella, what is the matter?'

Doña Isabella, slowly swung her legs down and sat up to face her. Automatically she ran her fingers through her hair, pulling the straggling strands back and into a knot behind her head. 'I'm really not in a good place to have visitors, Rosa. Please forgive me.'

'Nonsense. There's no need to apologise. Have the police been in touch?'

'About Jorge, you mean? No, but our solicitor telephoned me. He's with Jorge at the police station right now.' She pulled out a handkerchief and wiped her eyes. 'I don't know what to do, Rosa. I can't believe it's true. Why would Jorge do that to me? I could have been killed you know. Do you think that is what he wanted? To get rid of me?'

'No, I'm sure he didn't mean for you to be hurt,' said Rosa.

'I still can't move my left arm, you know. The doctor says it will take months for my shoulder blade to heal.'

'Mama, would you like me to ask María to make some tea?' Araceli asked.

'Yes please, *Cariño*. Unless you would like anything stronger,' she asked her guests. 'I'm going to have another glass of sherry.'

'Tea will be fine,' said JD. 'We won't stay too long, *Señora*, we just wanted to ask you a few questions about your brother. We are now sure that he was murdered, and before the police make an arrest we want to be certain that we have all the facts.'

'Murdered? My poor brother. He didn't deserve that. He was trying so hard to turn his life around.' She picked up her sherry glass and drank the remains. 'He used to be a bit wild when he was younger. Rebellious, if you can understand that. He had it all, he was the heir to a dukedom, never short of money, a good education. He should have been happy but he wasn't. We all loved him, but he could be hard work; he just would not conform to what Papa wanted.'

'But you say he had changed?'

'Yes. This last year he has been a different man. It began when Papa became ill; he decided then that he had to stop taking the drugs. It had started in a small way—all his friends took cocaine— but then he became dependant on it and was dabbling in other things as well. Papa spoke to him many times about the dangers; he even threatened he would find a way to cut him out of his will—of course that was not going to be easy —but it wasn't until Kiko finally realised just how ill Papa was that he decided to do something about his habit. Jorge helped him, you know.'

'Your husband helped Kiko to give up the drugs?' JD pretended to look surprised at this news.

'Yes, in a way. Jorge was once a very heavy smoker, you know; he had been all his life. Both his parents had died of lung cancer and when our family doctor warned him that he was developing the early signs of emphysema, Jorge decided it was time to stop. He heard about this clinic which had a reputation for curing addictions, so he went along and after six weeks he had given up smoking all together. I never thought it was possible; there were times when he had smoked forty cigarettes a day. Now he never touches a single one. He can't bear it if anyone else is smoking, either.'

'That sounds quite miraculous, but how did it help Kiko?'

'Well he took Kiko along to meet Doctor Delgado and he helped him to quit the drugs. It took longer than six weeks of course, but he was clean for quite a few months before his death. And he became an entirely different person.'

'I suppose being at the rehabilitation centre made the difference,' JD said.

'Yes, but Dr Delgado uses many different techniques, depending on the patient. Of course Kiko had to become an in-patient, so he could be monitored all the time. The patients go through a lot of physical therapy; Dr Delgado believes that a healthy body produces a healthy mind. And then there are the Mindful sessions and the hypnotherapy. He is very thorough and successful.'

'And it worked for Kiko?'

'Oh yes. Jorge seems to think my brother took his own life, but I refuse to believe that. If it had happened a year ago when he broke up with his fiancé, maybe I could accept it, but not now. He had everything to live for.'

'Did Kiko go back to the clinic afterwards? To see Dr Delgado about anything else?'

'No, not that I'm aware of. I'm sure Jorge would have mentioned it if he had.'

'Were Jorge and Kiko good friends?'

She hesitated. 'They were family. You know what families are like; there are always disputes but at the end of the day family is family.'

'Did they ever fight? Physically, I mean?'

'I don't think so. Jorge has a quick temper but I don't remember him ever getting violent.' She looked up as her maid came in carrying a tea tray. 'Thank you María. Just put it down on the table. We can help ourselves.'

'I'll see to it, Mama,' said Araceli, jumping up.

'Thank you, *Cariño*.' Doña Isabella placed her empty sherry glass on the tray and let her daughter refill it. 'But I can tell you that Kiko's attitude to life really annoyed Jorge, and more so since Papa has been ill. He refused to believe that my brother had changed and he was furious that it was Kiko who was going to inherit the family business, especially after all the hard work we had put into it.'

'I thought that the duke was going to leave the business to you?'

'Yes, that is what he suggested last year, but I'm not sure if it is specifically stated in his will. And of course we won't know that until he dies. So that made Jorge angry as well. We had tried talking to my father about it, but Papa didn't want to discuss it.'

'So you still don't know what will happen to the business when your father dies?'

'I suppose we don't, but I would imagine that now Kiko is dead it will go to me. After all we've been helping father to run it ever since he first became ill. Why would he leave it to anyone else?' She sipped some of the sherry and then added, 'Kiko was always his favourite, you know. No-one else in the family could get away with what he did. The drugs, the gambling and then humiliating the family with that wedding fiasco.' She sounded very bitter.

'Would you begrudge your brother the title, if he was still alive?' asked JD. She noticed her mother glaring at her.

'No, of course not. Why would you ask that? He was the eldest, that was all there was to it. Sadly he will not inherit the title now, and I will become the Duquesa de Roble when Papa dies, but it doesn't give me any great pleasure. I'm not sure I want all that responsibility, but it's not exactly a choice; I could never be the one to disrupt our family's lineage.'

'I think my mother needs to rest now,' said Araceli. 'Do you have any more questions for her?'

'Just one. Do you know where your husband was on the day Kiko died?'

'It was a Saturday, wasn't it? I expect he was doing what he always does on a Saturday, he would be para-gliding or some such sport. Is that all? My daughter is right, I really need to rest now.'

'Yes, I think we will leave it there,' said JD. 'Thank you for talking to us, Doña Isabella. I realise it has not been easy for you.'

'You don't think my husband had anything to do with Kiko's death, do you?' she asked, her eyes filling with tears again.

JD hesitated. Doña Isabella's father was dying, her brother had been murdered and her husband was charged with hiring someone to mug her. Was now the time to tell this woman what she really believed? No, even JD couldn't do that. 'I'm sure the police will have it all sorted out soon, and hopefully before your father passes away.'

'I do hope so. He so wants to know what happened to Kiko before he dies.'

Rosa and JD stood up, 'Thank you, Isabella. I hope you soon have some peace of mind. Do let me know if I can do anything to help,' said Rosa.

'Would you mind if I used your bathroom before we leave? It's a long journey back to Málaga,' asked JD.

'Of course not. It's just there, along the hall, next to the boot cupboard.'

'I won't be a minute.' JD knew exactly what she was looking for and she knew she had to be quick. She closed the door to the lounge behind her and hurried along the corridor. The door to the bathroom was ajar, so she opened the door next to it. Yes, it was the boot and shoe cupboard; all these big houses had them, a throw-back to the days when most of the gentry enjoyed hunting. She switched on the light and instantly saw them, a pair of lime green Air Jordan trainers tucked at the back of the cupboard. She took out her mobile phone and took a photograph. On their own they were not necessarily proof that Jorge was the mystery man, but along with the witness's identifications they did strengthen his link to the crime scene. Her mother's voice suddenly was louder and clearer; they were leaving the lounge. JD quickly closed the door to the boot cupboard and dived into the bathroom where she began to wash her hands.

'Ah there you are, Jacaranda,' her mother said. 'We really ought to get going; it's a long drive and I have an important engagement this evening.' She gave Doña Isabella a hug and said, 'I'm so sorry about Jorge, Isabella. To have this new worry on top of everything else, it must be very hard, but I'm sure they will sort it out.'

'I hope so. When Papa dies, I'd like you to come to his funeral, if you could,' Doña Isabella said, wiping her eyes. 'He would want you to be there.'

Rosa hugged her again and replied, 'Of course I'll be there. He is a dear friend, as was your mother.'

'I'll show you out,' said Araceli, opening the door for them.

Neither JD nor her mother spoke for a while; they sat in silence as Rosa navigated the crowded streets of Seville. At last, once they were on the motorway, Rosa asked, 'Did you find what you were looking for?' JD looked across at her mother in surprise. 'You didn't think I knew what you were up to, wanting to go to the bathroom before we left? You never use other people's bathrooms. Not even mine. So, tell me. What do you think? Is he our murderer?'

'I would think so. After all he had motive and I would say he had the means, but we need to speak to Doctor Delgado first; there are a couple of things I'd like to clarify with him,   and then I think we will hand it all over to the police.'

She felt her mobile vibrate in her pocket and took it out. 'Oh, that's good. Your neighbour, Margo has confirmed that Jorge was the man she saw with Kiko. She says she is absolutely sure it was him. She also mentioned he was wearing bright green trainers, most likely the ones I just saw at the back of their boot cupboard.'

'So, he was the last person to see Kiko alive, in that case.'

'It seems so.' JD could feel the excitement building up inside her again, although this time it was tempered by the sympathy she was feeling for Doña Isabella. How would she cope if her husband was charged with murdering his brother-in-law?

'You didn't ask her about her husband's gambling,' said Rosa, tooting her horn at a car which had just overtaken her on the inside. 'Bloody idiot.'

'You shouldn't just sit in the centre lane, Mama, not going at this speed.'

'Well?' asked Rosa, ignoring her daughter's comment.

'No I didn't ask her because I thought it was obvious that she didn't know and I didn't want to tell her anything else that would ruin her day. But I will ask Dr Delgado if he knows about it and if Jorge is seeking help.'

CHAPTER 24

Nacho had arranged for JD to see Dr Delgado at mid-morning. She sat at her computer flicking through the photographs of the Delgado Clinic which he had sent to her computer. 'It looks very expensive,' she said.

'It is. They charge €2,000 a week for a short stay, and slightly less for stays of more than a month.'

'Well it worked for Jorge. I suppose €12,000 was cheap for them.'

'And don't forget, it worked for Kiko too.'

'So why didn't he do something about the gambling as well?'

'You'll have to ask Dr Delgado. Maybe Kiko thought he could cure that addiction himself.'

JD continued to read through the Delgado Clinic's website. 'He has some impressive reviews. I am surprised that such well-known people would admit to going to a rehabilitation clinic.'

'Celebs like publicity, good or bad,' said Nacho.

'That sounds a very jaundiced view of the celebrity world.'

'Have you spoken to the *Capitán*?'

'Briefly, why?' She had in fact discussed the case with him as they lay in bed that morning, but she wasn't going to tell that to Nacho.

'Have they interviewed Jorge yet about Kiko's death, or is he still in Seville?'

'They are bringing him to Málaga this afternoon. I believe the police are going to search his home this morning. They are looking for the handbag.'

'Surely he will have got rid of it, by now.'

'Oh Nacho, how little you know about the fashion world.' Her assistant looked up from his computer, in surprise. 'It's not just a handbag, it's a Hermés Birkin handbag. They cost thousands, even the cheapest ones. Jorge will be keeping hold of it so that he can sell it at a later date and pay off some of his debts.'

'Have you given all the evidence to the *Capitán*?'

'I'm taking it over to him, after I've spoken to Dr Delgado. In the meantime, I'd like you to run through it and double-check that we have everything covered.'

'Will you be there for the interview?'

'I certainly hope so. Aristocracy or not, I want to see justice for Kiko. I don't want any last minute cover-ups just because he's the duke's son-in-law.'

'Good luck with that.'

'Did you speak to Linda?'

'Yes, she has arranged for her daughter to stay with Phil for a few hours, while she goes with you to see Dr Delgado.'

'Good, I'm not keen on psychiatrists. They always seem to be analysing you.'

Nacho laughed. 'Well watch out he doesn't hypnotise you as well.'

The door to the agency opened and Ricardo burst in. 'Good news,' he said, sitting down at JD's desk and depositing a tray of coffees.

'Coffee is always good news,' said Nacho, helping himself to the Capuccino.

'No, it's about the handbag. They found it. Jorge had hidden it at the back of his dressing room wardrobe.'

'He has his own dressing room,' said JD, jealously.

'So, he can't deny he was involved in the mugging; we have him for that at least,' said Ricardo.

'But we need more than that to get him convicted of Kiko's murder,' said JD. 'While we wait for Linda to arrive, let's take a look at what evidence we actually have that Jorge killed Kiko.'

'We now know he was there, paramotoring with Kiko when he died,' said Nacho.

'And he saw him in danger and did nothing to help him.'

'Nor came forward to tell the police that he was there.'

'Nacho.' She gave him a big smile.

'Okay, Boss.' He left his desk and began to write on the evidence board. There was plenty of room because JD had been busy deleting their previous ideas.

'We know he had been borrowing money from Kiko.'

'And he owed a lot of money to various loan sharks. Can you check that out Ricardo? Some names and addresses would help.'

'I'll see what I can do.'

'What else?'

'They had a fight, probably about money.'

'He didn't want Kiko to inherit the title and take over running the estate.'

'Yes, we do have motive, but it doesn't mean he killed him.'

'It doesn't seem a lot. All very circumstantial,' said Ricardo, staring at the evidence board. 'And it doesn't explain why Kiko agreed to go para-motoring in such a dangerous place.'

'Let's see if we can get anything else from Dr Delgado.' JD glanced at her watch. 'What time is our appointment?'

'Twelve o'clock.' As he replied, the door to the agency opened.

'Buenos días everyone. Sorry I'm a bit late. Are you ready, JD?' asked a rather flustered Linda.

'As I ever will be. Come on, let's see what our psychiatrist has to say about the deceased.'

The clinic was as lavish as it looked in the brochures. This was not a place for your everyday addict. She wondered, slightly nervously, what Dr Delgado would be like. In fact she didn't have to wait for long. A rather rotund figure in a white coat was waiting at reception to meet them.

'Señora Dunne?' he asked, looking straight at Linda.

'I'm Jacaranda Dunne,' JD said. 'I take it you are Dr Delgado?'

'Indeed. Delgado by name but not by nature,' he said with a smile. 'Would you like to come along to my office. Our receptionist will bring us some cold drinks. This summer seems to be even hotter than last year.' As they walked through the long corridors, where the walls were decorated with paintings of seascapes and mountain views—presumably to relax his patients—he continued to chat about the weather and how he was looking forward to his long overdue holiday. 'Here we are. Would you like to go in, Señora Dunne. Your companion can wait for you here.'

'I would prefer her to come with me,' said JD. 'You will understand when we get inside.'

The doctor looked annoyed at this, but opened the door and followed the two women inside. 'I prefer to speak to my patients on their own. The first interview is a very sensitive time for both the doctor and the patient.'

'I understand that, Dr Delgado, but you see I haven't been completely truthful with you. I am actually a private detective, and I'm working with the Guardia Civil. We are looking into the suspicious death of the Duque de Roble's son. I believe you treated him for drug addiction.'

The doctor's smiling face changed. 'I'm sure you know that I can't discuss any of my patients with you.'

'Yes, I know that. We just wanted a general chat about when you last saw him and how he was. Did he seem to be having any kind of relapse, for example?'

'Well, it's been some time since he left the clinic and he was completely clean of drugs then. I can assure you of that.'

'That is not in dispute. The toxicology report showed there was no sign of any drugs in his system at the time of his death.'

'I am relieved to hear it.'

'I wondered if you could describe to me the sort of treatment he underwent. You don't have to go into detail; I realise that would be unethical, just in general terms.'

'Well, if you have read our brochure you would see that we try to take a holistic approach to the patient's condition. You probably know that Kiko was a complicated young man, unsure about what he wanted out of life and burdened by his inheritance. The treatment consisted of many physical activities, yoga and meditation, as well as regular counselling with myself and some of my staff.'

'I believe I read something about hypnotism in your brochure,' she said. JD hadn't looked at the brochure yet, but she remembered Doña Isabella mentioning it in passing. The doctor crossed his arms and looked away from her, staring at something outside the window. 'Doctor?'

'Yes, well we do use it occasionally. Not all patients are susceptible to it. Some are most resistant.'

'And Kiko? Did you try it on him?'

'I did. I found he was actually very receptive to the treatment. It was the main reason he was able to give up the drugs so quickly; when I say quickly, he still required quite a few months of treatment in the clinic, but I am convinced that the hypnotism was a great help to him.'

'That is very interesting.'

'Why do you say that?'

She could swear the doctor looked frightened. 'Well drug addiction is a serious complaint. I find it surprising that a few sessions of hypnotism could cure it.'

'You misunderstand, Señora Dunne. I have already told you, it was a complementary treatment. I have never used hypnotism on its own, with any patient.'

'Did you use it with Kiko's brother-in-law, Jorge Domingo Montero?'

'I don't think I recall the name,' he lied.

'Of course you do. He was a patient here a couple of years ago. He came to quit smoking.'

'Oh, yes, I vaguely remember him. We have a lot of patients come through here, you know. It is not easy to remember all their names.'

'I am sure that you remember the husband of the Duque de Roble's daughter. What is it that's worrying you, Dr Delgado?'

'What is it that you want to know, *Señora*? Please come straight out and ask me.' The doctor heaved a huge sigh, and looked straight at her. 'I knew it was a mistake to trust him,' he said. 'I believed him when he said it was just so he could play a joke on him. I never imagined that he would do anything so dangerous. I really don't know what he was thinking about.'

'Who are you talking about? Jorge Domingo Montero?'

'Yes. He was a previous patient of mine and he came to see me a few weeks ago to tell me that Kiko was doing well as far as the drugs were concerned, but he had developed an addiction to gambling—this often happens, where one addiction replaces another one if the root cause is not tackled— and he wanted to help him. He said Kiko wanted to give up the gambling but he refused to go back into the clinic as a patient. He asked me to try hypnotism on him.'

'And you did?'

'Well, as I said, it had worked before for Kiko, so I thought I was helping him. I had no intention of harming him in any way, and Kiko himself was quite happy to give it a try. I must admit that I was impressed with how determined he was to stop gambling. He said something about that if he managed to do it, he was going to make amends to a girl whom he had hurt very badly. He didn't say how and I didn't ask.'

'So what exactly happened?' asked JD. She glanced at Linda who was busily writing down everything the doctor said.

'Nothing very special. We went through the usual procedure to put him into a trance and then identify the triggers that started the addiction. There could be many; in Kiko's case I think it was low self-esteem and the stress of being the duke's heir. Hypnotherapy helps to access the unconscious mind and find those triggers. The idea is then that I would work with Kiko to teach him how to manage them and break the negative patterns.'

'So, what went wrong?'

'Jorge insisted he stay and watch while I put Kiko into a hypnotic trance. The next time they came, he wanted to try to do it himself. I objected very strongly, but Kiko seemed to think it was all right for his brother-in-law to have a go. I don't think he thought he would be able to do it, but Jorge turned out to be a quite good hypnotist. He joked about it and said now he would be able to control the duke's son. I explained that it didn't work like that. It was only a tool to help the therapist access the patient's inner thoughts.'

'But he wasn't listening?'

'No. He didn't say anything else, but I was left with a very bad feeling about it.'

'So could you hypnotise a patient and make him do something he didn't want to do?'

'It depends on the patient. You can't hypnotise someone if they don't want to be hypnotised. If they agree, as Kiko always did, then it is not difficult to get them to do things under hypnosis that they might not usually do.'

'So, when you heard about Kiko's strange death, did you ever think it had anything to do with Jorge?'

The doctor now looked very uncomfortable. 'It did cross my mind.'

'So it could have been possible for Jorge to persuade Kiko to go up in the para-motor without doing all the usual safety checks?'

'Yes, it could be possible. But I can't say for sure.'

'And you didn't think to tell the police?' Now the psychiatrist began to look even more uncomfortable. 'Did he pay you to show him how to hypnotise Kiko?'

'Not exactly. He did say that he would make a substantial donation to the clinic.'

'And you believed him?' The psychiatrist made no answer. 'You do realise that Jorge was not just a liar but he had no money and owed thousands to various betting organisations. There was no substantial donation, then or ever. You were conned Dr Delgado.'

'I will probably lose my licence when this comes out. I should never have allowed Jorge to hypnotise Kiko in the first place, but I truly thought he was just trying to help him stop gambling. And Kiko was quite happy to go along with it. I mean it wasn't the first time he'd brought his brother-in-law to me for help.'

'But, sadly, it was the last, Dr Delgado.'

'What will happen now? he asked.

'I will tell the Guardia Civil what you have told me and I expect they will want to speak to you. I should let your lawyer know, if I were you.' JD stood up. There was nothing else to say. This was more evidence but was it enough to prove he deliberately killed his brother-in-law. Well, now it was down to Federico to get a confession out of Jorge. She couldn't see what else they could do.

CHAPTER 25

Nacho had gathered all their evidence together, ready to hand over to the captain. 'Are you sure you haven't missed anything?' JD asked. 'I don't want them to have any excuse to throw it out.'

'The *capitán* wouldn't let them do that, Boss,' Nacho replied. 'Don't worry, it's all there. Ricardo and I have been through it together.'

'What about Linda?'

'Yes, Linda as well. I assure you, Boss, we haven't missed anything.'

'The captain might not throw it out, but his superior might. They are very sensitive about upsetting a member of the aristocracy, never mind accusing one of them of murder. What about Kiko's bank accounts? Was there anything there?'

'Yes, there were two deposits made into Jorge's bank account, each for two thousand euros. They were in May but nothing since then, although in July, Kiko withdrew quite a few large sums of money. And I mean large. Five thousand one time and seven thousand the next time. I think that's probably when Jorge decided he wanted to be paid in cash.'

'He'll have the best lawyer in Spain, you know that.'

'What's the matter, Boss? I've never seen you so agitated about a case before?'

JD sat down and placed the folder on the desk in front of her. 'I don't know, Nacho. You're right, there's nothing to worry about; we've gone through it all thoroughly. Is Linda coming in today?'

'Yes, she'll be in later this morning. You could wait until she gets here and get her opinion, if it makes you feel better, but she'll say the same as me. We can't do any more. We have motive, means and opportunity. It's up to the Guardia now to charge Jorge with the murder of his brother-in-law.'

'You're right. Okay I'll take it over to him myself.'

'Does he know you're coming?'

'Sort of.' She saw Nacho lift one eyebrow. 'Okay I told him last night that we had solved the case. I felt more confident then.' She had been euphoric last night when she went through what they had discovered with Federico. So why did she feel so apprehensive now? 'What will you be doing?'

'I thought I'd pick up one of our outstanding cases that have been sitting on your desk since we heard about Kiko's death. The one about the boundary dispute is on the top of the pile.'

'You could give yourself a day off, you know,' she said. 'You deserve it.'

'No, I want to be around when the *capitán* opens the champagne. Then I might have a couple of days off and learn to paraglide properly.' He picked up his phone. 'It's Linda. Hi, what's up? You sound very excited. Okay, I'll put you on speaker.' He placed his mobile phone on the desk in front of JD.

'JD, are you there?' Linda's voice was unusually high-pitched.

'Yes, Linda. What's happened?' She hoped that Phil hadn't taken a turn for the worst.

'You know I've been trying to get in touch with Rachel, the English tourist?'

'Yes, why? Have you succeeded at last? It's a bit late we don't need her testimony any more. The other two witnesses have identified him.'

'No, it's not to do with our mystery man. Listen to this.
Rachel remembered something about the day that Kiko died. It didn't come back to her until she was on her way home and then the battery in her phone stopped working; it had been giving her trouble for some time. Anyway she took it to her local mobile phone shop and has only just got it back. That's why she wasn't able to ring me until today.'

'Okay, so what new evidence does she have?'

'She reckons that Kiko was wearing a body-cam.'

'What? A body-camera? Is she sure?'

'Yes. She says she only realised it when she saw that the policeman on duty in the airport had one.'

'If that's true then it's incredible news. But where is it now?'

That's the problem, nobody has reported finding one, have they?'

'Nacho, get on to Ricardo. Tell him we need to locate it, and quickly. Maybe SEMAR found it. Linda, did Rachel say when she saw the body-cam? Where was Kiko when she noticed it?'

'Yes, she did. It was just before he was blown over the harbour wall. It could be anywhere by now, and even if we find it, would it still be working?'

'We can worry about that later. First we need to locate it. Okay, let's go back over the scene again and this time let's look at everyone who could possibly have come in contact with Kiko or was at the scene of his death.'

'Are you going to speak to the captain?' asked Linda.

'Yes, we have no choice, we need all the help we can get if we are to find it.' At last, now they might have actual noncontroversial evidence that Jorge was responsible for Kiko's death.

When Ricardo and the captain were on their way to the interview room Federico was surprised to see his superior officer just leaving his office. '*Comandante*? Did you want something?'

'Capitán Rodriguez. Yes. A word, if you don't mind.'

'Of course, *Comandante*.' He turned to Ricardo. 'Don't go in yet. I'll just be a moment.' He followed his boss into his office and shut the door. 'What is it, *Comandante*? You realise we are just about to interview our main suspect about the suspicious death of the duke's son.'

'Yes, I do and that's why I wanted to make sure everything was in order.'

'I don't understand, *Comandante*. Why wouldn't it be?'

'Well, I heard that woman was involved in the investigation, again. I hope she has got her facts right.'

'The private investigator, you mean. I have been through her evidence and I can assure you it is watertight.' That was not strictly true but he was not going to admit it to the *comandante*. He knew JD would never have handed the case over to the police unless she was satisfied that she had done all she could. 'My *cabo* can vouch for that; he has been working closely with her and her team.'

'Ah yes. Her team. Does she still use that young hacker, Ignacio something?'

'Yes she does and he is no longer a hacker, I can assure you of that.'

'Very well, if you are certain you have enough to convict this man, you had better get on with it. Although I ought to remind you that this is very embarrassing for the force, having to arrest the duke's son-in-law.'

'May I remind you, *Comandante*, that the accused not only murdered his brother-in-law, the previous heir to the dukedom, but he also arranged for a physical attack on his wife, the new heir to the dukedom. It was sheer luck that she was not killed as well, then he would be facing a double murder charge.'

'Just go carefully, is all I'm saying,' the *comandante* replied, scowling at the *capitán's* impertinence.

'With your permission, *Señor*, I would like to get prepared for this interview.' Federico sat down at his desk and opened the report. He heard the *comandante* close the door as he left but didn't look up. What the hell had that been about? Was it a warning from his superior? Or from someone higher up? Surely he wasn't trying to influence the outcome of the interview. There were people who believed that some of the senior officers in the Guardia Civil were a bit too cosy with members of the aristocracy, but as far as he was concerned, it was all rumour. And he never allowed rumours to influence his work. True police work relied on verifiable facts.

JD dialled Federico's number. It rang a couple of times then went silent. Damn it, every minute was important now. They had no idea where the camera was or if it still existed, but any delay made it more unlikely they would find it. 'He's still not answering.'

'I'll ring Ricardo. We need them to go over all Kiko's possessions again and double check,' said Nacho.

'And get him to question Juan Felipe. He might know if Kiko wore a body-cam,' added Linda. 'I'm on my way over now.'

JD began cleaning the evidence board and listing the people that could possibly have come across the camera, while Nacho telephoned Ricardo. 'Thank goodness, Ricardo. The boss is getting pretty agitated. I'll pass you over to her.'

'JD, what's the matter? Are you worried about something?'

'Ricardo, at last. Yes I am, in a way. Listen carefully. We have a witness who says she saw Kiko wearing a body-cam on the day of his death. Can you get on to the forensic department and ask if they found anything. I would think that they would have told us if they had, but maybe it got overlooked.' She doubted that very much as María was very methodical in her work, but they had to try everything.

'Okay. Anything else?'

'If you are able to question Juan Felipe, ask him if Kiko was in the habit of wearing a body-cam. And as soon as you can, please, Ricardo. This could be the final piece in the puzzle.'

'Have you spoken to the capitán?'

'He's not answering his phone.'

'He was in a meeting with the comandante.'

'Oh, is that good news or bad?'

'Your guess is as good as mine, JD. But don't worry. I'll get on with it.'

'Okay. One more thing. Tell the captain that I have sent him the report. I was planning on bringing it over in person but I need to get on with this now.'

'Okay, JD, don't worry. He is reading it now.'

'Thanks.' She ended the call and handed the phone back to Nacho. Almost immediately it rang again, and Nacho began to speak to someone. 'Well?' she asked as soon as he finished.

'That was Marco, the president of the paragliding club. He said that a lot of them wear body cams. They get some wonderful videos from them. He didn't see Kiko that morning so he can't say if he was wearing one but he often did. He added that we should be looking for a very small, waterproof camera which Kiko usually attached to his glasses. A lot of the guys have the same model because it's economical and reliable.'

'And a microchip, I suppose?'

'Yes, Boss. Of course.'

'So if we can find the microchip, you can make it work, can't you?'

Nacho shrugged his shoulders. 'Well it depends how badly it's damaged, but yes, I expect so, Boss. But first we need to find it.'

'Okay, so who do we know for certain was at the harbour that morning?' She looked at the list Nacho had scribbled on the board. 'SEMAR. Okay you contact them. Rachel we can cross off the list. Who else? Where are the witness statements?'

'There's no mention of a body-cam in any of them, JD.' He handed her the file.

'I realise that, but let's work out who else was at the scene.' She picked up Rachel's statement first. 'Now she says that a small group of people had gathered at the harbour wall. I wonder if the police took any details of their names. If so, then we can question them about the camera.'

'What about that restaurant? The one where the foreigner was having lunch with his wife. The staff might have seen something.'

'Apparently not. They were very busy at the time. But maybe the foreigner knows something about it. Do we have a contact number for him?'

'Yes, I think so. Here it is. His name is Henry Wood. He gave a statement to the police at the time.'

'Why didn't he come forward to identify the second para-motorist?'

'Because he didn't notice him until he had flown past. He told SEMAR it was impossible to identify him by the time he arrived at the scene because he was already flying away and into the midday sun, so all he saw was a black silhouette.'

'Okay, well let's start with him. Unless he too has gone back to the UK.'

'No, it says here that he is a foreign resident. I'll ring him now.'

'Ask him to come in and see us. If he did find the camera, I want him to understand that he's not in any trouble. We just need to see it.'

'Okay Boss, I'll get on to it next.'

'Everything all right, *Capitán*?' whispered Ricardo, as he rejoined the captain in his office.

'As right as rain, *Cabo*.' He closed the folder he had been studying.

'I've just had a call from JD. I think you need to hear this before we speak to Jorge.' He proceeded to tell his captain about the missing body-cam.

'Well that might change everything. If we can find it, that is, although the chances of that are very slim. It's probably somewhere at the bottom of the harbour by now.'

'So what do we do?'

'Send Jorge back to his cell for now. You can tell his lawyer that some new evidence has come to light and we need time to verify it before we can share it with him.'

'But we haven't found it yet.'

'I know that, but he doesn't. Just do as I say, then go and give Jacaranda all the help she needs.'

CHAPTER 26

They were all huddled in the meeting room, Linda, Nacho, Ricardo and JD. 'Any luck, Linda?' asked JD.

'Yes, sort of. 'I've spoken to Henry's wife, at last. She says he's playing in a golf competition and he always has his phone turned off while he's playing, so we can't contact him until he finishes.'

'Which is when?'

'About three o'clock. She expects him home about four-thirty.'

'What? We can't wait until then. Ricardo you will have to drive over to the golf club and speak to him in person.'

'But, we can't do that, JD. We can't drag a man off the golf course for no good reason.'

'Of course we can and we have a very good reason. The sooner we find out what happened to the camera and know if it is still working, the sooner we will know if we have some new evidence to convict Jorge.'

'I'm not happy about it, JD. The capitán was not pleased when I searched Bob Free's storehouse without a warrant.'

'This is different. We just want to speak to the man. *Dios mio.*' The lance corporal continued to look doubtful. She understood why he was so reluctant. Many of the senior members of the Guardia Civil played golf and if Henry Wood was playing in a competition with one of them, word would get back to Federico. 'All right, I'll come with you, Ricardo. I'll speak to him and you just stand in the background and look menacing.'

'It's not a joke, JD.'

'All right. I'm sorry. But either I go on my own, or you come with me. Your choice.'

'I'll go with you.'

'I'll continue to check out the people who were by the harbour when Kiko crashed. I've had no luck so far, but there are still a few more to contact,' said Nacho.

'What about me, JD? What do you want me to do?' asked Linda.

'Perhaps you could give Nacho a hand checking that list of people at the harbour.'

Fortunately the golf club where Henry Wood was playing that morning was in Málaga so it did not take Ricardo and JD very long to get there. They drove up the drive to the impressive white *cortija* that served as the club house and parked outside. Instantly a man put his head out of the door and shouted, 'You can't park here. It's private. Can't you read.' Almost immediately he realised it was a police car and when he saw Ricardo getting out, wearing the uniform of a Guardia Civil officer, his tone changed and he said, 'My apologies, officer. People are always parking here, even though it clearly says No Parking. What can I do for you?'

'Do you know a member called Henry Wood?' JD asked. 'Which hole is he on, now?'

'Henry. I don't know.' He looked flabbergasted. 'Why has he done something wrong?'

'What time did he tee off? Surely you can tell me that?'

'Yes, of course, although they were all a bit late teeing off today.' He ducked back into the pro-shop and went to check the computer. 'Ah, here he is. Well, he wasn't one of the early ones; he teed off at 10.30.'

JD looked at her watch. It was now almost twelve o'clock so he would have played about six holes. 'So he's on the 7th tee?'

'Probably. I haven't seen them come through here yet, so they are still playing the first half. You won't have to wait long for them. Or I can get him to phone you.'

'Wait? We don't have time to hang about. Give me the keys to a buggy and we'll go out and speak to him ourselves.'

The man looked from JD to Ricardo and back again. 'I'm sorry, you can't do that. They are playing a competition. It's the *Copa del Año*. A very important competition.'

'I know what it is, but we can't wait for them to finish. This is urgent.'

'Yes, we won't be long. We just need to ask Mr Wood something and then we will be gone,' said Ricardo. He was looking very uncomfortable with the situation.

Reluctantly the man handed them the keys to one of the electric buggies. 'Do you want me to come with you to show you the way?' he asked.

'No, I know the way,' JD replied. She had played on that course on many occasions.

'Yes, I thought your face was familiar. It's JD, isn't it?'

She smiled at him. 'That's right. Look don't worry. The *cabo* is right; we will be gone before you know it.'

He did not look convinced and watched them as they drove away in the direction of the seventh teeing-off ground.

'I have a horrid feeling that we are going to regret this little adventure, JD. If the capitán gets to hear of it, I can kiss goodbye to any promotion, and I have the feeling that his boss would love an excuse to get rid of you, as well.'

'We'll worry about that later. Look there they are.' There were four men on the putting green, so she stopped the buggy by the next tee and waited until they had finished putting and were walking towards them.

'*Dios mio*. I recognise two of them,' said Ricardo in a whisper. 'I knew this was a mistake.'

'Just leave it to me.' She walked towards them. 'Excuse me gentlemen, I just need a quick word with Señor Wood. I'm sorry to interrupt your game but this is urgent police business. It won't take long.' It was obvious which of the men was Henry, with his pale northern skin and his hair the colour of ripe corn.

'Is this to do with the death of the young man the other day?' he asked, following her back towards the buggy.

'Yes, in a way. I believe you saw what happened to him?'

'I did, but I told all that to the police at the time. I didn't see much, you know. I was having lunch in a nearby restaurant.'

'We know all that. What I want to know was if you picked up anything from the ground? Did you find anything?'

Henry Wood hesitated. 'Nothing of any value.'

'So there was something?'

'It was broken. It had nothing to do with the dead man, if that's what you're thinking.'

'What did you find?'

'It was an old micro camera. Broken. It didn't work.'

'So why did you pick it up?'

'For my son. Toby loves playing at spies and I thought he'd like to play with it. It was one of those body-cams, like the police wear, but smaller. I thought he'd be pleased.'

JD turned and beamed at Ricardo. 'So, Mr Wood, does he still have it?'

'No, I don't think so. He said it wasn't worth having as it was broken; he wants me to buy him a new one. That's kids for you these days. They have to have the best. I would have been delighted to play with it when I was his age.'

'So where is it now?' asked JD.

'Probably in his bedroom. I'll look for it when I get home, if you want me to. I don't think it will be any use to you. It was pretty damaged.'

'No, that's okay. We'll ring your wife and see if she can find it. Sorry to have disturbed your game.' JD smiled at the other three men, whose expressions wavered between annoyance at having their game interrupted and curiosity about the reason for it. She climbed back into the buggy and whispered to Ricardo, 'There, that wasn't so bad, was it?'

'So, now we go and see the wife. This is turning into a wild goose chase, JD.'

'You drive and I'll ring Mrs Wood.' As he headed down the cart track back towards the club house, JD dialled the number that Nacho had sent to her phone. It rang and rang, but there was no answer. She was about to hang up when a breathless voice asked, 'Can I help you?'

'Mrs Wood? It's Jacaranda Dunne from the detective agency. We have spoken to your husband and he thinks you can help us.'

'Me?'

'Yes, if you don't mind.' JD proceeded to explain to the bewildered woman what they were looking for.

'Oh, I remember that old camera. Henry was a bit disappointed that Carl didn't like it, but I can understand why, it was in a dreadful state. Kids don't want cast-offs these days. Anyway I've promised to buy him one for his birthday.'

'Do you think he might still have it or would it have been thrown away?'

'I think it'll be kicking around somewhere. Whatever goes into Carl's bedroom tends to stay there until I get round to having a spring clean. What shall I do with it if I find it?'

'We're already in the area, so we will come round and collect it, if that's okay with you?'

'That's fine. Shall we say, fifteen minutes?'

When they arrived back at the agency they were greeted with two expectant faces. 'Well?' asked Linda. 'Have you found it?'

JD tried to keep a straight face, but it was impossible. 'Yes, we have. All we need now is for Nacho to work his magic on it.' She took the broken body-cam from her pocket and put it on the desk.

'*Dios mio*, that looks a mess,' said Nacho.

'And so tiny,' said Linda.

'But you can get into it?'

'I'll try but it depends if there's any water damage to the microchip. Well we'll soon find out.'

'Do you need me for anything else, JD? Otherwise I'll get back to work,' Ricardo asked.

'Nacho, do you need any help from Ricardo?'

'Not at the moment. If it's beyond my capabilities I'll ring you and maybe you can get one of your tech guys to take a look.'

'Better still, why don't you bring it back to the police station now and use our equipment; we have a much better set up.'

Nacho looked across at JD. 'What do you think?'

'He's right. The last thing we want is to spoil it for lack of the right equipment. I'm sure you would do a great job, Nacho, but as they say two heads are better than one. Just let me know as soon as you have something.'

'Of course. We're all desperate to know what actually happened that Saturday.'

CHAPTER 27

Nacho never entered the Guardia Civil building without a feeling of trepidation. He had kept on the right side of the law, more or less, for many years but he never felt completely at ease when he was within these walls. He knows he was very fortunate that the capitán had taken pity on him and pleaded his case. He often wondered what he would be doing now, if he had been sent to jail over hacking into the police computer base. Best not to dwell on it.

'Ah, Nacho. How are you?' asked Federico, greeting him with a customary hug. 'I hear you have something very special to show me.'

'Yes, it's not in great condition, but it's clear enough to stand up in court as evidence.'

'That's all that matters. Has Jacaranda seen it yet?'

'No, she and Linda are on their way over. In fact, there's something I want to tell you before they arrive.'

'Okay, what's bothering you?'

'It's about JD. You remember Antonio's bar, well it's a pop-up coffee shop now.'

'Yes, JD told me. So?'

'Apparently the barman there has been asking personal questions about JD. Where does she live, is she married, those sorts of things.'

'Have you said anything to her?'

'No, I wanted to speak to you, first. She sounded really upset when I told her that I'd found Steed's name listed as the owner. I didn't want to give her more to worry about.'

'I'll look into it. Thanks for telling me about it.'

'Oh, I think that might be them now.' The sound of clattering feet could be heard in the corridor. 'We're in here, Boss,' Nacho called.

The door opened and JD and Linda bundled into the room. 'Well done, Nacho. I can't wait to see what it has to tell us. Have you watched it all?'

'Yes, from the beginning but we can fast forward over some of it. It appears to be working fine, just a loss of sound in some places.' He could see how excited everyone was and prayed that he had managed to recover the whole film. He signalled for Ricardo to put the blinds down and switched on the computer. 'It's quite long, because Kiko had obviously used it on other occasions. Do you want us to go straight to Saturday or start at the beginning?'

'Start at the beginning. There could be something useful that explains why Kiko allowed himself to go along with it.' He switched the projector on, and it was as though they were flying with Kiko, seeing the world through his eyes. 'This was filmed earlier in the week. Jorge is not with Kiko at the moment. You can see that Kiko is perfectly able to fly the para-motor on his own. Proof that he was no novice.' They continued to watch for a while then Nacho said, 'I'm going to move it on to the Saturday when he died. This is the important part, where he is being prepared by Jorge. Look who is there.' The picture moved around the screen rather erratically, as though Kiko was unsteady on his feet. Then at one point the image became totally obscured as though the camera was blocked by someone's back.

'Who is it?' asked JD. 'That's not Jorge. *Dios mio*, what is she doing there?'

'I can't believe it; she knew what her husband was doing all the time. The two-faced bitch,' said Linda. 'How could she turn on her own brother.'

'So, they were in on it together,' said Federico. 'I hope you have got watertight proof that she was involved; accusing the duke's son-in-law is one thing, but his own daughter, that is a whole new ball game.'

'Don't worry Capitán, she soon incriminates herself.' They continued to watch as Jorge attempted to hypnotise Kiko. Nacho was convinced that he could feel the tension in the room rising. 'Listen to this.'

'Are you sure he'll do what you tell him?' asked Doña Isabella.

'Yes, he's very easy to put under,' Jorge replied. 'He thinks it's just another session to check his response before we can tackle the gambling.'

'Why are we wasting time like this? You've been working on him for weeks now. You do realise my father could die any day. We don't have time to wait.'

'It's not a waste of time. You want it to work don't you? He has to trust me for it to work. It's as simple as that. Anyway, this is the last attempt. This time I've planted the idea in his mind that he's going to fly out to a deserted island and land on the beach, but in reality he will be flying over the port. No more simple tasks like before.'

'And he has agreed?'

'Don't worry. He's quite relaxed about it.'

'But what if it doesn't work? What if he doesn't get into trouble and lands successfully? What then?' asked Doña Isabella.

'Nothing. We try again another time. He knows it takes time that's why he has agreed to be hypnotised by me more than once, I'm sure he'll agree to it again. He's so obsessed with stopping gambling, he's happy to try anything. The poor idiot is convinced that if he stops gambling that Italian bird will go running back to him.' He picked up Kiko's safety vest.

'You're not going to put that on him, are you?'

'But it will look suspicious if he isn't wearing it.'

'Rubbish. Nobody will even notice. All they'll see is someone who got caught up in his parachute and drowned.'

'All right, if you say so. Let's remove his knife as well. I'm not sure what will happen when he gets into trouble; he may come out of the trance and cut himself free.'

'You said it was foolproof. You said, by the time he came round it would be too late. Now you're telling me he could cut himself free?' Doña Isabella sounded very annoyed.

'Only if he has his knife.' He slipped the hook knife into his pocket.

'What about his glasses. Remove his glasses,' Doña Isabella told her husband.

'No, now that would look suspicious. Kiko can't see a thing without his glasses. You stop worrying about what he is wearing and just make sure he follows me off the cliff. Okay?' Jorge sounded irritated with his wife. He turned to Kiko. *'Okay old mate, are you ready to fly?'*

They couldn't see Kiko's face but there was a mumbled response. 'What did he say?' asked JD.

'I think he just repeated what Jorge had said, "ready to fly." That's probably the key phrase to activate him. And now we lose the sound for a while but the images continue.'

'Oh my God, he just jumped straight off the cliff,' said Linda, covering her eyes with her hands.

'It's okay, he is flying normally and following Jorge.'

'That's interesting. So if Jorge hadn't led him towards the port then he probably wouldn't have crashed,' said the captain. 'A clear indication of intent.'

'We'll never know. but it is quite clear that Jorge is controlling him and leading the way to the port. What a bastard he is.'

'I wish we could see Kiko,' said Linda.'Where's the body-cam positioned?'

'One like this is designed to be difficult to detect, and apparently he usually wears it on his spectacles.'

'Do you think Kiko had his suspicions about Jorge? Is that why he wore his body-cam that day?'

'We'll never know. All we know is that it was not unusual for him to film his flights and maybe he was just more comfortable with wearing it like that. After all, putting it on his spectacles gives him images of what he is actually seeing.'

'It's ironic but, if Jorge had removed Kiko's specs like his wife wanted, then we wouldn't have this film,' said Linda. 'We wouldn't have seen anything.'

'But why didn't they notice the camera on his glasses?' asked Nacho. 'If Rachel noticed it then why didn't they when they were prepping them?'

'Who knows. It could have just been the angle of the sun shining on the tiny lens that attracted Rachel's attention,' said the captain. 'Whatever the reason, I'm glad she saw it.'

'So what was Doña Isabella doing there? Didn't she trust her husband to go through with it on his own?'

'It sounds as though his wife stayed behind to make sure that Kiko followed Jorge off the cliff. Remember Jorge had to lead the way and there was nobody else he could ask to help him.'

'So they were leaving nothing to chance.'

'How come we didn't know that she was in Málaga that day? Did anyone check her alibi?' asked the captain.

'I don't think we even asked for one,' said JD. '*Dios mio, how could we have been so blind?*'

'Ricardo, get in touch with Capitán Montero in Seville and ask him to arrest Doña Isabella, at once. If he has a problem with that then to ring me and I will explain. Tell him I will go over to collect her this afternoon.'

'Okay Capitán.' The lance corporal reluctantly left the viewing room as the others continued to watch the uneventful filming of the coastline.

'They are gaining altitude,' said Federico. 'Why is that?'

'Jorge probably doesn't want anyone to recognise them. Look they're over the sea now and heading west.' It was hard not to become mesmerised by the scenery, the intense blue of the sky and the shimmering Mediterranean below. Nacho had to remind himself that this was a man deliberately leading his brother-in-law into a situation from which he would not escape alive. The calculated callousness of his actions made him shiver. 'I hope they send him away for a long time,' he muttered.

'Thanks to this footage, I'm sure they will,' said Federico. 'You've done very well, all of you.'

'I recognise that beach. They must be getting near to the port now,' said JD.

'Yes, they are dropping lower and lower.'

'Not Jorge. He's maintaining his height. Wait. Did he say something?'

'Damn, I think the sound has gone,' said Nacho. He fiddled with the controls to bring up the sound but all they got was a loud crackling. Then suddenly they heard Jorge's voice. '*You've arrived at the island, Kiko. It's safe to land. Safe to land.*'

'That has to be the signal for him to land. Look how he responds immediately,' says Nacho.

The images they were watching began dancing around the screen now. Kiko was being buffeted by the wind and was losing height rapidly. They had lost the image of Jorge and now all they could see were shots of the beach and people running wildly around, trying to avoid the out-of-control para-motor. 'There's Rachel,' cried Linda. 'She was so close to him.' The sound level was blanketed by the buffeting wind and flapping parachute, but then one heartbreaking cry reached their ears, *'Jorge, help me. Help me. Jorge.'*

'Oh, *Dios mio.* Kiko has come out of the trance. He knows he's in danger,' said JD.

One final image came on the screen as the wind tried to lift Kiko over the harbour wall. They saw Jorge in the sky above him, coldly watching the demise of his brother-in-law and so-called friend before turning away and flying on. Then the camera was spinning across the ground, displaying chaotic images of dozens of running feet, before finally going dead.

At first nobody spoke. They were all too stunned by what they had witnessed. At last Linda broke the silence, 'What happened there?' she asked. 'At the end?'

'I don't know. Do you think Kiko threw the camera into the crowd, hoping someone would find it?'

'It's possible. That cry for help makes me think that he eventually realised what Jorge was up to. Maybe he hoped someone would give it to the police,' said JD. 'This must be one of the most tragic cases we've ever had. Well, at least you have enough evidence now to convince the *comandante*, don't you?' She looked straight at Federico.

'Most certainly. You and your team have done an excellent job. Now it's up to us to make sure that they don't wriggle out of it.'

They all stared at him. 'Surely there's no way they can deny what happened now?'

'You have to understand that we are dealing with two very powerful people, but I promise you that I won't relax until they are both in prison. I am convinced that with this film as evidence we have more than enough to convict them.'

'We need to find that hook knife,' said Ricardo. 'I bet Jorge still has it.'

'I'll arrange a warrant for you to search his home,' said the captain.

JD stood up, 'Okay in that case we will leave you to speak to the prosecutor and we'll get back to work.' As soon as she was outside, she telephoned Tim.

'JD, this is an unexpected pleasure. Do you have any news for me?'

'Not at the moment, Tim but I hope to have a juicy scoop for you in the next twenty-four hours.'

'So what do you want?'

'When you told me the duchess was seen hanging about the offices of the Voz de Málaga, which led you to believe she had asked the editor not to print any details of Kiko's death, whom exactly did you mean?'

'The duchess of course, Doña Isabella.'

'You weren't referring to the real Duquesa de Roble, Leticia, the duke's wife, the current duchess, in fact?'

'Oh God, I'm always doing that. These fancy titles tie me in knots. I was referring to the sister of the dead man, Doña Isabella. Sorry if I sent you down the wrong track, JD.' He chuckled.

Had he deliberately misinformed her? She wouldn't put it past him. 'Okay, Tim, let's get this clear. It was Doña Isabella who spoke to the editor and persuaded him not to publish details about Kiko's death?'

'Yes. Why is that important? Is the sister involved in his death somehow?'

'When I know, so will you,' said JD, and hung up abruptly. She vowed not to give him any more details about the investigation. If he had told her before that it was Doña Isabella he had seen then they might have looked at Kiko's sister a little more closely earlier in the investigation instead of seeing her as a tragic sibling grieving for her brother.

'What's up JD?' asked Linda, 'You look pissed off with someone.'

'I am. To be specific, with Tim. I've found out why there was nothing in the local papers about Kiko's death,' she replied. 'Because Doña Isabella told them not to report it. She didn't want any publicity about what they had done. Tim lied to me.'

'So that's him off your Christmas list,' said Linda. 'Well it's his loss. I can't think he's ever been much good as a source of information, anyway. Look on the bright side; this is just another piece of the puzzle in place.'

'That's probably why she wanted the body released early, so she could get the funeral over,' added Nacho.

'You're right, guys. Okay let's go back to the office and see if there are any more loose ends to tie off.'

CHAPTER 28

The interview followed the usual pattern, a protestation of innocence followed by a plea for a reduction of the charge to manslaughter as, according to Jorge's lawyer there had been no intent to kill the deceased. It had been a simple prank which went wrong.

'Very well, indulge me Jorge. How did this prank work out? You are an experienced para-motorist, you know the rules about flying over water, yet you allowed Kiko to break all of them. What was the intention of this prank, if that is truly what it was? When would Kiko wake up from the trance? What did you expect him to do when he did wake up? Do you expect me to believe that you led him into a very dangerous situation, paramotoring over the sea with no life vest and a forty-kilo motor strapped to his back, and thought it would end well? You knew it was a tremendous risk even for someone who was wide awake.'

'I'm sorry. I was just having a joke. I never thought he'd get caught up in the parachute,' said Jorge, giving a sideways glance at his lawyer.

'Okay. Now, I want you to talk me through what you actually did.'

'What do you mean?'

'How did you hypnotise him? We know that Dr Delgado had allowed you to do it before, but that was in the safety of the clinic and under the doctor's supervision. What did you say to Kiko that made him fly over the harbour?'

'I…' He turned to his lawyer, who nodded in agreement. 'Once he was in a hypnotic trance I told him that we were going to fly out to an island and land on the beach. I thought it would be funny when he realised that he was in the port, near the cruise ships. It would give him a fright.'

'Well it did more than that. So you intended to go with him?'

'Yes.'

'When you saw he was in trouble why didn't you stop and help him? It was a prank after all. Why leave your friend to drown when you could have landed and helped him to get free?'

Jorge turned helplessly to his lawyer, who responded by stating, 'My client has no more to say on this matter. I suggest you either charge him or let him go.'

'Very boldly said. Well, you will be pleased to know that I will do exactly what you suggest.' He looked straight at Jorge. 'Jorge Domingo Montero, I am charging you with the murder of your brother-in-law, Gabriel Francisco Mendoza de Goya Pérez and the attempted murder of your wife, the Duquesa de Roble.'

'But, I'm innocent,' he protested. 'I told you; it was a joke that went wrong. I wouldn't kill anyone.'

The lawyer stood up and said, 'You are making a big mistake, Capitán Rodriguez. My client is not a murderer. It was an ill-thought prank that resulted in the death of his friend and brother-in-law. There is no way that the charge will stand up in court without more concrete evidence.'

'Well, in that case I'm pleased to tell you that we can now provide that evidence. I apologise for not showing this to you sooner Señor Campos, but this piece of evidence has only just come to light. I think if you check your emails now, you will see that there is a new file for you to examine. I will leave you and your client to study it at your leisure. Afterwards you might like to consider getting your client to change his plea, and you may want to take on another client as well, as I'm sure Jorge's wife is going to be in need of your help. And may I add, Señor Campos that if this is what Señor Domingo considers a friendly prank, then I am glad that I don't have friends like him.' Federico stood up and continued, 'Good day to you, both.'

It was another week before Federico went to the agency to give them an update on the case against Jorge.

'*Buenos días, Capitán,*' said Nacho. 'Good news I hope?'

'I wanted to tell you all in person, that despite the best efforts of Jorge's highly paid lawyer, he has been charged with the first degree murder of his brother-in-law, Gabriel Francisco Mendoza de Goya Pérez. Doña Isabella has also been charged with the lesser crime of conspiring to injure her brother, the heir to the Duque de Roble. The prosecution is still trying to bring a charge of conspiracy to murder, but her lawyer is claiming that she was bullied into it by her husband.'

'But we have their conversation on the recording. It's obvious that she's the one in charge,' said JD. 'Did she have an alibi for where she was on the Saturday?'

'Not really. She said she was in Málaga for the Feria with her daughter, who was staying with a friend, but Araceli didn't meet her mother until some time later in the afternoon. However they are claiming that the recording could have been tampered with, and as such is unreliable evidence. But we are not finished yet. We have agreed to an independent analysis of the tape. If they accept it as genuine then it's an open and shut case. Also, Ricardo found Kiko's hook knife in Jorge's bedroom, clearly identifiable as his by Kiko's initials on the handle and with fingerprints both from Kiko and Jorge. By the way, we have also charged Doctor Delgado with unprofessional conduct which led to the death of one of his patients, for which he will lose his licence to practice medicine. He has promised to be a witness at Jorge's trial.'

'Has anyone told the duke, yet?'

'Yes, your mother went over there yesterday to speak to him. She was just in time, apparently.'

'Why was that?'

'I had a call from the duke's wife half an hour ago to say that he passed away last night, in his sleep. She wanted to thank you all for giving him some peace of mind before he died. She also said a special thank you to you, Jacaranda and that if you give your bill to their solicitor he will see that you get paid.'

'It can't have been very comforting to know that your own daughter and her husband conspired to kill his son and heir,' said Jacaranda.

'Maybe not, but she said that the duke had had some suspicions about Jorge for a while now; that the man was never content with what he had, no matter how much, he always wanted more. He said, Jorge always flew too close to the sun.'

'Well I wish he had shared his suspicions with us,' said Linda. 'What did Jorge have to say for himself when you interviewed him?'

'He protested his innocence at first, but the evidence was so stacked against him that his lawyer told him to confess, and plead mitigating circumstances.'

'Mitigating circumstances? What mitigating circumstances?' asked JD, astonished at this news.

'I think they still have to work on that. But that's not our concern. That's up to the prosecution and the defence lawyers.'

'He's not going to get away with it, is he?'

The captain shrugged. 'I hope not; he deserves a long prison sentence. They both do, but that's not up to us. We've done our job, or should I say, you've done your job and found the evidence to prove them guilty.'

'Don't you find that frustrating?' she asked. 'We all know he's guilty. We have proved it. Please don't tell me that some highly-paid lawyer will get him a reduced sentence.'

'You're not new to this, Jacaranda; you know what can happen. We just have to wait and see how it pans out. One thing I feel certain about is, with the weight of the evidence that you have collected, the case will not be dismissed out of hand. He will be found guilty. That's our job done. Then it's up to Leticia's lawyer and whatever is in the old duke's will that will decide the outcome. But I expect that the dukedom will eventually pass to Antonio once he is old enough. As for us, now we move on to something new.'

'And if they're not found guilty?' She saw him look at her in surprise; she knew this was unlike her to get so emotional about a case. After all it was out of their hands now. What was the matter with her?

'They will be. Now it's time to drink to an excellent team of investigators,' he said, popping the cork on the very expensive cava he had brought to celebrate the closing of the investigation. 'Ricardo will join us in a few minutes; he had some business to tidy up first.'

'Hey, he must have heard the cork popping,' said Nacho, as Ricardo opened the door to the agency and joined them.

'Well done, everyone,' he said, accepting a glass from his boss. 'Cheers.' Once everyone had relaxed and were talking about what they would do next, he turned to Federico and said, 'May I have a word, *Capitán*?'

'Of course, what is it, *Cabo*?'

'There was a message for you from Interpol. Jean-Paul tried to phone you, but you were engaged. He wants you to ring him. The gendarme in Marseille have found Thomas Steed's body.'

'His body? You mean he's dead? Well that's a surprise. Okay, thanks, Ricardo. I have to go back to the station anyway; I'll ring him from there.' He glanced across at Jacaranda; she looked more relaxed now and was sipping her cava and chatting to Linda. He emptied his glass and said, 'Sorry folks, but I have to go back to work. Well done all of you. I know this was a tough case, but you cracked it nevertheless.' He picked up his cap and started to leave, then stopped and said, 'Jacaranda, do you have a moment?' She followed him outside and shut the door behind her. 'Is everything all right?' he asked her.

'Yes, why do you ask?'

'You seemed very agitated just now. You're not still worrying about Steed?'

'Of course not,' she replied, but not very convincingly.

'Well, you don't need to worry about him anymore. They found his body in Marseille. He's dead. I'm just going to talk to Jean-Paul and get the full story, but I thought you would like to know straight away.'

A smile, more of relief than pleasure spread across her face. 'Thank goodness. I just hope it's really him and not a case of mistaken identity.'

'I thought you would be pleased with the news.' He took her hand in his and whispered, 'Maybe now it's time we sat down and talked about the future?' She continued to smile at him, but did not reply. 'You know how much I want to marry you, *Cariño*. I love you,' he continued.

She leant towards him and kissed his cheek. 'Yes, I love you too. Let's talk about it tonight. I have something I need to tell you.' So Federico still wanted to marry her. No matter what her head was telling her, as she watched the captain put on his cap and leave the agency, her heart wanted to call him back and say yes, yes, yes. She looked around at her team and smiled. How lucky she was to work with such an enthusiastic group of people, but how would they react when she told them she was pregnant? Would they believe it? She could hardly believe it herself, but one thing was certain, whatever decisions she made, her life was going to change.

Federico's head was buzzing, what with solving the murder of the duke's son, the news of Steeds death and Jacaranda telling him she had something important to tell him, he found it hard to concentrate. Nevertheless, as he parked his car in the police car park, and walked into the building he was determined to focus all his attention on Steed. He owed it to Jacaranda to find out exactly what had happened to this man who had been a torment to her for the last three years.

The police station was very quiet but Luis was there, waiting outside his office and immediately came over to him. '*Capitán*, I'm sorry to drag you away from the celebration, but your colleague in Interpol said it was very important. Here's his number. He wants you to ring him right away on this number.'

'Thank you Luis.' He sat down at his desk and took out his mobile phone. That was strange. He had Jean-Paul's contact details in his address book, why was he being told to telephone him on a completely different number? Nevertheless he dialled the number he'd been given and almost immediately he heard Jean-Paul's voice.

'Federico. You received my message then? Good. I don't know what's going on here, but something's not right, which is why I sent you my personal number.'

'You reckon that Thomas Steed is dead then? Are you sure it's him?'

'We checked the DNA of the cadaver and it matches the DNA on file.'

'How did he die?'

'Execution style. A bullet to the head and another in the chest

'What about the fingerprints? Have you checked them?'

'Ah, I see I haven't explained myself very well. That's not so easy. The body we found has been dead for over two years; it is not in a very good condition for taking fingerprints.'

'What do you mean, over two years? He can't have been dead that long.'

'Well, by the state of his body that's what the pathologist believes.'

'But that means…'

'Exactly he died very soon after he was given early release. We've been trying to track a dead man all this time.'

'But it doesn't make sense. We were so sure that it was Steed who had put the spyware on JD's computer last year. If it wasn't him, then who was it?' This was not the news he was hoping for.

'Didn't you tell me something about him opening a bar in Málaga, as well?' asked Jean-Paul.

'A pop-up coffee shop. Well that's what we thought. Someone is obviously playing games with us. Whoever opened the pop-up, it was not Thomas Steed.'

'I'm sorry not to have better news for you, *mon ami*, but at least you know where he is now. In the morgue in Marseilles. So he won't be bothering JD again.'

'Well, that's true in a way, but there is someone out there who is trying to scare her. But who is it?'

'From what I remember of JD, she doesn't scare easily. Give her my regards. And if I hear anything further, I'll let you know.

By the way, keep this phone number. It's best to use it if you want to contact me about Steed or anything else to do with this case. I'm not sure how secure my other number is, right now.'

'Okay. Well thanks for keeping me informed. I'm still trying to get my head round the fact that we've been chasing a dead man for almost two years.'

'*Adieu, mon ami.*'

'*Adios, amigo.* I'll let you know if I find out anything.' He closed his mobile and sat staring at his desk for a while. What was he going to tell Jacaranda now? At least before they knew whom they were looking before, now they would have to go back to the beginning. He wondered if Bill knew that Steed was dead, and if he did, how long had he known? Was it possible that Bill had been behind all this subterfuge? No, that seemed far too outlandish. He had not a speck of proof that Bill was involved in anything; the man even had a solid alibi for the day Jacaranda's husband was murdered. Yet there was still something bugging the captain. And the news that Steed had been dead all this time and neither the Met, Europol or Interpol had known anything about it, felt very strange.

THE END

Thank you for taking the time to read TOO CLOSE TO THE SUN. If you enjoyed it, please consider telling your friends or posting a short review. Word of mouth is an author's best friend and much appreciated. Thank you, Joan Fallon.

CONNECT WITH JOAN FALLON ONLINE AT:
http:// www.joanfallon.co.uk

Too Close to the Sun